## SWORD OF DOOM

ALSO BY JAMES JENNEWEIN
AND TOM S. PARKER

# RUNEWARRIORS
## SHIELD OF ODIN

# SWORD OF DOOM

## JAMES JENNEWEIN AND
## TOM S. PARKER

WITHDRAWN

**HARPER**
*An Imprint of* HarperCollins*Publishers*

Library of Congress Cataloging-in-Publication Data
Jennewein, Jim
     Sword of doom / James Jennewein and Tom S. Parker. — 1st ed.
          p.      cm. — (RuneWarriors ; 2)
     Summary: In the fortress of King Eldred the Moody, Dane the Defiant receives honors
and a magical rune sword that belonged to his father, but he also finds treachery that sends
him and his friends on a quest to retrieve the sword from a thief who hopes it will lead to
a fabled treasure.
     ISBN 978-0-06-144939-0 (trade bdg.)
     1. Vikings—Juvenile fiction. [1. Vikings—Fiction. 2. Adventure and adventur-
ers—Fiction. 3. Voyages and travels—Fiction. 4. Fathers and sons—Fiction. 5. Kings,
queens, rulers, etc.—Fiction. 6. Fate and fatalism—Fiction. 7. Fortune telling—Fiction.
8. Humorous stories.] I. Parker, Tom S. II. Title.
PZ7.J4297Swi 2010                                                    2009012027
[Fic]—dc22                                                                    CIP
                                                                               AC

Typography by Carla Weise
10   11   12   13   14      LP/RRDB      10  9  8  7  6  5  4  3  2  1
❖
First Edition

*For Margery B.*
—T.P.

*For my brother Augie, the kindest soul I know*
—J.J.

# AUTHORS' WARNING

## Young Readers Beware!

Please think twice before letting your parents read this book. If they are easily frightened by gruesome and hair-raising acts of Viking violence, or are offended by graphic, gross-out humor, then this book is not for them. After all, if young people don't protect the delicate sensibilities of grown-ups, who will? Enjoy!

*"The problem with humankind is it's not very kind."*
—*Lut the Bent*

*"The headaches I get from thinking are always worse than any I get from drinking."*
—*Drott the Dim*

| NAME | PRONUNCIATION |
| --- | --- |
| Astrid | AZ-trith |
| Bothvar | BOTH-vahr |
| Drott | DRAHT (rhymes with "hot") |
| Dvalin | duh-VALL-in |
| Eldred | ELL-dread |
| Fulnir | FULL-ner |
| Geldrun | GEL-drun |
| Godrek | GOD-reck |
| Gudlaf | GOOD-lawf |
| Hrut | Huh-ROOT |
| Kára | CAIR-uh |
| Lut | LOOT (rhymes with "boot") |
| Prasarr | PRASS-ahr |
| Ragnar | RAG-nahr |
| Rognvald | RHONE-vald |
| Skrellborg | SKRELL-boorg |
| Svein | Suh-VINE |
| Thidrek | THIGH-dreck |
| Ulf | OOLF |
| Vidarr | VIGH-dahr |
| Voldar | VOLE-dahr |
| Voldarstad | VOLE-dahr-stahd |

# SWORD OF DOOM

# PROLOGUE

# A VIGIL
# OVER THE VILLAGE

Though they called her a Goddess of Slaughter or Chooser of the Slain, the name she answered to most was Mist, and it seemed to befit her airy personality. And though she looked resplendent—riding astride her pearly steed, her coal-black hair spilling from her golden helmet down over a breastplate of bronze armor, her cloak of swan feathers aflutter in the rush of wind—she was anything but confident. Indeed, although she looked every bit the part of one of Odin's corpse maidens, she did not feel as though she was ready to perform her duty. Her job, she knew, was not only to transport the fallen dead to Valhalla but to choose only the bravest warriors, for there were very high standards among the dead in Viking heaven. The worst mistake Mist could make was to choose a cowardly soul instead of a courageous one. If she erred, if she ferried the chicken-hearted through the gates of Valhalla, she would be stripped of rank and forever made to serve

1

*as a lowly galley wench, lugging buckets of mead in Odin's hall of heroes, a fate nearly as demeaning as being bound in wedlock to a one-legged troll.*

*So Mist had to be careful. As she was new to the sisterhood, this was her first solo assignment. Today, in this very village, it would be up to her and her alone to choose whom to ferry to the afterlife. She peered down upon the simple thatched-roof huts, watching the carefree children at play in the rain and the older folk going about their business. Though it was the very picture of a village at peace, Mist knew it would not last. Soon innocents would be killed and the blood would run.*

# 1

# A DOWNPOUR
# OF INSULTS

"We're doomed!"

"We're dead!"

"The gods are against us, thanks to the defiant one!"

"It's *his* heroics that got us into this mess—"

"—and thus his duty to fix it!"

"Perhaps we should banish him—before it gets worse!"

Surrounded by the many angry faces of the elders, Dane the Defiant stood in anguish in the center of the room, wishing they would all just stop talking and leave him alone. All right, so things in his village had gone terribly, horribly wrong. But why heap all the blame on him? It wasn't fair! Outside, it was pouring rain, and inside, it was pouring insults, and Dane had had enough. He stood listening to their grumbles, gripes, and personal attacks, trying to avoid the accusing stares of the graybeards, and all he wanted to do was run. Run away and hide from all the trouble and turmoil. Hide from his failures and his responsibilities. Hide from everything and everyone. Life had become a nightmare from which he could not escape. And it had only been a few short months since they had hailed him a hero.

He heard a *crawk!* and, looking up, saw Klint, his black-feathered raven, perched on a crossbeam high off the floor. Ah, his friend understood him! Dane watched as the bird hopped along the beam, drawing nearer the smoke hole in the center of the roof. Fixing Dane with a look, the raven flapped his wings and gave a scrawk, as if to say, C'mon, let's fly. And out the hole he flew, disappearing into the great outdoors to spend his time and enjoy his freedom as he pleased, leaving Dane bitterly wishing that he could do the same.

Just the past spring he had defeated the tyrant Thidrek the Terrifying and freed the people from his evil rule. Did that not count for anything? Thidrek had taken posses-sion of Thor's Hammer, the earth's most powerful weapon of mass destruction, and threatened to use it to crush all his foes and conquer the world. But when Dane defeated him in combat, Thor sent down a mighty whirlwind to scoop up the hammer and return it to the heavens, where it belonged.

And, oh, how they had cheered him. "Huzzah for Dane the Defiant!" they had shouted as they carried him on their shoulders. Dane had tried to explain that he hadn't been the only brave one. All his friends had helped, too—Jarl the Fair, Fulnir the Stinking, Drott the Dim, and others. But since Dane had personally dispatched Thidrek in front of the whole village, it was he who was decreed a hero. This, of course, had pained Jarl no end, for he hated when others received more praise than he did, especially when they actually deserved it.

During the week of celebrations, Dane had felt on top of the world. Kingly, in fact. Children came from leagues around to hear him speak and to touch a real live hero. Women, too, had found him especially desirable. But the skies had darkened, and it had begun to rain. Not a light drizzle, either. A downpour. The black sky burst open and down came a deluge. Night after night, day after day, the rain fell. Relentless torrents for weeks. The village became a river of mud.

Instead of letting up, it got worse. Winds blew. Lightning tore open the sky, soon followed by ear-shattering booms of thunder—Thor's anger hurled earthward, or so the people believed. And then came hail, balls of ice as big as a baby's fist. Crops were flattened, thatched roofs caved in. Panicked villagers took cover under the overturned hulls of their boats. Frightened cows and goats stopped giving milk and hens stopped laying. Even the fish in the sea sought to escape the fury and went deeper, beyond the villagers' nets.

And still it rained.

Thor, the people said, seemed to be making up for all the time his hammer had been lost to him. Like a child who had found his favorite toy again, it seemed that now the god could do nothing *but* play with it, banging away until humans below begged for him to stop. And when he didn't—when Thor's storms continued unabated and the village had begun to go without food—the people did the only thing that made sense to them: They pointed accusing fingers at a scapegoat. Dane the Defiant.

And now he stood there inside the village meetinghouse, watching silently as they railed against him. The elders sat on benches in a wide circle round the fire in the center of the lodge as the younger members of the community stood shoulder to shoulder behind them. Though smoke from the fire wafted up through the roof hole, the room was still thick with haze and abuzz with conversation.

"If not for you, Thor wouldn't have his blasted hammer back!" spat Gorm the Grumpy, shaking his fist.

"You just *had* to be the hero, didn't you?" stormed Hakon Large Nose. "And now look at us. Ruined crops! No milk! No eggs! No fish to catch!"

"And not *one* hour of sleep thanks to ceaseless thunder and lightning!" lamented Prasarr the Quarreler, always one to complain. "If only Voldar the Vile were still among us. He'd know what to do."

Dane sat there enduring their ire. He knew Prasarr was right. If Dane's father, Voldar the Vile, *were* alive, they wouldn't be in such a fix. It was only when Dane tried to fill his father's shoes that events had spiraled out of control.

Dane's two best friends, Drott and Fulnir, rose to speak. "Now listen!" Drott began with authority. "There's something you're all forgetting here." They waited for Drott to continue, but he'd forgotten his point and gave Fulnir a panicked look. "Uh, you first."

"What Drott means," Fulnir said, addressing the room, "is you can't blame Dane for all our misfortune."

"Oh, no?" asked Hakon. Holding up a slab of wood, he pointed to the runic inscription carved on it. "The invitation to today's meeting says 'A Gathering to Blame Dane.'"

"Wait! Wait!" Drott blurted. "I just remembered my point—"

"Sit down!" Gorm spat. "You're wasting our time!"

Astrid, daughter of Blek the Boatman, stepped inside the circle of men. Tall and blond, she was a young woman of rare and dangerous beauty whose deadly skill at axe throwing had given her the nickname Mistress of the Blade. She hefted one of her razor-sharp weapons and said, "Let them speak."

To which Gorm snorted, "We'll listen to whomever we like, young lady"—only to scream in fright an instant later as Astrid's axe came flying past his ear, slicing off a hank of his white hair as it buried itself in a beam just behind him.

"Oh, did *I* do that?" said Astrid innocently. "How clumsy of me." Dane, of course, knew that, had she wished, she could have lopped off Gorm's whole ear. It amused him to see the other elders suddenly cease complaint as she retrieved the axe and turned back to her friends.

"Go on," she told Drott and Fulnir.

"I know times are hard," Fulnir said, continuing, "but think how bad things would be if we *hadn't* defeated Thidrek the Terrifying."

"Exactly!" said Drott, regaining his faculties. "Have you forgotten what Thidrek had in store for us? Beheadings? Floggings? Being forced to dance with farm animals? Not *my* idea of a good time."

The one known as Jarl the Fair thrust himself forward. "No one disputes that ridding ourselves of Thidrek was a good thing. A deed for which, I might add," he said, cocking an eye toward Dane, "we *all* deserve plaudits for taking part. But winter nears and our food stocks are low. This calls for action, not words! And being Norsemen of pride and thunder, I say we raid and plunder!" A year older than Dane and half a hand taller, Jarl cut quite a fair figure, his gleaming white teeth and jutting jaw made all the more striking by his mane of long golden hair, which he kept well glossed with frequent applications of bear fat. And much to Dane's chagrin, Jarl's godlike looks were further complemented by an expertise in archery and swordsmanship that Jarl never tired of telling others about.

"We must strike now," continued Jarl, strutting before the gathering, "lay waste to our enemies and seize what we need before the winter snows!" Hooting in loudest approval were Jarl's pals, the massive twins Rik and Vik the Vicious Brothers. Always keen for a fight, the twins' favorite contact sports were bloodletting and advanced bloodletting.

"So it's agreed," Jarl proclaimed. "We will take up the sword and shield and show no mercy!"

Rik and Vik began a war chant, banging their ale cups together as they cried, *"No mercy! No mercy!"* Dane knew it was madness. For even if a raid was successful, many villagers would die in the doing. He remembered what his father had once told him: that if you steal a man's bread, he and all his kin will be your enemy forever. "But help a man feed his family, and you not only have a friend for life, but also many invitations to dinner," Voldar had also quipped.

Now more council members, Gorm among them, took up the chant. Dane wanted to jump to his feet and tell everyone how foolish and reckless and dangerous it was. But since the elders had already blamed him for all that had gone wrong, he knew few would be eager to take his advice. No, the only one who could talk sense into these people would be the village soothsayer, the *eldest* of the elders, Lut the Bent.

Dane's eyes found Lut seated across the room. The ancient one was leaning against a post, eyes shut, mouth wide open, and snoring. Dane picked up a pebble from the earthen floor and covertly tossed it Lut's way, meaning to bounce it off his bald head and rouse him. The pebble flew straight into Lut's open mouth and down his throat. Suddenly the old man began to choke and gag, and Dane rushed over and pounded him on the back with the flat of his hand. The pebble shot from Lut's mouth and flew across the room, hitting Gorm in the face, drawing cries of pain from the grumpy one.

Lut recovered, getting his bearings. "What in Odin's name just happened?"

"You swallowed a pebble," Dane said.

"How did a pebble get in my mouth?"

"I aimed higher. Listen, Jarl is calling for a raiding party. You have to speak."

Lut nodded—this was serious indeed. He cleared his throat and the room quieted, for every villager valued the wisdom of him who had endured one hundred and three winters, not to mention six wives.

"So Jarl wants to go raiding, eh?" Lut said. "A fine idea!" Dane shot Lut a look of surprise, having expected an argument *against* Jarl's plan. "What do *you* think, Dane?"

Dane hesitated, not knowing what to say.

"We know too well what he thinks," Jarl said. "That *he* should lead us. Be the *hero* like always. But this time this is my idea and *I'm* leading." The Vicious Brothers hooted approval, waving their swords about, nearly wounding a couple of elders.

"Very well," said Lut decisively, "so you shall lead us." Again Dane gawked at Lut. Had the old man finally succumbed to senility? But Lut beamed an insincere smile and said, "Tell us your *plan*, Jarl." And it was then Dane realized Lut's stratagem.

"Yes, Jarl," said Dane, eagerly turning back to face the pompous one. "We're only too glad to follow *if* you tell us your plan of attack."

"Well," said Jarl, taken aback, not expecting Dane to give in so easily, "it's like I said. We're Norsemen! We should pillage and—"

"Plunder, right," Dane interrupted. "Can't do one without the other. But if we're to follow you, we need specifics. Exactly *who* and *where* do we strike?"

Jarl's face went blank. He turned to Rik and Vik, who just gave him shrugs in return.

Dane made a suggestion. "Forgive my presumption—I know you're in charge, but perhaps it's unwise to go north. It's nearly winter, so the storms could be fierce and—"

"That was my thinking," interjected Jarl. "We'll go south."

"Right," said Dane. "But of the two villages we'll pass, which should we attack?"

Again Jarl looked at Rik and Vik for help. The Vicious Brothers were blunt instruments not known for strategic thinking or, for that matter, *any* kind of thinking. Their puzzled looks told Jarl he was on his own. "We'll attack . . . the first village?"

"The first village is well fortified on all sides and has over eighty men in its guard," said Dane. "The second village is larger, better fortified, with one *hundred* men. Both villages will see us coming and will fight and die to the last man, woman, and child to save their food. *What* is your plan of attack, Jarl?"

Jarl was clearly flummoxed. Silence settled over the room. The elders who had been earlier so roused by the prospect of mindless violence wore furrowed brows, now seeing the foolishness of the endeavor.

As support for his attack drifted away like the smoke through the roof hole, Jarl did the only thing a good Viking could do when logic and good sense were against him. He swept his sword heavenward, struck a heroic pose, and shouted, "Who will follow me to the gates of Valhalla?"

The only ones stupid enough to fall for this ploy were Rik and Vik, who raised swords and cried in unison,

"Valhalla!" Everyone else either quietly eyed the floor or worked on hangnails. As the embarrassing silence grew, even Dane pitied Jarl. Finally, mercifully, Fulnir the Stinking emitted a roof-raising thunderclap of flatulence that cleared the room quite handily. Preferring to stand in the pouring rain rather than stay inside breathing in Fulnir's stench bomb, everyone including Dane rushed for the exits. Everyone except Fulnir, that is. He alone stayed behind, relaxed and relieved, giving truth to the old Norse proverb: "Every man loves the smell of his own wind."

Later on that gray morning, in the hut he shared with his mother, Dane sat morosely by the fire, picking out the same mournful tune on his wooden pipe. His mood was dark, for he knew that although he and Lut had stayed the cries to go a-viking, soon his hand would be forced. If the village food stores continued to dwindle, the elders would side with Jarl, and then everyone would have to strap on swords, take to their boats, and go steal grain from their neighbors.

Everyone but the elders, of course. While the young men oared off to do the dirty business of pillage and plunder, the graybeards would warm themselves before their home fires, waiting for the boats to return with booty.

Outside, the torrential rains continued lashing the hut's sodden roof, sending rivulets of water dripping down the inside log walls. *If only this ceaseless storm would stop!* Dane thought. *Then perhaps the fish and game would return before the snows came.* Peals of thunder shook the hut, further darkening Dane's mood, and he cursed the elders. "Like it's my fault Thor's throwing a fit! They can all go drown in pig slop!" His raven, Klint, gave an agreeing *crawk!* from his perch in the rafters.

Dane's mother, Geldrun, a handsome, fiery woman still in her early thirties, gave her opinion on the subject. "Remember what your father said about our people?"

"I believe he said, 'They can all go drown in pig slop.'"

"That," agreed his mother, "and that a leader's life is thankless. No matter how well you keep the people fed, their children safe, and their pets free of ticks, a village will always find reasons to complain. It's always 'What have you done for us lately?'"

"So why even *be* a leader then? All they do is blame you when things go wrong." Dane's eyes went to the Shield of Odin hanging on the wall. In its center was a many-faceted jewel, the Eye of Odin, which was said to magically protect the shield holder against every hack and thrust of enemy axe and sword. Whoever possessed the shield was entrusted with great responsibility and honor, for it was his sacred duty to protect the village and its people. Voldar had held the shield with distinction and valor, and when he had fallen, it had been passed to Dane, the people hoping that he had inherited his father's greatness. But wearied by the burden of such an inheritance, Dane now took the shield from its peg on the wall and told his mother he was going to turn it over to the village council. They could decide who now best deserved it.

"Perhaps Jarl should carry it now," he said.

"You will put that back," said Geldrun with iron in her voice. "Giving up so easily does dishonor to your father. I didn't raise a son to be a whimpering, whipped dog." She took the shield from his hands. "All men get beaten, son, life does that. But the strong risk failure again and again, refusing to *remain* beaten."

The icy rain pelted his cheeks as he sloshed through the river of mud, leaving the village behind and ascending Thor's Hill, seeking some peace from his torment. This was the spot where Thor's Hammer had last touched earth before being blown heavenward by a mighty godsent wind, and it was the one place where Dane would go to think.

Reaching the top of the hill, he gazed down at the deep impression still visible in the earth, the sizeable imprint Thor's Hammer had made when it had fallen. To be here on this hallowed ground never failed to fill him with awe. But now, with the impression filled with rainwater and nearly gone from sight, it only filled him with sadness, for soon all proof that he had once been a hero would be gone.

He stood alone under the soot-gray sky, gazing out over

the village to the bay waters beyond, thinking on what could have been. On this very spot, he remembered, his people had planned to erect a great granite runestone in his honor. Upon the stone there was to be carved the tale of his grand triumph over Thidrek the Terrifying, thereby commemorating for all time the heroism of the Rune Warriors of Voldarstad. What glory might have been his! But now, Dane knew with bitter certainty, the runestone would never be erected. The unceasing rains had washed away that plan and killed so many other hopes and dreams as well.

Clutching his Thor's Hammer amulet at his neck, Dane lifted his face skyward. "Mighty Thor, I beg forgiveness!" he cried to the heavens. "You see before you a man fully chastened, disgraced, and made humble by your supreme omnipotence! I get the message! Now if you could just show some mercy and stop the deluge, I do think we've suffered enough!" For a moment Dane heard nothing but the rain. Then a sudden *KA-BOOM* of thunder sounded, as if Thor were saying, "*I'll* decide when you humans have suffered enough!" And adding further insult, the rain instantly turned to hail, the iceballs pummeling Dane's upturned face.

Dane dropped to his knees and closed his eyes, this time beseeching someone he hoped was listening from his ale bench in Valhalla. "Father! If you hear me . . . I've done my best to fill your boots . . . but I've made a mess of things, if truth be told, and, well . . . maybe my destiny is not to be a leader of men after all . . . which would suit me fine, really it would. Perhaps Jarl is better suited for it. I know he's a fool at times . . . well, *most* of the time, but perhaps he'll have better luck than I have. He wants to go raiding for food, but . . . is that the right thing to do? If you could just give me a sign . . . a thunderclap? A bird call? A chirping of crickets? Anything!"

The hail ceased, the rain eased a bit, and a moment later Dane felt a warm glow upon his face. He opened his eyes and saw a bright, shimmering light hovering above him, as if the thunderclouds had suddenly parted and the sun maid Sol had shown herself. The light filled him with tranquility, until it dawned on Dane that it wasn't the sun warming him but an entity of an altogether different nature. He rose unsteadily to his feet and reached up to touch the thing within the dazzle of light, when a female voice cried, "Behind you!"

And turning too late, all Dane saw in his last moments of consciousness was the blur of a swiftly advancing stranger bringing a club down upon his head.

# 2

# A Deadly
# Arrival

In the woods beyond the village the ten-year-old quietly stalked the enemy. There! A mere hundred paces away he spied him. The boy ducked behind a tree and drew an arrow to his bow, knowing this would be a difficult shot in the rain. Pulling back the bowstring as far as strength would allow, he let the arrow fly.

It landed a good thirty paces shy of his target—an ancient pine.

William the Brave swore at how badly he had missed. He had been sneaking off to the woods every day to practice against imaginary enemies, gradually building his arm strength to hit targets farther and farther away. From seventy paces or less he was deadly, but he lacked the muscle to launch an arrow accurately beyond that. Until the day he could kill reliably from at least a hundred paces, he would not be deemed a warrior worthy to stand in battle beside Dane the Defiant, the young man whom he had come to idolize in the short time he had known him.

William had been a Saxon orphan whom Dane had rescued from slavery just months before. William had shown a particular act of courage—an act inspired by Dane himself—and Dane then had dubbed him William the Brave, a name the boy longed to live up to. And so daily he visited these woods in secret to practice his art, even in the pouring rain.

He strung another arrow, envisioning an attacker skulking up behind him. He whirled to shoot—and was surprised to see a strange man standing there wearing a chain-mail shirt and helmet, brandishing a shield and war axe. Behind this stranger stood a dozen others. William had been so intent on his imaginary invaders, he hadn't heard the real ones creep up. *Thwack!* An arrow hit the tree behind him, just missing his shoulder.

William ran. He heard the hiss of arrows as they shot past into the trees and brush. Behind him he heard the attackers crashing through the woods in pursuit. He knew he had to alert the village but was too far away to be heard. Emerging from the trees, he raced like a hare across the open field toward the village perimeter, expecting any moment to feel the impact of an arrow shaft. As he ran, he threw a quick look over his shoulder. The attackers were just reaching the tree line and were coming fast. But not being weighed down by chain mail as they were, William knew he had the advantage. And thus he ran, and gave a blood-curdling cry so high and loud, it scared even him to hear it.

"*Attack!* ATTAAACK!"

Geldrun rose from the goat pen to see her village under assault. Villagers, including Astrid and Jarl, Rik, Vik, Fulnir, and Drott, had quickly found weapons and engaged the invaders but were being pushed back by the onslaught. Immediately Geldrun thought of the children. In a blink she was racing through the village, taking control of the panicked women and wee ones, herding them away from the fighting to the ships beached on shore. If the village was overrun, she knew, the only escape route would be over water.

Hearing a familiar voice, she turned to see Lut the Bent emerging from his doorway, dragging a sword. The frail one planned to do battle, though he could barely lift the war blade. Geldrun grabbed the weapon from his hands, saying, "Get to the boats!"

"No!" Lut barked. "I will defend the village!" And he grabbed the sword back from her with surprising swiftness, iron resolution in his watery blue eyes.

"But the women and children!" she urged. "You must get them to the ships and away!" Geldrun knew he would give his life to see that no harm came to the children. He nodded briskly and started off, then suddenly stopped.

"My dagger," he said, patting his cloak. "It's inside." He started back toward his hut, but Geldrun rushed in to retrieve it instead, knowing she could find it faster. Inside she rooted around and soon found his sheathed dagger beneath his furs. Rising again to her feet, she heard a scuffle. A cry of pain. Moving to the door, she saw Lut now sprawled facedown in the mud. Three attackers stood over him, holding the sword they had seized from him, and Geldrun heard their derisive laughter.

"Your blade weighs more than you, old man!" she heard the tallest one say. This drew more chuckles, and he lifted the sword over his head to plunge it into Lut the Bent. But before the laughter died in their throats, Geldrun flew out the door and thrust the dagger up under the tall one's arm, the one place she knew a man in mail would be most vulnerable. He bellowed in pained surprise, falling to his knees. One of his cohorts whirled and slashed at her with his sword, knocking the dagger from her grasp. "Kill her!" the wounded one shrieked.

Geldrun backed away as the other two came toward her, swords drawn. But her back hit the wall of the hut. Her throat tightened. With nowhere to run, she knew it was over but still refused to cower. As they neared, she girded herself for the killing blow, too proud to look away from their blood-spattered faces, a brief thought of her son flashing through her mind. Both men raised swords to strike. Then the nearest one gave a sudden grunt, Geldrun just as

21

shocked as he was to see a bloody arrowhead sticking out of his chest. The arrow had gone right through his chain mail. And her attackers barely had enough time to exchange looks of shock when—*thhhummmp!*—another arrow skewered the other man through his neck. Both men tipped over like stone statues, dead before they hit the ground.

Too stunned to speak, Geldrun was further struck to see, emerging from the smoke, a strange but striking figure in a white cloak, stringing his bow with a new arrow as he walked. Behind him strode twelve more hard and battle-scarred men loaded with spears, knives, and swords, the business of killing clearly their chief stock-in-trade.

Geldrun rushed to help Lut to his feet, relieved to find the old one shaken but unhurt. And when she heard a voice asking how the old man was, she lifted her eyes to find the one becloaked in white standing before her. There seemed a great grandeur in his bearing, his smoky brown eyes and broad smile giving off a warmth that somehow seemed faintly familiar. A moment passed as she studied his face and he hers. She felt her knees go weak.

"Oh, Odin be praised," she said, "is it really you, Godrek?"

His face lit up as he nodded and said, "The years have been good to you, Geldrun. It seems I have arrived just in time." But this was all they could say to each other, for the enemy came charging in and Godrek and his men went to work with ruthless efficiency.

Oh, how it hurt her to see the boy clubbed from behind. Because he had turned suddenly, the blow had been only a glancing one but still enough to send him spilling down the hillside, disappearing down the embankment, perhaps to his death. How awful it had felt to watch, and how surprised she had been by the intensity of her emotion. And when she caught sight of the horde of attackers pouring over the hill toward the tiny village beyond, it felt even more horrid.

She sent her horse splashing down into the shallow stream, stopping beside the body, which lay motionless. This was all so new to her, this dark business of seeing people die. And this one was just a young man, she judged, and quite easy on the eyes. Not at all like the other warriors she had ferried during her brief apprenticeship. Most had been hairy, louse-ridden brutes who smelled like the wrong end of a bear. But this one—this one was so sweet and kind-looking, so regal and ripe with potential.

Why had she tried to warn him when he was about to be clubbed? Had she . . . *feelings* for him? No! Perish the thought! The vows of the sisterhood strictly forbade any interference in the fate of a human. Her duty was to select and ferry the bravest of the war dead to Valhalla, not to *protect* them from death! She had to keep her feelings out of it! She had a duty to perform, and perform it she would.

Her eyes again fell upon the young one's mud-spattered form lying unmoving in the stream. Such a pity. He was dead and that's all there was to it. She might as well accept it and get on with it. She bent to take his spirit-body, but a sudden moan escaped his lips and she jumped back, startled. His eyelids cracked open, peering up with a dazed, glassy stare. "Who are you?"

Momentarily tongue-tied, she considered fleeing but had to be sure. "So . . . you're *not* dead?"

The young man felt his body. "I . . . don't think so." Suddenly eager to leave, she started to walk away. "Wait!" said the young man. He sat up, wincing in pain as he felt the side of his head. There was no blood, she saw, and the wound appeared not to be serious, no doubt due to her ill-advised warning about the blow.

"Who *are* you?" he asked again.

"No one, really. Forget we even met."

"Your voice . . . I heard you warn me."

"No, no! I didn't!"

"Yes . . . it was you. You said—"

"Wrong! I said *nothing*. I just happened to be in the area, saw you lying here, and—" Mist realized she was only making matters worse. First she saves his life, now she's standing here having a chat with him. Exactly how many rules of the sister-hood was she going to break today? She should just knock him senseless with a rock so he'd forget he'd ever seen her, but she couldn't bring herself to cause him any more pain.

His vision, she noticed, seemed to be returning. He was gazing at her in growing astonishment, as if only now noticing her feathered cloak, bronze chest armor, and golden winged helmet. Turning his head, he spied her majestic steed grazing nearby, and she saw his eyes widen further in disbelief.

"By the gods . . . ," gasped the young man, "you're a *Valkyrja*?"

"Your village is under attack!" she blurted out, gesturing to the plumes of gray smoke rising above the trees, and hurried away.

At the sight of smoke Dane got to his feet, his head still too dizzy and aching for him to get his legs working. But then, as his mind cleared, he was struck by another bewildering sight: The maiden and her mount had vanished. Had he been dreaming? Had she indeed been a phantasm of his mind brought on by the knock on his head? He had no time to puzzle it out. Looking again at the rising plumes of smoke, he roused himself and dashed off.

Crashing through the forest, Dane had no idea who or how many were attacking. He had no weapon, so he'd have to improvise when he got there. But when he emerged from the trees and rushed headlong into the village, he saw he was too late. The battle was over and the invaders had already been routed. He saw Blek and Prasarr the Quarreler lifting a half dozen bodies of enemy dead onto an oxcart. Moving past them, he saw that the remaining attackers, a good twenty of them by his rough count, had been rounded up and put in one of the livestock pens. They had been tied together in pairs and forced to lie facedown in the mud and the muck, the hogs and chickens running about them, snorting and squawking. Guarding them were men Dane had never seen before, men who sported the fine weaponry and polished armor of warriors in service to a lord. He watched them for a moment as they stood round the pen perimeter, poking and prodding their captives with their spearpoints and chuckling at each cry of pain. They stopped and stared at Dane, and as the liegemen met his gaze, he saw in them a coldness, an emptiness in their eyes, and it struck him that the guards seemed more vicious than the prisoners they were guarding. But this thought soon passed, as Astrid ran up to welcome him back.

"Dane!" Astrid cried, overjoyed to see him alive, throwing her arms around him.

"Axe!" Dane cried in pain.

"Oh, sorry," she said, quickly dropping it. She'd been so happy to see him, she'd forgotten the war axe in her hand. "I thought, since you were on Thor's Hill— Oh, but you're here! You're all right!" Overflowing with emotion, she embraced him again, impulsively kissing him on the cheek, barely able to contain herself.

"I'll have to return from the dead more often," he said with a knowing smile, and as he squeezed her hand, she felt herself blush, warmed by his touch. Their moment together was interrupted as Drott and Fulnir approached, equally excited to see him.

"We were just about to send a search party!" Fulnir said.

"Thought you might be bound for Valhalla!" added Drott.

"I did too," Dane said. "I got hit on the head, and when I woke in the creek, I saw this beautiful—" Dane caught himself and gave a nervous laugh. "For a moment, I actually thought I was talking to a Valkyrie, but it must have been my imagination." Dane laughed uncomfortably, and Astrid felt a sudden prick of jealousy. A Valkyrie? Although Dane wasn't one to lie, this seemed hard to believe, even rather ridiculous. It had to be from the bump on the head, she told herself, and she dismissed all further thought of it, wanting instead to fully feel the pleasure of having him safe and alive.

"Well, *look* who missed the festivities," said Jarl the Fair, striding up, sword in hand. His tunic was streaked with blood, and he proudly wore a few superficial wounds slashed across his muscled arms. "Where were you, out picking flowers?"

Dane ignored Jarl's taunts. "How are the others? Did we lose anyone?"

"No lives were lost," said Astrid, "though the fate of the wounded is still in doubt."

"Good news is," said Fulnir, "Lut, Ulf, William, and your mother all were unhurt."

27

"Answer my question, Dane," said Jarl, insistent. "Where were you while *we* were defending the village?"

"He need not explain his whereabouts to you," Fulnir said.

"He engaged the enemy up on Thor's Hill, Dane against a score of invaders!" Drott said dramatically, miming the scene with thrusts of his sword. "He killed one! Two! Am I getting this right, Dane?"

"Not exactly—"

"And then! He was overcome! A blow to the head sent him reeling down the ravine! And he woke to see a Corpse Maiden!"

"A Valkyrie?" smirked Jarl. "*You* saw a Valkyrie."

"I *said* I *thought* I did," said Dane. "I'm sure I imagined it."

"Course you did. Since the Corpse Maidens visit only those most courageous in battle—and you were nowhere to be found! Hah!"

Dane flared in anger, Astrid seeing he wanted to smash Jarl in the face.

"We believe you, Dane," she said, pulling him away, not wanting to spoil the moment with a fight. They walked toward Dane's hut, she, Drott, and Fulnir, Dane still smoldering.

"So the Valkyrie," Drott said. "What did she look like?"

"Was she *pretty*?" teased Astrid.

"Can we drop it, please?" Dane said, irritated, his attention now turning to the liegemen who stood round the livestock pen, polishing their axe blades and tossing insults at the captives. "Who are those men?" he asked.

"They came out of nowhere to aid us," Fulnir said.

"The invaders would have taken all our food had the lord and his men not arrived in time," Astrid said.

"What lord? Where does he hail from?"

"No one knows," said Astrid, "but he has a striking white cloak. When I first saw him and his men, I thought they were against us too. But then, as if sent from the gods, they were *with* us." It felt good, she realized, to be telling him all that had happened, and it reminded her just how terrified she'd been at the thought that he might be dead. "I've never seen men fight as they did," she continued. "Their lord killed three with one slash of his blade; then the rest threw down their arms, begging for mercy. The lord gave the order that they all be butchered, but your mother stepped in and said, 'There has been killing enough for one day.'"

"She did?" said Dane in disbelief, finding it inconceivable that his mother, a commoner, would countermand the order of a lord. "What did the lord do?"

Astrid said, "He bowed and said, 'As you wish, my lady.'"

And by the look on Dane's face, she could tell he was intrigued to meet this man.

# 3

# A ROYAL
# SUMMONS

Dane stood in the doorway of his hut, trying to take in what he was seeing. The stranger lay before the fire, naked to the waist, oozing blood from a gash in his side just below his ribs. Dane's mother knelt beside him, using needle and linen thread to sew up the nasty wound. Dane watched for a moment, amazed that the stranger didn't flinch as the needle worked through his flesh. Though in obvious pain, he had nothing but a smile of easy contentment on his rugged face.

"So what's this then?" Dane said at last.

Geldrun rushed to her son, hugging and kissing and making a teary fuss. Dane said he was fine and allowed himself to be hugged, waiting for his mother's tears to subside, silently meeting the stranger's gaze. At last his mother released him from her embrace. Drying her tears, she gestured to the stranger and said, "This is Lord Godrek Whitecloak, son. He and his men helped save our village."

For a moment Dane did nothing but stare. Godrek was first to speak.

"An honor to meet the son of Voldar the Vile," Godrek said. He started to rise to show his respect, but Geldrun rushed back to stop him.

"Don't stir till I'm done, or you'll start bleeding again." She resumed stitching the wound, and Godrek eased back onto the furs with a chuckle and a sheepish shrug. Dane took a seat in his father's old cedar-post chair as Godrek took a swig from the ale jar beside him.

Dane turned his gaze to another curious object, a bright white cloak hanging in folds on the back of the door. Made of bleached leather and trimmed in snow-white fox fur, it looked to Dane like a rather fancy piece of clothing for a warrior like Godrek. Did he wear it to show off the splattered blood and gore of his enemies? When Dane looked back, he found Godrek studying him.

"I see your father in your face," he said with a grin. "In your red hair as well."

"You knew my father?"

"Like a brother. War-mates, we were. Years ago. Before your mother's charms lured him away." At this Geldrun gave him a playful swat on the head.

"Thank you for saving our village," Dane said.

"Thank yourself," Godrek said. "*You're* the reason I'm here, son."

"Me?"

"Much as I like a good fight, we weren't just riding the countryside looking for one. I came here to fetch you. King Eldred wishes an audience with the one and only Dane the Defiant. He's heard of your exploits—and you know how it is," Godrek said, laughing. "Someone performs a heroic feat like slaying a sea monster or, in your case, returning the hammer of the gods, kings have to meet the hero, parade them around their court, throw a feast or two in their honor. That's what he has planned for you."

Dane looked at his mother for a moment, dumbstruck. With a note of suspicion, he asked, "Why would the king honor me for returning Thor's Hammer? Everyone *else* blames me for months of bad weather. Is it a banquet he has in mind or my execution?"

Godrek laughed. "The king doesn't blame you for a god's tantrums. This princeling Thidrek would certainly have been a threat to all the kingdoms eastward, so the king wants to thank you for making our lands safe again. And look." Godrek pointed to the doorway that was now alight with late-afternoon sun. "Perhaps Thor has shown mercy, or maybe he wearies of his stormcraft. Either way, 'tis a good omen for our journey."

It was the first sunshine Dane had seen in months. Perhaps his prayers had been answered.

"Then it's settled," said Godrek. "You will come."

It sounded so enticing. To leave behind the demands and complaints of ungrateful villagers. To be celebrated in court instead of castigated by commoners. Feted instead of spat upon. Eating and drinking in kingly content, while skalds serenaded him with poems rejoicing in his heroic deeds! How sweet! But one sobering look from his mother was all it took to end his reverie. That dreaded responsibility thing! How could he even think of leaving when his people were wanting? *Why do I have to be Voldar's son?* Dane thought in despair. *Anyone else could skip out with nary a look back.*

"There's something else you should know," said Godrek. "King Eldred wishes to gift you with an item of great value. Your father's war chest." Godrek explained that he and Voldar had once been liegemen to Eldred many years ago, when he was a lord and not yet a king. Over many successful campaigns, Eldred's brother, who *was* king, was forced to flee and Eldred seized the throne. For his service, Voldar was offered a lordship and command of the king's guards, but he had grown disenchanted with the sword path and its constant bloody battles. He declined the lordship, took Geldrun as a wife, and vanished to a peaceful little village by a bay. "But before he went, he entrusted his war chest to King Eldred, who swore to hold it, unopened, until the time he came back for it. Now that your father has gone to his reward, the king believes the war chest, and all its contents, must be passed on to you."

"So whatever is in there . . . is *mine?*" Dane was entranced.

"Yes. And, who knows, perhaps there's rich plunder inside. Maybe even arm rings of silver and gold. Imagine what a young man could do with such treasure."

Imagine indeed! The thought of such plunder sent Dane's mind reeling. His mother brought him back down to earth. "You could buy food and livestock for the village," Geldrun said. "It's what your father would have done." Yes, Dane glumly realized, he would have to share the wealth with his people. The elders would squabble and fight over how to divide it and who should get the largest share. This had to be the reason his father had kept it hidden all these years.

"You'll want your friends to meet the king, too, won't you?" Geldrun asked. "They're every bit as heroic as you."

"Of course they are," Dane agreed. "If I go, they go, too."

"Bring an entourage, for all I care—make a party of it," Godrek said, chuckling. "The king wants to meet *all* the heroes of Voldarstad."

Dane gazed thoughtfully into the fire. He saw Godrek open a leather pouch and shake some of the powdered contents into his cup. *"Wenderot,"* he said in explanation. "Helps ease the pain of battle-wearied bones. Something you might have to use someday too, if you're lucky." He gave Dane a wink.

Later that night Dane sought out Lut the Bent and found the old one in his hut, recovering from his bout with the invaders. They sat by a smoky fire, sipping barley ale, Lut applying a yarrow-root paste to the scrapes on his arm as Dane relayed news of the white-cloaked one and his father's war chest.

"I knew of this chest," Lut said, "but nothing of its contents. Your father rarely spoke of it to me, nor to anyone else, I gather." The old one's eyes grew misty. "It was as if his war chest held something he no longer wanted to possess or be reminded of. A part of his past—a piece of himself—that he wanted to keep locked and hidden away, perhaps as much for his own good as anyone else's." Lut gave Dane a penetrating look. "I believe your father would never have opened that chest again," he said with emphasis, "and perhaps neither should you."

"Not *open* it?" said Dane in surprise. "But if there's treasure inside—"

"Some secrets are best left unknown, son." Dane wanted to speak, but the fire in Lut's stare silenced him. "That which happened in your father's past, before you were born—how much do you know of it?"

Dane shrugged. "I know that in his youth he followed the sword path. He was a brave warrior who served with distinction and honor, but he spoke little of it to me."

"True, your father sent many to their deaths."

Dane took this in and then said, "I must have asked him a hundred times to tell me of his glories and victories. But he would only laugh and change the subject. It hurt me, like he didn't believe I had the stuff to fully understand what he had done. Or do it myself."

"Perhaps he was protecting you," said Lut, "from something he knew might only cause pain. Fathers are funny that way, only wanting the best for their sons." This last was said with a playful smile. His mother, Dane knew, had respected her husband's wishes to let the past be and had rarely spoken of it, at least in Dane's presence. But oh, how Dane had yearned to know all he could about the man he revered. And why not? Wasn't it natural for a son to learn about his father? To hear of his grandest exploits and, yes, even his lowest failings? To examine every broad stripe and torn thread from the tapestry of his life? How else would he ever come to know the one who had fathered him—or come to know himself, for that matter? And with his father dead, that chance was gone forever. But now the chest gave him a final opportunity to peer into his father's mysterious past.

"I *must* know what's in the chest," said Dane. "Perhaps we should consult the runes."

"I already have."

"You *have*? But how'd you know—"

"—that you'd come pestering me with questions? When *don't* you?"

Dane smiled. It was true. Hardly a day went by that he

didn't ask Lut's advice on any number of subjects, from girls to cures for scalp itch. Despite being decades older than most elders, and having a long white beard and more wrinkles than a bucket of prunes, Lut possessed the light heart and playful nature of a much younger man.

"So," said Dane, staring at Lut in the firelight, "*was* there a message in the runes?"

Lut stifled a yawn, then nodded soberly. "They said, 'The secret of the chest will change your life.'"

Dane took a long moment to consider this; then he spoke.

"So it means I might find treasure, or . . ."

"Or something," Lut said with finality, "you'll wish you'd never laid eyes on at all."

# 4

# HUNGER ENDS
# AND A JOURNEY BEGINS

They journeyed northeast along a river fed by distant glaciers, their horses climbing a trail that gradually rose into the mountains. Dane's entourage included his mother, Lut the Bent, Astrid, William the Brave, his friends Drott, Fulnir, and Ulf, as well as Dane's rival Jarl with his cohorts Rik and Vik the Vicious Brothers. Godrek and his men rode at the front and rear of the caravan as a precaution against attack by rogue bands of thieves known to ply the trails. And above them all flew Klint, Dane's faithful raven.

It had been only a week since the attack on Voldarstad, but to Dane it seemed like ages, such was the change in his people's fortune. The storms had abated; the fish returned to the villagers' nets. The men captured in the attack had been ransomed for more food stocks, enough to see the village through until spring. Godrek had officially put Voldarstad under his protection, warning other villages in their fjordlands that any more attacks would be brutally dealt with. But even this had not satisfied the village elders; they had also demanded that Dane leave behind the sacred Shield of Odin so that its mystical powers would safeguard them.

As they had ascended Thor's Hill, Dane had taken a last look at his home, relieved to know that his people were safe. And now, well under way on his new adventure, he felt an even greater relief. He was free! Free of the rancor, the criticism, the responsibility. He was leaving behind all the burdens of leadership he had come to resent and was soon to be feted by a king, no less. And given a chest of unknown treasures! How his luck had turned!

At midmorning the party stopped for the *dagmál*, the day meal. Dane sat with his friends eating flatbread, cheese, and dried fish. He heard his mother's laughter and saw her enjoying the meal beside Godrek on his blanket. Dane had seen a change in her since Godrek's arrival. For months Geldrun had been unable to shake the dark shadow of grief over losing her husband, Voldar the Vile. Not one to weep or rend her garments, she instead suffered in silence.

During Godrek's days of recuperation in Voldarstad, Dane saw his mother's pall of grief gradually lift. She attended to Whitecloak's wounds and went on long walks in the woods with the man. Dane had been surprised to learn that Godrek had courted his mother years before, when he and Voldar vied for her hand. Now it seemed that the courtship had renewed itself, and though gladdened to see his mother's smile again, Dane also felt uneasy when he saw her in Godrek's company. And after their midday meal, Dane sought out Lut the Bent, who was moving among the trees, picking mushrooms, hoping the seer could help him understand the conflict in his heart.

"You are of two minds," said Lut. "One part of you wants to see your mother happy." Lut brushed the dirt from a mushroom and placed it in his leather shoulder sack. "Another sees her with Whitecloak and feels she is somehow being untrue to your father. That pains you."

Dane thought for a moment. "But what if Godrek isn't the right man for her?"

"Would you approve of *any* man who would replace your father?" Lut asked sagely.

"No one *could* ever replace him," Dane said.

"In *your* heart, son," Lut said gently. "But you must trust your mother to do what's right for hers."

Dane acknowledged that Lut was probably correct. He didn't *dis*like Godrek. On the contrary, Dane was fascinated by him. During the days of Godrek's recuperation in Voldarstad, he and Dane had shared many meals and talks. Dane had yearned to know what he knew of his father, and after some gentle prodding, Godrek told him. "Yes, in our youth we rode and raided together," he said. "We were fast friends at one time. I looked up to him as if he were an older brother, I suppose. No one showed more courage in battle or more humor when among friends. And few men enjoyed such favor, shall we say, with the ladies."

Godrek had gone on to tell of the many adventures he had shared with Voldar. He spoke of the time when, in their early twenties, by happenstance they had rescued the twin sons of a Gottlander king from kidnappers, and of how the grateful king had richly rewarded them with arm rings of silver and made them members of his own personal guard. For five years they had served as the king's sworn liegemen, harrying the coastal villages to the east and the south, reaping kingly tribute, and guarding their lord king on his many trips abroad.

There were good times and there were bad, said Godrek; a few narrow scrapes that, at the time, he'd feared might mean their end. Once, he and Voldar single-handedly stood off a score of Saxon warriors, killing them all. Another time they spent six months in a Frankish dungeon and dug their way to freedom using nothing but their bare hands. He also told of a fateful voyage to the north they had taken: Their ship had become wedged between two icebergs, and to survive they had had to kill and eat a giant polar bear before it killed and ate them—and it had been Voldar himself who had bravely dealt the beast the fatal knife blow. Through it all, Godrek said, Dane's father had been ever true and trust-worthy. "But then," Godrek had told him, his face darkening as he stared into his ale jar, "we parted ways."

Dane had asked, innocently enough, what had caused their parting.

"As I said, he met your mother."

"I have a feeling there is more to it," Dane had said, press-ing for an answer. And it was then that Godrek's eyes went cold and he flashed Dane a savage look. An instant later he had composed himself, laughing it away, but that sudden ruthless look had stuck with Dane.

In all words and actions, Godrek had proven himself honorable. He had rescued Dane's mother from certain death and saved the village as well. But there was something about the man, lurking beneath the surface, Dane could not fathom.

The man's cloak had been another curiosity to Dane. Why did he wear it and how had he come to possess it? And one night, after Godrek caught Dane staring at the garment as it hung on the wall, he got his answer.

"You wonder why I wear such a garment," said Godrek. "What its meaning might be." Godrek had then thrown the snow-white cloak over his shoulders, tying its leather cords at his neck, and given Dane a look. "Once, this very cloak saved my life, and so I wear it as a reminder."

"A reminder of what?" Dane had asked.

"That death is always nearer than we think."

They crossed grouse moors thick with heather and hawthorn and late autumn grasses, and by the next afternoon they found themselves in a primeval forest so dense with massive, moss-covered trees that only an occasional shaft of sunlight reached the ground. They passed great granite stones the size of a longhouse, the circular patterns of pale green lichen that clung to the rock like nothing Dane had ever seen. Pale brown toadstools the size of cabbages nestled in the tree roots, and covering the ground were great clumpy patches of green moss, the moss in places so thick and hairy, it seemed to Dane like the fur of some forest-dwelling creature that might soon awaken to terrorize them. Later, after they had stopped to water their horses near a stream, Whitecloak stood among them and gave a warning as if he had read Dane's mind.

"Shadowlands like this one," Godrek said loud enough for all to hear, "the thickest forests which never see the sun, are the dominion of wights." And then, after a pause, "Creatures with a taste for human flesh."

Dane felt a cold lump form in his throat.

A choking sound came from Drott. "Uh, did you just say what I *think* you said? These *wights* are . . ."

"Man-eaters, son," said Godrek, "savorers of human flesh. And once they've caught you, they don't bother with cooking you over an open fire, either. They tear you limb from limb and suck the marrow right from your bones."

"Well," said Fulnir, always one to look on the bright side,

"at least it's over quick."

"Actually," said Godrek, "they usually start with your extremities and save the head and heart for last. So in truth, a man being devoured can stay alive for a good long time, for wights are known to be rather slow eaters who never hurry a meal." As Godrek paused to drink from his goatskin, Dane spied the sickened faces of his friends. Drott and William seemed especially disturbed. He noticed that a deeper stillness had seemed to fall on the forest, the creak of the trees going unanswered by so much as a single twittering bird.

Chief among these night creatures, Godrek went on to explain, were the shape-shifting *varúlfur*, men bitten by wolves, forever doomed to roam the forests as half man, half wolf, preying on anyone stupid or unlucky enough to be out alone in the dark. "At least that's what my mother's second father, Kelki Sharp Tooth, always told us," said Godrek with a wry smile, "if one can believe a man who lived on nothing but ale and horsemeat."

"What of the *svartr dvergar*?" Drott said. "My father feared them most of all."

"The dark dwarves?" said Godrek. "The most vicious of all, they say. They live in caves and hunt in packs by night. They also say that if dark dwarves don't take shelter by daybreak, they curl up on the ground and turn to stone. Come midnight, they regain creature form, and woe betide anyone caught in their midst."

Nothing else was said on the subject, and soon they

remounted and rode on warily through the darkening forest, Dane's friends talking louder and joking among themselves, trying to keep their moods light and their minds occupied by silly talk. Ulf the Whale mumbled old war chants to ward off the frights. Fulnir made a game of seeing who could count the most mushrooms. Drott and William, riding side by side just ahead of Dane, tried to comfort themselves with conversation.

"You think it's true, Drotty?" he heard William say. "*Are there wights about?*"

"Of course not," said Drott, waving his hand with a casual air. "It's just talk."

The riders fell silent as they slowly passed a pair of squat, lichen-scarred boulders just to the left of the path, each about the size of a hunched-over child. Dane heard William whisper to Drott that he thought he'd seen faces appear on the surfaces of the boulders. Had his mind been playing tricks? Fulnir, overhearing, said it was nothing but the shadowplay of the trees throwing shapes on the rocks, no reason to worry. But a moment later Dane heard Drott whisper in answer, "I saw them too, William. I saw them too." And Dane would have found their superstitions amusing had he not felt a tinge of worry himself.

Late in the day Godrek called a halt in a small clearing, announcing they would camp here for the night. His men gave orders to Dane and his friends, dispatching Jarl, Rik, and Vik into the forest to chop wood and telling Dane, Drott, and Fulnir to water and feed the horses. Dane bridled a bit at being so roughly ordered about, but did as he'd been told to please Lord Whitecloak. Ulf the Whale, being of serious heft, was put to work rolling a circle of stones together for a cook-fire pit. Not long after, a ring of fires was lit round the camp perimeter to ward off any wild beasts or wights, and Godrek gave the order to his men to take turns keeping watch during the night.

"I'll keep watch too," the eager William said, drawing derisive snorts from the men.

"Sentry duty is man's work," said Thorfinn, one of Godrek's men. "Little *boys* need their sleep." The other men guffawed at this, and Dane saw William's face color in embarrassment and anger. William was small for his age, and Dane knew he resented being thought of as puny and helpless.

The boy went off to sulk, and Dane found him sitting on a downed log at the edge of the clearing, sharpening his arrowpoints on a piece of granite.

"Going hunting?"

"Any of those wights attack, *I'll* bring 'em down," William said sullenly. "Then nobody will laugh at me."

Dane gave the boy a pat on the shoulder. "Those wights won't stand a chance." William looked up at Dane, managing a smile, then went back to work on his points.

After the *náttmál*—the night meal, consisting usually of hot stews and roasted meats—with the horses watered and fed, everyone sat round the large fire in the center of camp, grouped in friendly conversation. Jarl stood at the perimeter, watching Godrek's warriors with a mixture of envy and admiration. They carried themselves with such sturdy and quiet confidence. He was fascinated by them, and a bit fearful as well. He not only wanted to be *with* them, he wanted to *be* them. He chose his moment and, with his boys Rik and Vik beside him, Jarl approached a particularly impressive-looking pair of Godrek's warriors.

The warriors were playing a board game called *hnefa-tafl,* or king's table. They balanced the square game board on their knees and strategically moved carved pieces made of ivory from one square to the other, each trying to capture his opponent's pieces. Addressing the one known as Ragnar the Ripper, who bore an ugly white knife scar from the corner of his mouth to his left ear that made him seem always to be wearing a sickeningly crooked grin, Jarl begged his pardon and asked how he might enlist in their company.

Ragnar spat and studied the board.

"Join us?" said Ragnar, not looking up. "What? And leave your nice little village?"

"I want a life like yours," said Jarl. "A warrior's life. Full of adventure, bloodletting, and pillaging."

"We're particularly keen on the pillaging part," added Rik.

"Pillaging, eh?" said Ragnar, warming to the subject. "Pillaging does have its diversions, but it's not all a bed of lilies. For instance, take the taxes."

"Taxes?" said Jarl.

"Yeah. Say I plunder a merchant ship and find a nice fat cache of silver. I can't just pocket it all and call it a day!"

"You can't?"

"No! A third must be paid in tribute to our sovereign King Eldred, another third to our liege lord Whitecloak, and me, I'm left with a pittance for my trouble. Then I have to pay all my personal costs out of that. Like feed for my horse, new boots for my feet, or ale for me and any lady companions I might entertain. Then there's repair costs to my armor, costs for keeping my weapons sharpened. And if I fall ill or get cut open in battle, do I get to use the services of the king's surgeon? No! I must pay for my *own* healer. And in my old age, when I am no longer able to plunder, will the king give me as much as a comfy bed to rest my weary bones? No! So, believe me, the plundering life isn't all it's cracked up to be—"

"Are you *playing* or talking?" asked his opponent, Svein One Brow, a pock-faced brute with one giant eyebrow above his nose. "Quit griping and move already, ya piss-hole." Ragnar grumbled and looked back at the board. Svein grinned up at Jarl and said to pay no mind to Ragnar's nitpicking. The warrior life had it all. "Freedom. Travel. Women. Fresh air. Excitement. Did I say women?" One Brow admitted it wasn't perfect. The hours were often too long, the food undercooked, and most were lucky if they saw their twenty-fifth year.

"Yes," said Vik, "but what's the downside?"

After the others had eaten and left Dane and Godrek alone by the fire, Dane again asked about his father. What was his best quality? His worst? His finest moment in battle? Godrek was slow to speak on these things, preferring one-word answers and cryptic smiles. Still, Dane felt honored to be having this private time with his lordship, and even brief glimpses of his father were better than none at all. Curious then about another matter, he asked what had happened between them to end their friendship.

For a long moment Godrek drank from his ale jar and said nothing, contemplating the past. "Your father could have been a great man," he said at last, his eyes on the fire. "A man of wealth and distinction beyond measure. He stood on the threshold of a life few can imagine. He could have grasped the stars." Godrek fell silent. "But he threw it all away. Turned his back on greatness and retired to your sleepy little backwater village to live a dullard's life."

The words hurt Dane, and noticing this, Godrek softened his tone.

"I'm sorry, son," he said. "I don't mean to belittle you or

your people. But you must understand there is a life beyond the one you know. One of limitless glory. Since I last saw your father, I've lived ten whole lifetimes, become a lord of my own lands. Tested myself in ways few men ever do. Seen and done things that change a man forever, that make you change your view of life itself. Suffice to say, son, I've had my share of adventures. . . ."

*Adventures!* The very word was so tantalizing to Dane, it seemed as though a new doorway was opening right before his eyes.

"The question is," said Godrek with a glint of fatherly wisdom, "do you want to stay in your little village of farmers and fishwives and while away your days in indolent domesticity? Or do you want to see the world? Maybe even *conquer* a piece of it?"

Dane couldn't speak; his heart swelled with yearning. Was *this* what he wanted? Was this his true destiny? Godrek rose, stretched his limbs, and said, "Some men keep their heads in holes all their lives and never even know it; others lift their eyes to the stars." And it was these words most of all that Dane lay in his bedroll thinking about deep into the night.

William lay in his bedroll, determined to stay awake and prove his worth in the event thieves or godless wights chanced attack. For a time he heard distant hoots and night calls, and imagined the beasts of prey both furred and feathered that might be stalking the teeming forest. He heard the snuffles and snores of his comrades, as well as nocturnal rumblings from Fulnir, who lay nearby. Even Klint the raven, perched in a nearby birch tree, slept soundly, his head tucked under a wing. The only other one awake, William saw, was the sentry on duty, who sat in a crouch on the far edge of camp, stoking a fire and drinking from an ale jar. It was Thorfinn, the one who had laughed and ridiculed him for being a *little boy.* Oh! How William wanted to show him he was wrong.

But it would have to wait. Perhaps, he thought, he should get some sleep before daybreak. He turned over in his blankets—and spied something that had escaped his attention before. Two squat boulders, similar to the ones they had passed on the trail that day, sat together just within the perimeter of the camp. There was nothing strange about these rocks, except for the fact they looked identical, like twins. Their surfaces were weathered and pitted just like ordinary stones. And, of course, that's just what they were. Harmless, ordinary rocks. And this was why he hadn't noticed them before.

He burrowed snugly in his blankets to ward off the cold and closed his eyes. Soon, very soon, he vowed to prove his mettle and show what he was made of. Fading into slumber, the boy conjured images of the day Godrek and Dane would grip his arm warrior style and tell him he'd done well. . . .

An eerie whisper jolted him awake. He sat up. How long had he been asleep? He darted looks around the camp. All was quiet. Even the sentry appeared to be dozing. Then he saw something that sent an icy shiver down his neck.

The twin boulders were gone.

He started to shout an alarm but caught himself. What if he was mistaken? What if the boulders he'd seen earlier were not where he thought they were but somewhere else along the perimeter? If he awoke everyone on a false alarm, he'd be yelled at, if not laughed at again. No, he would do the right thing and first make certain.

He quietly pulled on his boots, strung an arrow on his bow, and crept off to the spot where he thought the twin boulders had vanished from near a thicket of brambles. He stopped. Listened. On the wind came that eerie sound again . . . faint whispers, rising and falling as if in chorus, the sounds just short of being words. The night, it seemed, was speaking a strange language he had never heard before . . . a language that seemed to be calling to him.

He crept closer to the thicket, to where the forest merged into blackness. That's when he saw them: eyes staring out at him. Six pairs of tiny ovals ashine in the darkness. William wanted to run, but he seemed rooted to the ground. And then he saw deathly white claws tipped with sharp talons reaching out from the darkness toward him—and something grabbed him from behind. He let out a piercing scream, whirled away from the grasp, and fell to the ground.

Dane was staring down at him. "William—what are you doing!"

"I—I saw them!" William sputtered. "They—they—they were here!"

His scream had roused the camp. Godrek and his men came running, weapons in hand, followed by Jarl, Astrid, and the others.

"What is it, boy?" Godrek demanded. "Why do you wake us?"

William excitedly pointed to where the rocks had been. "The rocks—they moved! So I went to see and    " He gestured to the woods. "They were there! I saw them! I heard their voices! The dark dwarves!"

Godrek turned to Thorfinn, the man on sentry. "Did you see or hear anything?"

"No, my lord. I saw the boy go to the perimeter, I thought to relieve himself. But nothing more."

"He saw nothing, my lord, " William responded, "because he was sleeping."

"He lies!" Thorfinn bellowed. He came at the boy, hand raised. Dane stepped in front of William, catching Thorfinn's wrist before he could strike. With his other hand Thorfinn went for his knife, and Godrek shouted, "Enough!" The liegeman froze, hand on knife handle, glaring at Dane. He was older than Dane, a good five years his senior, but both seemed evenly matched.

Thorfinn jerked his wrist from Dane's grasp and let the knife handle go with the other, still staring hard at Dane. "The boy lies. I demand satisfaction from his protector."

"We'll have none of that," Godrek said. "As for the boy, I'm sure it was a dream he had."

"No! It wasn't!" William protested.

"Quiet!" Godrek barked, his glare turning William mute. For an instant William felt Godrek himself was going to strike him, but the man collected himself and turned to Dane. "Inform your charge about the dangers of a loose tongue." With that, Godrek and his men went back to their bedrolls. Thorfinn followed, but not before he gave Dane a final sneering look that said, *This is not over.*

Before William could speak, Dane turned on him, his eyes livid. "Never challenge a liegeman unless you're man enough to fight him. He'll kill you—and be within his rights!" Dane strode away, leaving William standing alone. He peered into the woods where he thought he had seen the eerie, glowing eyes. There was nothing there but darkness.

# 5

## DAYLIGHT BRINGS
## NEW DANGERS

By midmorning the following day the party emerged from the woods into an alpine meadow. In the summer it would be alive with bright flowers and lush grasses, but the winter freeze had turned everything brown and dead. No one cared that the landscape was so lifeless or the air biting cold; they were all thankful to be out in the bright sunshine and away from the gloomy, dreaded forest. Dane noticed that everyone's mood had brightened and there was laughter now among his friends.

"Think there'll be many girls in Skrellborg?" asked Fulnir as he rode beside Dane.

"Lots," Dane replied. "You'll have your pick."

"Our *pick*?" asked Drott the Dim. "You mean if I try to kiss one, she won't hit me with a rock?"

"You can't kiss her right off," Dane said. "You have

to make conversation first. Girls in Skrellborg are more refined."

"More refined than *who*?" Astrid chimed in as she rode up alongside them. "We *simple* girls from Voldarstad?"

Dane blushed. "Uh, I *like* simple girls from Voldarstad."

"Sure of that, Dane?" she chided. "And when all those Skrellborg maidens *throw* themselves at your feet? What then?" She pulled her hair and wailed in comic exaggeration. "'Oh, Dane! Dane the Defiant, you have stolen my refined heart!'"

His friends hooted in laughter, and Dane noticed it even drew a smile from Ragnar the Ripper.

Dane grinned. "Astrid, you needn't worry."

"Worry? Why would I worry?" she asked. "I'll be too busy with the refined *boys*."

There were more guffaws, the laughter free and easy, the kind shared among good friends, and Dane couldn't remember when he had last felt so carefree and happy.

The path continued to climb through the woods; an unruly wind arose, and it grew colder. Dane noticed that Lut the Bent had turned pale, so he took his woolen scarf and wrapped it round the old man's face and neck. Lut nodded in gratitude, but there seemed something weighty on the old one's mind, something more than just the chilly weather.

"I was thinking about how wolves choose their leader," Lut said. Dane sensed another life lesson coming. "Did you know the lead wolf is born to its place? Just as those who trot behind are born to theirs?" Lut nodded toward the front of the procession, and Dane saw Jarl on his mount ahead, leading the party up the trail as if he were the lord of the troop.

"So you're saying men are the same? They're born to their position? I thought you said a man could choose his *own* destiny."

Lut sighed. "Did I say that? I'm old and I forget things."

Dane knew Lut's mind was as sharp as ever. He only feigned forgetfulness to win arguments. "I have a choice, Lut. I can lead farmers and fishwives, or I can strike out on my own and see the world. Godrek says some men keep their heads in holes all their lives, others lift their eyes to the stars."

"Hmm" was all Lut said for a while as their horses trod on. Dane thought perhaps the life lesson was over. Then Lut said, "Your father took a wife, raised a son, *and* led farmers and fishwives. Find out why he made that choice, and you will know what your destiny should be."

Dane thought for a moment. "Could the answer lie in the chest, Lut? The secret that will change my life?"

"A distinct possibility, son. A distinct possibility."

The party climbed ever higher up the mountain, the vegetation growing sparse and the footing treacherous as the path led them across the blue ice of a glacier. Deep crevasses in the ice could be hidden by thin snow bridges, so two of Godrek's men went ahead on foot to probe the ice with pikes and spears to be sure it was solid. Godrek ordered all to stay in single file and not stray from the path, for if anyone were to stumble into a chasm, death was certain.

The riders guided their mounts with care up the icy path to where the glacier reached its highest point between two mountain peaks. They crested the ridge and made their way down the gently sloping path. Dane spied a fortress far in the distance at the glacier's southernmost edge. He had never seen such an impressive structure. The timbered walls encircling the city stood at least five times the height of a man. He glimpsed, within the walls, more huts and a high-roofed lodge of wood and stone that surely was the lair of the king.

"Behold Skrellborg," Godrek announced with pride. "King Eldred's abode."

Dane exchanged looks of awe with Drott and Fulnir. The fortress was far grander than they had ever imagined. Dane envisioned himself passing triumphantly between its massive front gates, sitting before the king's roaring fire, a cup of hot mead in his hand, and servants attending his every need as he regaled the king with stories of his exploits. He could hardly wait.

"It'll be nightfall before we make it down," Dane heard Drott say. And looking over, he saw Drott was thinking the same thing that he was thinking: *Let's get there already!*

Drott raised his eyebrows and said, "There *is* a faster way."

Drott eagerly jumped off his horse and sank to his knees on the downward-sloping ice.

"Don't be a muckhead," Fulnir said, realizing what he was about to do. But Drott wasn't listening. "Last one down's a moldy maggot pie!" he shouted as he launched himself face-first down the icy slope, gleefully screaming at the top of his lungs.

Not to be outdone, Dane leaped from his saddle, and soon he too was shooting down the ice slope, deaf to his mother's cries of alarm. What a thrill to be going so fast, the exhilaration of wind whipping his hair, making him feel free and unfettered. The slope abruptly dropped away, he went airborne—and in a sickening moment of clarity he realized this perhaps had not been such a wise idea. Flying in midair, he saw dark, jagged shapes fast approaching. Rocks. Huge slabs of granite jutting up out of the ice. In one panicked moment, he cursed himself for forgetting that his friend was named Drott the Dim for a very good reason: *He was an idiot!*

Missing a jutting rock by a hair, Dane crashed hard onto the ice slope again, tumbling ass over ale cups down the ever-steeper slope. Again he went airborne, flew *over* Drott, who lay spread-eagled, and slammed down on a crusty stretch of snow. At last he came to an abrupt halt, crashing hard into a snowdrift piled against a boulder.

He was still breathing, at least. That was good. But

when he rose to his feet, he saw Drott wasn't moving. He hurried back toward where his friend lay, but before he could reach him, Drott cried, "Stop!" Dane froze. He heard deep cracking sounds coming from somewhere beneath them. Evidently this was one of the snow bridges Godrek had warned them about. Any sudden moves and the bridge could collapse, sending Drott falling hundreds of feet to the bottom of the crevasse.

"Get away, Dane! It's gonna fall!"

"Don't move! I'll reach you!"

"Stay back!" Drott yelled again.

Dane hushed him and put an ear to the ground. Faintly he could hear a creaking, cracking sound coming, it seemed, from deep within the glacier, traveling up through the fissure in the ice. He crawled forward on his belly, inching closer to Drott. The cracking sound grew louder. Dane knew he was right at the fissure's edge but not nearly within reach of his friend. Any farther, and his added weight might collapse the bridge, and then he, too, would never be found until the earth warmed and the glaciers melted. Like that could ever happen.

There was only one thing for Dane to do—he took off his pants. Grasping the end of one pant leg, he tossed the other one over to Drott, who grabbed it. "Hold tight, Drotty." Slowly Dane pulled Drott forward.

Then the snow bridge collapsed.

Drott disappeared, nearly pulling Dane down with him.

But Dane held tight to the ice cliff, keeping a firm grip on his end of the pants as Drott dangled over the chasm, holding tight to the other leg.

"Hold on, Drotty!"

Dane pulled with everything he had. Drott rose a bit—until the deerskin pants began to rip at the crotch, the threads giving way. Dane made a wild grab for the scruff of Drott's coat. The pants fell into the chasm. With a final heave, Dane pulled his pal up and over the edge to safety.

They scrambled away a short distance and slumped down, exhausted, Dane's bare buttocks freezing as they touched the snow.

"You're a fool, boy!" Godrek's voice rang out as he pulled up his horse, having raced down the glacier to Dane's aid. "You!" he said, angrily stabbing a finger at Drott. "You are a half-wit! But you," he said, glaring at Dane, "*you* are the son of Voldar the Vile and *should* have more sense!"

The others rode up, and when Dane saw Astrid, he sheepishly cupped his hands in front of his privates. Jarl let out a guffaw. "Well, won't you be em-*bare-assed* when you meet the king." Godrek's men laughed heartily.

"I'm just wondering how he's going to wave to the crowd," Astrid said.

"All right, all right, I guess I deserve that," Dane said.

"You deserve a good birching, that's what you deserve," Geldrun scolded.

"I have a spare skirt if you need it," Astrid said. Her sense of humor was often as sharp as her axes. Right now, as he stood freezing, this was *not* one of the qualities Dane loved most about her.

"Thank you, Mistress of the *Jest*, but I packed another pair of pants. Why don't you all ride on and I'll catch up."

"Maybe you could point us in the right direction," she added.

Dane gave her a scowl.

After the others had ridden ahead, Dane went to his horse to retrieve his pack. He untied it and found an undershirt, a tunic, two pairs of leggings . . . but no trousers. Frantically he dug through the pack, tossing his things willy-nilly trying to find the missing garment . . . but with no luck. Sickened, he realized that in the excitement of leaving for the trek, he must have forgotten to pack his deerskin dress trousers.

Now what was he to do?

Alone on the freezing glacier, his bared buttocks turning to ice, Dane spied his loyal raven, Klint, circling overhead.

"Klinty!" Dane called. "At least *you* won't abandon me, eh, boy?" But as soon as the cry had left his lips, the bird took wing toward the fortress, letting out a *scrawk!* that to Dane sounded every bit like mocking laughter.

# 6

# A Foreboding
# in the Fortress

At the far end of his cavernous lodge hall, King
Eldred the Moody sat brooding on his oaken
throne, his brow creased in worry. His long,
unruly gray hair fell about his shoulders, and his face bore
a most fretful scowl. He cast suspicious looks at the many
servants and mead maids scurrying about, making ready for
the grand banquet to honor Dane the Defiant, the young
man who he hoped would prove himself worthy to inherit
his kingdom. By any measure, this prospect should have
given him reason to smile. But Eldred suffered such moody
fits of melancholy, it was often said a team of oxen would be
hard pressed to lift his spirits.

That morning he had conferred with his team of oracles.
They had arrived wearing their filthy cowled robes, stinking
of the various methods they employed to divine the future.

One of them read the omens found in the reeking entrails of chickens. Another counted the maggots on sun-baked slabs of rotting meat. A third seer, having long forsaken his former technique of studying squirts of ox urine, now read the irises of sheep's eyes floating in sour milk. Even though their prognostications often proved of dubious value, Eldred knew that a king's power and prestige was measured by how many paid consultants he had on staff. So he suffered the strange odors and gave ear to their pronouncements, if only to sustain his regal aura with the commonfolk. But the king himself was not without his superstitions. Once, believing the lumps in his oatmeal to be an omen that he would die of hiccups, he issued an edict requiring that all visitors to his court hop on one leg when in his presence. Another time, a wolverine appeared to him in a dream and told him to eat nothing but mud. This he did for an entire week until, tiring of his diet, he took a dozen bowmen into the forest and for months hunted nothing but wolverines. He put on weight that winter eating nothing but wolverine stew.

"Well, what have you divined?" the king asked the three seers gathered before him. "What have the fates foretold?"

The Chief Oracle, whose name was Sandarr the Seer, stepped forward. His gaunt visage, fiery green eyes, and forked beard gave him a daunting look. And as he prepared to speak, he angled his head backward in such a way as to make it seem as if the twin points of his beard were aimed directly at the king. The king found this habit highly annoying, hating it almost as much as the sulfurous odors that followed the seer around, but he desperately needed the talents his seers possessed and so indulged their many eccentricities. "Lord," said Sandarr, "we have labored day and night to read the signs, going without sleep or nourishment—"

"Yes, yes, I *know* predicting the future is *such* hard work," Eldred said irritably. "Just give me the results!"

Sandarr turned to his subalterns, exchanging hushed whispers. Then he faced the king again and said, "It is as you wish. The party that nears the gates brings you promise of a worthy heir."

"Brings me *promise*? What precisely does that mean? Is this Dane the Defiant the *one* or not?"

"My lord, the fates speak in obscurities. Perhaps he is. Then again—"

"Would you care to be roasted on a spit?"

The three exchanged whispers, and then Sandarr said, "No, my lord, we would not."

"Spare me the weasel words. *Will* a worthy heir to my kingdom soon show himself?"

Again the oracles bowed their heads in conference. It irked Eldred no end that they never gave clear answers to his questions, always spouting convoluted pronouncements that were open to interpretation. And the king well knew why. In this way, if their prediction proved wrong, the oracle could blame his boss for the misinterpretation. *They believe themselves so clever,* thought Eldred the Moody, *but I am the king and I can have each of their heads delivered to me on a pike if I so choose,* and he made a mental note to see about having it done someday soon. Or should he have them drawn and quartered? Hmm. Decisions, decisions.

At length the soothsayers ended their conference and Sandarr faced the king. "The answer to your question, my lord," intoned the seer, raising his eyebrows, "will be written in blood."

Further angered by the obfuscations, Eldred picked up a gold drinking cup to throw at them. They ducked and cowered, but then Eldred froze, suddenly grasping the oracle's words. "So, what you mean is . . . this Dane fellow will spark a fight among all those who aspire to be my heir . . . and the winner will be he who survives."

"Brilliant, my lord!" mewed Sandarr. "Such rare wisdom you show! May we kiss the hem of your robe?" They all moved forward, but the king put up a hand to stop them, further repelled by their stench.

"I'd rather you didn't. I just had this cleaned." Eldred abruptly dismissed them, and they scurried away like cockroaches, the king deciding then and there on decapitation.

Now Eldred sat alone on his throne, fretting over his oracles' pronouncements. *The answer will be written in blood?* If this was true, someone was sure to die soon. His unsuspecting guest of honor, Dane the Defiant, might even find his hero's welcome turn into a hero's demise. Well, such was the way of kingdoms. They needed leaders. Unfortunately, *his* realm seemed sorely lacking in kingly vigor and virtue, all his trusted lords being too interested in possessing power for its own sake to wield it wisely. Even Godrek Whitecloak, his trusted friend for so many years, seemed distracted. Eldred's dreams of late, as well as his old man's aches and pains, had told him that his time on this earth was drawing to a close. Years? Months? Exactly how long he had he didn't know, but he had to get his house in order. He had to find someone worthy to wed his niece and take the reins of his kingdom. Preferably a younger man, someone he could still mold to his liking. Someone of fiery strength and firm character, a man whose virtues far outweighed his vices. But time was running out, and if he failed to soon find a candidate strong enough to fight and defeat all the other pretenders, he feared, his lands would then be plunged into civil war and chaos.

Upstairs in her dressing room in the royal lodge, Princess Kára, the king's niece, gazed into her hand mirror of polished silver, practicing her smile. She had to practice, because smiling was not something she often did. The pout she usually wore expressed how little she liked living in a frigid fortress so near a glacier. Having reached marriageable age, Kára desperately longed for romance and travel—and life in a place where she didn't have to crack the ice on her porridge to eat it. And who better to rescue her than this brave and valiant Dane the Defiant? He *had* to have more going for him than the motley louts of Skrellborg, whose biggest excitement in this frozen wasteland was watching icicles melt.

Because her uncle the king had no heirs, she was being offered as bait to attract a man who would prove himself worthy to inherit the Skrellborg royal house. Thus she was to be regal and compliant and act in every way the fragile porcelain doll, protected and sheltered from the outside world. How tedious and tiresome! At times she felt like a prisoner.

So far, the candidate most likely to win her hand was Bothvar the Bold, the spoiled, humorless son of a powerful local lord. He wasn't bad to look at, but he wouldn't win any prizes for spouting poetry or even making conversation. To prove his worth, Bothvar had won several duels over her, some resulting in serious injury. But Kára cared little that blood had been spilled on her account. "You maimed *who* in a duel? Eirik Thordarsson?" she'd said to Bothvar. "*That's* supposed to impress me and make me want to marry you?" He could win a hundred duels for her, but it would never win her heart. The last thing she wanted was to be stuck in Skrellborg for the rest of her life, playing the compliant wife of a doltish brute.

As her ladies-in-waiting fussed over her hair and dress, she studied her smiles in the hand mirror and vowed she would escape the life they had planned for her. It was *her* life. She would live it the way she wished. A sudden blare of horns sounded the arrival of guests. Her pulse quickened. The famed young man who had returned Thor's Hammer had come to take her away, or so she hoped.

On the steps of the royal lodge hall, Princess Kára tingled with anticipation as she stood beside her uncle, waiting to receive the hero. Every commoner had turned out to cheer the arrival of Dane the Defiant, lining the lane that led from the fortress gate to the lodge hall steps. Young women wore their most alluring outfits, hoping to catch the hero's eye. Kára caught sight of Bothvar the Bold and two others, Espen the Loud and Ottar Threefingers, who had fought for her hand in marriage. Poor Ottar had come out the worst of it. During one duel he had lost one finger and acquired the name Fourfingers. After another he became Threefingers. Such was his swordsmanship, Kára feared, that sooner or later he'd be known as Ottar the Stump or, worse, Ottar the Dead and Buried.

Casting a sidelong glance their way, she saw her trio of jealous suitors standing together, glowering as the procession passed, for although they were rivals, they were united in their contempt for the one who had come to steal their princess. *Their* princess? Ha! She was about to meet the one who would put these boastful fools to shame.

Riding first in the procession was her uncle's chief liegeman, Lord Godrek Whitecloak. When Kára laid eyes on the young man following him, her heart leaped. He was pleasingly, ruggedly, *impossibly* handsome! With rippling muscles, chiseled face, and glossy golden hair, he rode tall in the saddle, waving and smiling grandly to the cheering crowd. She clutched the king's hand and whispered, "Uncle, he's everything I imagined!"

The king nodded, equally impressed. "He certainly has the look of a hero, doesn't he?"

Kára reconsidered how best to present herself when greeting this Dane the Defiant. *Smile, yes, but keep it modest,* she thought. *Understated. Nothing too flashy or impassioned. Perhaps merely a half-interested nod his way, nothing more.* For a girl in her position should never give a man the idea that she could be too easily won.

As the procession neared, the blond one spurred his steed ahead of Godrek's so that he was first to reach the lodge hall steps. He jumped from his mount and went down on one knee, bowing his head before the king and Kára. "Lord King, greetings from Voldarstad. Your humble servant is most pleased to make your acquaintance. To be here in your radiant presence is indeed an honor." The light reflecting off his golden mane was almost as dazzling as the gleam of his teeth, and Kára made a mental note to ask him if bear fat was his secret.

The king bade him rise. He came up the steps as cheers from the townspeople rose in intensity. He turned and waved to the crowd, drinking in the adulation, Kára thinking he was more than a little full of himself.

The king cleared his throat, finally drawing his guest's attention away from the cheers. "Young man, I wish to introduce you to my niece, the Princess Kára." When he turned to her, she expected the usual reaction she got from young men: instant adoration. Instead, with an air of self-admiration, he gave her a cocky, arrogant smile, as if *he* were the prize to be won here, not her. The impertinence!

Then, unseating himself from his horse, Godrek Whitecloak strode to the king, gave a bow, and uttered something in his ear. Eldred gaped in astonishment, then held up his hand to silence the crowd. "I call out Dane the Defiant," the king shouted. "Show yourself!"

"Here!" a new voice rang out. Kára saw another horse trotting up the lane. Upon it was an altogether different-looking young man. A head of unruly red hair. A strong jaw. A manly smile. And wrapped round his waist was something that looked like—could it really be? Yes, it *was*—a horse blanket. Stopping at the lodge hall steps, he climbed down off his mount but failed to see that his horse had stepped on the trailing hem of his blanket. And as he strode forward, the blanket covering him was suddenly yanked off—and to Kára's shock, she saw he wasn't wearing pants! A gasp arose from the crowd as, for one shocking moment, the redhead stood in the altogether, his nether regions exposed to the world. But in the next instant, the embarrassed one quickly freed the blanket from beneath the horse's hoof and wrapped it around himself again—but not before the townspeople exploded in laughter. The king gave Godrek a baffled look, as if to say, Who is *this* buffoon?

The red-haired one approached the king and went down on one knee in the mud. "I beg your forgiveness, sire," he said with surprising dignity, "I am Dane the Defiant, your most humble and honored servant. No disrespect to your lordship is meant by my attire. You see, there was an incident on the trail and—"

The blond one with the jutting jaw interrupted, as if anxious to bring attention back to himself. "If I may explain, your majesty: I fear Dane disobeyed Lord Godrek's orders to stay on the path over the glacier." He paused, allowing the frown to deepen on the king's face. "As you know, there are dangerous pitfalls, and he quite rashly and foolishly—"

"—saved my life!"

To everyone's surprise, another young man from the party came stumbling forward, a chubby but cheerful-looking sort who somewhat clumsily took a knee beside the one wearing the blanket. *Now what?* thought Kára.

"Uh, majesty," said the clumsy one, "I mean, *your* majesty, your kingliness, your most royal, lordly highness—*I* was the dolt who strayed from the path. I would've fallen to my doom had Dane not sacrificed his own pants to pull me out. That's the kind of brave soul he is, lord. The kind who'd give up his breeches and freeze his backside to save a friend."

After a long silence, with all awaiting his response, the

king broke into a chuckle. The king laughing? Kára couldn't believe it; it was as if they'd just heard a donkey tell a joke or a beaver break into song. Never had such sounds of jollity come from Eldred the Moody. People were even more taken aback when his low chortle soon became a loud, braying guffaw that grew into great waves of full-throated, belly-shaking laughter. His mirth contagious, Kára and the crowd joined in with the king.

The only one *not* laughing was the young redhead in the blanket. He was still kneeling in the mud, Kára saw, looking shamed and hurt, apparently believing they were all laughing at him. So this was the real Dane the Defiant, the true hero who would steal her heart away? Well, if he was found wanting, there was always the blond one. Even though he seemed awfully stuck on himself, she knew she could tame him. She had never met a man she couldn't. She would play the redhead off the blond and let the best man win.

She caught Dane's eye with the coyest of smiles, then whispered to her uncle that they should do the hospitable thing and help him look his best for the banquet.

The king signaled to a pair of personal assistants, and they whisked Dane away to be bathed and garbed by the royal tailors. Dane smiled at her as he passed, but Kára caught a look from the pretty girl in his party, the tall, athletic one in braids and furred vest who radiated a warrior's strength. The look she gave Kára was one of mild contempt, as if she were well aware of Kára's romantic schemes. But Kára, coolly realizing this was her rival for Dane's affections, gave the girl a haughty smirk in return, a look that said, Silly girl, no one bests a princess at her own game.

# 7

# ROASTS, TOASTS, AND BOASTS

S oon after the visitors from Voldarstad had arrived, the king gave them a formal welcome, greeting them by grasping their arms in turn, warrior style, as was Viking custom, and presenting them each with their own personal drinking horns with pewter-embossed rims and hand-tooled leather shoulder straps, which he had had made just for the occasion. Geldrun raised an eyebrow when William too was handed his own drinking horn, but a look from Godrek told her that rejecting the gift of a king was not at all wise, and so she later whispered to one of the serving wenches to bring the boy only nonalcoholic drink.

Dane was led in by the king's assistants, and the sight of him took Geldrun's breath away. Gone were the mud-spattered horse blanket and torn coat. His hair washed and brushed, he now looked resplendent in a whole new wardrobe—brown breeches of the finest wool, a linen undertunic, a green and white silk overtunic with silver clasps at the chest, a gold-buckled leather belt, and brand-new brushed-suede boots. "A wardrobe fit for a prince," said King Eldred in compliment as he greeted Dane warmly, and Geldrun's heart swelled with pride.

The king bade everyone eat. Cheers of "Hail, Eldred!" went up and the feast began.

Seated at the king's table, Geldrun and Godrek were treated like royalty, with servant girls attending to their every wish. It was soon explained to her that King Eldred had invited all the nobles and liegemen from Skrellborg and the surrounding countryside to join in the feast and honor his guests from Voldarstad. There was Thorkelin the Chin, whose massive jaw gave women pause until they heard the off-color oaths that flew from his mouth. There was Arndórr the Clever, a poet who spoke only in rhymed couplets, even when ordering more mead, and his simpleton brother, Gnúpr the Happy, who laughed for no reason and spoke only to the pet piglet he kept in his lap. Geldrun had also made the acquaintance of Sandarr the Seer, the king's fork-bearded soothsayer, who was going from table to table telling fortunes for gratuities.

The invitations had stipulated that this would be a polite affair and not the typical Viking banquet where knife fights were common and men ate and drank to the point of vomiting, then continued to eat and drink to the point of more vomiting. Since there were to be women of refinement present, weapons were to be surrendered at the door, and if people wanted to vomit, they would have to do it outside and not in the traditional tableside bucket.

Despite these severe restrictions and the insistence on table manners, it seemed to Geldrun that all in attendance—the lords, the ladies, and the few commonfolk who had wangled an invite—were enjoying themselves immensely. The king's poets-in-residence—they were called skalds—entertained the gathering, declaiming in voices rich and sonorous the epic song-poems of wars and warriors, of love and the death of love, stories they had spent their entire lives learning and perfecting, as was the oral tradition. And, oh, the music! A quartet—a father and his three sons named Kvígr and the Kinsmen, all smartly attired in matching forest-green tunics, playing a flute, lyre, cow horn, and hand drum— had begun to fill the hall with the most pleasing music. She felt the gentle caress of Godrek's hand on hers and turned to find him holding out a juicy morsel of ox steak for her to eat. She opened her mouth and took it in, the adoring look in his eye making it taste all the more delicious.

Lut the Bent had never seen such an abundance of food and drink. There were salted whale and ox steaks, roast pork and reindeer, whole chickens stewed in beer. There were giant lamb shanks, meat pies, and—the king's favorite, he was told—boiled squirrel. Table upon table was piled high with plates of smoked trout, pickled herring, sliced turnips, barley flatbread, honeyed nuts and bilberries, cheeses mild and sharp. Even more appetizing, he thought, were the shapely serving wenches who circulated through the hall with endless pitchers of ale and mead, and he eyed them with interest, admiring their every billow and bulge.

He watched in amusement as Svein One Brow challenged Ulf the Whale to an eating contest—and Ulf lived up to his name and amazed the crowd by eating twenty-six squirrels at one sitting, seven more than Svein had managed to put away. When William went missing, Ulf was accused of eating *him*, and everyone had a laugh when the boy, exhausted by the day's ride, was found asleep in the corner.

One of the king's jesters then delighted the gathering by putting on a display of strength, lifting an entire seating bench over his head—while *three* of the plumpest women were sitting on it. The room exploded in cheers, the women most appreciative, and the jester, yearning for more laurels, further impressed the crowd by juggling torches. Two, three, four, five at a time he had going, until his cloak caught fire and someone had to drench him with a bucket of water, which, of course, only drew more laughter.

Seated beside Lut, Drott and Fulnir were so agog at the grandiosity of the feast and so busy craning their necks at the girls, they barely touched their food. Fulnir noticed two local maidens eyeing them from an adjoining table. "Those girls are staring."

"What, I got a booger?" Drott asked, wiping his nose clean of any unsightly material.

"No, I think they want to meet you," Lut said.

"*Meet* us? Why?"

"You're heroes," said Lut. "Young men of courage. They have no notion of your, uh, limitations." The boys looked at each other, realizing that here perhaps they could escape their reputations.

"Lut's right. *They* don't know we're dim and stinking." Fulnir finger combed his hair and got up to go over to the girls.

Drott stopped him. "So what do we call ourselves if we're *not* dim and stinking?"

Fulnir shrugged, not having any idea.

"Well," offered Lut, "how about Drott the Dangerous and Fulnir the Fierce?" The boys considered this for a moment, then grinned.

"Dangerous and Fierce we are," Drott proudly proclaimed, and off they went to try out their new, improved personas at the girls' table.

A serving wench drew near to refill Lut's ale jar, and any lingering concern he had about what lay within Voldar's war chest instantly left his head.

Though the hall was alive with gaiety and laughter, Jarl sat brooding, glowering over his ale horn. "I can't believe it," he grumbled. Beside him, Rik and Vik were deep into their drink and vigorously trying to outbelch each other. Rik paused long enough to ask Jarl what exactly he couldn't believe.

"Dane!" said Jarl. "He walks into town dressed like a buffoon—and now look at him!" Jarl gestured to the king's table, where the newly refurbished Dane sat with King Eldred on one side of him and the king's radiant niece on the other.

"Looks right princely, he does," said Rik admiringly, and his brother Vik agreed, which only drew more oaths from Jarl. Vik wondered aloud how much Dane's outfit might cost on the open market if one lacked the services of a king's tailor, and they agreed it would cost upward of ten pieces of silver or a score of goats at least. Rik said that if he had that much silver or that many goats, he would rather spend them on a new steel fighting sword or casks of his favorite ale, and his brother told him that that was why he would never be seated beside a woman as beautiful as the one seated beside Dane. Rik said he was probably right, and Jarl exploded in rage.

"It's not *fair*!" he fumed. "He loses his trousers and everyone makes him out to be a hero! Even when he does something *stupid*, he lands on his feet!"

Rik finished his hornful of mead and belched loudly. "Would you give up your pants to save *my* life?"

Jarl thought for a moment. "If I had a spare pair, I would."

Astrid watched Dane in the seat of honor, drinking from the king's own silver goblet. Seated beside him, the princess seemed utterly entranced by Dane, hanging on his every word, her eyes never leaving his face, as if he were the only person in the room. There was no denying it: Princess Kára was a rare beauty. Delicate boned, with dark brown tresses framing her creamy, pale skin, Kára radiated the kind of girlish vulnerability that made men want to protect her. She had Dane in her sights, and he didn't appear to be resisting.

Astrid touched the Thor's Hammer locket that hung around her neck. It had been only months since she had walked in the woods near their village with Dane and he had given her the locket as a symbol of his love, pledging that they would be together forever. But now, she feared, he was falling under the spell of another. Astrid caught a brief glance from the princess, a self-satisfied smirk that said, *See? I have turned his head and there's nothing you can do about it.*

Dane's head was spinning. Everyone was so polite, so accommodating. The food. The drink. The music. The regal setting. And the attentions of Princess Kára! She was so interested in everything he had to say. To be drinking mead from the king's own silver goblet and to have so many people—noblemen, no less—treating him as the center of attention. It felt wonderful to be freed from the needy complaints of the villagers of Voldarstad. For the first time in months he had begun to feel like his old self again. Talkative and self-assured, funny and free.

For a moment or two he had thought of Astrid and his friends, and felt guilty he hadn't come down off his regal throne and spent any time with them. But with Kára and Eldred asking him so many questions, his attention was drawn back to them again and again. Plus his friends did seem to be enjoying themselves.

"So you actually *saw* Thor's Hammer?" Kára was saying, her eyes wide with admiration. "How fascinating!" And then a young man pushed his way forward, intent on introducing himself. His name, he said, was Bothvar the Bold, and Dane quickly surmised he was a suitor of Kára's. Bothvar began to belligerently pepper Dane with questions, insisting on knowing which weapon Dane preferred in hand-to-hand combat. Kára deftly extricated them from this embarrassing moment by turning to the king and blithely asking, "Oh, Uncle, is it not time for our guest of honor to speak?"

"Indeed!" said the king. Clapping his hands to silence the music, Eldred stood and proclaimed in a booming voice, "Dane the Defiant will now present his heroic tale!"

The hall fell silent. With all eyes suddenly on him, Dane was at a loss. *His* tale? He was totally unprepared. His mind went blank, his mouth dry. The princess gave his hand a little squeeze, and seeing her reassuring smile, Dane nervously stood, searching his mind for a good place to start.

"It was a struggle of good against evil—"

"We can't hear you!" said a voice in the back of the hall.

Dane cleared his throat and began anew, his voice louder but still shaky. "Good against evil! Of honest, hardworking people fighting a despotic ruler with—with little regard for . . . for—"

"Get to the bloody parts!" a new voice shouted.

Dane heard the crowd growing restless. His friends began to shout suggestions.

"Tell them about the storm at sea," cried Fulnir, "and the frost giant!"

"The ice rat!" yelled Rik. "Tell them about that!"

"And how I drank the water and got wisdom!" shouted Drott.

"Don't forget the doomfish!" yelled Ulf. Klint too gave an encouraging *crawk!*

Now Dane was even more confused. A dagger look from Bothvar rattled him further.

"It was a quest for justice and revenge!" Jarl suddenly said in a booming voice, climbing atop his table and commanding the attention of the room. "Decreed by the gods! We sought to find wind, wisdom, and thunder! And indeed, we not only found the thunder in our hearts, for bravery did abound—!"

"But we found the thunder of Thor's Hammer!" cried

Dane from atop his chair, now spurred into action by Jarl's attempt to steal all the attention. "The greatest power on earth!"

"But first we braved the labyrinth of the legendary Well of Knowledge!" said Jarl, not to be outdone. "Facing down an evil troll and a giant ice rat with jaws as big as a whale's!"

"Successfully retrieving one goatskin of precious wisdom water and one of idiot water," said Dane. "And I don't have to tell you which of us was the idiot!" Dane grinned and swelled his chest, and the crowd roared in delight. They saw Jarl's deflated frown and knew he had been the loser. Dane pressed his advantage, delighting the crowd further by jumping atop the king's table itself and telling the story of how Drott the Dim had been touched by the gods and made smart by the wisdom water, the hushed crowd awed by the gems of wisdom Dane brought forth. Now filled with confidence, there was no stopping him, and Dane proceeded to further entertain the king and his guests with their escape from the Aegirdóttir sea demonesses during the storm in the Shallow Shoals of Peril. Then Jarl got back into the act, telling of their escapade with the deadly flesh-eating doomfish *and* their escape from a real live frost giant. And so back and forth it went, Jarl telling one part and Dane another, each interrupting and trying to outdo the other, exaggerating and embellishing the details each to his own advantage. But as they neared the end, Jarl made it seem as though he and he alone had freed Dane and his friends from the executioner's axe—and as though when fighting Thidrek and his men atop the ramparts, he had fearlessly fought and killed twenty men single-handedly. According to Jarl, *he* was the sole hero. Dane bristled. It was a ridiculous bald faced lie, he knew, but the crowd was eating it up, cheering and chanting, "Jar-rl! Jar-rl! Jar-rl!"

"But then you *failed*!" cried Dane, seizing back the spotlight. "Thidrek overpowered you and pushed you off the ramparts—and he launched Thor's Hammer at our village!" And knowing then he had them in the palm of his hand, Dane launched into his own dramatic reenactment of the final battle between him and Thidrek, his heroics every bit as overblown and bigheaded as Jarl's had been, wowing the crowd even more by using a carving knife like a sword and leaping from tabletop to tabletop, bringing to life every thrust and parry. Dane caught flashes of his friends' faces falling in dismay as they heard him taking all the credit, yet on he went. And in a moment most inspired, he fell upon a whole roast pig that still lay uncarved, an apple in its mouth, and pretended the pig itself was Thidrek, moving its mouth up and down while mimicking Thidrek's frightened voice.

"Please don't kill me, Dane, sir—please spare me!"

"*Spare* you?" Dane cried in his own voice, throwing back his head in exaggerated laughter. "But you're swine! And swine like you have but one fate—to be slaughtered!" And with both hands, he thrust the carving knife down through the roof of the pig's head, the apple popping out and rolling away as Dane stabbed again and again, the crowd on its feet in ecstasy, cheering wildly. Dane sawed off the head at the neck, impaling it on the carving knife and raising it over his head for all to see, and the place exploded. "Dane! Dane! Dane!" they cheered, and pounded the table. Dane felt himself lifted upon the shoulders of a dozen strangers, men and women alike, and they paraded him round the hall, chanting his name, everyone on their feet and reaching up to touch him, Dane feeling every bit on top of the world.

When Dane was deposited back at the king's table, Godrek gave him a proud smile. The king himself patted his shoulder and said he'd done well indeed. He heard the music start again and looked around, eager to find Astrid for a dance. He felt a tug on his hand and, turning, found it was Kára, staring dreamily up at him with her princess smile. She raised herself on tiptoes and gently kissed his cheek.

"Honor me with a dance?" she said, batting her lashes, and all thought of Astrid emptied from Dane's head.

"He used our real names!" complained Fulnir.

"He called me dim!" said Drott.

"And me stinking!" said Fulnir.

Astrid listened to them grouse, feeling bad for her friends. There had been snickers of laughter at their expense, and the girls they'd been sitting with had promptly deserted them, not wanting to be seen with boys so idiotic and odiferous.

"The way he told it," Fulnir continued, "it seemed he alone was the heroic one—and all we did was hold his coat."

"Well," said Drott, "I did hold his coat that one time, remember? When we were—"

"I *meant* he belittled us," said an irritated Fulnir.

"Oh, right," said Drott.

"And you, Astrid," Fulnir said between gulps of ale, "he never mentioned you by name even once."

"Yes, I noticed," she told him, trying to appear unhurt. "I'm sure it was just an innocent mistake. When you're that excited, it's easy to forget the details sometimes."

"I guess you're right," Drott said, not convinced.

"It's bad enough being made fun of by strangers," said Fulnir, still upset. "But your best friend?" Saying that the feast was no longer to his liking, Fulnir walked off, followed by Drott.

Astrid noticed that her friends weren't the only ones annoyed by Dane's tales. Another young man in the crowd was giving Dane dagger looks. She asked a passing mead maid the young man's name. "He is Bothvar the Bold. He presumes the princess is his bride-to-be," she said with a grin, "but it seems another has laid claim."

This put an entirely new face on the matter. Was the princess merely using Dane to make Bothvar jealous? Or was she throwing herself at Dane to escape an unwanted marriage? Astrid considered warning Dane—but what would she say? If she began tossing around accusations, she herself would appear a schemer, the wounded sweetheart who'd say anything to discredit her rival. Oh, how Astrid hated these stupid games. If the little vixen's attentions had blinded Dane, so be it. He deserved to suffer the consequences. Just as his stupidity on the glacier had lost him his pants.

Oh! Her head was pounding now. She slipped from the mead hall, going to her quarters to sleep. Maybe by morning, she thought, things would be a whole lot clearer.

# 8

# A Door to the Past
# Is Opened at Last

The time had come for Dane to peer into the mysterious past of his father.

The king had waited until the feast had ended and most of the guests had tottered off and gone home. As she bade him good night, Princess Kára had surprised Dane with a kiss, saying that her dreams would be sweeter because she knew they would be spending *many* more nights like this together. And as she swept away, all Dane could think to say was "Good night, my princess." Because truth be told, he had enjoyed her company and for a time had even fallen under her spell. But as the evening had worn on, he had begun to sense there was a practiced calculation in her attentive charms, as if she were a hunter stalking prey. He'd even tried to break away during the evening to be with his friends, but Kára had started to pout, and Dane knew it unwise to upset the niece of his host.

Now that he was free of her, he sought out his village mates. He called out to Fulnir and Drott just as they were leaving the hall. They turned, their faces cold and sullen.

"What's wrong?" Dane asked.

"We're tired," said Drott, his eyes on the ground. "We thought we'd turn in early."

"But you mustn't leave," Dane said. "I'm about to open my father's chest. Don't you want to see what's inside?"

"Why should that interest *us*?" Fulnir asked flatly.

"Because if there's treasure, I want to share it with you."

"*You* want to share it?" Fulnir said. "Just as you shared your heroism tonight, I suppose? You should go buy a hat."

"A hat?"

"Your head's so swollen, I'm sure you'll need a new one," Fulnir said. He and Drott turned to leave but Dane stopped them.

"I'm sorry. I got a little caught up in the telling of the tale and—"

"Why'd you have to call us by our names?" Drott asked. "We have new names now. I'm Drott the Dangerous and he's Fulnir the Ferocious."

"Uh, it's Fulnir the Fierce," Fulnir corrected him.

"Since when?" Dane asked.

"Since two girls smiled at us. At *us*!" railed Fulnir. "And they were pretty!"

"Mine had all her teeth. And seemed free of lice." Drott sighed dreamily.

"But then you had to call us *dim* and *stinking*, and they ran from us like pigs on fire!"

"How did *I* know you weren't dim and stinking anymore?" Dane shot back.

"And what about Astrid? You didn't even *mention* her," Fulnir said. "You were too busy playing up your part and making eyes at the princess."

Dane felt a hand on his shoulder. He turned and saw Godrek, who said, "The king bids you to come." When Dane turned back, Fulnir and Drott were out the door and gone. For a moment he wanted to catch up to them and somehow make things right. He wanted to find Astrid and tell her his feelings for her had never wavered. But Godrek was giving him an insistent look, and he knew that a king like Eldred the Moody was not to be kept waiting.

Dane, Geldrun, Lut, and Godrek were led by two of the king's guardsmen up a winding staircase and into the king's private chambers. The king waited for everyone to enter. The guardsmen closed the door and stood watch beside it.

"Son," said the king, "we gather here to remember your father, Voldar the Vile, a great man by any measure. We knew him well, Godrek and I did. We rode with him. We ate and drank with him. We spilled blood with him. And, Odin knows, we chased skirts with him! I remember a time—"

There was a loud cough from Lut, and the king changed the subject.

"Uh, what I mean to say is," continued the king, "he entrusted me with some of his most personal items, namely the contents of his sacred war chest. Something I have kept under lock and key these many years, awaiting the day when I might meet him again. Sadly, he has been taken. But now it's my honor to reunite you, his only son, with a piece of your father. To give you his war chest, your birthright, as your proud father would have wanted." He gestured then to his men, and they drew back a gray velvet curtain. And there on the floor, lit by a shaft of moonlight from the window, lay the war chest of Voldar the Vile.

Dane saw it was rather small and ancient-looking, caked in dust, its scarred and weathered pine planks reinforced with rusted iron bands. There was a musty odor about it that made Dane wrinkle his nose. He had expected something more majestic, a chest made of fine hardwoods, decorated with silver and gold, perhaps plundered from a wealthy lord and spattered with bloodstains. But then it came to him that this modest pine chest perfectly matched his father's true nature—simple and sturdy, bearing the scars of many campaigns. That was the man Dane had known and loved, and standing there before it, he found that the sudden closeness of it made his father come alive in his mind: memories of his hearty laughter and colorful curses, and most of all the mystery in his eyes. Dared he open the chest and see what dark secrets lay within? He caught a look from Lut and knew that it was time. The king and Godrek seemed excited by the sight of it, too.

Atop the chest lay a key, milk white in the moonlight. Dane knelt before the chest and lifted the key. Tense with anticipation, he inserted it into the rusted lock. He paused, suddenly fearing the truth of his father's past, a past perhaps better left buried. Once the chest was opened, there was no turning back; he would have to face whatever he found. Dane turned the key. He heard a *click.* He raised the lid, its aged hinges creaking in complaint. Dust rose. He stared down into the chest. For a long moment he didn't move; the chest appeared to be empty.

"What? What is it?" he heard Godrek asking impatiently from behind.

Dane reached into the chest, for a moment finding nothing at all. Feeling around, his fingers bumped something. An object cold to the touch. Slowly he lifted it into the light. It was a sword, sheathed in a scarred leather scabbard marked with burns and bloodstains. And coiled in bas-relief round the hilt was the snakelike figure of a sea serpent, its bronze scales gleaming in the moonlight, its tongue becoming the sword itself.

"This is all there is," Dane said, holding up the sword for all to see.

Godrek rushed to the chest and peered inside. "That's it?" he said in pained disbelief. "What mischief is this?" Taking the sword from Dane, he grabbed the hilt and pulled it free of its scabbard. To everyone's surprise, the sword was broken off halfway down the blade, the piece from middle to tip completely missing. Godrek gave a bitter smile and handed the sword back to Dane. "I can nearly hear your father's laughter," Godrek said, staring up into the moonlight, as if up into Valhalla's corpse hall.

Dane looked at the broken sword in his hand. *This* was his inheritance? His legacy? *This* was the thing that was to change his life? Why had his father kept such a useless weapon? Had it been a keepsake of some kind? Did it somehow represent the reason he had turned away from the warrior life? Or perhaps it had no meaning at all. Perhaps, as Godrek said, his father was just having a wink and a laugh. Dane had come all this way hoping the chest would contain insight into his father, or, if not that, something of monetary value he could use to help his village. But now he had neither—just a broken, worthless sword that revealed nothing.

"Lut, I guess you were right about my father never wanting to open this chest again," Dane said, unable to hide his disappointment. "Why would he, since he knew the only thing inside was a useless sword?"

"It *is* a mystery, I'll give you that," Lut said.

"Perhaps not," said Geldrun. "Your father rejected the

warrior's path. A broken sword could mean he hopes you will, too." His mother left the room with Godrek. The king approached.

"I wouldn't read too much into this," the king said, nodding at the sword. "And besides, you're young—you've plenty of time to make your fortune." And then, leaning in closer, the king whispered, "I'd suggest a new seer as well—yours is a bit dotty." The king hurried out followed by his men, and Dane was alone with Lut. As the boy held the blade, the old man bent down to examine it, paying especially close attention to the serpent-coiled handle. A look of concern crossed his face.

"What?" Dane asked.

"It's just a feeling." Lut shrugged. "The answers will come by living the questions."

"I hate when you say that," said Dane.

"If there is one constant in this life," Lut said, "it is uncertainty. Best get used to it, son, for it will be your ever-present companion." Lut bade him good night and tottered away, mumbling that it was late, he was tired, and he feared he had had one too many plates of creamed herring.

Outside, snow had begun to fall, and the frigid night air fogged his breath as Dane walked away from the lodge hall. A dim shine from the partly clouded-over moon silvered the frozen footprints in the mud. Despite the late hour, Dane couldn't sleep, and he had decided to find Astrid and tell her that the promises he'd made when he gave her the locket were still held in his heart. Then a figure darted out and stopped in front of him, a small boy looking up at Dane with eager eyes, no doubt another worshipful urchin wanting to touch a real live hero.

"Are you Dane the Defiant?" the boy asked.

Dane said he was.

"You are to follow me to the princess."

Dane gave a weary sigh. He had had enough of the princess that evening and wanted nothing more than to be with Astrid. "Tell her I will see her in the morning."

"Her ladyship says it's urgent," the boy said. "She says your life is in danger."

Dane tried to get the boy to say more, but he started away, bidding Dane to follow. Snow flurried thicker now, and the boy led Dane to the far side of the lodge hall, around to a building that housed the royal stables. "In there," the boy said.

"She's in the stables?"

"Her secret meeting place." The boy held open the door, and Dane saw light inside. Passing the boy, he moved through the open doorway—and suddenly the door slammed shut behind him. Dane spun round to see two youngish brutes brandishing swords, the tips just a hand's length from his face.

"What is this?" Dane demanded. "Who are you?"

"They're my seconds," a voice said behind him. He

turned, and there, stepping from the shadows, was Bothvar, the glowering suitor he had met at the feast, wearing a haughty sneer. "I, Bothvar the Bold, challenge you to a duel." He drew his broadsword, whipped the air with it, and did deep knee bends to limber up. "Do you wish the rules of *Hólmgang* or *Einvigi?*"

Dane just stared at him. "You can't be serious," he said.

Bothvar slashed at Dane's tunic, cutting a neat swath through the silk. "Bow to me, you maggoty cur!" Dane felt a sword tip thrust onto the back of his head. He pitched forward, landing on his knees in front of Bothvar, who pressed his sword into Dane's neck, using the blade to lift Dane's chin. Pinned between two swords, front and back, Dane decided any sudden moves were out of the question.

"I'm afraid you have me at a loss," Dane said, trying to keep a reasonable, nonthreatening tone, "since I've no idea why I have caused offense."

"I take offense to rank, ill-bred scum who don't know their place. Who think because they sit at a king's table, they have rights to the king's niece as well."

Now Dane knew what this was about. This swell-headed he-goat—or *brusi*, as his father would have called him—was in love with the princess and feared Dane was encroaching on his territory. "Bothvar, you are wrong to think I have designs on the princess."

Bothvar pressed his sword tip deeper into Dane's neck. "I care not what *your* designs are. Only that her eyes reveal what her heart feels for you." Bothvar abruptly pulled back his sword tip, and Dane felt the sword pressed to the back of his head release, too. "Since you will not choose the rules of our duel, I will," he announced. "I choose *Einvigi.* Which means there *are* no rules."

"And I choose not to duel," Dane said, rising. "Whatever you're trying to prove, I want no part of it."

"Draw your weapon, coward," said Bothvar, pointing his sword at Dane, "or I will slay you where you stand."

Dane saw there was no reasoning with this fool; and if he tried to escape, the man's seconds would hack him down for sure. He picked up the scabbard from his father's war chest and drew out the sword. Bothvar grinned, seeing the blade was broken off and therefore only half as long as his. "The fool brings a dagger to a sword fight."

"The blade is broken," Dane said. "If I'm to fight, at least let me have a proper sword."

"'Tis only fair, Bothvar," said one of his seconds. "He can have mine."

The second moved to give Dane his sword, but Bothvar shouted, "Stay where you are! In *Einvigi* the man fights with the weapons he brings." Bothvar brought his sword around in a mighty stroke to decapitate Dane and end the contest promptly. But Dane ducked it, feeling the whoosh of air over his head. Dane thrust his broken sword upward, aimed at his opponent's belly, but Bothvar easily parried it. Now Bothvar came hard at Dane, slashing powerfully, using the advantage of his sword's length over Dane's pitifully short weapon. All Dane could do was backpedal and deflect the blows, unable to fight back. His only hope was to stay beyond the deadly arc of Bothvar's sword and pray his opponent's attack would fatigue him. But Bothvar was well practiced with his weapon, and his strength unrelenting. Dane realized he was severely outmatched, and would have been even if he had a full sword. Bothvar pinned Dane against a wall—and raised his sword to cleave Dane's head in two. Dane lurched sideways, and his enemy's blade embedded in the log wall. He smashed the pommel of his own broken sword across Bothvar's face, the blow bloodying his nose and stunning him, but just for an instant. Bellowing in fury, he yanked his sword free from the log and swiped at Dane, slicing through his left sleeve, drawing blood. The two circled each other, their heavy breaths frosting the air, Dane recalling a piece of advice he'd once gleaned from his father.

"Know what Princess Kára thinks?" Dane sneered. "That you're a churlish lout with hair lice and foul breath." Enraged, Bothvar lunged wildly. Gripping his sword in his right hand, Dane parried Bothvar's blade and with his left smashed Bothvar's nose again, crunching bone. "'Bothvar the Boar-Pig' she calls you, because that's what you smell like." Blood gushed from Bothvar's broken nose, turning his tunic crimson. "And now you look like a stuck pig," Dane mocked.

"Motherless bastard!" Screaming in fury, Bothvar came at Dane like a madman, both hands on his sword, swiping wildly, blind with rage. Again Dane heard his father's words—*He who fights blindly will be defeated*—and though he had no shield for protection, in a blink Dane saw his opportunity. When Bothvar swung his heavy blade in a wide arc, it took him an instant to stop its momentum and swing it back. Dane leaped forward and thrust the tip of his broken sword into Bothvar's side under his ribs. Bothvar screamed and stiffened, but Dane held his sword fast, watching the blood streaming from Bothvar's wound over the blade. Their eyes met, and Bothvar knew he soon might die, for a further thrust of the blade was sure to kill him.

But Dane buried the sword no deeper. Instead, he withdrew it, and Bothvar collapsed to the ground.

Dane heard a sound and whirled to face Bothvar's seconds, expecting an attack—and would have gotten one if Godrek hadn't barged through the door. Godrek's eyes went from the wounded boy to the bloodied sword in Dane's hand. "Perhaps your father's sword *is* of some use," he said dryly.

The seconds rushed to attend to their friend, and Dane began to tell Godrek what had happened. "No need to explain," Godrek said. "I know a duel when I see one. Lucky I heard the ruckus as I was passing. His seconds would've killed you if—" Godrek abruptly froze, his gaze fixed on Dane's sword in amazement. "The blade!"

His hands feeling suddenly hot, Dane looked at the broken sword—amazed too by what he saw. Along the surface of the blood-smeared blade, forming a mysterious inscription, a long row of rune figures had appeared, a dozen or more, each glowing a pale orange as if lit by a fire from within the blade itself. Awed by the sight of it, Dane knew not what to think. It had to be magic of some kind. Godrek touched a finger to the blade and smeared the blood down the rest of the sword—and on whichever part the blood touched, more glowing rune marks appeared. Dane saw a fevered look come into Godrek's eyes as he stared transfixed at the blade. Under his breath, Godrek mumbled a few disjointed words, as if he were trying to decipher the runes.

"Can you read it?" Dane asked. "What does it say?" Godrek appeared not to hear him, so lost he was in the glowing runes. He reached for the sword handle, but Dane pulled it back, alarmed by Godrek's possessive manner.

"My friend Lut is a runemaster, m'lord," Dane said firmly. "I shall take it to him in the morning." The runic figures began to fade and disappear. And as they did, the fervid look in Godrek's eyes faded too.

"Indeed," said Godrek, nodding. "It's your sword—do as you wish with it." He nodded at the wounded boy being attended to by his friends. "I'm guessing the duel was his idea, not yours. But this Bothvar comes from a powerful family. Give me time to talk with his father, to let him know his son was the instigator. I'll come for you in the morning. Until then, stay out of sight and talk to no one."

Agreeing to do as Godrek said, Dane shoved the sword into its scabbard and left the stables, hurrying through the falling snow to his room in the royal lodge hall. Along the way he suddenly found that his hands were shaking, less from the cold, he realized, than from the fact that he had just narrowly escaped death. A broken sword bequeathed him by his father, a weapon Dane had thought worthless, had saved his life. Then blood—whether by godly magic or some darker curse—had revealed its runic message. This alone had been thrilling. And when Godrek had caught sight of the runic figures, he had taken on the look of a man possessed; clearly he must have some clue to their import. Dane was now determined that, until he learned its secrets, the blade was not leaving his sight.

# 9

# THE SERPENT
# AWAKES

I t wasn't yet dawn when Dane found himself awake
and unable to sleep. He lay in bed, adrift on thoughts
of his father. He pictured a time in his youth when
Voldar had first taught him how to "bring fire." For that
indeed was what his father had said as he struck his flint
rock against his axe blade, sending sparks down into the
tinder brush he had collected. "Man cannot *make* fire; only
the gods do that." The tallow candle near Dane's bed was
still aglow, and the candlelight shone on the sword that lay
beside him on the bed. He watched it gleaming there in
the light, its blade edge dulled and dented by time, yet still
capable of delivering a deathblow if dealt correctly. How
many men had been killed with this ancient blade? How
had his father come to possess it? And who *now* possessed
the other half of the sword?

His eyes fell on the bronze serpent's tail coiled round the handgrip, the beast's horned head forming the pommel at the end of the handle itself, the two gems set in its eyeholes seeming to glow redder. Something within it seemed to be whispering to him. And then he saw it move! Slowly the serpent's tail uncoiled, unwrapping itself from the handle, the whole sword then becoming the serpent itself! Unable to move or cry out, Dane watched in growing horror as the thing slithered onto his leg and began to coil around his calf, his knee, and then his thigh, tightening itself ever tighter. Why couldn't he move? Had the snake—or whatever it was—bitten him with some paralyzing poison? Fearing for his life, he braved another look at the awful creature, its head now sliding slowly up his belly, coming straight for him. Its ruby eyes glowing like hot coals, the serpent's mouth yawned open, and instead of a tongue, Dane saw his very own head emerge from its mouth, and on his face a look of utter terror—

—Dane awoke with a start, bolting up in the bed, his heart hammering. His breathing calmed as he realized it had only been a nightmare. But what a horror! The serpent come to life? His own head? What did it mean? His eyes went to the sword, which still lay where he had left it, sheathed in its scabbard beside him, its serpent's-head pommel intact and unmoving just as before.

Was the sword telling him something? Warning him?

Was it a portent, an omen of danger to come? Whatever it was, it had begun.

Dane quickly rose to get dressed and go see Lut. The old one would know what to make of it all, he thought, and he anxiously pulled on his breeches. But before he could open the door to leave, he heard footsteps out in the hall and a loud knock. He opened it to find his mother, looking very much upset.

"You must leave at once," she said urgently. "The boy you wounded still lives. But Godrek says his father is just as hotheaded as his son and fears he'll come after you. Hurry now—dress yourself! Your horse is being readied. Godrek and his men will get you out the gates and safely away."

Dane started to throw on the rest of his clothes. "But what about my friends?"

"There's no time to rouse them. They'll catch up with you later."

"You'll be coming with me, won't you?"

She looked at him for a moment, gathering her words. "After you're safely away, I'm going with Godrek to his village. I've decided to marry him." All he could do was stare at her, openmouthed, shocked to the core. "Godrek is a good man. And he has power and influence. He offers to make Voldarstad a trading port. Our village will be under his protection, it will grow and prosper—"

"Don't do this, Mother. You do *not* know this man."

"I've known him for as long as I knew your father."

"Do not compare him to my father. That insults his memory!"

"I will never stop loving your father. But neither will I grieve forever. It is time I set aside that pain."

"But you do *not* love him!"

"Love is a luxury, son," she said gently. "Perhaps one day I'll feel it again. This tie will be good for our people. . . . It will be good for me, too, for I'm not so young anymore."

Dane felt his world collapsing. His father was gone and now his mother was leaving as well, marrying a man not for love but for—what was the term? *Practical reasons?* She was trading herself to further the safety and prosperity of her people. It was equally true she was also insuring *her* future, for Godrek was a man of means and property who could support her in comfort. Did it matter that Dane felt no kinship for the man? Or that Dane felt there was something within Godrek that could not be trusted? Perhaps he would feel like this toward *any* man who was taking away his mother. But the thought that she would no doubt live far away from him in Godrek's village was almost too much for him to bear. For he knew he would never again enter his hut at home and be greeted by her warm smile and hug. Or feel his mother's gentle kiss when she tucked him into his blankets at night. Just as never again would he hear the stories his father would tell or the booming laugh that often accompanied Voldar's favorite expression, "Well, I'll be dipped in weasel spit." He had taken all of it for granted when he was growing up, all those moments with the two people who loved him more than anyone else could. He would give *anything* to have just one more night with them together at home, eating, talking, and laughing before the fire. But it was all lost. Everything was changing, his life falling apart.

He came out of the lodge hall to his waiting horse. Godrek and three of his men were mounted and eager to be off. Dane stowed the broken sword in the pack behind his saddle and mounted up without even a look Godrek's way. If the man was expecting approval of his upcoming betrothal, Dane just couldn't find the words. He knew he was being sullen and selfish, but he was not about to smile falsely and say good luck and congratulations to the thief who was stealing his remaining parent. He wanted to go and get Lut's counsel about the sword, but with new danger pressing, he knew that would have to wait until they were all back safe in their village.

Dane looked to the skies for his raven, Klint, hoping to have at least one friend with him on his flight away. "We've no time to wait for your raven," said Godrek, "but I'm sure he'll catch up. Nesting with a new lady friend, no doubt."

They rode out between the gates of Skrellborg as the first rays of morning sun peeked over the eastern mountains. They rode hard and fast, which suited Dane, for he wanted to put distance between his newly hardened heart and the tearful boy who bade his mother good-bye.

Leagues from the Skrellborg gates, on the icy path leading up across the glacier, Godrek ordered the riders to stop. Looking back now at the distant fortress, they could see no riders in pursuit, and Dane knew this was where he and Godrek would part company. Dane turned in his saddle to face the man who had saved his mother and now, it seemed, had saved him. "I want to thank you, Lord Godrek, for all that you've done."

"I do what is honorable," said Godrek, "whenever I can."

"Then you will honor my mother. Or I will—"

"What? Come to wreak vengeance?" Godrek grinned. "I rather doubt that, boy."

Thorfinn reached down and grabbed the reins of Dane's horse, jerking them from his hands. Another man came alongside and pulled Dane from his saddle. He fell to the ground onto the carpet of new-fallen snow. In an instant the three men were on him, pinning his arms. And it was then Dane saw they were near the same crevasse into which Drott had nearly fallen.

"What're you doing? What is this?" But his words just echoed off the ice hills.

Godrek calmly dismounted and went to Dane's horse, finding the scabbard and sword from Voldar's war chest. He drew out the sword, gazing in worship at the broken blade. "You wish to know why your father and I parted company? He was a coward."

"No!" Dane said, struggling against the men who held him.

"He found this—a talisman that would lead to the greatest treasure on earth. But he lacked the courage to follow its path. I didn't know what form this thing took, and he said it didn't exist, but I knew he was lying. I knew I would have to torture him to get the truth. But he disappeared—to a place I never found. Until Eldred revealed he had left a chest and that I was to fetch his son." Godrek chuckled, and Dane once again saw the cold emptiness of his character. "If you hadn't been such a hero, boy, I never would've found you—that's the amusing part." With a flick of his wrist he gestured to his men.

Dane struggled to fight his way free, but Godrek's men were too strong to overcome. Thorfinn drew his knife and, putting it to Dane's throat, said, "Defy *this*."

"No," said Godrek, looking up from the sword, "too much blood." He gestured to the gaping crevasse. "There."

"Godrek, *you're* the coward!" screamed Dane as they dragged him across the snow to the mouth of the chasm. "Face me, you bastard! Face me!"

The men pushed Dane to his knees. Godrek came and stood before him. He nodded to his men, and they released Dane's arms. "Last words, boy?"

Dane looked into Godrek's pitiless eyes. "You had it planned all along. Saving my mother's life, pretending to love her so she would want me to trust you!" Dane started at Godrek, but Thorfinn thrust the knife against his throat, stopping him.

"I had to deliver you alive to Eldred," Godrek said, "so the chest would be opened and I could see the contents."

"You'll not succeed with this treachery!"

"No one will find you, boy, not even that winged wretch you call a pet. I saw to that." Godrek's smirk told Dane that Klint was dead. The shock of it left him bereft, shrunken. Yet a spark of yearning, his desire to live, made him attempt one last bargain.

"The blade is yours. Take it, I don't care. Take it and let my mother and me . . . let all of us return home, and I swear I will never see you again."

"Let you live? You'd come after me. You're Voldar's son."

Dane realized it was true; he *would* pursue him to the ends of the earth. There was nothing more he could say to save his own life, but perhaps he could save another's. "Swear you'll not harm my mother."

Godrek thought for a moment, and a sickening smile came to his lips. "Harm her? But dear boy, that's exactly what I *must* do." There was the thrust of Godrek's boot as it hit his face, a brief, backward stumble, and then a sudden plunge downward into darkness.

# 10

# BOY AND BIRD
# IN LIMBO

Rudely shaken awake by Drott, Fulnir gave a
snort and turned over, trying to return to his
blissful dream of being kissed by the girl in
the king's lodge hall. But Drott gave him another insistent
nudge. "It's Klint! He—he might be dead!"

Moments later they were rushing across the iced-over
snow to Lut's lodgings. They bustled in the door, and a lump
came to Fulnir's throat when he first saw the bird's limp,
lifeless body. Lut had the raven wrapped in a blue woolen
blanket and was cradling him in his arms beside a toasty
fire. Ulf and Astrid were standing solemnly by.

"Is he . . . ?" Fulnir asked, his voice cracking.

"He lives, barely," answered Lut. "Odin loves the raven,
and I have prayed he spare this one."

Lut told them that that morning he had gone to find

Dane, only to be told by Geldrun about the circumstances of his hasty departure. She had also told him about her decision to marry Godrek and leave that morning with him for his home village. "You can imagine my surprise when I heard it," Lut said. "Walking back to my room, I was in such a fog that I almost didn't see poor Klint lying in the snow. I put a thumb to his breast and felt his heart still beating."

"What befell him?" Fulnir asked.

Lut shook his head. "He was perhaps made ill by spoiled meat."

"He had his fill of roast pork at the feast like everyone else," Astrid said. "We'd all be sick too, wouldn't we?"

"Or perhaps he just has a bellyache from too much eating," Drott volunteered.

"Ravens never eat more than their bellies can hold," Lut said.

"Unlike some people," Fulnir added, casting a glance at Ulf, whose gurgling stomach was still digesting the twenty-six squirrels he had gorged on the previous evening.

Klint's head moved feebly. His beak closed and opened, but no sound came forth. "I've sent William for curatives," said Lut. "Perhaps they will purge him of the poison."

"Poison? Who'd poison Klinty?" Fulnir asked, his eyes welling.

Lut shook his head, stroking the bird's feathers. "I'll do my best to save him."

William hurried in holding the small canvas pouches of

herbs he'd been sent to buy, and Lut went immediately to work, mixing a concoction of blackberry-root bark and rue. Fulnir took the raven, cradling him gently by the fire, whispering to the beloved bird, "Klinty, you're going to make it, you hear me? 'Cause if you don't, it would kill Dane. It would just kill him."

Dane could no longer feel his feet. He could scarce feel his fingers either, for that matter, being so cold he could barely think. His whole body shaking, he lay curled in a ball with his greatcoat pulled over his head, trying to keep his body warmth as contained as possible. There was a fierce throbbing in his head and a shooting pain in the elbow of his right arm that rendered it near useless—both injuries from his fall down the crevasse. He remembered the fight with Godrek, getting pushed, and then the long, sudden slide into the heart of the chasm. He dimly remembered awakening some time later to find himself in eerie darkness, completely disoriented. When he'd tried to crawl toward the light, all he had done was slip backward, sliding farther down the ice slope to the place he now lay, in utter blackness.

For a long time he had yelled for help, screaming as loud as he could, hoping that by sheer chance, someone might pass by close enough to the mouth of the crevasse above to hear his cries. Though he feared it was folly, it was the only chance he had for getting saved. Godrek wouldn't tell anyone what had happened; Godrek *wanted* him dead. And it was only Dane's burning hatred of Whitecloak that was keeping him alive. He imagined doing all sorts of violence to Godrek and his precious white cloak, things that he never would have wished on anyone before. But now things were different; his innocence had left him vulnerable to the cunning scheme, and it looked like he would pay for this mistake with his life.

He had wept for a time, for all the things he would never live to see. A life with Astrid. Children. And then he had stopped thinking much of anything. Too tired and numb with the cold, he had just given up and lain there shivering and shaking, listening to the strange kind of silence that surrounded him, his every groan and whimper echoing through the ice chamber and even the sound of his own shallow gasps for air coming back to him. And then, fumbling blindly through his pockets, he had found an old friend to help keep him company.

*Caw! Caw!* Klint's call echoed across the glacier. The raven poked his head up from within a fur-lined box that was tied atop Fulnir's horse behind the saddle. Fulnir turned and held out a berry, and the bird snatched it in his beak and gobbled it down. "You're not well enough to fly yet, so just lie back and enjoy the ride." Fulnir gave him another berry, and Klint settled down into his luxurious nest and went to sleep.

It had been less than a full day since Lut had found the

bird in the snow. His herbal brew had miraculously purged whatever poisons had afflicted Klint, bringing the hardy raven back to life. Fulnir fashioned the travel box, and soon he, Drott, Astrid, William, Lut, and Ulf set out to catch up with Dane. Jarl and his cohorts Rik and Vik stayed behind in Skrellborg. For when Princess Kára learned that Dane had deserted her, she threw her interest Jarl's way, and he was glad to bask in her attentions.

The horses passed the crevasse where Dane had lost his pants and followed the trail up the sloping glacier. Fulnir marveled at the many shades of white there were out on the ice field and at how the clopping sounds of the hooves on the ice seemed to echo back and forth across the frozen hillocks. There seemed to be a different kind of quiet out here on the glacier, each place in nature having its own kind of sounds and its own kind of quiet as well.

Fulnir felt excited to be going home. The trek to Skrellborg had not been without its excitements, but he missed his family. And he knew if they rode hard, they should catch up with Dane before dark and they could all camp together for the night. He hoped they could all put their hurt feelings about the banquet behind them.

The raven suddenly poked his head up from his box and gave a call. "Hungry again, boy?" Fulnir got another berry from his pocket and turned to feed the bird. He was gone. He had hopped from the box onto the horse's rear end and down onto the snow. "Klint! Come back!"

The raven hopped away across the snow, flapping up snowflakes with his wings. Calling after Klint in exasperation, Fulnir dismounted and went trudging after the raven, the others now curiously watching this comic spectacle.

"Why's he running from Fulnir?" asked Drott.

"Maybe the fumes got to him," replied Ulf.

Klint had stopped, Fulnir saw, and was hopping up and down, squawking furiously. Finally catching up with the bird, Fulnir himself stopped when he saw where the bird was: on the edge of the deep crevasse. What was more, to his alarm, he saw there were two furrows in the snow and footprints on both sides of the furrows leading to the edge of the crevasse. He spied an object glinting in the bird's beak and bent down to examine it. He put out his palm, and into it the bird dropped a brass button, a button Fulnir was certain had come from Dane's coat.

The ice beneath him and air around him was so bitterly, bone-chillingly cold, Dane had found the only escape was to occupy his mind by playing songs on the wooden pipe. He had found it in his pocket and had played for so long, he could not remember when he had started. Now it seemed that just gathering the strength to blow a single note was beyond him, each breath a mammoth task.

Then a voice told him to keep playing.

Dane looked across the chasm to see the dim outline of a familiar figure. The Valkyrie was perched on an icy ledge.

"Hello . . . figment," he croaked, too cold and weak to be surprised. "We must stop meeting like this."

"And you must stop falling into trouble," she said crossly. "I weary of watching you hover near death all the time."

"You have something better to do?" he moaned.

"I am *not* your personal corpse maiden! Right now there are bloody battles taking place, dead souls waiting to be ferried. I can't take time out of every busy day to deal with *your* mortality. I should let you freeze to death and finally be done with you!"

Again his eyes fell shut as he gave in to sleep. He felt a rap on his head and cracked an eye open to see the befeathered image of his Valkyrie hovering before him. "Keep playing!" she ordered. Too weak to argue, he put the pipe to his cold lips and blew.

*"Dane! Daaane!"* Astrid stood at the rim of the chasm, beside herself with anxiety. Had Dane fallen in? Or worse, been *pushed*? If so, was he already dead? Astrid didn't want to believe it. He *had* to be alive! But she knew that crevasses such as these could be hundreds of fathoms deep. And then, wafting up from the icy depths, came music . . . was it the wind? No!

"Dane's pipe!" she cried to the others. "He's alive!" She cupped her hands to her mouth and called down into the blackness. "Dane! Daaane! We're here!"

Immediately a rescue effort was launched. One end of a

rope was tied to the saddle of Drott's horse, the other end to Fulnir, and he was lowered into the mouth of the crevasse. "Careful, Drotty," said Fulnir, holding a lit torch. "Drop me and I'll never forgive you!"

Drott pulled on the reins and his horse began backing up. Astrid watched as the last of Fulnir disappeared down into the mouth of the crevasse. "Dane!" Fulnir's voice boomed. "Dane, you *down* there?" They all fell silent, aching to hear a reply. None came. Just the snuffling of Drott's horse and the sound of Fulnir's voice echoing into silence.

Dane heard his name being called, but he could barely muster a response. Once, twice, he tried, his voice but a whisper. Where was the Valkyrie? Had it really been her, or just his imagination? Oh, to be so close to rescue now, but too weak to speak! He even recognized the voice. It was his good friend Fulnir, the warmth and closeness of him filling Dane with hope. And then he heard the voice of Astrid again.

*"Dane! Daaane!"*

Ah, so sweet it was to hear her again. And then—

*". . . if you're down there, ANSWER me!"*

The urgent command in her voice—the iron strength of her plea—struck a similar chord inside him. Roused anew, he filled his lungs with air and gave out the greatest cry he could. . . .

He waited, hearing nothing. Had it been but a dream? He saw a light descending toward him, the warmth of its glow as comforting as if it were the hand of Thor himself reaching down to him. And then the sight of Fulnir's own face came into view. Dane felt such a surge of love and gratitude, it was all he could do to croak a greeting to his friend and listen to the comforting talk Fulnir made as he busied himself in tying Dane's body securely with a rope. Next thing he knew, he felt himself pulled upward, the blaze of sunlight above growing brighter, and within him grew the hope that he would soon see Astrid and his friends—and that one day soon he might have the chance to take the life of the one who had tried and failed to take his.

# 11

# THE CURSE
# OF DRAUPNIR

In the king's lodge hall, Dane was laid beside a roaring
fire and covered with furs to restore his body heat.
For most of that day and into the evening he was in
and out of consciousness, and Astrid never left his side. She
thought for certain he would die, and she found herself saying prayer after prayer for the gods above to spare his life.
Lut made a curative of bog myrtle and mulled wine and
forced a good bit of it down the boy's throat to give him
strength. For hours Dane was out of his head, mumbling
nonsensical things about magic runes and slithering ser-
pents. Astrid sat up with him the whole time, holding his
hand and mopping his feverish brow, never so in distress as
the hours when death hovered over him.

She asked Lut if Dane would live, and the old one rasped,
"If the gods so decree it."

"But why wouldn't they?" she asked. "Surely they should look upon him with favor."

"There is no 'should' when it comes to the will of the gods, girl. 'Tis only their wishes that decide our fate."

"But Dane said that *you* said, 'Perhaps a man could change his fate.' That what the gods willed could sometimes be overcome."

Lut paused, deciding how best to answer. "Yes," he said, recalling the events of the recent past with a rueful smile. "I *did* say that, and I believe it still to be true. Perhaps."

Early the following morning, Jarl, Rik, and Vik came in to check on Dane's condition, and it touched Astrid to see the genuine concern on their faces. For although Jarl and Dane had been rivals for years, engaged in a constant game of one-upmanship, in truth she knew neither wished real harm on the other.

The door burst open and in came Princess Kira. Seeing Dane lying there, pale and motionless, she threw herself upon him, weeping and wailing and pleading to the gods to spare her beloved hero. Astrid could easily see from the hurt look on Jarl's face that he thought *he* had secured the position of her beloved hero. Apparently, having heard of Dane's return, Her Fickleness had given her affections back to him, showing less loyalty, Astrid thought, than a praying mantis shows its doomed mate.

Jarl stalked out in a huff, followed by Rik and Vik. As soon as Jarl had gone, the princess abruptly stopped crying, pointed at Dane, and matter-of-factly asked Lut, "Uh, this one *is* going to live, right?"

"If not, you always have the blond one," Astrid said tartly.

"Right. Well, keep me posted." She made a face at Astrid, gave Dane a peck on the forehead, and was out the door.

"I could strangle that little minx," Astrid heard herself say.

"Never thought she'd leave," whispered another voice.

The words, she realized, came from Dane. He was awake now, his eyes wide open, color returning to his cheeks. Astrid gave a cry of delight and embraced him.

At the sound of Dane's voice, Lut's heart leaped. He joined Astrid and the others now, gathering round his bedside in celebration. From his perch on the bedpost, Klint gave a *crawk!* of his own.

"Klint!" Dane croaked. "You're alive!"

"Good thing, too," said Lut. "We never would've found you had he not heard you piping."

Dane's face clouded with alarm, and he struggled to sit up, looking round the room. "My mother! Where is she? Is she safe?"

Lut laid a calming hand on his shoulder. "Did you not know, son? I'm afraid she has gone away with Godrek."

"We must go after them!" he cried, struggling again to rise. "Her life is in danger!"

Lut admonished him that he was in no condition to travel yet and gently pushed him back down. Astrid lifted a cup of warm mead to Dane's lips. Lut waited for him to take a few swallows, and then he asked what had happened out on the glacier. Dane told them everything, his eyes burning in anger. "He means to kill her, Lut," said Dane, and again he tried to rise. "Let me go! We must go after him!"

"We *will*, son," said Lut, "once we know where he is going."

Dane slumped back on his bed, exhausted. "He is following the runes."

"What runes?" Lut asked.

Dane told of his fight in the stables with Bothvar and what had happened when the boy's blood had touched the broken blade. "Runes appeared, as if by magic. . . ."

"It's a *rune sword*?" Lut said, jolted. For a moment he couldn't speak. Lut had heard of such things, of the great magic that lay within these blades, but in all his years he had never seen one himself.

Dane nodded and said, "There, in my greatcoat. I made a drawing after my fight with Bothvar." Fulnir quickly brought Dane's cloak to the seer. With shaking hands, Lut drew open the cloak and ran his eyes along the calfskin lining. His gaze fell on a series of runic symbols that Dane had scratched into the leather. Lut couldn't believe his eyes. Reading them, he felt his heart race.

"So what's it mean?" he heard Dane ask with impatience,

and the old one brought his gaze back to Fulnir and Dane.

"From your look, I'm guessing it's not good," Drott said.

"I'm afraid," Lut uttered gravely, "we are all in terrible danger."

"For once," Drott moaned, "I wish I hadn't been right."


Later that afternoon, Dane stood with his entourage before the king in the smoky lodge hall, Dane barely strong enough to stand.

"The rune sword," Lut told the king, "is a map that leads to nothing less than the greatest treasure known to humankind, the legendary Draupnir. . . ."

Cloaked in gloom, King Eldred sat motionless on his oaken throne, gazing at the floor. At length he spoke, his voice barely above a whisper.

"Are you certain?" Eldred's voice quavered. "Odin's magic ring?"

"Yes, my lord," Lut answered. "It is said the arm ring was made for Odin himself, but its magic was so great, it caused jealousy among the gods. So Odin hid the ring somewhere on earth, and it was said that if any man be so brave and bold as to find it, he will hold the key to riches greater than any man can imagine."

The king's face paled in dread as he contemplated Lut's words. "Seer, have you any notion what power Godrek would have if . . . ?"

"He found Draupnir?" Lut said gravely. "I can well imagine. The massive ring is said to be fashioned of solid gold. And every ninth day it drips eight *more* gold rings large enough to encircle a man's arm."

"You mean . . . it actually *makes* gold?" asked an astonished Drott. "Like a cow makes milk?"

"Something like that," said Lut.

"Sounds good so far," said Jarl with a cocky grin, drawing smiles from Rik and Vik.

"Except," said Lut, now raising his voice and silencing Jarl with a look, "there is a curse upon it."

Drott threw up his hands. "Well, of course! Anything *really* good, there's *always* a curse on it!"

"If it sounds too good to be true, it usually is," said Ulf.

"It is said," Lut continued, "that he who possesses Draupnir goes mad with jealousy, for he suspects that everyone is plotting to take his treasure away."

"I wouldn't be mad. I'd be happy," said Drott. "I'd share my gold with everyone." Drott caught a doubting look from Fulnir. "Did I *not* share my hunk of cheese with you last week?"

"The moldy part," Fulnir griped.

"I'm sure Godrek has no plans to share the gold with anyone," Eldred snapped. "With such wealth in hand he'll raise an army. No earthly person or kingdom will be safe from his tyranny."

125

"So the rune sword leads to this lost treasure. What was my father doing with it?" Dane asked, almost afraid to hear the king's answer.

The king looked at Lut, gathering his words. "Years ago Voldar was a far different man from the one you knew as your father. We had heard talk that he had found a map to riches of some kind and had left to seek it. And after a long absence he returned here, entrusted his war chest to me, and left, saying only that he had found love and was bent on keeping it. 'There is no greater treasure than love.' Those were the last words he ever spoke to me. I released him from service, and that was the last I saw of him."

"Why did he not throw away the rune sword, instead of leaving it in the chest?" Dane asked. "I mean, if the treasure is cursed and whoever possesses it goes mad—"

"Perhaps he never knew of its magic," Eldred answered. "Or if he did, perhaps he wisely resisted its call. Or maybe lacked the courage to seek out the treasure to which it led. Godrek, however, is not a man given to fear. He will stop at nothing to seek this Draupnir. And if he succeeds"—the king's face went pale—"it will mean the ruin of my realm and all others."

"My lord, we must speak!" Dane heard a voice say. He turned to see a man in a dirty cowled robe, staff in hand, leading two other men in similar robes across the floor. As they approached, Dane's nose was assaulted by an awful smell, and he shot a look at Fulnir, thinking he might be the culprit. But Fulnir also wore a sour look—which meant even *he* was repulsed. The robed men, who Dane now realized were the source of the smell, came and bowed before the king. "We have read the omens, lord king!" the one with the staff proclaimed.

"Have you now, Sandarr?" the king said in irritation, roused from his moroseness. "Yet you gave me no warning of Whitecloak's treachery. Is that not your job description, to foresee the future?"

"My lord, I beg you remember our admonition," mewled the one called Sandarr. "We said, 'The answer will be written in blood.'"

"Bah!" the king spat. "You could have just as easily said, 'Beware Godrek!' *That* would have been more helpful!"

Lut stepped forward, crinkling his nose from the stink. "My lord, we waste precious time. You must send men after Godrek now."

Sandarr looked indignantly at Lut. "Heed not this rustic charlatan, lord king. I'm sure his methods of divination are laughably primitive." Sandarr pointed the end of his staff at Lut. "Begone, you feckless fool! Or I shall visit you with great boils and pustules!"

Lut just looked at him for a moment, then turned to the king. "You're actually *paying* this man?"

"Him *and* his assistants," the king grumbled. "But it strikes me that a change might be in order."

Sandarr indignantly jutted his chin toward Lut and

harrumphed. "Perhaps you'd like to tell us *your* methods of prognostication."

Lut said simply, "I read the runes."

The cowled ones hooted in laughter. "The runes, you say!" mocked Sandarr. "How quaint!"

"Let me guess," Lut said. "You consult pig innards?"

"*Chicken* entrails," one assistant said with a snooty air.

"And I, maggots on rotting meat," sniffed the other.

"And I," added Sandarr, waving his staff in Lut's face, "have had enormous success with sheep's eyes floating in sour milk—a technique far beyond your silly runes."

Having had enough, Lut grabbed the staff and thumped Sandarr across the skull. It made a sound like an axe handle striking a hollow log. Sandarr just stood there, too shocked to move. "Begone, the lot of you!" Lut thundered. "Your fakery delays us! Begone!" Within moments the cowled figures and their odors were sent fleeing like rats before a flood.

"I should have done that long ago," Eldred said with a slightly amused smile. "Now, where was I?"

"Dispatching men after Godrek," Lut said.

The king thought for a moment, his brow knitting. "Godrek is cunning and ruthless. I would have to send fivefold the men that he has to have a chance against him. Even then he would probably kill them all or recruit them against me. No, Godrek will return, and I must keep *every* man within these walls to defend my kingdom."

Dane approached the king, flaring in anger. "Your kingdom? What of my mother's *life*!" Two of the king's household troops came forward, thrusting lances at Dane's chest.

"Emotion has clouded his judgment, sire," said Lut quickly, pulling Dane away. "He means no disrespect."

"But your majesty, we are here at your behest, are we not?" Dane said. "And so it seems only right that you then share blame for my mother's capture!"

Two more guards advanced on Dane, seizing him, but Eldred waved his hand and ordered them to stand down. There was a tense moment, the king gathering his words. "I pity your mother's plight, son," he said at last, "but it is as I said: Every man I send after Whitecloak will either join him or be killed. What would you have me do?"

Dane nodded, respecting the king's sincerity. And so what he said next he said with the utmost calm and control. "My lord, if you will provision us, I will hunt down and kill Godrek Whitecloak." Dane caught jeering looks from two guardsmen; clearly they believed him too callow for such a daunting task.

"*Kill* him?" the king said. "I don't think you understand, son. Godrek and his men are death merchants. Masters of warcraft and weaponry. He has butchered more men in a single day than most men ever do in a lifetime. I've seen him in many a duel and—"

"What will you offer for his head?" Jarl stepped forward

with his usual swagger, flanked by Rik and Vik. Catching his eye for an instant, Dane surmised that Jarl wasn't about to let Dane get all the glory by going on a suicide mission alone.

"Very well," the king said with a sigh, realizing his admonitions were useless. "I will pay one hundred silver pieces for Godrek's head."

William stepped from behind Ulf. "B-begging your p-pardon, my lord," he said, his voice quavering. "But I was the thrall of Thidrek the Terrifying, and I saw him offer *five hundred* pieces for a one-armed horse thief."

Murmurs of disbelief ran through the room, Dane as shocked as everyone else that a mere stripling lad would be so brash as to imply his eminence the king was being miserly. King Eldred's cheeks darkened. He stared hard at the boy, but William didn't blink.

"No disrespect, sire," William continued, "but you have to admit Godrek's head is worth at least twice that."

The king's eyes bulged. "You have dangerous gall, boy!"

"*Three* times!" said Drott, coming to the boy's rescue.

"Yes, sire," said Fulnir, chiming in. "It was you yourself who said Godrek was such a death merchant, a master of warcraft and—"

"Fine!" Eldred barked. "A thousand pieces for the man who brings me Whitecloak's head! Make it *two* thousand pieces! Not that I'll ever have to pay it!"

"You are a most generous king," William said, bowing. "I will sing your praises to my dying day."

"Pursue Godrek and that day shall arrive sooner than you think," observed King Eldred the Moody.

# 12

# A Mystical Misunderstanding

A gust of icy wind blew open his coat as Dane reached the top of the riverbank, still feeling a fierce pain in his arm from his fall down the crevasse. He set down the bucket of water he had brought for his horse and, pulling up his woolen hood, stood a moment, taking in the scene. A hazy sun hung low in the western sky like a shimmering bronze medallion. Looking southward, down the sparsely treed ridge line that ran alongside the winding river, he saw Fulnir, Drott, Ulf, and the others all spread in a line, tending to their horses and their own thirst as well. And he could still see, far on the southernmost horizon, the dot that was Skrellborg, the king's fortress whence they'd come.

All day they had ridden, and all of it uphill. Soon they would have to find a safe place to build a fire and camp for the night, somewhere near the water but wooded enough as well. With winter coming on, ice had begun to form on either side of the river, growing wider and thicker the narrower the river became. He looked upriver, into the rolling hills that lay northward, past the tree line to the icy peaks beyond. Were they headed on the proper course? What would Godrek do to his mother? And what would happen when he did catch up with the man—how would he fare against one so heartless?

That morning they had set out on their journey from Skrellborg, following the runic inscriptions Dane had marked on the leather lining of his cloak. Deciphered by Lut, the message turned out to be a cryptic verse:

> *Travel east or west or south*
> *And ye'll not see the Serpent's Mouth.*
> *To go forth to find Drownir*
> *Face you must your darkest fear*
> *O'er moonless water, white as bone,*
> *Find the secret writ in stone.*

Though the words *Serpent's Mouth* had disturbed him, reminding him of his dream, Dane joined his friends in the daunting task of decoding the message.

"'Travel east or west or south,'" said Fulnir, as they huddled in a circle outside the fortress, "'and ye'll not see the Serpent's Mouth'?"

"Well, that's easy," Astrid had said. "It means we go north."

"But north of where? And what is the Serpent's Mouth?" asked Dane, remembering the sword hilt. "Does it mean the serpent on the sword itself? Or . . ." A frustrated silence had followed; no one seemed to know the answer.

Then Lut had spoken.

"My father's father, Umleth Blacktooth, was something of a fisherman. All day he spent in his skinboat, plying his trade up and down the waters of this very region. He was a bad fisherman, but he did love his rivers. Whether shallow or deep, marshy or swift, he loved them all." The others had begun to roll their eyes, expecting another of Lut's rambling stories that went nowhere. Dane knew better.

"He would say that a river is like a person," Lut told them. "And that each had a character all its own. Umleth named each river according to its own particular nature. If I'm not mistaken, the name he gave to the river that lies north of here was the Coiling Snake."

"So the Serpent's Mouth is the end of the river," said Dane, solving the riddle. "And when we reach the end, it's there we'll find the 'moonless water.'"

"What about the facing-your-darkest-fear part?" asked Ulf. "Is that something we should discuss now, or—?"

Jarl threw back his hair and declared, "Let us hie to the hills! And may our blades find Godrek's head!" And without another word, they had mounted their horses and begun the trek northward, Dane letting Jarl, Rik, and Vik ride out in front at first, to let them feel that they were somehow in charge. By noon, they had found the serpentine river and followed it to the spot where Dane now stood. He bade everyone remount and move on, wondering again what lay ahead.

Just before sundown, in a tiny grove of alder and pine beside a bend in the river, they stopped to make camp, everyone too weary to go on. Still atop his horse, Jarl began to give orders to the others. "You and you—gather some wood!" "You two—set up the tents!" "You there—get started with the meal!" Catching irritated looks from Ulf and Fulnir, Dane just shrugged as if to say that it was better for Jarl to be bossy about the little things than about anything really important.

Joining Drott and William in the woods, Dane began to help them collect wood for a fire, pulling down dead tree limbs and chopping them into kindling. He quelled their complaints about Jarl, complimented William on his diligence with his long-handled axe, and thanked him for his challenge to the king back in Skrellborg.

William grinned and said, "The king could well afford it." And as Dane turned to begin work on another tree, he found Astrid was already there, chopping off the lower limbs with one of her hand axes. They worked together, side by side in silence, until Astrid finally spoke.

"It's sweet," she said, nodding to William, "the way he

135

looks up to you. They all do, you know. They'd rather follow you than Jarl any day."

"Even after my performance at Eldred's banquet?"

"You mean when you puffed up your heroics and became a vain, self-lauding ass?"

Dane smiled. "Exactly."

"I think they forgive you."

"Do you? I see you still wear the locket."

She fingered the locket for a moment, thoughtful. "Do I have reason to remove it?"

"No. I'm more sure of *that* than ever."

He held her look, the birdsong in the treetops all at once going still, and for a moment it seemed they were alone in the world, she and he enfolded in the glow of affection they felt for each other. And then the spell was broken by a clamor of voices from the camp.

As he and Astrid came back into the clearing, Dane could scarce believe his eyes. Beside the supply sled, surrounded by Lut, Fulnir, and the others, stood Kára, the very girl he thought he was finally free of. Wrapped in the finest white fox-fur hat and coat, she was complaining that she hadn't eaten all day and was so ravenous she would die for a plate of hot mutton stew. "The quicker the better," she said, "and don't forget the vegetables. But no radishes or carrots; they don't agree with me—and no greasy meats, either; they're bad for my skin. Oh, and a double mug of mulled cider with just a pinch of cinnamon, and a clove or two if you have it."

Rik and Vik stumbled over themselves to fetch it all for her. Seeing Dane approach, she threw her arms round him, kissing and hugging him so tightly, he had to pry himself free of her.

"Well?" Kára pouted. "Aren't you glad to see me?"

But before Dane could speak, Jarl arrived on the scene and erupted. "What is *she* doing here?"

Kára spun on Jarl, her eyes afire. "*She?* You will use proper language when addressing a princess!"

"Do forgive me," said Jarl with a courtly bow. "Is *pompous brat* a better term?"

Astrid laughed. Kára now turned to Dane and ordered, "Put this man in chains for his impudence."

"Princess, no one is putting anyone in chains," Dane said. "In fact, we don't *have* any chains."

"Well, you can just behead him."

"Princess," said Dane delicately, "might you perhaps tell us *why* you are here?"

She began to explain, rather melodramatically, how she hated her life in Skrellborg, could bear it no longer, and craving the company of real adventurers, she had hidden in the supply sled beneath the folded canvas tents. There she'd lain all day long, quietly enduring the bumps and lurches along the way, her mind alive with visions of what she would encounter in the days ahead.

"But what of your uncle the king?" Jarl growled. "When *he* discovers you missing, he'll know exactly where you went!

He'll send men after you—and no doubt blame *us* for your escapade!"

"My uncle will send no one. He left this morning to raise troops in the west lands. And he gave orders that no man remaining was to leave the fortress. By the time he returns, I'll be so far from home, there's no way he'll find me. Isn't it delicious?"

"It stinks!" Jarl bellowed. "You're just one more mouth to feed. A drain on our resources. Excess baggage that's just going to slow us down and make us more vulnerable than we already are!"

"Excess *baggage*!?" Kára seemed about to explode.

"You're going back," Jarl said, "and if you refuse, I'll tie you to a tree and leave you here."

"You just try it," Kára shot back.

"Now where was that rope?" Jarl said, starting for the sled.

"I can easily tell Uncle you kidnapped me," said Kára with an arched brow.

Jarl froze in his tracks. He looked in shock at Dane and the others. Would this mollycoddle be capable of such a bald-faced lie? "I will tell Uncle, ever so tearfully," she continued, sniffing mock tears, "that you were angry with him for not sending troops with you. So you seized me—took me hostage—with plans to sell me and raise money for more men. Such treachery would never be forgotten, much less forgiven. For as long as you lived, there'd be prices on *your* heads."

Kára stood there, arms folded, a proud, self-satisfied smirk on her face. Then Astrid spoke, casually running her finger along the sharp blade of her axe. "Perhaps you should consider *this*, princess. If you died out here and the wolves ravaged your pretty bones . . . who in Skrellborg would even know what happened to you?"

Kára held Astrid's unblinking stare. "I had thoughts of making you my maidservant, but you prove too coarse even for *that* lowly a position." Astrid's eyes flashed, she raised her hand at Kára, and the girl rushed to Dane for protection, throwing her arms about him. "I am Princess Kára of the Skrellborg royal house!" she spat to all. "And I bid you build a fire— *now* —for I am cold!"

Dane just stood there, sheepish, Jarl and Astrid staring daggers at him. What was he to do? He looked to Lut for help, but the old one merely shrugged and tottered away, leaving it to Dane to figure out for himself. Yet another moment that made Dane hate being a leader.

Astrid lay awake in her tent, listening to the low murmur of the river, too upset to sleep. For hours she had lain there, turning this way and that beneath her furs, her mind astir.

That night they had debated what to do with the stow-away. Sending her back to Skrellborg would take horses and manpower, and their ranks were too thin already. Also there was her kidnapping threat to consider. Jarl argued that they should just hang her upside down from a tree and let the wolves and wights have at her, but Dane had insisted that that was too harsh. At length it was decided: They had no choice but to take her along. And although Astrid knew there was no wiser alternative, she could not help but notice how hard Dane had argued for it.

What did he feel for this girl? She was silly and spoiled, it was true. But she was of uncommon beauty *and* a princess. Whoever won her might very well gain a kingdom and all its riches. Dane had assured Astrid that he still loved her; but now, with Kára in their midst, Astrid feared the brat would be tempted to use her enticements to try to turn Dane's head.

Astrid pushed it all from her mind, telling herself that it would work out. That they would save Dane's mother and get back safe and sound, and return Kára to Skrellborg where she belonged. But when at last she was just starting to drift off to sleep, she heard something. Footsteps? She peeked outside the tent, past the dying embers of the fire. Nothing. No one. All seemed quiet. But just as she was about to turn away, she saw a figure that looked to be a female approaching Dane's tent.

Astrid sat up in disbelief. Had Dane lied to her? Or was Kára acting on her own to force a rendezvous? Astrid got to her feet and threw back the flap of her tent. Upon hearing this, the figure froze. In an instant she turned and was fleeing toward the river. Astrid had her boots on in a wink and was out of the tent, determined to set this girl straight, princess or not.

Reaching the ridge that ran along the river, Astrid crept behind a tree and peered down at the water. What she saw took her breath away. The most magnificent horse she had ever laid eyes on: Monumentally tall and as white as pearls, he was most definitely not one of their mounts. Astrid now saw that the figure moving toward the horse wore a white-feathered cloak, and on her head a helmet of some kind.

Who on earth was this? A spy?

Wasting no time, Astrid was down the bank in a flash, and as the figure was climbing onto her horse, Astrid grabbed her from behind. The cloak came away in Astrid's hand. The girl gave a cry and tumbled backward into the wet grass. Astrid put a foot down onto her chest, which she saw was covered in gleaming armor. This was no girl, but a woman, with big green eyes and a fine bloom of jet black hair spilling out from under her winged helmet.

"Who are you?" Astrid demanded.

"No concern of yours!"

"I'll decide that. Why were you in our camp?"

Before Astrid could react, the woman grabbed her foot and flung her backward onto the grass with amazing power. In an instant Astrid was on her feet again—but the woman was gone! "Give me my cloak!" Astrid looked up, alarmed to see the woman was now seated on the horse—floating in midair over her head, well out of reach. The floating woman sighed with irritation. "No, I'm not real. You're asleep and dreaming."

"You're . . . you're a Valkyrie," Astrid gasped.

"I am but a phantasm of your imagination. The cloak! Give it up and I'll disappear."

Astrid looked down and saw she still held the feathered garment and sensed she might have bargaining power. "I think I'll keep it."

"You have no idea who you are dealing with!" the Valkyrie shrieked. "I shall rain down grief and agony upon you if you do not obey!"

"Still keeping it."

Realizing Astrid would not be so easily fooled, the rider changed her tone. "All right, fine. The truth in return for the cloak?" Astrid nodded.

"My name is Mist. And yes, I am a Valkyrja."

So Dane had been telling her the truth! He *had* seen a Valkyrie! All her life she had heard tales of how Odin's Shield Maidens would descend upon the field of battle and take the spirit-bodies of the fallen war dead up to Valhalla. As a girl she had even dreamed of joining the sisterhood. But her father had quickly disabused her of this notion, saying it was highly unlikely she would live to be a goddess. Those of lowly birth like her could never reach the godly realms, although her mother might have come close.

But now, standing beside the river, gazing up at the vision of the warrior-maiden, a Chooser of the Slain, another, more troubling thought occurred to Astrid: *Someone was to die—or perhaps already had.*

"If you're a Valkyrie," she said, "that must mean someone is to die. Who are you here . . . to take?"

Mist was silent for a moment. "The red-haired one. The one they all look up to."

Astrid felt something break inside her. Suddenly light-headed, she had to seat herself on a nearby rock. As she waited for the weakness to pass, the horse floated to earth and the Valkyrie dismounted and stood before her. Mist stretched out her hand for the cloak, but Astrid clutched it tighter. "When will he die?"

"I must take him now."

"No!" Astrid stood. "I won't let you!"

"His time is already past. He was fated to die twice already, but when the Nornir learned he was *still* alive after the fall into the crevasse, they ordered me to remedy the situation."

Hearing her speak of the Nornir, Astrid felt the awful finality of it all. The Norns, Astrid knew, were the Goddesses of Time, caretakers of the Past, Present, and Future, the godly forces who fixed men's fates.

So it was done; her beloved was to die. She felt a weight pressing down upon her, the weight of an inescapable sadness. Memories of their times together flashed through her mind, the pain unbearable. She saw Mist's hand reach for the white-feathered cloak—when a thought suddenly rose from the depths of her memory.

"Wait! *I* know why you need your cloak!" Astrid said,

jumping away from Mist. "The legend says that if a human steals a Valkyrie's feathered cloak, she must grant a wish to have it returned."

"That legend has been repealed," Mist spat. "Give it to me!"

Again Astrid jumped back, eluding her grasp. "My wish is you let Dane live."

"Impossible. Only the Norns can grant that wish."

"Well . . . take me to the Norns."

Mist's eyes went wide with fear, and Astrid knew that she indeed had the leverage to have her wish granted. "Are you mad? The Norns—they live in another realm and accept no visitors. It's quite out of the question; no one gets to—"

"*I* have your cloak and *you* owe me a wish," Astrid said, holding her ground. "And *my* wish is to see the Norns."

In desperation the Valkyrie began to whimper. "Don't you see? The Norns are already angry at me for delaying Dane's fate. If I go against their decree one more time—"

"So it was *your* mistake! Why did you spare him?"

Mist looked off. "Can you blame me? He was so youthful and handsome and full of promise. I just couldn't bear to see—"

"So you love him, too."

Mist reluctantly nodded. "A Valkyrie must have no feelings. Dead men should be nothing more than stones to be gathered." Astrid saw tears of frustration in her eyes. "I am *trying* to be callous! I really am!"

"Will you take me?"

Mist sighed in resignation. "I can't imagine the Norns will even see you . . . but, yes, I'll do it." Mist closed her eyes and drew her palms upward. Astrid felt a sudden sleepiness overtake her, and looking around, she saw that a vapor had suddenly descended upon them, enshrouding them both, and the thicker the strange fog grew, the sleepier Astrid got, until she felt a hand upon her arm and all went dark. . . .

When next she opened her eyes, Astrid found herself moving through thick clouds, showing blue and silver in the moonlight. She had the sensation of flying, and her heart raced in excitement. Was she dreaming? Moments later, she broke through the billowing mists to find a night sky aglitter with stars, countless sparkles of light, each beckoning for her to come and dance with them. Glancing downward, she was further thrilled to see the pearly disk of the moon reflected in a river as she was passing over it. *Over* it? Yes, she was *flying*! Several leagues high in the sky, she was, seated behind Mist on the back of the Valkyrie's horse. Oh, how they flew! What sweet euphoria as she soared over a mountainside forest of spruce and below her saw the silver-tipped trees in the moonlight! The feeling was indescribable. Such freedom and wonder. And just as quickly, the night sky disappeared as they plunged again into misty cloud fluff. Soon a white flaming light appeared, the glow growing brighter as they flew toward it. Astrid was filled with sudden warmth as the celestial steed sailed ever nearer into the heart of the light.

# 13

# A Spirited Debate
# with the Fates

Before Astrid could even see, she heard it: the frothing burble and bubble of falling water, the sound soothing to her ears. Then the thick veils of vapor parted to reveal a kind of paradise such as she'd never seen. She stood in what could only be a garden of the gods.

Before her there was a moss-hung grotto surrounded by dazzling lilacs and lilies and other blooming plants. From a ledge above, water cascaded down over large smooth stones, emptying into a series of pools, each alive with flashing shapes of silvery fish and leaping toads. There was birdsong and crocuses and the faint croaking of frogs, and around the pool a bright green apron of plush dewy grass that felt soft as velvet underfoot. And arching over it all, a shimmering rainbow—just like ones she had often seen after a spring rain, only this one was bigger and brighter and ever so much nicer. A tiny blue bird alighted on her shoulder for a moment. *Tweep-tweep*, it said, and just as quickly flew off to flit and play in the rising spray of the waterfall. Mist and her steed were nowhere to be seen amid the thick curtains of vapor that surrounded her.

On the pond swam the loveliest pair of snow-white swans. And as the mists slowly receded, Astrid was further awed to see, rooted in the ground and rising up like a kingly tower, an ash tree of unspeakable size, its gray-brown, moss-covered trunk looking as wide as the length of fifty men. Gazing upward, Astrid saw that the tree was of such monumental height, it disappeared up into the mists, its uppermost limbs not even visible. Astrid felt the hairs on her arms rise. Could this be it? The storied Tree of Life? Yggdrasil? The center of time itself? How utterly thrilling, she thought, to be in the sacred place where all phases of time—past, present, and future—came together.

Astrid stood a moment, calmed by the lulling sound of the waterfall and the swans that swam upon the water, marveling at the sight of the pink and blue butterflies that flitted from lily pad to lily pad on the fringes of the pond. Such peace she felt. And such a sense of wonder. And then a new sound: the murmur of voices, low and indistinct. Drawing closer, she saw dim shapes appear. Just across the pool, at the base of the giant ash tree, was a trio of seated figures.

Three women, Astrid could now make out, sat side by

side, each garbed in a flowing robe of remarkable color and beauty, each with her hair wrapped in a headdress of a different color. The woman on the left, wearing a pale yellow headdress, was bent over a loom of sorts, working to weave a silken fabric the color of gold. The lady on the right wore a hair covering as blue as the sky and was feeding the swans with food she drew from a bag at her feet. The woman in the center, scarfed in bright red, was bent over what looked to be a large book, its pages flapping back and forth in the breeze. Each absorbed in her task, the women gave off a relaxed but regal air. They had not yet noticed her at all, Astrid realized; it was as if she were not really there; as if she were merely visiting them in a dream. Was she? But it all felt so real. She crept closer.

And then from out of nowhere Mist appeared at her elbow, explaining in hushed and reverent tones that these were indeed the storied Norns, the Goddesses of Time, the Fates. The one on the left, she said, was Urdr, her name meaning "That Which Is Past." The one on the right feeding the swans was Verdandi; her name meant "That Which Is Now." And the red-headdressed lady in the middle, the one with the dark and penetrating eyes, she was Skuld, so named for "That Which Shall Be."

"Aren't they also called the Wyrd Sisters?" Astrid asked.

"Don't *ever* call them that," Mist said, cringing. "They hate it. Oh, look at their dresses. Aren't they just dreamy? I wonder who makes them. I could use some new summerwear."

She gestured to the pond. "This is known as the Well of Future Reflections. Fate is revealed there and recorded in the Big Book of Life." Mist nodded toward Skuld, who held the book in her lap. Astrid was about to ask another question, but it was then the Norns made themselves heard.

"Hallo! Who speaks?"

"Pray thee make yourself known!"

"Who dares invade the sanctity of our realm?"

The prickly edge in their voices gave Astrid pause. She anxiously watched Mist move forward to the rim of the pond to greet them. What would they do? What powerful magic would they wield?

"Mist? Is that you?" Urdr said, recognizing her. "Have you done as we ordered? Has the red-haired one been ferried to Valhalla?"

Sputtering apologies and begging their godly pardons, the flustered Mist bowed in deference and tried to explain. "Well, that's just it—I was about to fulfill your decree, I really was, but . . ." Mist turned and gestured to Astrid. "But *she* stole my cloak and fouled the plan."

The Norns turned their penetrating gaze upon Astrid, who stood there, terrified.

"H-h-hello," she stammered. "I am Astrid, Mistress of the Blade. I have come to beg for—"

"Silence!" thundered Urdr.

Astrid trembled. She had never been so frightened. She saw the Norns whispering to each other, and Verdandi looked at her and said, "Come forward."

Astrid did.

"Why do you dare to trespass in our world?"

"Well, I—"

"What could possibly be worth our precious time? We are the Fates. We and we alone wed men to their futures—"

"Let her *speak*!" This from Skuld, whose voice had the ring of ultimate authority.

Astrid took a moment to calm herself, then began, her voice still shaky. "I'm here to ask a favor. Actually, it's rather big, so I'm kind of afraid to ask—you being goddesses and all, and me just a lowly mortal of modest birth. . . ."

"Go ahead, child," Skuld said in a voice more soothing than the waterfall. "Ask it. That which is in your heart must be heard."

"It's about the red-haired one, the one who was ordained to die. I want you to change your minds. I want him to live."

A sudden choking cough was heard from Urdr, but Skuld shushed her and, smiling at Astrid, motioned for her to continue.

"He is the love of my life and is too good to die so young. Why, even your Valkyrie," Astrid said, motioning to Mist, "thought him too ripe with potential to suffer death."

Mist muttered from the side of her mouth, "Leave me out of this—you're on your own."

Astrid continued. "But it's not just I who will feel his

loss. He's beloved by so many others. He is a hero to his people. Fated to become a Rune Warrior. A man who brings hope and strength to all who know him. Just last spring he returned Thor's Hammer to Thor himself! And if you have any feeling for humankind, you'll see the error of your ways—the very slight error—and grant this humble girl before you this one simple wish. Please, I beg of you. Let him live."

Astrid then bowed her head in respect, and when she raised her gaze again to the Norns, she saw looks of deep concern on their faces. A quiver of hope leaped in her heart. They understood! Then the Norns erupted in laughter, high shrieks of raucous gaiety. So amused were they that for several moments the Norns did nothing but roll about on the ground, holding their sides, convulsed in whooping peals of derisive laughter.

"Change our *minds?*" Skuld cackled when she finally regained her powers of speech.

"Never in all my days!" crowed Urdr.

"And did you see the look on her face?" Verdandi cried, collapsing into more laughter. "So earnest and heartfelt!"

"*He's too good to die so young,*" Skuld said, mocking the plaintive tone in Astrid's voice. "Now *that's* priceless!"

"*He's the love of my life,*" mimicked Verdandi, exploding in giggles. "So pathetic!"

Astrid felt a cold fire rising in her belly. Something inside her snapped, and she advanced on the Norns in fury.

"*You* are the ones who are pathetic—who should be laughed at and scorned! You hold such power over so many lives, yet you understand nothing. Human pain and suffering? Joy? Beauty? Love? What do you know of these things? Nothing! And because you care nothing, you're less than we mortals! You truly *are* the Wyrd Sisters!"

"How *DARE* you!" Skuld roared.

Mist covered her mouth in shock, fearing Astrid had gone too far.

"How dare I what? Disagree? Talk back? Tell the truth?"

"We've heard enough!" Urdr spat, eyes ablaze. "I command thy tongue to silence!"

Mist tried to pull Astrid away, urging, "We should be going now—"

Astrid was having none of it. There was no stopping the venom pouring out of her now. "You haven't even heard the beginning!" she cried. "That which is in my heart must be heard, right? Isn't that what you said? Well, my heart is screaming that you're wrong—*wrong*! Dane the Defiant can *NOT* die! He's too hungry to *live*!" Astrid shot a look at Mist, hoping she'd jump in here, but the Valkyrie waved her off, wanting no part in this insurrection.

Astrid saw Skuld furiously flipping pages in her Big Book. "You want to punish me now for my outrageous sin of honesty, go ahead. Punish me. I don't care anymore—"

At that moment she saw Skuld slam her finger down onto a page of her book—and suddenly Astrid couldn't speak. Her jaw wouldn't move. In fact, her whole body, she was alarmed to realize, had frozen still as a statue. All but her eyes had been rendered immobile. Scowling, Skuld stood over the Book, the long bony finger of her right hand pinned to the page, a look of utter ferocity and victory on her face. And in a flash, Urdr disappeared from her seat across the pond and in the next instant was standing right beside Astrid.

"In case you were wondering," Urdr said in smug satisfaction, "my Sister has frozen you in time. Pinned you to this page of your life. You can't move, so don't even try."

Verdandi was suddenly standing on the other side of her. "Don't you *get* it?" she whispered in Astrid's ear. "It is Dane's own nature—his daring heroics—that decides it. His own behavior is the thing that dictates his fate. The risks he takes. His insistence on going on these ridiculous quests! Climbing mountains, falling down ice crevasses, fighting to save his mother! It's his own fault!"

Astrid wanted to protest that it was Godrek who had pushed him down the ice crevasse and that one's mother is an honorable thing to fight for—but she couldn't move. She couldn't speak. And it crossed her mind that she might be nearing the end of her own life. Despite her fear, she marveled at the wonder of it all. To be here in this godly realm, interacting with the Goddesses of Time themselves! She only wished that she knew more about the mysterious inner workings of the Book and the nature of time itself. And just as this thought went through her mind, the Norns all suddenly turned their heads and looked at each other.

"She wants to know how it works!" said Urdr.

"So let's show her!" said Verdandi.

They shrugged and both looked at Sister Skuld.

"Behold, the Book of Life!" she cried, and rising up over the open book, she pointed the outstretched fingers of her right hand directly over it. Astrid heard an eerie hum. A sudden wind came up—a tiny storm, Astrid noted, that blew only around Skuld herself—ruffling the Norn's headdress and the folds of her robe. Amid the whistle of the wind, Astrid heard a flapping sound and saw that the pages of the book had begun to turn all by themselves! Faster and faster they flew, pages turning at whip speed, until all at once they stopped. Awakening from her trance, and without even looking down, Skuld stabbed her finger down on a particular spot on the open page. And as soon as she did, Astrid instantly felt free—she could move again. A feeling of ease swept through her and she began to giggle like a child. And then, looking down into the pool, she saw that she *was* a child. She had magically been transformed into a little girl of seven years, her yellow hair falling over her shoulder. Oh, how light and happy she felt.

"Well, how does it feel?" asked Urdr with a knowing smile.

"It's wonderful," Astrid heard herself say in a voice so girlish, it took her breath away.

"Sister Skuld has paged you back into your past."

In the pool Astrid saw herself with Dane at the same age, sitting side by side on a tree branch. She saw Dane impulsively give her a kiss on the cheek, and saw herself slug Dane in the side of the head, knocking him off the branch.

"The first kiss!" Urdr mocked. "How precious!"

Astrid smiled at the memory. "What do you expect from seven-year-olds?"

Skuld again closed her eyes, raised her finger above the book. Again the wind blew and the pages turned and suddenly stopped. In the pool Astrid saw herself as she had been just six months before, walking in the forest with Dane and holding hands. This made her happier still.

"But don't get too comfortable," Verdandi said with an oily smile. "Time has a way of getting away from us all."

Catching a look from Verdandi, Skuld made the pages move once more, but this time they went the other way, from front to back, fast-forwarding into the future. And moments later the pages stopped. The wind died. And Skuld's finger fell onto the page. And just as before, Astrid felt a sudden transformation, mind and body all at once slipping into new feelings altogether. An ache was the first thing she felt, a pain in her back, and a general feeling of fatigue. At first hesitating, she braved a look down into the waters of the pool. Old! She'd become a doddering old woman! Her hair white, her back stooped, her eyes watery, and her face a mass of wrinkles. Worse, she saw Dane's body too, a dried-up corpse long dead and withered, lying beside her.

She shut her eyes and turned away, and when next she opened them, Skuld was once more over her Book and pages were starting to fly. And in a blink Astrid found herself returned to the present, every bit herself again.

"As you have seen, the red-haired one's fate has been written," Verdandi said. "And you have wasted our time enough with your petty mewlings. Mist, take her back, and this time do not fail to return with the boy!" The Norns turned their backs on Astrid with finality.

"But I was told a human can fool his fate!" Astrid cried, not giving up. "That his own acts can determine his life and his death!"

Skuld turned back, wearing a mocking grin. "Who told you this, girl?"

"Our village soothsayer, Lut the Bent. He is a very wise man, and I believe him."

Skuld traded calculating looks with the others, as if they were hatching some plot. "I suppose there has been a time or two when we have allowed fate to be—how shall we say— rewritten? Played out by chance."

"Of course," cautioned Verdandi, "chance has its own perils, and certainly no guarantees. Say we let the boy live for the present. Tomorrow, he *still* might die of his own doing anyway."

"What our Sister is saying," continued Urdr, "given that he is young and inexperienced and going on a dangerous journey to retrieve an item of immeasurable value, it is quite likely he *will* perish. These so-called quests he keeps going on aren't exactly bettering his odds for survival."

"That's what *I* keep telling him," Mist said, forgetting she was on thin ice with her superiors already. "But, no, he *has* to keep plunging headlong into danger—" She caught a fierce look from Urdr and fell silent.

"Yes, he's headstrong, impulsive," agreed Astrid, "but he's only trying to do what's right. Surely you can see that. There must be *something* you can do—some deal that can be struck to give him another chance." At this the Sisters suddenly bent their heads together and began whispering in earnest, every so often sneaking looks back at Astrid. Astrid sensed that they were on the verge of some kind of decision. Had she swayed them?

"You brazenly come here and ask us to make—" At a loss for the word, Skuld looked to Urdr for help.

"Concessions."

"Concessions, yes," said Skuld, "in the usual way we mold time. But if we are to let chance take its course regarding his fate, we require . . . a little something in return."

"Anything," Astrid said.

*"Anything?"* asked Skuld.

At the desperation of her plea, the eyes of the Norns shone with animal desire. And despite the ominous chill she felt, Astrid managed to say, "What is it you want of me?"

The chill night air felt good to Lut the Bent as he stepped from his tent and began his walk through the camp. The embers of the evening's fire still glowed a dull amber, and the smell of woodsmoke on the air stirred his appetite. He'd been awakened by something—a bad dream or a bad case of indigestion, he wasn't sure which—and now he had resorted to fresh air to calm the disturbance he felt in his spirit. The moon, he noticed, was half shrouded in mist, a sign, he often thought, of an omen in the offing. Climbing the slight ridge toward the river, he looked back for a moment at the silent tents, all still in the moonlight, and it gave him comfort to know that his comrades all seemed in safe repose.

As he turned to crest the hill, something came crashing through the brush just ahead—and before he could react, a body collided right into him. He was knocked backward for a moment and gave a frightened gasp—until he saw it was only Astrid. But etched on her face was a look of extreme distress.

"What is it, child?" Lut asked in concern. "Have you seen a ghost?"

Astrid flinched, her face growing paler than the moon. "*Three* of them," she said to him. And then, quickly excusing herself, she brushed past him and strode down the hill, returning to her tent. Lut stood there a long moment. What was *that* about? That look in her eyes—he'd never seen that before. Astrid was no tender flower; she was tougher than most of the men he knew. Whatever had spooked her was very out of the ordinary. But what? Back in his tent, he thought of her haunted look until at last he was overtaken by sleep.

The next morning, watching her carefully across the fire, he tried to read what it was that might be troubling her. She seemed to be staring off into some other realm entirely. And when Dane greeted her that morning, the look she gave him was a strange one indeed, full of longing and dread. Still later, after they had packed up and were on their way again, Lut observed that Astrid insisted on riding right alongside Dane, never letting him leave her sight. Strange, Lut thought. *Three ghosts?* What could it mean? He tried to convince himself that she must have had a bad dream, but something kept telling him otherwise, and he couldn't shake the feeling that whatever it was would be worse than he wanted it to be.

# 14

# GODREK UNCLOAKED

The ride northward had been long and arduous, across a steeply pitched ridge line, but Godrek had scarcely noticed. He had been riding beside Geldrun, relaying his knowledge of the many herbs and plants they passed and eliciting her laughter as well. What a joy to once again hear the voice and see the smile of the only woman he had ever loved. Such was his pleasure, in fact, that for short periods of time he actually forgot that her days were numbered. And whenever it came to him that she was doomed to die by his own sword, he felt a pinprick of remorse, but the moment passed quickly. This is what great men must do, he told himself, to gain their ultimate desire. The life of a loved one was a small price to pay to at last have his emptiness filled, to have his soul made whole. After a lifetime of killing, it would hardly matter to add one more to his score. He would gladly kill tenfold the women, queens even, if this would gain him entrance to Draupnir's lair, for such were the bottomless desires of one born a slave. And as the long ride wore on, he thought of these things, the dark and ugly things that had formed him, the things he had told no one. . . .

His mother had been a thrall, a lowly servant girl owned by King Volund, a powerful warlord in a land far to the south. Although born into slavery, as a child Godrek had been anything but submissive. He had endured daily thrashings meant to beat the insolence out of him; the beatings, however, had only hardened his resolve for revenge against his masters. At age ten he had been put to work on one of the king's warships as an ash boy—an *askeladden*—or fire keeper. He was told that if he let the cook fire die, even in a raging storm, he would be thrown overboard, as had been the boy before him and the boy before that. Such was the fate of the ash boys, for there was always another boy to be pressed into service in the next port, especially for an all-powerful king like Volund.

But the toughened-up ten-year-old had done his job well and—yearning to one day escape thralldom and become a warrior himself—had even found time to study the warriors on board and the way they used their weapons. One night in his twelfth year, as his ship fortuitously came to land near his home village, he got his chance. He stole a sword and jumped ship, with plans to escape north. Before he left, he went to find his mother to say good-bye, for she was the only person to ever have loved him.

To his great shock and sorrow, he had found her on her deathbed, her body but a stick, wasted by disease; and that very night, from trembling lips, she had whispered to him the name of his father. It was King Volund, she said. *He was the son of a king!*

Instantly all his plans for escape changed. He would go to the royal lodge hall and present himself. Once Volund saw what a fine boy he had sired, the king would surely embrace him as his own. No longer a thrall, he would thenceforth be called Prince Godrek, with all the royal property and privileges his birthright bestowed.

But his fantasies were soon dashed. The king had no desire to admit his blood flowed in the veins of a dirty, rough-hewn slave. Instead of accepting the boy as his own, to dodge disgrace he ordered that Godrek that very night be killed. The boy narrowly escaped into the frigid, snowbound countryside, stealing a white cloak from the king's court to keep himself warm. The king's men rode hard in pursuit, a dozen liegemen on horseback hunting him. And they most certainly would have caught him—no doubt drawn and quartered him as well—had it not been for the royal cloak. For, hearing the approach of horses as he crossed a treeless moor, Godrek had lain down in the snow and hidden himself beneath the cloak, the white leather seamlessly blending with the snow, rendering him invisible. The horses had thundered past, just steps from where he lay hiding, and thus he had escaped.

From then on he lived alone, befriending few, trusting no one, learning to kill for his living, and in time he grew to be a cold and cunning warrior, a king's liegeman but never a king. And ever after, he wore the white cloak to remind him of his true destiny, the just rewards of his birthright, the gloried summit he one day would reach. Now, with Odin's Draupnir within his sights, he would soon possess the wealth and might to be a king ten—nay, a hundred—times over. And then he would return to Volund's kingdom—and any other kingdom he liked—to seize what was rightfully his.

Ragnar the Ripper stood with the horses at the mouth of the mountain cave, awaiting his lord's return. At this elevation the wind was biting cold, and he drew his furred coat tighter round his shoulders, contemplating Whitecloak's devilish scheme. They had left the boy's mother, Geldrun, with two men in a thicket of pines a league or so ahead. Godrek had kissed her and lied, saying that while she rested, he would bring back fresh game for *náttmál*. But as Ragnar had ridden back in this direction with his lordship, toward the cave mouth, he knew it was not meat they were after, but the very cave writ on the rune blade; therein Godrek hoped he would find the clue as to where to go next.

Ragnar had been surprised to find himself feeling sorry for the woman. It had made him uneasy to watch Godrek chatting with the mother of the boy he had killed, unbeknownst to her, just days before. Believing they were journeying to Godrek's birth village for their marriage ceremony, she had no notion of the real truth: that Godrek had stolen her son's rune sword and was following its message on a quest to find the most magnificent treasure on earth.

Why, Ragnar wondered, did Godrek, a man capable of monstrous cruelty, keep up the ruse with her? Perhaps because if she learned the truth, she would be a prisoner and no longer such pleasant company? All too soon she would discover Godrek's cruel intentions—that she was but a pawn in his grand scheme—and what then would he do?

At that moment Godrek emerged from the cave, the rapturous look on his face telling Ragnar that they had found it. Indeed, Godrek was talking excitedly about having found "the next piece of the map," as he called it, and he brandished a vellum scroll onto which he had copied rows of runic figures.

"It's here!" he uttered, barely able to contain his excitement. But before he could speak another sentence, the sound of horse hooves was heard approaching from the south. Everyone quickly drew their weapon, tensing for a fight. But then they spied the dark gray stallion, slick with sweat, as it rounded a giant outcropping of rock, the rider none other than Svein One Brow. Wisely, Godrek had stationed him a day behind to guard their rear flank and scout for any pursuers. Ragnar held his friend's steed as Svein dismounted and moved immediately to his lordship to deliver his news.

"A party a day back, m'lord," One Brow said. "I counted eleven." After an apprehensive pause, he added, "Voldar's son is with them."

Ragnar saw Godrek stiffen. "How can it be?" Godrek said in disbelief. "He could *not* have survived the fall!" One Brow said he was certain that the party was led by Dane the Defiant; he had made sure to get close enough to see. Godrek fell silent, and everyone waited to see what their lord's next move would be. A moment later Ragnar saw the grin re-forming on his master's face and the usual glint return to his eyes.

"Shall we ambush them, my lord?" asked Thorfinn, one of the younger liegemen, eager for blood. "Lie in wait and kill them all?"

"Or poison their horses and let them freeze to death?" asked another man.

"No, that takes too much of our time," Godrek said, his grin growing broader. "I have a more . . . amusing way to stop them." And after Godrek had explained his plan to the men, Ragnar had to admit it was ingenious.

# 15

# A Light at the End
# of Darkness

A day and a half later Dane's party stood uneasily at the cave mouth, staring into the maw. That morning they had reached the river's end, the "Serpent's Mouth" writ on the rune blade. From there they picked up the tracks of horses, followed them into the ridge line of mountains to the north, and found the cave entrance.

Examining the ground, Lut saw traces of fresh footprints going in and out of the cave. "They did not try to cover their tracks," Lut said, "which means they *want* us to enter."

Was it a trap? Dane saw the apprehension on the faces of his friends. Sharpening their dread was the cave mouth itself, which resembled the gaping jaws of some savage beast ready to swallow whoever dared to enter.

"Why is it," asked Drott, "these journeys *always* lead into dark, frightening places? Couldn't we once just end up in some sunny meadow somewhere?"

"Not likely," said Ulf.

"Because a quest," Lut said, "is a test to see whose bravery is best."

"Yeah. If it was easy, everyone would do it," Fulnir said.

Princess Kára stared into the dark mouth of the cave. "Will it be dangerous?"

"What?" Jarl asked mockingly. "Afraid it might *muss* your hair, your highness?"

"*You're* the one afraid to muss his hair."

"I am not!"

"You comb it every half hour, you preening ass!"

"Oh, and who's the one staring at herself in her hand mirror every five seconds?"

"I do not!"

"Do too!"

Dane broke in. "The question of who cares *most* for their hair can be settled later. For now the cave awaits us." Jarl petulantly ran his fingers through his golden mane, caught himself, and stopped. Dane turned to the princess and said, "It's likely danger lies within, so I think it best you stay outside."

"But that's the very reason I came!" Kára retorted. "Don't you understand? I've had enough of the boring sheltered life of a princess. I want danger! Peril! Excitement! Adventure! The stuff stories are made of!"

"The stuff death is made of, you mean," said Ulf.

"You could get hurt, Kára," said Dane.

"Yeah," said Jarl dryly. "That's why they call it 'danger,' princess."

Kára gave Jarl a withering look. "I don't care. I've made up my mind. I'm going in and that's that."

"Consider yourself warned," Jarl said, "and don't expect any of us to come hold your hand if you get frightened of the dark." Kára stuck out her tongue at Jarl and he at her. And though it was clear that Jarl was sorely pained to have the princess along, Dane could also see that it wasn't because he disliked her. Quite the opposite. By the way Jarl and Kára each stared when the other wasn't looking, Dane could tell that they had feelings for each other. But nothing they would ever admit, of course. They were both too vain, too lacking in curiosity, and altogether too pigheaded—in short, made for each other. And Dane hoped they would soon stop playing their silly little game so that Astrid would once again know that he had eyes only for her.

After he and Jarl agreed that Rik and Vik should ride ahead to scout for signs of Godrek, Dane told William to stay outside with the horses.

The boy protested. "Why must I stay outside?"

"Because the horses need watching, that's why."

William kicked the ground. "'Cause I'm the youngest? I *don't* need protecting!"

"Just do as you're told," Dane said sharply. "Picket the horses and stay here. It's an important job and I'm giving it to you." Resentful and grumbling, William snatched up the reins and went to tether the horses. Dane understood William's yearnings; not long ago he himself had felt just the same. But Dane had grown up too much to let hurt feelings get in the way of responsibility. The job he had to do was impossible enough as it was—the last thing they needed was an impulsive boy taking unnecessary risks.

Equipped with weapons, ropes, and torches, Dane started in, only to find Astrid scooting ahead of him. "Wait, I should lead," Dane said as he jumped in front of her.

"Where is that written, in the quest rules?" Astrid said, hurrying to lead the group.

"There may be peril ahead," he said, elbowing his way around her.

"I'm *just* as good with peril as you, Dane!" she said, forcing her way past him. "Maybe even better!"

Dane stopped her. "What's wrong with you? You've been acting odd lately."

"Perhaps I'm tired of you hogging the glory."

"We *all* are," cracked Jarl, walking past them.

Dane gawked at Astrid. "I do *not* hog the glory."

"You're always first into danger," Astrid accused. "As if you think the gods will always spare the *great* Dane the Defiant." Although her tone and words were hard, as he met her gaze, Dane saw a hint of something else in her eyes. Was it fear? He decided he would wait till later to find out, and he let her walk ahead.

With Jarl and Astrid leading, the party went deeper into the passageway, the air turning colder as the tunnel widened, and the princess griping that if she'd known it would be this chilly, she'd have brought her ermine coat and sealskin gloves. The footing became wet, with small pools of icy water to avoid. Soon they came across the skeletons of long-dead animals, their bones scattered about as if they had been dragged there, stripped of their meat, and sucked clean of their marrow. Amid the detritus of death Dane spied small misshapen skulls, vaguely human, but before he could ask Lut what kind of creature these skulls could be from, Astrid said, "Stop!" and signaled for silence. Eerie echoing whispers came floating on the air.

"What *is* that?" the princess blurted. Everyone shushed her and they listened again. To Dane, the whispering seemed to be a strange, guttural language, full of growls and squeaks, as if the speakers were more animal than human.

"Dark dwarves," Lut said, gesturing to the small, human-like skulls mixed with the strewn-about bones. "They eat animal flesh, and sometimes even their own." Lut tossed his torch high in the air, and the light swept the ceiling to reveal a chilling sight. A score of the awful creatures, small, squat, and deathly pale, perched like gargoyles directly above them. They screeched, shielding their eyes from the glare, and quickly scuttled back behind rocks. Dane heard the princess gasp in fright. Drott began to hiccup, his usual response when suddenly shocked. So it was true what Godrek had

told them! The dark dwarves were all too real and dangerously close.

"They'll not come near the firelight," Lut said, picking up
his torch. Warily the eight of them continued on, huddled
together. Soon Dane spied a dim, ghostly light ahead, a glow
that grew brighter as they approached. Abruptly the tunnel
opened into a large, cavernous chamber, and peering upward,
they gaped in amazement.

Above them were stars, seemingly hundreds, each giving
off a shimmering pale blue glow. Dane wondered how this
was possible. They were inside a cave—at midday, no less!
Feeling some act of courage was in order, Dane stepped forward, and his torchlight revealed something even stranger.
Hundreds of silken strands hung like fine ropes from above,
glistening eerily in the torchlight. The silence was broken by
a chilling shriek, and as he turned to the sound, Dane's torch
cast its light upward, causing everyone to gasp at what they
saw. It was a dwarf creature, caught in the sticky strands. It
struggled to free itself, but its desperate gyrations served only
to entangle it further.

"It needs help!" the princess cried.

Before anyone could decide what to do, the trapped and
terrified creature was drawn upward, like a fish on a line.
Dane saw what was on the ceiling. The points of light weren't
stars; they were the luminous tail sacs of giant insects. They
resembled monstrous, hairy caterpillars, their pale pink
segmented bodies the length of two grown men and as big

around as a mead barrel. And from each creature hung dozens of the silken snares that it used to trap prey. The insect's mouth rapidly gobbled in the strands that had trapped the pitiful dark dwarf, pulling the creature higher and higher, its awful shrieks growing louder and more desperate, until at last it was enveloped in the monster's mouth and its screams were heard no more. Just the sounds of bones being crushed. Dane noticed that Princess Kára was not the only one to turn away from the gruesome sight.

"Remind me not to die that way," said Ulf the Whale.

"Don't worry," said Fulnir. "They could never lift you."

"And who knows," said Drott, "you might get so hungry, you'd eat one of *them* instead."

Moving on, careful to stay clear of the forest of snares, they descended steps cut into the rock that looked to have been carved in ancient times. Down they descended until the steps gave way to a rocky ledge, Dane halting the group as he discovered that just paces ahead the ledge dropped away to a large subterranean lake perhaps thirty paces below.

"The moonless water," Astrid said. "The thing we seek must be near." They searched the area by torchlight, but they could see nothing bearing runic inscriptions.

Lut lowered his torch to the ground and pointed to parallel lines newly scraped in the rock. He followed the lines to the ledge that fell away to the lake below. He retraced his steps, pointing to where the lines started. "A great slab of rock stood here—most likely the runestone we seek. But it was recently moved, dragged across here"—his fingers traced the lines to the edge—"and thrown into the lake below."

A torch was tied to the end of a rope and lowered down over the ledge so they could see where the great stone had landed. To their surprise, the lake was frozen, and ice had re-formed over the hole where the stone had crashed through. They threw a sizeable rock down, and it broke the new ice, disappearing under the water. Astrid was tethered to a rope harness and lowered over the hole in the ice, but her torch-light could not penetrate far enough into the blackness of the water to see the stone at the bottom of the lake.

"It could be ten or a thousand fathoms deep," Astrid said after she was pulled up. "There was no way to see."

Dane began stripping off his clothes, and Astrid asked what in Odin's name he was doing. "I'm going to swim down and find the runestone. I'll attach a rope and we'll pull it up."

"Great plan, except for two things," Astrid said. "The water is so cold, you'll freeze before you reach bottom. And even if you *make* it to the bottom, there's no light down there to see anything."

"I don't care—I have to try," Dane said, continuing to strip off his clothes.

"Must you always be the hero?" Astrid cried. "You'll die!"

"She's right," Fulnir said. "It's too dangerous."

Lut put a hand on Dane's shoulder. "Son, even if you found

the runestone, it's probably too heavy for our ropes to lift."

Dane stood his ground, angry they were giving up, his frustration turning to fury.

"There is only one way to know Godrek's destination! And that is to read the runestone. There must be *something* we can do, because I am not ready to go home and let my mother's life be sacrificed."

Outside the cave, William sat and glowered. He was dead sick of being treated like a child. He was just as brave and capable as any one of them! But when would he get a chance to prove it? The cave entrance beckoned. He knew he should stay and do as Dane had ordered, but what was the harm of having just one little peek? Besides, he told himself, what if Dane and the others had fallen into a trap and needed his help? They could even be calling to him now, *William! William! Rescue us!*

A short time later, carrying a long-handled axe in one hand and a torch in the other, he crept into the cave. His bow and quiver of arrows slung over his back, he splashed through shallow pools of water, feeling the air grow colder. His torchlight fell on a mass of animal bones. He halted, spying the small, humanlike skulls. And then came a sound so terrifying, he dropped his torch into the water and all went dark.

He fell to his knees, groping for the extinguished torch in panic. He found it and got his flint steel working, but the torch was too sodden to relight. He heard it once more from the darkness: eerie, growling whispers. It was the sound he had heard in the forest . . . the sound of the dark dwarves. The whispers grew louder and came closer. William could almost feel them reaching out to strike. He swung the axe blindly—*whoosh!*—and felt it hit flesh. He heard a shriek of pain. Something grabbed at him, he chopped down with the axe, and another cry pierced the blackness.

He ran, stumbling, falling, feeling clawed fingers grasping at him. He swung the axe, heard animal cries of pain, and felt the spatter of hot blood on his face. He ran, not knowing in what direction, his only thought being escape. He ran until he thought that nothing was chasing or grabbing at him. He found himself in a huge cavern under a starlit sky.

William gazed up in awe at the stars above, too many to count. How could this be? When he was a thrall in Thidrek's castle, he had heard stories of the mystical dwarf Laurin, who ruled an underground kingdom lit by jewels. Yes! This must be it, thought William. He wandered deeper into the cavern, drawn by the twinkling luminescence overhead. He felt something slap his cheek, something sticky. Now, to his horror, he saw he had wandered into a forest of ropelike vines hanging from above. Trying to pull away, he entangled himself all the more. He swung his axe, trying to cut himself free, but now the axe too became caught in the strands. He felt himself pulled up off the ground and he heard himself screaming, a cry of full-throated terror.

*"Help! Help!"* Eerily, his words came back to him, echoing

off the cavern walls, as higher and higher he went. To his horror, he now saw that above him the lights were not glistening jewels after all, but the glowing tails of giant insects, and that one of them was sucking the vinelike strands into its mouth, pulling him ever upward. Shouting frantically, he grabbed for the knife in his boot but could not bend to reach it. As he rose higher, he saw the insect's mouth had pincers on each side that acted like hands gathering up the silken thread, bringing him closer and closer toward its gaping jaws. From above its mouth, the creature's two feelers dipped and touched William's body, as if taking measurements of its next meal. William saw the thing's mouth open—he was going to be eaten alive.

*Fffhit!* An arrow shot past William's ear, burying itself just below the insect's mouth. *Fffhit! Fffhit! Fffhit!* Three more arrows hit the thing's body. It writhed violently like a snake, and William, hanging just below its mouth on the strands, felt himself swung roughly to and fro. Awakened from his paralyzing fear, he realized the shaking had loosened the strands binding him. He got hold of the knife in his boot and struck it upward, slicing through the insect. To his surprise, out poured a mass of pale green goo that fell *splat* on his face and head, the stench of it nearly making him retch.

"Behind you!" someone cried from below. Twisting round, William saw another caterpillar crawling across the ceiling toward him. Another arrow hissed upward, striking this one behind the head. The insect's body arced; its tail shot round, whipping at William, who now saw the thing's glow sac had a needle-sharp stinger at its end. William hacked with his knife, slicing off its tail and glow sac, which fell away to the ground.

He heard more cries from below and saw more of the creatures crawling across the ceiling toward him. His knife hand now free, he hacked desperately at the remaining strands. Although he was high off the ground and would probably break both legs in the fall, he knew he'd rather suffer broken bones than be insect food. He swiped the blade through the last strand still hanging from the dead insect above him— and plummeted.

As fortune would have it, the boy fell right into the rather large and waiting arms of Ulf the Whale, who caught him as easily as if he were an apple falling from a tree. And what relief William felt as, safe at last, Ulf set him down and he was surrounded by the faces of his friends, happy to see him unscathed. All save for Dane, who was furious for having been disobeyed, and William thought Dane might actually throttle him good. But Lut stepped in, pushing Dane away and pointing to the severed glow sac that lay throbbing on the ground, throwing light on their feet.

"Let's get busy," Lut rasped. "We have our light."

# 16

## THE RUNESTONE
## REVEALED

It was decided that Ulf—being a learned reader of runes and insulated by his prodigious fat—would be lowered into the lake. Using sealskin cords taken from his own boots, Dane tied the glow sac around the end of an extinguished torch stick. Rocks were thrown down to widen the hole in the ice. A rope harness was fastened around Ulf's torso, and Drott gave him the glow-sac torch. Straining to hold on, Dane and the others lowered Ulf through the hole in the ice. Dane watched anxiously as the eerie blue light of the glow sac faded from view; and they continued to let out more rope, sending Ulf deeper and deeper into the frigid lake, until at last the rope became slack. He was on the lake bottom. But had he found the runestone? They could only wait, praying for Ulf's safety.

Time wore on. Dane feared he had sent his friend to an

untimely end, when—*kuh-sploosh!*—they heard the blow of air below and with relief saw Ulf's great bulbosity bobbing in the icy water.

Up they pulled him, and it felt to Dane as if they were hoisting up a full-grown ox, the ropes nearly snapping from the strain of his weight. But at last they managed to pull Ulf the Whale up and over the ledge to safety, where they immediately went to work rubbing his vast expanse of skin to restore circulation. At length Ulf regained his powers of speech and haltingly recited the astonishing message writ on the runestone. It proved every bit as mystifying as Dane had expected. . . .

*Trek to where all teardrops shed*
*Freeze into mountains much in dread*
*Where death adorns a kingly throne*
*Ye'll find a king as still as stone*
*Within him rests the blade of runes*
*To lead you to the serpent's doom*

"Why must it *always* be so complicated?" Drott complained. "Couldn't we for once have some *simple* directions, like, 'Go fourteen leagues, make a right, and you're there'?"

"You're sure?" Dane asked Ulf. "That's everything on the runestone?"

"To the word," Ulf said.

"Did you check the other side?" Drott asked. "Maybe that was just Part One."

"I couldn't exactly *lift* it to turn it over, Drott," Ulf said testily. "Maybe you could've done better? Oh, wait—*you* can't read!"

Dane patted the big man's shoulder, reassuring him that he'd done a fine job.

"'. . . Teardrops shed . . . ,'" said Lut, thinking aloud, "'. . . freeze into mountains much in dread.' . . . Hmm . . . frost giants. They're said to be created by the tears of the gods."

"'Mountains of dread,'" said Dane. "Sounds right to me."

Dane saw their faces fall—everyone had guessed where the next part of the quest would take them. All except Drott, who asked, "A sunny meadow? A balmy beach? *Tell* me that's next on the itinerary."

They rode north, Astrid keeping to herself now. If only she could tell Dane what Skuld had said and how she had tricked her. When Skuld made the bargain, she already *knew* where the quest would be taking them. And it wasn't the safe, warm climes Drott wished for. No, it was Utgard, the legendary fortress of the frost giants! The old witch must be cackling now, telling her Sisters how she really put one over on the naïve blond girl from Voldarstad. *Thinks she can save the boy's life, does she? Let's see him try to survive in the yawning abyss of cold and ice!*

181

It was impossible to tell Dane not to go. His mother's life was at stake. And just months before, he had flung himself into equal peril to rescue her from Prince Thidrek. That's what Dane always did—if danger loomed or someone needed help, he always put himself front and center. Yet it was his very selflessness now that would make it difficult for her to keep him out of harm's way. Back in the cave she had tried to convince him to let her lead by calling him a glory hog. And she had hated seeing how her words had hurt him—even though he *had* become big-headed of late, and the attentions of the king's flighty niece weren't helping. Now they were trekking to one of the most perilous places on earth, and protecting him would be even harder. No one knew exactly where Utgard was, only that legend said it lay beyond Mount Neverest, in the trackless, frozen north. They could wander for weeks, and Dane would never give up until Skuld snipped his thread of life.

Cresting an ice-crusted hillock, Dane signaled everyone to stop. From her place at the rear of the long line of horses, Astrid watched Dane conferring with Fulnir and Jarl. And the mere sight of Dane standing there in the wind only worsened her agitation. And what of the Norns? Although she dearly wanted to, she *knew* she could not tell him of the deal she had made with them. News of it would only weaken him at the very time he needed strength and confidence most. And what if she had to make good on her side of the bargain? The thought was too horrible, and she pushed it from her mind.

The *scrawk* of Dane's raven caught her attention. She saw that Dane had placed the bird atop his shoulder and was whispering to him, patting the bird's head and fluffing his feathers. And she knew that he was bidding the bird good-bye, no doubt sending Klint on an important mission. The raven gave a squawk, and in a sudden flapping of wings, up and away he went, his flight so swift that in a matter of moments the bird was but a speck in the sky. Seeing the raven had gone in a northwesterly direction, toward the peak of Mount Neverest, she knew then what it meant. He had been sent to find an old and faithful friend. The only one who perhaps could help them get where they needed to go. She said a silent prayer, wishing Klint godspeed and good weather, for if he failed to find their friend, she feared they were certainly doomed.

From the position of the sun hanging low in the winter sky, Geldrun saw they had subtly changed directions. Godrek had told her his birth village lay northwest of Skrellborg, over the ridge of mountains that bisected the land, and down to the opposite coast on the northern sea. But then they had taken a path that veered due north, toward the distant ice-locked mountains. She asked Godrek why they had changed course, and he assured her nothing was amiss, that the normal path to his village went through mountain passes that would be blocked by early-winter snow, so they must detour north around the mountains. "In a few days we'll be in my village, snug round a fire," he assured her with a kiss.

On the following afternoon she overheard two of Godrek's men grumbling about their provisions running low. "This keeps up," one said, "we'll soon be eating our horses." Geldrun thought this strange. When helping to prepare *dagmál* that very morning, she had seen there was more than enough food to last the few days Godrek had said it would take to reach his village. Why then had the men complained of provisions running low? It was as if they knew their trek would be lasting *much* longer than Godrek had told her.

Geldrun pondered this, staring into the nighttime campfire. Perhaps her thoughts were awry, and everything Godrek had told her was true—that he loved her and soon would take her to be his wife. Why would he lie and take her on this journey if it weren't for that? What possible other purpose could her presence serve?

Glancing up, she caught one of the men gazing at her from the other side of the fire. It was the liegeman, Ragnar the Ripper. He immediately looked away, self-consciously showing her the unscarred side of his face instead. For a moment he glanced back at her, holding her gaze, his eyes revealing a hint of intelligence and empathy. Then, as if feeling he had revealed too much, it was gone, replaced with the usual empty stare of a warrior. He rose and left the campfire.

Godrek sat beside her and made pleasant conversation as he ate his meal, pausing from time to time to caress her cheek with the back of his hand. And though she smiled and returned his affection, her mind wandered to the words her son had spoken when last they were together: *"You do not know this man."*

Dane dipped the bucket into the river, filling it with water for the horses. And as he drew the bucket up again and turned to take it away, he was surprised to see who was standing before him. Godrek Whitecloak. Seemingly from out of nowhere. His smug grin gave Dane a chill in his vitals. Then another surprise—Godrek drew out a sheathed sword from beneath his cloak and threw it to Dane. Dane caught it, and putting his hand on the coiled serpent handgrip, he pulled it out of the sheath. It was the broken-off rune sword, the one Whitecloak had stolen from him. The one with the curse upon it. Godrek came at him, slashing hard with a blade of his own, unrelenting in his charge, and the fight was on. *Clang!* The cry of steel on steel rang out as the two swords came together, the force of Godrek's attack pushing Dane backward. Losing his footing, down the embankment Dane stumbled, falling with a cold splash into the river, still holding the rune sword. He came up gasping for air, fully expecting to find Godrek crashing down upon him to finish him off.

But Godrek, he was surprised to see, was gone. The

riverbank was empty. He stood in the icy water, catching his breath. And then felt the sword move in his hand.

He looked down at it, seeing that the entire sword had come alive. The steel had turned into a long, scaly-tailed serpent, cold and squirming in his hand. Next he noticed that indeed the thing was growing larger and longer—its tail end now wrapping itself round his wrist and its head dropping into the water, its body as thick as his thigh. He desperately tried to uncoil it from his arm, but to no avail. Suddenly the creature yanked him into the water, pulling him upriver. Faster and faster he went, the water choking him as it was forced down his throat, a panic rising as he realized he couldn't breathe and in moments might drown. He saw the beast's head rise up out of the water, growing ever larger, it seemed, its rough, pebbled hide like that of a lizard, and from behind he watched as two giant horns sharp as thorns grew out of the top of its head. He took in more water, choking violently. The beast turned. Dane saw its merciless reptile eyes, as big around as war shields, and—

Dane awoke suddenly, much relieved to find he lay in his furs beside the cold fire of the camp. It was morning. Another nightmare about the serpent, this more horrific than the first. He would have to talk to Lut.

"Cozy?" Astrid stood over him, holding a load of kindling she had gathered. Dane now saw that Kára had snuggled up next to him in the night for warmth. He immediately jumped up, looking sheepish.

"I had no idea she was there," he said to Astrid.

"Right," Astrid said, moving off to make a cook fire.

Kára stirred, still half asleep. "Bring me warm stones to heat my blankets," she mumbled, as if she were still at home and servants were standing by. An iron cooking pot landed on the ground near her head, abruptly waking her. Jarl had thrown it.

"Oh, *princess*," Jarl said mockingly. "Go fetch water from the stream."

Kára sat up, looking offended. "Fetch?" She tossed the pot back, and it landed near Jarl's feet. "That is work for lowborn *dogs* like you."

"What is your function on this trek, *m'lady*?" Jarl inquired, barely controlling his temper. "We all contribute—what *exactly* do you do?"

"I . . . make observations."

"Really. Well, here's one. You're a selfish child more spoiled than a basket of rotting fish!" With that Jarl kicked the pot back at her and walked away.

"He favors you," Dane said.

"Of course he does," she scoffed, as if it were impossible for any man not to and even less possible for *her* to care. But Dane noticed that her eyes stayed on Jarl as he strode away, and he saw on her face the faint but unmistakable stirrings of affection.

That day the trail northward descended into a windswept mountain valley where only stunted trees and sparse scrub grass grew. Ahead of them lay the mountainous, foreboding realm of Jotunheim, the so-called Land of the Frost Giants, a land of mists, blizzards, and savage beasts—the largest and most fearsome of all being the frost giants themselves—or so Dane had heard from his father as a child during countless story times round the fire.

Dane brought his horse alongside Lut's mount. The old man's eyes were closed. He looked to be dozing in his saddle. Dane rode for a few moments, not wanting to interrupt his nap, but then, without even opening an eye to see who was there, Lut asked, "You have a question, son?"

Dane smiled and said, "Do I smell that bad?"

"Your scent is vexed. Is it a girl who sparks your worries? When I was your age, that's all I thought about."

"I had a bad dream," Dane said.

"Ah, dreams," said Lut, "the whispers of the gods. I don't know about you, but sometimes I wish they'd just stop their whispering and leave us alone."

Dane told him of his nightmare, of the sword that turned into a serpent. It had all seemed so real, Dane said. The feel of the serpent asquirm in his hand, the water filling his lungs, the panic, the look in Godrek's eye as he'd slashed down with his blade. What did it all mean? Was the rune sword talking to him in some way? Telling him something? And if so, what? He could have dismissed the dream as meaningless had it not been for the first dream he'd had—of the sword coming alive, trying to harm him.

"*First* dream?" Lut asked in concern.

Dane described the dream that he had had on the night he had first opened the chest. Lut listened in silence, his eyes narrowing. Dane finished and waited for Lut to speak, but the old one said nothing.

"'To lead you to the *serpent's doom*,'" said Dane. "This was the last line from the runestone in the cave. The serpent on the stone, the serpent on the rune sword, the serpent in my dreams. What does it mean? There has to be some connection, doesn't there? Is this a warning from the gods?" Again Dane waited, eager for Lut's response. Lut's eyes popped open.

"I kissed a walrus once," said Lut, his eyes atwinkle.

"Really," Dane said, having no clue what this had to do with his very pressing problem.

"It was long ago in my youth," Lut said, "when a man has his greatest dreams. Every night I dreamed I kissed a walrus that turned into a beautiful maiden, whom I then took as my wife." Lut cocked an eye at Dane. "Have you tried kissing a walrus? Or just getting your arms around one? Not an easy feat. Crippling injuries can occur. But, being an impetuous youth, I believed in that dream so fully that finally I snuck up on a colony of walruses sunning themselves on a beach and kissed one right on its god-awful mouth."

"And *then* what happened?"

"The dream came true, of course," said Lut.

"The walrus turned into a beautiful maiden?"

"Well, not exactly. There were some village girls watching from a nearby bluff. The ridiculous sight of a grown man kissing a walrus made one of the girls laugh so hard, she tumbled off the bluff and fell down onto the colony of beasts below. They started barking and biting the girl, I came to her rescue, and *she* became my first wife."

"Was she beautiful?" asked Dane.

"She was a good and loving wife, if only slightly better looking than the walrus."

"Oh, " said Dane, not sure what the story was meant to convey. Lut saw the puzzlement on his face.

"Son, sometimes dreams aren't *exact* foretellings of one's fate. Perhaps this serpent from the rune sword represents an adversary you will one day face."

"You mean Godrek?"

"Perhaps. Or an actual sea beast. Or perhaps merely some flaw within yourself. Maybe it's all three."

"Well, thanks for clearing it up," said Dane wryly.

"Yes, well, the answers will come by living the questions. But one thing is certain: Whatever this is, you mustn't shy away from it. For, like all inner truths, it will consume you if you don't confront it."

Dane slowed his horse a bit, allowing Lut to ride on. It was amazing, Dane thought, how one conversation with the wrong person could really ruin your mood.

# 17

# A GHOSTLY
# ATTACK

The trail had narrowed treacherously, and staring down into the steep ravine, Dane wondered how he got into these increasingly dangerous situations.

They had ridden through the windswept valley, climbed higher into the craggy mountains, their path soon narrowing into a thin ledge where a sheer ravine fell away to their right. A howling wind had blustered up, threatening to blow riders off their mounts, and Dane had ordered that everyone dismount and walk in single file. They had been walking like this, hugging closely to the mountainside, the horses skittish as they led them on. Dane had tried to push all thought of his mother out of his mind, but it hadn't worked.

Dane heard a shout. He spied Fulnir in lead position holding up his hand, calling for a halt. Leaving his horse for Drott to hold, Dane threaded his way to the front of the line to find Fulnir standing stock-still before a patch of snow soaked with what looked like blood.

Dane pushed his gaze a bit farther up the trail and, through the falling curtain of snow, there saw a huge she-wolf lying on her side across the path. Nearly the size of a bear, the wolf lay stone dead, her snow-white fur streaked with blood from the arrows shot into her, fangs protruding from her half-open jaws.

Coming forward, Lut took one look at the dead wolf and said gravely, "We must turn back."

"Turn back?" Dane asked. "Why?"

*"Draugurwulfn,"* Lut said, now joining them. "Ghostwolves. They'll come for revenge." He scanned the craggy rocks above them. "They may be watching us now."

"But we didn't kill it," Dane said.

"No, Godrek's men obviously did—and left it here so we dared not cross its blood."

"What happens if we do?" Fulnir asked, sounding worried, his hands smeared in wolf blood.

"We'll be marked and the *draugurwulfn* will surely follow the scent," Lut said. "It is said they are the bastard offspring of Odin, made partly of snow and partly of shadow. A *Völuspá*—a female seer I knew in my youth—warned me of their ways, of their thirst for blood."

There was a pause. "It's a chance we'll have to take," Dane said. "I'm not turning back."

Jarl exchanged looks with Rik, Vik, Ulf, and the others, then turned to Dane and nodded. With no other trail into Jotunheim, they had to go forward.

Dane pushed them onward, trying to lead their horses past the dead wolf on the trail. But the horses refused, shying away from the body of the she-wolf. Only after Jarl, Rik, and Vik dragged the wolf's body from the path and threw it over the cliff would the horses finally proceed, though the scent of the beast's blood made them greatly uneasy as they trod over it.

Even with the trail darkening into night and a heavy snow beginning to fall, Dane led them onward along the ledge, desperately seeking a place wide enough to make camp. To Dane's dismay, the wind became a roaring blizzard, with particles of whipping ice so sharp, it stung their faces and greatly limited visibility. For a time Kára whimpered in complaint, the poor pampered thing numbed by the freezing winds, and Dane worried they might have to carry her. But after Jarl had bundled her in more furs, she soldiered on in silence, much to everyone's surprise.

Dane saw that the trail was starting to broaden, and it seemed that perhaps soon there would be space enough to pitch tents and take refuge from the punishing storm. Over the howling wind Dane heard a sharp shriek behind him. Turning, he peered back into the whiteness, barely able to see anything in the blizzard. Moving closer down the trail, he caught sight of Drott's horse furiously rearing and kicking, a vivid slash of blood on its neck. The terror-struck horse frenzied the other mounts. They reared, trying to jerk their reins free from their human leaders. One animal bolted, but the path was too narrow and it slammed into the two horses pulling the sled; all three panicked and lost their footing, and suddenly they were gone, sled and all, falling off into nothingness.

Above the screaming wind Dane heard a chaos of shouts. But all he could do was grip the reins of his terrified horse to keep it from bolting too. Directly ahead, Jarl was doing the same with his mount. From behind him Dane heard a sudden sound—hoofbeats—and turned just in time to see the crazed eyes of another horse, its nostrils flared in terror, thundering up the path straight for him. It slammed him back against the rocky ledge, and he fell to the ground, dazed, as his horse and the other one ran off up the trail.

Astrid tried not to panic. The ghostwolves had come out of the blizzard unseen, leaping from above, attacking the horses and creating havoc on the narrow trail. In the chaos Astrid and her friends were forced to retreat as the wolves turned their attack upon them. She and Fulnir slashed blindly with swords, knives, and axes, but the white fur of the wolves was nearly invisible in the whiteout, and it was like fighting phantoms.

Before their horses fled, Rik and Vik grabbed their shields from their saddles. Made of hard limewood and reinforced with iron, the shields were placed side by side across the path, edges overlapping to form a wall, and everyone took refuge behind them. The wolves leaped at the shield wall, battering it, but the Vicious Brothers dug in their heels, using all their muscle and size to hold back the onslaught. One wolf rammed his head and front legs between the shields and got his snarling, snapping jaws onto Fulnir's arm, but Drott rushed forward, thrusting his sword straight down the beast's throat, and the beast stumbled away, howling in retreat. The wolves repeatedly tried to smash through or leap over the shield wall, but each time, swords and knives drove them back. Finally the attack ceased; Rik and Vik peered over the shields and could see nothing but the blinding white ahead.

In the tumultuous confusion of the attack, no one had noticed those missing.

"Dane and Jarl," said Astrid, realizing, "they're still out there!" She made a move forward to get past the shield wall, but Rik stopped her.

"So are the ghostwolves," he said. "Stay behind the shields."

"But we can move forward together, behind the shields," she said.

"Ahead the trail widens and our shields won't give full cover," Vik said. "We'll be vulnerable to a side attack."

"He's right, Astrid," Lut said. "Until the snow blindness lifts, here we must stay . . . and pray they made it away." She would have to hope that, for once in their lives, Dane and Jarl had let drop their rivalry to look out for each other.

And then the voice of Kára broke the silence. "Uh, are we stopping for food anytime soon? I am absolutely famished. Nothing too elaborate, mind you. Some big juicy elk steaks might be nice, with roasted beets. Or perhaps cold poached salmon and a nice stew of leeks and potatoes."

The looks the others gave her said they might cook *her* for dinner.

"On second thought," said Kára, "I'm really not that hungry. Later is fine."

# 18

# TALL, FROSTY,
# AND HANDSOME

Dane lay in the snow, trying to regain his bearings. His head throbbing, the shrieking gale filled his ears and he saw nothing but a wall of white. He called out, first up the trail where he'd last seen Jarl, and then behind him to where he thought the others were.

His words died on the wind, and no one called back.

He drew his sword and started back up the trail when two ghostwolves came loping toward him, halting in their tracks. They were even larger than the dead she-wolf, Dane was chilled to see, with fur so white, their eyes and blood-smeared jaws seemed to hover before him, disembodied. The wolves began to circle him, heads slung low, baring their canines, watching Dane's eyes. His sword in his right hand, Dane drew his knife with his left and turned with them, trying to keep both wolves in view, for he knew the moment he lost sight of one, it would attack.

Then the one on the left, the female, made a quick, sudden feint at Dane and he slashed at her, missing. He felt teeth ripping into his boot heel as her mate attacked him from behind. He stabbed wildly backward with his knife, the blade hitting fur, and he heard a yelp of pain. The female now lunged forward, locking her jaws on Dane's left arm, sinking her teeth into the stiff, padded sleeve of his sealskin coat. His knife hand now unusable, Dane smashed the pommel of his sword into the wolf's snout. The enraged beast shook him like a dog shakes a rat, Dane's sword flew from his grasp, and he felt himself slammed to the ground. The she-wolf held him there, jaws clamped tightly on Dane's arm to prevent escape, waiting for the other wolf, the one Dane had wounded with his knife, to come and kill his prey. He came into Dane's view, and he felt the wolf's hot breath as he opened his jaws to rip out his throat.

And then a sudden chill came over him. Dane felt himself rising up off the ground. *Am I dead?* he thought. *Am I being taken to Valhalla?* But where was Mist, his Valkyrie? Shouldn't *she* be here to ferry him? He realized that both the wolves were airborne too, and that he was still dangling from the jaws of the one that refused to release him. He saw them: the massive, ice-frosted fingers that were wrapped around their necks, and Dane's spirits rose as he was lifted higher and higher and soon found himself looking into the pale blue eyes of a dear old friend.

It was the frost giant Thrym, the same friendly grin on his face, his beard of icicles even longer and frostier than the last time he'd seen him.

Dane heard a *scrawk!* and saw Klint perched on the frost giant's shoulder.

"Klint found you!" Dane said.

Thrym nodded, smiling, and his eyes went to the bird.

Just then Jarl trotted up, returning from the path ahead. He saw Thrym holding the white wolves by the scruffs of their necks, and Dane dangling helplessly from the mouth of one of them. "Look who's almost *náttmál*," Jarl cracked.

"Ha, ha," said Dane dryly. "Where were *you?*"

"Retrieving the horses. Hey, Thrym."

"Jarl. Looking good. Put on some weight?"

Jarl slapped a hand to his chest. "Muscle. *All* muscle."

"I thought your *head* was all muscle," said Thrym.

"*Thrym,*" said Dane impatiently, "a little help here . . . ?"

"Oh, sorry," said Thrym. He lowered his head to eye the wolf in question. "Drop it!" the frost giant said, exhaling a huge cloud of icy vapor that instantly frosted the wolf's entire fur coat. Whimpering like a scolded puppy, the wolf got the message and opened her jaws, releasing Dane. He dropped, landing with a painful thud on the hard ground.

"Bad wolves! *Bad!*" scolded Thrym. And Dane watched as Thrym turned to a ridge line on a lower elevation all the way across the ravine, and there he set down the wolves where they could no longer do any harm, further shaking his finger at them. Dane could hear the wolves bark and snarl; and then, realizing they had been beaten, the ghostwolves slipped away, disappearing into the snowy whiteness.

Kára knew that frost giants existed. She'd heard Dane tell the story of how Prince Thidrek had traded Astrid to Thrym in return for Thor's Hammer, and how Dane and his villagers had rescued her from Thrym's cave atop Mount Neverest. And finally how Thrym had bravely come to their aid and stopped an avalanche from destroying Voldarstad. Hearing it had been one thing; but actually *laying eyes* on the towering creature, and trying to make sense of what she was seeing—a living, breathing man of ice? Her senses were so overwhelmed, all she could do was sit and stare in wonderment, having lost all power of speech.

This delighted Jarl no end, of course, and he joked that at last his prayers had been answered. "Thrym, you did the impossible," he said, laughing. "You shut her up!"

"I seem to have that effect on people." Thrym sighed, his breath forming a giant cloud of frost that settled over the icicles of his beard, making them grow even longer.

When William saw the *frostkjempe*, he too stared up in awe and disbelief. So the stories were true! The creatures did exist! He marveled at the frost-encrusted giant, amazed that all that ice could be alive. The others welcomed their friend and thanked him for coming to their aid, no one happier to see him than Astrid.

"Thrym, I could kiss you!" she said.

Grinning, the giant bent down and offered his cheek. Astrid coquettishly kissed it—and instantly her lips froze to the spot. Not realizing she was stuck fast, everyone was made uncomfortable by the lengthy show of emotion.

"She *really* likes the guy," she heard Drott whisper to Fulnir. Even Dane looked askance at their seeming display of affection.

Finally Astrid managed to free herself with a cry of pain, leaving a piece of skin from her lip still stuck to Thrym's cheek. The giant grimaced in sympathy.

Last spring, when Astrid had first arrived in his lonely ice cave, Thrym had been so taken by her that he'd hoped they could get over their size and temperature differences to become man and wife. Astrid told him that he was a nice giant, but girls who preferred cozy nights by the fire and guys who melted whenever they even drew *near* one were not exactly the ideal match. Thrym had been angered by her rejection—he'd pouted, stamped his feet, punched holes in the walls—but in time he had realized she was right. They could never be mated. Yet he had never stopped loving her, and this, Astrid knew, was what Dane had been counting on when he had sent Klint to find him.

"When I saw the bird," Thrym told her, "I knew you needed me." The summons had worked the first time, and so it had once again.

It was night and the blizzard had subsided. Thanks to Thrym, making camp had been amazingly easy. They had watched Thrym scoop a large handful of snow from the mountainside and form a cave shelter for them all, marveling that he could do in mere moments what it would take them several hours of labor to accomplish. Then everyone—the people and their horses—had climbed into the snow cave, and Thrym had lain across the top of it, instantly blocking out the freezing winds. Thus shielded, they had felt a cozy feeling come into the cave, the combined heat of everyone's bodies helping to keep them all so warm and toasty that Astrid had said they probably wouldn't even need a fire, and she had been right. Nor would they have made one, out of respect to what it might do to Thrym.

Now Dane sat comfortably atop his furs, glad to have some warmth back in his bones. Ulf was snoring away, and Kára seemed fast asleep beneath her furs, wearied but unhurt by the day's ordeal. Drott was teaching William a game of dice, and from what Dane could tell from Drott's frequently muttered oaths, the boy was beating him handily. With great interest Vik and Rik the Vicious Brothers were watching Jarl comb his hair, and even from across the cave, Dane could easily see the long, glossy strands agleam in the few shafts of moonlight that fell past Thrym's massive body.

Fulnir, he noticed, seemed rather irritable and unable

to sleep, and lay rolling around in his bedroll, vigorously scratching at his arms and legs and even his privates, as if he had been bitten by a load of fleas. But Dane's attention was drawn away as he heard the shifting of an even larger body—Thrym's. Dane saw that the giant had moved so that his face was peering down at them in the cave, the moon visible just over his left shoulder, a look of deep affection on the frost giant's face.

"Now you are safe," Thrym said in his soothing rumble, his voice sounding to Dane like air blown through a giant flute.

"This is the second time you've saved our lives," Dane said.

"I can count," the frost giant said with a growing smile.

Dane had something of a ticklish favor to ask of Thrym, and he looked to Astrid and Lut, who sat beside him, partly hoping that one of them would ask it. They had discussed it earlier and agreed that one of them would have to do it. Astrid gave him a "so ask him already" look. Lut just looked down and began to pick at his fingernails. Dane knew that it was up to him, and he tried to come straight to the point.

"Thrym, I have to ask a favor. . . ." Dane saw Thrym's giant brows arch upward in anticipation of his question. "I was wondering if you could, I mean if you had nothing better to do . . ."

"Yes . . . ?" asked the frost giant, looking as if nothing Dane could say would change his happy mood.

A look from Astrid made Dane get right to it. "I wondered if you could lead us to Utgard."

Thrym's glacial blue eyes went white. His prodigious brow knitted in anger. Hairline fractures of ice spiderwebbed across his face and neck. "You want *WHAT*?" he roared, his frosted breath blowing into the cozy cave, blasting everyone instantly awake. "No! Never!" He stood and crashed his fist into the mountainside, causing a small avalanche, then stalked away into the night, his footsteps shaking the ground. With Thrym gone and thus exposed to the elements, everyone sat up, pulling their furs around them for warmth and giving Dane annoyed looks. Now they'd never get to sleep.

"Good job, Dane," said Jarl.

"Yeah, way to sweet-talk him," said Fulnir.

"You *know* how hesitant he is about returning home," said Astrid.

"All *right*, I get it," Dane flared in frustration. "I should have eased my way into it. Bad strategy on my part." But then they heard the heavy footfalls returning. Dane traded looks with his friends. "Or *not*. Maybe he's thought it over and will agree to—"

Thrym thrust his massive hand into the cave. Dane suddenly felt himself being plucked up and pulled out into the freezing cold wind. For the second time that day Dane was brought face-to-face with the frost giant, and this time Thrym was anything but cordial.

"You *DARE* ask me to take you there? To *Utgard*?" boomed the giant, his breath frosting Dane's face and hair, turning them white. "Have you no heart? No compassion? Have you forgotten I am hated there? That they'll kill me if I ever show my face? Utgard is a death sentence! I save *your* life and you now ask me to risk *mine*?" The giant's icy fingers gripped Dane tighter. "Tell me why I should do this! Tell me!"

Dane was so cold, he could barely think, much less speak. He stared up at the irate frost giant, his teeth chattering, searching for the one answer that wouldn't get him hurt. "Because, uh . . . because *she* wants you to!" Dane pointed down to where Astrid stood on the ledge just outside the ice cave. Astrid gave Dane a look, as if to say, "Thanks for throwing the problem in *my* lap."

"Well, Thrym," she said, cautiously choosing her words, "we all know that with your prodigious strength, you could easily kill Dane with your teensiest little finger, or just rip his head off if you so chose, and I can certainly see why you might like to. Dane can be awfully full of himself at times, fully deserving of such treatment, and there's been many times I've wanted to rip his head off, too."

*Not helping my case, girl,* Dane thought in panic.

"But," Astrid went on, "that would be too easy, now, wouldn't it, Thrym? Because those of giant-size power crave giant-size challenges, something great and noble and worthy of their stature. Something like, well, the one that awaits you back in Utgard." Dane held his breath, waiting to see how the giant would react. To his relief, he saw warmth returning to the giant's eyes as Astrid continued. "For though we all have fears from time to time—terrifying, paralyzing fears—those like you, Thrym, those with true strength of character, are strong enough to face those fears head-on, because they know they are capable of great things if only they try. And that is why we look up to you, Thrym, and revere you, and yes, even love you, now and forever, whether you choose to lead us to Utgard or not. . . ."

Thrym was so affected by her words he began blubbering real tears. Dane watched in awe as they rolled in great rivulets down his cheeks and froze solid right there in his beard, a sight he would not soon forget. They waited for Thrym to regain his composure, and for the longest moment Thrym stared down at Astrid, a smile growing bigger and bigger on his face. The next thing Dane knew, the frost giant had gently set him back on solid ground, and bending down, Thrym brought his face so close to Dane's that their noses practically touched.

"So when do we leave?" Thrym asked.

# 19

# A SECRET
# DISCOVERED

Geldrun knew it would be her end if they heard her crying, and so it took everything she had to hold in her tears.

It had happened quite by accident, as they were making camp at sunset in a wooded canyon. Geldrun had been idly watching Godrek, enjoying the gentle way he had with his stallion, talking to his horse as he removed his saddle and patting him on the head. And then, as he removed his pack, she'd seen it poke through the blanket. A flash of bronze caught the light for the briefest moment, but it was enough for her to recognize it.

The hilt of Dane's rune sword!

What was *he* doing with it? Godrek had quickly covered it up with a blanket and thrown a look to Geldrun, but she had given no sign that she had seen it. Though her heart was pounding, she had simply smiled and calmly gone about cutting the dried deer meat into edible chunks and gone into the trees to gather wood for the fire. Only then, safely out of sight and out of earshot, did she finally break into great muffled sobs, knowing something had gone terribly wrong and fearing her son likely dead. Why else would Godrek not want her to see it? The very sword from the war chest? And why had he kept it hidden? Dane would never have freely parted with it, unless . . . Clearly, there was something Godrek did not want her knowing, and harking back to what she had heard while eavesdropping on the men—that they were running short of food—she knew that Godrek was no longer to be trusted.

She felt swallowed in darkness. She had lost her dear husband just last spring—and now her son? It was all too much to bear. She felt the urge to run and throw herself off the nearest precipice. And blinded with grief, she would have followed her impulse had not some hopeful inner voice reached out from the darkness and pulled her back from the abyss. Perhaps Whitecloak had only stolen it from Dane, she thought, or maybe something else had happened—a fight, a disagreement. Again the voice spoke to her, and she felt new strength arise within, the urge for self-preservation and revenge. She must save herself.

Her sobbing subsided. Regaining some clarity of mind, she recalled the moment Dane had opened the war chest. Godrek's eyes had flashed with covetous desire when he snatched the scabbard from her son's hands and shown disappointment that the blade was broken. Had Godrek discovered some secret about the weapon? And, if not marriage, what did he want with *her*?

"Geldrun."

Chilled by the voice, she turned to see him standing on the rise, looking down at her. For a moment his face was expressionless, and she could not tell if he had seen her crying. But then he smiled and in a playful, chiding tone said, "A fire will not make itself, my love."

She affected a smile and said, "A woman can't have time to think?"

"That depends on where her thoughts might stray."

"I pledge you my heart," she said, returning his chiding tone. "But my thoughts remain my own." She beamed him the brightest smile she could muster, turned her back, and continued her wood gathering. When she looked back, he was gone. It was then she decided that whatever purpose Godrek had for her, she would not wait to find out. The question now wasn't *if* she would flee, but *how*. She was one woman against thirteen hardened warriors. To get away unnoticed seemed impossible, but then a notion presented itself. It was daring and dangerous, yet she had to try it.

That night before *náttmál* Geldrun waited for her chance, and when Godrek was busy dressing down one of his men, she slipped unseen to his bundle and stole his bag of *wenderot.* She had remembered that he carried a supply of the dried herb to ease the pain of his "battle-weary bones." He swore by its pain-easing properties; but would his medicinal cure work the way she hoped it would?

Later that evening Geldrun lay still in her bedroll, pretending to sleep. The fire had long since dwindled, and now the camp was still, everyone asleep, or so she hoped. Beside her, lying motionless beneath his great bear-fur bedroll, Godrek lay asnore. Still she waited. The venison and barley stew she had made in the big iron cook pot had been so enjoyed by the men, many had asked for second and third helpings, which had only given her scheme confidence. Goatskins of wine had also been passed round, and she had seen to it that the men had drunk to their heart's content. It hadn't taken long for the men to take to their blankets, and not much longer for them all to fall asleep. All save the sentry assigned first watch. And sneaking a look now, she could see that the guard, wrapped in a brown woolen blanket, sat with his back against a rock and was using his dagger to pick at stones on the ground. Would he ever fall asleep?

She hadn't been sure how much *wenderot* to put in the soup. What would be the proper dose for thirteen men? Worried she might not have enough and with no time to spare, she had hurriedly dumped the whole contents of the bag into the bubbling pot and just started stirring, quietly hoping her desperate plan would prove effective. Now, lying there under the stars with a chill wind at her back, she knew that she would have to make her getaway soon. Again she cracked open an eye and looked across the camp at the sentry. He slept. It was time. She slipped from her blankets and crept toward the horses with the bundle of dried fish and flatbread she had packed, gaining more hope with every step.

Ragnar watched the woman as she saddled her horse, not knowing what to do. Had she decided Godrek was not good husband material and wanted out? Or had she discovered the plot against her? Perhaps one of the others had secretly told her of it and they were going to escape together. He glanced round the moon-shadowed camp, but all the others were fast asleep. So she was escaping on her own. This woman had fine looks *and* grit.

He lay watching, unable to take his eyes away from her. He had seen her crying in the woods. He had eyed her taking the pouch of *wenderot* from Godrek's bundle and had surmised what plans she had for it. And pretending to eat that evening, he had instead dumped his venison stew in the bushes. Much later, he saw her make her move after the sentry had fallen asleep.

Where would she go? A woman alone in this cold, harsh clime would be lucky to survive. And when Godrek discovered her missing in the morning, he'd go after her with a vengeance. She had no chance. But what could *he* do? Would he not be risking his own life to aid her? Torn, he prayed that the *wenderot* was sufficiently potent.

Moments later Ragnar came up behind her and thrust a hand over her mouth. Instantly she swung around with a knife to plunge it into the unscarred half of his face. He caught her hand a hair before the blade broke skin and whispered, "Your son lives."

She stared at him, her eyes afire. Ragnar was unsure whether she believed him.

"He's two days behind us," he said, seeing her look soften.

"Why do you tell me this?"

"Because you're a good woman. Go now."

She held his eyes for a moment, the way women used to in his youth, and said, "I was right about you."

Watching her mount up and ride off into the night, he spied in alarm the handle of the rune sword poking out from the pack behind her saddle. *By the gods, she has taken it!* Godrek's vengeance, he now knew for certain, would be swift and merciless, and he was relieved to realize that he could easily escape his lordship's wrath by pretending to have been drugged like everyone else. But escape for Geldrun, he feared, would be far less likely.

As Kára rode on the pine-log sled pulled by the frost giant, she thought about something that had never concerned her before. Jarl had said that everyone in the party had a role, everyone contributed in some way. Well, what did *she* do to help? The very idea of helping others was odd to her. Being noble born and accustomed to commanding others to help *her*, she had never had to perform a menial task. She had no notion of what it felt like to fetch or lift or mend or clean. She was never taught to do anything of a practical nature; she had servants to do those things. So why was she even remotely bothered by this?

After Thrym had agreed to lead them to Utgard, he went down into the ravine and retrieved the supplies from the poor dead horses. Five of them had been lost in the wolf attack, and it was decided that instead of riding tandem on the remaining horses and straining them further, they would build a new, much larger sled to carry people and provisions. Thrym strode away across the mountains and, in no time at all, returned with a bundle of pine trees he had uprooted. Everyone had set about stripping the trees of branches and lashing the logs together.

Everyone but Kára. She had done nothing but sit and watch, of course, physical labor of any kind being below her station. Jarl had actually dubbed her Kára the Idle, and she had stuck out her tongue at him as the others had laughed. Watching now, she began to notice how everyone actually enjoyed the communal effort. Even William, all of ten years old, eagerly pitched in. And she couldn't help but notice that

Astrid worked hardest of all, expertly chopping off branches with her axe and stripping off the bark. Kára had marveled at how quickly they had lashed together a sturdy-looking sled and was especially struck with the pride and pleasure they had taken in such backbreaking work. Even Jarl and Dane, not always the best of friends, she had noticed, heartily clapped each other on the back, as if brought closer by the cooperative work. Though it had been too cold for the men to go shirtless while wielding their axes, she had noticed, not to her displeasure, that Jarl seemed particularly well sinewed through his arms and chest.

Now, riding the sled with Astrid, Will, Lut, and Drott, Kára mused on what it might be like to have a role, or "function," as she had heard it called. Perhaps she might find it amusing. She turned to Astrid and said, "I want you to teach me a skill."

Astrid appeared surprised. "A skill? *You?*"

"Something I can excel at."

"Other than being a royal pain?"

"I am *trying* to be civil. All I ask is for—"

"You *didn't* ask."

Kára gave a petulant sigh. This was far too much trouble. She gathered her words, forcing them out with the utmost calm. "I want you to . . . I mean, *would* you teach me how to . . . *do* something?" Astrid just looked at her, expectantly. Through gritted teeth Kára said, "Please."

"Was that so hard?"

"Yes."

Astrid smiled. "What would you care to learn?"

Her eyes went to Astrid's sling of throwing axes. "Perhaps how to use one of those?"

"What for?"

"To kill obstinate commoners," she said wryly.

Astrid drew forth an axe and placed Kára's hand on its handle, showing her how to employ her thumb for throwing leverage. The wood felt rough in her soft, dainty hand. As Astrid let go, Kára was surprised at how heavy the axe felt in her hands, yet there was an excitement to it, an anticipation of what the weapon was capable of, and what *she* might be capable of doing with it.

"Best to use both hands at first," Astrid said.

Kára grasped the handle, hefting it with two hands. "I will keep this . . . I mean, may I keep it for a while—to practice?"

"You may keep it forever. It is yours."

With a careful finger, Kára touched the edge of the blade, thrilled by its lethal power. She had received countless gifts before—furs, jewelry, once a full-grown dancing bear— but this one, she thought, was the best gift of all. She was reminded that there was a certain something one was supposed to say in these situations, but what was it? Oh, yes. The words came, but none too easily. "Thank you, Astrid."

"You're most welcome, Kára."

Kára? What cheek she had, addressing a royal by her first name! Kára had half a mind then to dress the girl down, but looking again at the axe, she decided to let it pass.

Later, as they stopped to rest and water the horses, Astrid noticed Lut eyeing her intently. Ever since the night she had surprised him in the brush after visiting the Norns, the old one seemed to be watching her, studying her more closely than ever. And every look he gave her reminded her of what the Norns had told her—of the offer they had made to her—and it made her sick with worry. Had it really happened? At the time it had seemed so real—the women, the pages of time in the book, her reflection in the pool, the waterfall.

Now, two days later, whenever she allowed herself to think of it, it seemed like a bad dream. Something her mind had fabricated to help her cope with her fear of Dane's death. But she knew it *was* real. It *had* happened. And in time, if she chose to, she would have to pay the consequences.

She turned to walk back, surprised to find Lut standing before her, blocking her path. The look on his face told her that they weren't going to talk about the weather.

"I think it's time you tell me," he said. "About the ghosts."

"Ghosts? I said I had seen *goats*," she replied as blithely as

216

she could, hoping she could bluff her way out of this. But as she tried to walk past him, he caught her arm in his hand, his fingers surprisingly painful as they dug into her flesh.

"I know you, girl. I've known you all your life. I know how you look when some boy has irked you or you're so mad you want to chop off someone's arm or even when you're afraid for your life. This was worse. And it's haunted you ever since, hasn't it?"

She nodded, a single tear running down her cheek.

"Is it about Dane? I see the fearful way you look at him."

"A Valkyrie was about to take him, but—but I couldn't let her."

She fell into the old man's arms, more tears came, and the story spilled forth. About Mist and the Norns. Everything. And choking out the words through her tears, she told him the worst of it. If Dane was to die, when the time came she would be given a choice: To save his life she would have to pledge her own instead. And for nights now she had been unable to sleep, tortured by the question she soon would have to answer: Whose life was more important, hers or his?

Lut held her at arm's length. His eyes were wet and he let out a deep, mournful moan. "Oh, child," he said, barely able to speak, and she fell into his arms again and stayed for a time, sobbing out her tears.

✦

217

Geldrun's roan, Freyja, chestnut and white, was much smaller than the brutish mounts bred for battle that Godrek and his men rode. During the journey, these warhorses had tried to have their way with Freyja, biting and bullying her. But the little roan would have none of it, using her teeth and sharp hooves to give back in kind. Freyja was brave, but also calm and dependable, qualities Geldrun needed the night she escaped, for the trail was strewn with rocks and pitfalls, and she had to trust that her mount would not be spooked by shadows or a sudden hoot from an owl. Still, the going was slow, and when the dark veil of night lifted, Geldrun quickened the pace, riding as fast as Freyja would abide, for she knew Godrek and his men were already on her trail. And their horses were trained to ride hard for days, if need be, to relentlessly hunt down an enemy. Freyja was simply not capable of galloping without stop for long distances. She was game and gave it her all without complaint, but Geldrun had to often stop to give the horse respite.

Late in the day she dismounted and broke the ice on a stream so Freyja could drink. Giving the animal rest, Geldrun climbed a steep rise that afforded a view to the south for leagues. All there was to see was the harsh terrain of mountains, rocks, and snow she had traversed before. Had Ragnar lied to her? Was Dane out there somewhere, or was she riding into a wilderness in which she could not possibly survive alone? Despair overtook her, and she felt her escape foolish and impulsive. Just as her agreeing to go away and marry Godrek had been. How blind she had been not to see his true motives!

In the midst of berating herself for all that had gone wrong, she glimpsed something moving far in the distance. Something big . . . no, *gigantic*. A frost giant! Yes! And it seemed to be pulling something behind it . . . perhaps a sled of some kind? Then she saw horses and riders, and knew the frost giant was Thrym and that Dane was with him.

# 20

# WHITECLOAK'S REVENGE

The five men on their mounts crested a ridge. It was nearing nightfall, they had ridden all day without rest, and their horses were glistening with sweat. Man and animal alike were hard-bitten warriors, accustomed to pushing themselves past exhaustion in the pursuit of prey, for their leader never gave up, never retreated until he had either killed or captured what he was after. And he expected no less from those in his service.

In the dim light, movement in the rocks below caught Godrek's eye. It appeared to be the roan, maybe a league up the trail. He saw a figure on foot, hurriedly mounting the horse. For a moment she looked his way, and he was sure she saw them, silhouetted on the ridge, for she immediately spurred her horse and took off at a gallop.

The pursuers spurred their mounts on, the heady scent of the chase filling the nostrils of both man and beast.

Geldrun knew her only hope was to reach her son before they ran her down from behind. Once they saw the frost giant, either they would turn back or, if they chose to fight, their weapons would be useless against a gigantic man made of ice. Thrym would crush them.

As if sensing new urgency, Freyja, tired but game, raced south, her golden mane and tail flying. When Voldar had presented Geldrun with the horse, he'd suggested naming her Shining Mane, after the steed that pulls the chariot of the sun across the sky. But Geldrun chose the name of her favorite deity, Freyja, the golden-haired goddess of love.

She heard a hiss and saw a white-fledged arrow fly over her head. She knew it was a warning shot, a message telling her the chase was over, they were close now and there was no escape. But with safe harbor so near, she was not about to stop. She rounded a turn on the trail and spied Thrym in the distance, the soft amber light of the setting sun coloring his ice-clad body. She was only a half league away now, but it was too dark for Dane and the others to see her.

Another arrow flew by. She heard hoofbeats thundering ever closer behind her. And then she was panicked to see Godrek himself coming up beside her on the right, riding his coal-black stallion. At full gallop she rammed Freyja into his horse, trying to knock him off the trail and into the ravine below. Both horses stumbled, Godrek's massive war mount veering into her little roan, biting her neck in fury. The roan's teeth flashed, biting back the stallion on the soft, tender flesh of his nose. Godrek leaned in and grabbed her reins, trying to pull up the mount. Geldrun fought him with her fists and went to draw her knife from her belt, when a vicious backhand from Godrek sent her tumbling off Freyja to the ground.

She lay dazed for a moment, then got to her feet and ran, screaming, *"Dane! Dane!"* Godrek leaped from his mount and caught her, wrestling her back to the ground. His men rode up, Thorfinn gasping, "Lord, look!" All eyes followed his petrified gaze. There in the dusky light they saw the colossal monster down the trail in the distance.

*"Frostkjempe!"* Svein uttered, touching the Thor's Hammer amulet around his neck.

All the men looked stricken with terror, even Godrek. Geldrun tried to call out again, but Godrek clamped a hand over her mouth. She was quickly dragged away, her mouth stuffed with cloth, and was lifted back atop Freyja. Godrek made sure the arrows they shot were collected, so as to not give away they had even been there. Her hands were tied to the saddle and the reins given to one of Godrek's men to lead the horse away. Godrek gave the order to retreat, but half his men were already galloping away, fleeing in fear of the frost giant.

Dane heard a cry in the distance. He ordered everyone to stop so the air was not filled with the sounds of horse hooves and the loud scraping of the log sled over the trail. He listened for it again, hearing nothing but the brush of cold wind on his face.

"What is it?" asked Jarl.

"It sounded like someone calling my name." They heard the distant cry of what sounded like an eagle.

"Bad omen," Jarl said. Dane shot him a questioning look, and Jarl explained, "Well, you know, 'feed the eagle' means to die in battle. So if you hear the bird call your name, you're maybe going to die."

"Thanks for sharing that with me," Dane said.

"Next time I see an omen, I'll keep it to myself," Jarl said tartly.

"You do that, Jarl."

Was it an eagle's cry, or had his burning desire to see his mother again made him *think* he'd heard her call to him? *Was* she near? He wanted to press on, but darkness was upon them, another storm was approaching from the west, and they had to make camp for the night.

Ragnar kept wondering when and if Geldrun would reveal his complicity in her escape. After they had captured her and retrieved the rune sword, he tried to covertly meet her eyes a few times while they rode away from her son's party and the frost giant. Her return look was sullen and hostile, which only increased his disquiet.

She was tied to a tree when they returned to camp so she could not escape. Godrek went and spoke alone to her. Although unable to hear much of their conversation, Ragnar did catch a few of her loud curses. Godrek stood, and his hard eyes found Ragnar across the camp. In that instant Ragnar thought his only chance of escape was to run to his horse. But he saw it was picketed with the other mounts and knew that by the time he got it free, he'd be cut down. Why had he shown mercy to her? Didn't he *know* mercy always makes trouble for a warrior? Godrek was now walking toward him, and he thought it a good time to compose his death poem.

> *O mighty Ragnar!*
> *Once handsome and plucky*
> *Then a Jutlander's knife*
> *Left him scarred and unlucky*

Though it was still a bit rough, he knew there'd be no time for revisions as he saw Godrek striding toward him, and he girded himself for the thrust of his lord's blade.

"Guard her—never let her out of your sight," Godrek said as he walked past. Ragnar's guts unclenched. His feelings of relief were momentary, however, for soon he realized she still held the proverbial axe over his head—and could spill the beans about him yet. Well, at least now he'd have time to work on a second draft of his death poem.

At *náttmál* he brought her food and untied her hands so she could eat. He spoke in whispers and turned his head so the others, eating round the campfire, could not see he was talking with her. "Why have you not told Godrek?"

"Because you will help me escape," she whispered back.

"Again? Have you not noticed there are only eleven liegemen? Godrek executed the sentry who was supposed to be watching you last night."

Her eyes flashed concern. "But I drugged him. It wasn't his fault—"

"Matters not to Godrek. I'll be dead, too, if I help you again. Or if you tell him what I did the first time."

As Ragnar turned to leave, she whispered, "The rune sword—why does he need it?"

"It leads to great treasure. Enough to make him invincible."

"But why does he need *me*? Why can't he let me go?"

Ragnar shook his head and started away.

"Tell me!" she whispered loudly. "Or shall I call Godrek?"

Ragnar glanced at the men at the campfire, hoping she hadn't drawn their attention. "*This* is what I get for aiding you? What—I'm just an ugly brute that you threaten?"

She looked away for a moment; then her eyes returned to him. "Forgive me. I'll not do it again." *Was* she sorry, or

225

merely playing him? Realizing that if he were in her place, he'd say or do anything to gain his freedom, he decided to tell what he knew. "To unlock the treasure, Godrek needs a woman's blood."

He read the shock on her face. *"My* blood?"

"It has something to do with the rune sword. That's all I know," he said, and hurried away.

Later, Thorfinn took sentry duty and the others bedded down to sleep. Since it was Ragnar's duty to guard Geldrun, he made a place near her. She was shivering, so he took one of his blankets and wrapped it round her and made her as comfortable as possible, even though she remained tied up.

"You're not like the others," she whispered.

"What, *they're* easier to look at?"

"Very touchy about that scar."

"It's what people see."

"Some people. I see other things. Like you, off by yourself, writing in your book."

"You're mistaken," he whispered brusquely. "I cannot write or read."

"Why do you keep it a secret?"

"Do you want me to gag you? I'd like to get some sleep." Ragnar settled into his blankets. It was cold, and he wished he hadn't given her his heaviest one. This mercy business was getting out of hand. It was vexing him plenty, and more so now that she had another arrow aimed at his head. She knew his secret.

It had begun two seasons ago, when he and the rest of Godrek's troop were raiding and burning a Saxon town. Mid plunder, he happened to look down and see a leather-covered rectangular item lying there. He knew the name of this thing—men called it a "book." He opened its pages and was stunned by the lifelike drawings, beside which were figures he knew to be "writing." He wanted to know the meaning of these figures, so over the following winter he asked a Saxon thrall to teach him how to read and write.

For his entire adult life he had been an illiterate warrior, but now a more exciting and fascinating world stretched before him. This was not the world of a mindless, duty-bound warrior, of course. Reading made a person think, and thinking led one to ask questions. And a liegeman who questioned his lord's orders was dangerous and subversive. For his own safety, he kept silent about his newfound abilities.

"Do you pen poetry, Ragnar?" she whispered.

"I *will* gag you if you continue to speak," he hissed. From then on she lay still. His mind then wandered to his death poem, and he started his revisions.

Dane felt his stomach lurch as he looked down the sheer rock face of the mountain. He and Jarl were suspended on ropes slung like a necklace round Thrym's neck as the giant climbed upward, using his massive hands to grab purchase on the mountain's rocky crags. Dane looked over at the grinning Jarl, who seemed to be enjoying the experience.

"I bet no one's *ever* been this high!" Jarl marveled. "They look like ants down there!"

Dane fought the urge to spew. The rest of their party was waiting below, and he was quite sure they wouldn't want bits of vomit raining down upon them. That kind of thing could ruin someone's day and even break up friendships.

They had been journeying two days since Dane had thought he heard his mother call his name. The trek had carried them deeper into the frigid abyss of Jotunheim, with no sign of Godrek's party. Without even a horse's hoofprint seen on the frozen ground, Dane began to doubt they *were* on Godrek's trail.

"Is it possible," Dane asked Thrym, "Godrek has taken a different route?"

Thrym gently shook his giant head and said, "No, if he's going to Utgard, this is the only way there from the south."

During the journey, as they drew closer to the frost giant fortress, Dane had detected a growing apprehension in Thrym. He knew about Thrym's crime—that he had accidentally caused a female frost giant, his beloved, to go below the snow line. She had died, and he was convicted of involuntary death by melting. Since then the exiled giant had lived alone, far from his kind, doomed to forever be without love. Well, until Astrid had shown up, that is, but that hadn't worked out too well either, for obvious reasons.

Thrym reached the crest of the cliff and pointed north.

They gazed across a thickly wooded valley to see a sheer wall of white rock, gleaming in the sun, curved and rising up out of the trees, the sides of it so smooth and sheer, they seemed impossible to climb. And the top of it rose so high that the peaks disappeared into the very clouds themselves.

Dane and Jarl stared for a moment, too entranced to speak. Thrym explained that what they were seeing was but the outer wall of the frost giant realm, that Utgard, the fortress itself, lay inside this mountain crater.

For once Jarl was silenced, greatly humbled by the sight.

"It's a fortress within a fortress," Thrym said.

"So how do we get in?" Dane asked.

Thrym pointed to a spot at the base of the cliffs just above the far edge of the woods.

"Entrance is through a cleft in the wall. But it's hard to reach, for first you must go through there." Thrym gestured to the thickly wooded, snow frosted valley below.

"Where? *There?*" said Jarl, believing a pine forest no barrier at all. "All I see are trees."

"It's what you don't see," Thrym said. "Trolls. Thousands of them."

"*Trolls?*" Jarl exploded, nearly falling out of the rope harness. "You never said there'd be trolls! I *hate* trolls! Despise the very sight of them! They're hairy and smelly and—and, well, they're just plain disgusting!" Dane too grew sick at the thought. Months before, he and Jarl had had a very nasty encounter with one of the malicious little monsters down in the Well of Knowledge, and neither wanted to come face-to-face with another, much less a whole slew of them, ever again.

"There must be an alternate route," Dane said.

"There isn't," Thrym replied. "You either go through the valley or go home."

From Jarl's anxious expression, it looked like he was leaning toward home. Usually he was not one to shy from danger or deadly beast, but ever since the Well of Knowledge incident the previous spring, he had developed a fear—or *phobia*, as Ulf had called it, using a Greek word he had gleaned from his readings—of the noisy, noxious beings.

"We go forward," Dane said. "Jarl, if you want to stay back—"

"Stay back?" Jarl snapped. Dane knew the best way to get Jarl to do anything was to question his mettle. It worked every time. "No! I will lead us through the troll forest!" Jarl proclaimed, drawing his sword, holding it up to the heavens in a heroic pose. "My blade is Trollslayer! And scores of the vile vermin it shall smite! Mighty Trollslayer will bring death and destruction—"

"Jarl, we get it. You're on board."

# 21

# A GRUESOME
# WARNING

The forest was deathly quiet. Not a bird was heard chirping nor even a breeze stirring the ancient, towering firs. Dane and his friends crept on foot, leading their horses across a muffling layer of fresh snow, the eerie silence compounding their dread. To Dane it seemed their every step was being watched by unseen eyes. Even the skittish horses seemed to sense an evil presence waiting to strike.

"It's quiet," said Jarl ominously.

"Too quiet," said Rik in answer.

"*Be* quiet," shushed Dane.

They walked on, Dane noticing that the usually cool-headed Astrid seemed particularly on edge as she crept, axe at the ready. She caught his look and turned away, unable to meet his gaze. Why was she so agitated around him? He looked to Fulnir behind him, who gave a scowl in return. What was happening? Were they still upset over the boastful way he had acted in the king's mead hall? If so, they weren't very understanding. Had they no notion of the strain he was under? The burden of so many expectations! He wasn't perfect! Didn't they know that?

The forest became so dense, the sled and its contents had to be abandoned. The towering spruces and pines grew so close together in spots, Thrym had to turn sideways at times to squeeze between them. Everyone held weapons, including Kára, who carried the throwing axe Astrid had given her. She'd been practicing diligently, and her aim was deadly—especially to those who drew too close; she'd nearly killed Drott and Fulnir in throwing accidents. The sight of the weapon in Kára's hand only raised the group's anxiety, and Dane didn't know what was worse, fear of attack by trolls, or fear of dismemberment by Kára.

"Did you hear that?" whispered Fulnir.

"Hear what?"

"*That!*" Fulnir snapped. They listened but heard nothing. Fulnir grew more irritated. "What's wrong with you people? Have you gone deaf or something? Get the wax from your ears and listen!"

Dane watched with interest as Fulnir raised up his nose and sniffed at the air, at the same time vigorously scratching at his privates. Ever since they had escaped the ghostwolves, Dane had noticed a change in Fulnir. First there had been the itching and scratching, as if he had contracted an invisible rash. And then Fulnir had grown unexplainably irritable, fighting with others for food and blankets, being not at all his usual self. At first Dane had thought his friend just out of sorts, his strength sapped by the strains of the journey. But Fulnir had begun hearing sounds that weren't there and sniffing the air and reacting to scents no one else could smell, and Dane had begun to wonder what was going on.

And then they came upon a most gruesome scene. A row of spears sunk into the ground, and atop each, a human skull, the eye sockets dark and empty, the jaws hanging open in silent screams. He could see the skulls were weathered and flensed of flesh, so Dane knew these unfortunates were not from Godrek's party.

"Well, look at that," said Ulf. "A welcoming committee."

"Welcome?" Drott said. "I think it's a warning to trespassers that doom awaits." Drott caught a wry look from Ulf. "Oh, you were joking. So it *is* a warning that doom awaits. Everyone agree?" Drott raised his hand to solicit a vote. "Hands?"

Rik and Vik raised their hands in agreement, both saying, "Warning—doom awaits."

"We *don't* have to vote!" Jarl said. "It's *clear* it's a warning."

"I just wanted to feel some unity," Drott said, hurt.

Dane told them all to be quiet, and they moved on deeper into the troll forest, everyone on edge. They walked for a long time, and Ulf started to get hungry, asking if they could stop and have a snack. Jarl rounded on him.

"*Snack?* You want to *snack* in the troll forest?" he asked, getting in Ulf's face. "Hundreds of those hairy, repulsive things lurking about, eager to rip our guts out, and you want to . . . *SNACK?*"

Ulf shrugged. "Maybe it can wait."

They walked for a while longer. Then, as if a curtain had lifted, the trees abruptly ended and everyone stopped and stared in shock.

Before them stood the troll village, or what was left of it.

The crude little huts were smashed, some crushed flat, as if an overwhelming force had recently swept in and destroyed the entire village without mercy.

"Seems the trolls and frost giants are at war again," Thrym said grimly, pointing to the trees on the north side of the clearing. A large path had been torn through the forest where apparently the frost giants had bulled through to wreak their destruction. Uprooted trees used to flatten the village lay among the destroyed huts.

The scene of gloomy devastation lifted Jarl's spirits. "Maybe I won't need Trollslayer after all. Little buggers have all cleared out."

And as soon as the words had left his lips, a dozen flaming arrows flew out of the woods behind them, striking Thrym up and down his back. The arrow tips, Dane saw, were coated in fiery pitch that splashed across his ice-clad body, melting holes in him. Shrill ear-piercing screeches filled the air. Dane turned to see a horde of troll warriors rushing toward them, faces smeared in war paint, carrying clubs, axes, and scythes, and no troll more than half Dane's height.

Dane, Thrym, and the others fled in panic, their horses scattering.

*Bzing!* More fire arrows fell, most of them raining down on Thrym, embedding in his legs and torso, the flaming pitch eating holes in his frost, the sudden gushes of melting water flowing like blood. His only hope was to find cover. He lumbered through the destroyed village, his footfalls shaking the ground, Dane and the others running behind him toward the trees on the far side of the clearing. The terrifying, discordant chorus of war cries swelled in volume as another wave of the screeching homunculi swarmed from the forest in front of them, cutting them off.

Hemmed in from front and back, Dane looked to his right and saw yet another tide of attackers flooding toward them from out of the woods. In moments they'd be completely surrounded. "This way!" Dane shouted, pointing left to the only possible direction of escape. They rushed across a meadow toward the trees, with Thrym backpedaling, protecting the rear. Weakened from water loss, the frost giant lifted one of the uprooted tree trunks, swinging it in a wide arc to keep the onrushing troll warriors from swamping them. Dozens more flaming arrows hit the tree. It burst into flames, forcing Thrym to drop it.

Looking over his shoulder as he ran, Dane saw the frost giant behind them, his body shielding them from most of the fire arrows. Then *ka-BOOM!* As Thrym stepped forward, Dane saw the ground give way beneath his feet, and with a thunderous crash the frost giant fell straight out of sight, his entire body disappearing down into what Dane now saw was a massive pit so deep it was twice Thrym's height.

A cheer went up from the trollfolk. They turned away en masse from Dane and his human friends to surround the rim of the huge pit. They screamed and danced in glee, firing flaming arrows down at the trapped frost giant.

At this sickening sight, Dane and the others stopped. They were just a few paces from the safety of the trees and possible escape, but the trolls were attacking their friend.

Knowing they had to help, Dane thrust his sword skyward, crying, "Trollslayer!"

"Wait—*my* sword is named Trollslayer," Jarl protested.

"Let's see which blade *earns* the name, eh?" Dane said.

Everyone followed suit, raising their axes, knives, and swords skyward, all shouting "Trollslayer!" Rik, Vik, and Jarl leading, they made a mad dash back across the meadow toward the mass of troll warriors celebrating round the frost giant trap. Lut tried to keep up, but at a hundred and three years old he couldn't really muster a mad dash—his looked more like a mild saunter.

The trolls turned and saw the humans bearing down on them. A command was shouted, and they quickly formed a defensive wall with their tiny shields, standing side by side, ten trolls wide and five lines deep, their backs to the rim of the pit. Rik, Vik, and Jarl never broke stride and mowed down the shield wall like boars charging through a field of daisies. The furious little creatures were trampled under or sent flying in all directions. Many were knocked over the edge into the pit.

Now that the pursued were fighting back, many trolls turned and fled. Dane and the others waded in with slashing blades against those who remained, and understandably, the diminutive beasts would not stand their ground and fight one on one like men. They were brave only in groups and would not press an attack unless the odds were overwhelmingly in their favor.

Astrid, Kára, and William rushed to the edge of the pitfall and saw Thrym lying at the bottom, barely moving. He had many holes in his legs and torso, melted away by the fire arrows. What was left of him was now being attacked by a score of the trolls who had fallen into the pit. They furiously hacked at his body with their tiny axes and scythes, chipping away more ice. William shot an arrow, knocking a weapon from a troll's hand. Astrid let fly two of her axes, causing the little beasts to scurry for cover. But in moments they were attacking the giant again.

"Thrym! It's Astrid!" The giant managed to turn his head, and Astrid saw her silhouette reflected in his eye. The look on his face was pitiful, as if this great giant knew his end was near. "Thrym! Raise your hand to me!"

Stirred by her voice, with great effort he slowly lifted his arm toward the sky, his fingers reaching out to touch her. Two trolls leaped upon his chest, chopping at the raised arm. Astrid heard Kára suddenly give a war cry, and the princess, in the throes of bloodthirst, threw her axe. And although the blade did not find flesh, the wooden handle of the axe brained one of the chopping trolls.

"I hit one! I hit one!" Kára yelled, jumping up and down as if she'd won a prize at the Skrellborg town fair. But the other troll continued his vicious work, obscured by Thrym's arm, so neither William's arrows nor Astrid's axes could find him.

"Higher, Thrym!" Astrid cried. "Reach higher!"

The giant struggled to raise his arm higher, though it shuddered with each hack of the axes. At last his upturned palm reached high enough, and Astrid, Kára, and William jumped into it. He began to lower them in his hand, when *CRR-AAACK!* his arm fell away like a mighty tree. Astrid, Kára, and William crashed hard onto Thrym's chest. Kára rolled off, landing with a thud on the ground next to Thrym's severed arm. She was sitting in something wet and saw it came from a troll who had been crushed by the falling arm.

"Ew, troll blood."

Three trolls sprang up, scrambling over the top of the dismembered arm, coming at her with axes. She screamed, and William's arrows drove them back. Astrid reached down and pulled Kára up onto Thrym's chest. Kára retrieved the axe she had thrown, and she, Astrid, and William now stood guard over the fallen giant. The trolls retreated like rats into the dark recesses of the pit, where they hissed and hurled insults, their pink, malevolent eyes glowing out at them in the dark.

Thrym's eyes were mere slits, his vaporous breath reduced to a bare whisper. Astrid patted his cheek, horribly scarred by the troll axes. "We'll protect you, Thrym," she whispered, "we'll protect you." And it gave her heart hope to see the tiny smile that he managed to make in answer.

After Dane saw that Astrid, William, and Kára were down in the pit protecting Thrym, he turned his attention to the troll army, which was regrouping for a counterattack. Their commander, a vicious-looking fellow with beady eyes and fat, puffy lips who strutted about in gleaming chain mail and a plumed silver helmet, barked an order. The troll army quickly took positions, encircling the humans. Dane and the others drew together, and everywhere they looked, there were trolls five rows deep, banging loudly on their shields and shouting. Not knowing a word of the troll tongue, Dane could only assume they were spouting obscenities, for their faces twisted into scowls as they spoke and they spat the words as if they were poison.

*"Exbla teva blombah karreggaha!"*

"What are they saying?" Drott asked.

"I'm familiar with the southern dialect of the troll tongue," said Lut, "but these being northern trolls, I can't make out exactly what they're saying. It's either 'Come, share a leg of mutton' or 'We wish to make furniture from your bones.'"

"I hope it's the first one," said Drott.

Dane now saw that the trolls had wheeled four catapults into position, forming a rear guard behind their ranks. The throwing arms of the siege engines were cranked back, weapons loaded. The troll commander raised his hand, preparing to signal the launching of the catapults, when the troops behind him parted and out marched a phalanx of soldiers fancily attired in black-plate armor. Dane took them to be the royal guard, for behind them strode someone who could only be their ruler, the troll chieftain, a noble-looking fellow of regal bearing, ruddy cheeked and rather stout. His eyes shone with bright intelligence and he carried in his left hand a long kingly staff that bore on its end the head of a wild boar carved in amber. Over his tunic he wore a woolen tricolor robe, and over his shoulders a bearskin cloak fringed with white fox fur. Ringlets of gold and silver jangled from his neck and wrists, and when he opened his mouth to speak, Dane saw that his two upper canines were made of glistening gold. Crowning it all was a magnificent turbaned headdress made of woven silks and feathers, and sunk in its center, Dane saw, was a hollow-eyed troll skull.

"Cease!" the troll chieftain demanded. All the troll warriors immediately stopped thumping their shields and went down on one knee, bowing their heads in obeisance.

The troll commander, irked by his chieftain's command, neither bowed nor knelt. He looked insolently at his ruler and said, "We *must* press our advantage."

Surrounded by the troll army, Dane and his friends could not hear all the words, but they grasped that the leaders were arguing over their fate. "The one with the headdress, he's the king?" Drott asked.

"That would be my guess," Ulf replied.

"I'm rooting for him."

Dane now saw the king and the sour-faced commander walking toward them, flanked by ten members of the royal guard. They halted a safe distance away and the ruler spoke. "I am Dvalin, Lord of the Trolls, ruler of all weefolk in this forest realm, chieftain of all that you see. And this is the captain of my troops, Commander Greb."

Harrumphing a greeting of his own, the commander angrily spat at the feet of the humans. Jarl stepped forward and spat at Greb's feet. Greb spat. Jarl spat. They spat until they were all out of spit.

"Well, now that we're done with that," Dvalin said airily,

"perhaps we can proceed. I have no wish to see you harmed. Leave your weapons and go the way you came."

"But the frost giant is *ours*," the commander snarled. "You leave without him."

Dane exchanged looks with his mates and saw they all thought as he did. "Thrym is our friend," he said firmly. "He has no part in your war."

"He's a filthy frost giant!" barked Greb. "Our prisoner!"

"We won't leave without him," Dane said.

"As you wish! Then you'll *all* die," said Greb with a grin, showing his sharp, pointed teeth. "You've made my day." And with that, Greb stalked away alone. The chieftain stood somewhat uncomfortably with his guard.

"What is your name?" Lord Dvalin asked.

"I am Dane. Dane the Defiant."

Lord Dvalin's face lit up. "Oh, but you are legend here! You returned Thor's Hammer to the heavens."

"He had *help*," Jarl snapped, looking down with scorn at the troll lord.

"It is said that in ancient times, my kind *made* the Hammer for Thor, did you know that?" Dvalin said.

"The legend we heard was that dwarves made it," Jarl said, unwisely calling Dvalin a liar in front of hundreds of his armed subjects.

"A gross misassertion!" Dvalin shot back. And then he gave a forlorn sigh. "We once made many wondrous things, but now . . . we *have* no magic."

"Magic is indeed a precious commodity, your lordship," Lut said with authority. "I am Lut the Bent, runemaster and sage. We have journeyed far and trekked here not to harm trollkind, nay, but to rescue this boy's mother, who was taken by a foul band of brigands! Surely they have come this way?"

"We saw no one come before you," the troll chieftain said.

"Or their heads would be on poles too, hmm?" said Jarl.

"I have cast the runes and the gods have spoken!" Lut said in a threatening tone. "Our cause is just, and those who impede our journey will be—will be visited by . . ." Here he faltered, and Dane quickly realized what words he sought.

"Boils and pustules," Dane whispered, recalling the lurid curses of King Eldred's oracles.

"Yes! Great boils and pustules!" Lut thundered. "Their insides will rot and their eyeballs explode! And that's just on the first day; it gets worse."

Lord Dvalin considered Lut's warning and said, "You see what ruin the giant ones have wrought here. Our village and countless families destroyed. And when they retreated, they took many of my subjects captive. My people are demanding revenge."

"Thrym is a peaceable fellow," said Dane. "He had no part in the attack. If you are a just leader, you cannot punish him for what he has not done."

"I have offered you freedom," said the Lord of the Trolls, his cheeks reddening. "If you choose not to take it, then it is out of my hands." He turned and quickly strode away with his guards.

"I left out unrelenting diarrhea!" Lut shouted after him. "The runes never lie!" But Lord Dvalin continued walking as if he didn't hear or care about Lut's warnings.

"We should attack now," Jarl said.

"That's your answer to everything," Dane said.

"I wasn't the one screaming 'Trollslayer,' Dane. It was you."

"That was before I knew they weren't all savages. The chieftain—"

"Is a troll—and the only way to deal with a rump-fed troll is with the point of a blade. And by the way, I won't allow infringement upon *my* sword name. I claim Trollslayer *and* all the other names with troll in it, such as Trollkiller, Trollslasher, Trollcrippler—"

"You can't own the *whole* troll category," Drott protested.

"Trollmaimer, Trollbutcher, Trollannihilator—"

Fortunately a sharp command from Commander Greb interrupted Jarl's litany of sword names he claimed were his. The troll forces rose from their knees and snapped to attention. They stood there, unmoving, poised for battle, their pink, unblinking eyes all fixed on the only target before them: humans.

"Let's rush them," Jarl said. "They'll scatter like rabbits."

"They'll expect that and flank us before we reach their lines," Dane said.

"Well, whatever we do, let's do it soon," said Fulnir, "'cause I'm itching to kill something."

Again Dane was struck by Fulnir's uncharacteristic aggression, and even the very hair on Fulnir's face seemed to bristle in anger. Feeling the urgency of the moment, Dane turned to Lut, eagerly hoping the old one might have some solution.

"Don't look at me," Lut said. "You saw how well *my* idea fared."

Commander Greb's voice rang out. "Ready!" He raised his sword skyward for a moment, then whipped it down, screaming an order in the troll tongue.

In quick succession, the throwing beams on all four catapults shot forward, launching their payloads.

Dane saw four large bundles soaring upward, and curiously, a troll was atop each one. The bundles arced downward, coming straight at the circle of humans. They tried to scatter, but it was too late. Atop each projectile, the trolls sliced through a cord and the bundles sprang open, revealing nets ringed with iron weights. The nets plunged down over Dane and the others, trapping them like so many helpless quail. They desperately tried cutting and slashing their way out, but in moments, the troll army rushed in, and when given the chance to drop their weapons or be hacked to death by a sea of angry trolls, Dane and the others surrendered. Last to give up was Jarl, of course, the idea of surrender—to trolls, no less!—so abhorrent to him that the shame he felt made him sick to his stomach.

# 22

# A PITIFUL
# SITUATION

S o it had come to this, Dane thought. Trapped for
hours now in a dark pit with unscalable walls, the
night air freezing cold and getting colder, everyone
miserable and aching with hunger. They'd been given neither food nor blankets—not that either of these would have
raised their spirits much—and everyone had descended into
a bitter silence. But at least they were all together and alive,
Dane thought, although poor Thrym was failing fast. For
hours the frost giant had lain motionless nearby, his frosted
breathing growing increasingly labored.

And then, to Dane's alarm, it got worse. Seemingly
unprovoked, Fulnir began to argue with Vik, saying that he
could tell by his smell that Vik was hiding food.

"Fresh hazelnuts and salted fish!" said Fulnir. "I can nose
it! Check his clothes!"

Vik vehemently denied he was hiding any food, and soon they came to blows, Fulnir erupting, snarling and snapping like a wild hound, trying to bite Vik. The others pulled them apart, and it took five of them to hold Fulnir down on the ground.

"His teeth!" said Rik pointing at Fulnir's face. "Look!"

Dane was horrified to see that Fulnir's canines appeared to have grown longer and sharper. Worse, his hair was growing thicker, stiff bristles of it appearing on his hands and arms and all over his face. Fulnir continued trying to bite them, fighting with an animal fury, his teeth bared and frothing. "Tie him to the log!" Dane ordered, and it took all hands to tie him to an uprooted tree that had fallen into the pit so he couldn't harm himself or anyone else. Lut examined him in what light there was, then took Dane aside.

"It's bad," Lut said. "The marks on his arm show he's been bitten by a ghostwolf. It's only a matter of time."

"A matter of time before *what*?" Dane asked, worried for his friend.

"Before he becomes a *varúlfur*," Lut said, "doomed to spend the rest of his days roaming the forest as half man, half wolf, with a savage taste for human flesh." Dane could only stare in disbelief. His best friend a murderous beast? Such was the legend, Lut told him; he who was bitten by a ghostwolf was doomed to become one. In a matter of days the transformation would be complete. Lut's father, Lundrin the Wise, had once told him of the legend of the ghostwolves, and now he was seeing it firsthand.

"There must be something," Dane said. "A poultice? An incantation? Some kind of cure?"

"The only cure I know," Lut said, sadly shaking his head, "is a quick and merciful death. For now, all we can do is watch and wait."

Dane waited for Fulnir to fall asleep before discussing the situation with the others. It was agreed they would keep a close eye on Fulnir for signs his condition was growing worse.

"What do we look for?" Ulf asked.

"If he starts howling at the moon, he's no longer one of us," said Jarl. "And then we do what we have to do."

"What—*kill* him?" Drott said, his face hardening. "No one is touching my friend. I don't care if he grows a tail and starts licking his privates. Nobody touches him!"

"I agree!" insisted Dane. "He's risked his life too often for us to turn on him now!"

Rik too sided with Dane. "I say we keep him alive as long as possible," said Rik, "before we put him out of his misery." Surprising everyone, he turned on his brother. "And you! You say you have no food? Prove it! Empty your pockets!"

"I'll do no such thing," said Vik with an iron stare. And then, to no one's surprise, the brothers instantly fell to fighting. For a time it was all fists and elbows as the two threw each other around in the dark, spitting and cursing, until at last Rik got the best of Vik and forced him to hand over the food. Vik shamefully did, and Rik shared the nuts and fish with the others, insisting that Vik apologize, which he did and then went off to sulk.

The few bits of food were quickly eaten, and a sullen silence again descended on the group. Later, when Fulnir awakened, Dane went over and found his friend feeling better. He had no recollection of what had happened, he said, and was saddened to hear of what he had done. His fits seemed to come and go, and Ulf said that perhaps when he was in their grip, he lost his mind. Drott said he sure knew what *that* felt like, not having much of a mind himself, and Fulnir laughed and said Drott didn't have much of a face either, and everyone else except Drott laughed at that too.

Dane saw a stone fly down from above, and heard more derisive hoots. He looked up to see a dozen or more trolls dancing along the rim of the pit, throwing taunts and rocks down at them.

"*Slavia crupto et kumgh bah!*"

"Lut, what are they saying now?" Drott asked. "They wish to make footstools from our skulls?"

"Close," Lut said.

"Dirty trolls!" Jarl shouted. He picked up a stone and winged it back up at his captors. Dane heard a cry of pain from above, followed by more unintelligible troll oaths. Rik and Vik joined Jarl in hurling more stones, and soon the trollfolk tired of their game and drifted away, no doubt joining the loud victory celebration that could be heard, the steady drumming sounds growing louder.

It was hours later now. Fulnir was awake as well, still tied to the log but talking as if nothing were the matter, calling out the sounds and smells his heightened *wulfen* senses could detect.

He sniffed the air, catching a scent. "Celery root. Willow bark. Turnips pickled in brine . . ."

Ulf's stomach growled like a hungry bear. "Sounds like they're having quite a feast."

"Or *preparing* for one," Jarl said ominously.

"Fishwife tales," said Lut, dismissing this with a wave of his hand.

"But the skulls we passed?" asked Ulf. "What do you think they did with the bodies?"

". . . honey, barley cake, berries and cream," Fulnir said, still sniffing.

Princess Kára finally caught on. "Are you . . . are you telling me that—that—trolls *eat* people?"

"*If* they can find the right seasoning," said Lut, trying to lighten the mood.

"Or the right person," said Ulf.

"But worry not, princess," Jarl said. "They'd never eat anyone obviously as spoiled as *you*!"

Kára glared at Jarl. "*You'd* be cooked first if they prefer eating *dumb animals*!"

This brought chuckles at Jarl's expense, but the mirth

didn't last. They were all too cold, hungry, and tired for much of anything. Fulnir piped up again with one of his food reports, and Ulf snapped at him to shut up already, he was too hungry to hear it, and soon the mood of the group sank into the dark gloom of the pit.

Seated off by himself, Dane mused on other problems they faced. He wondered if their fate was being debated at that very moment by the trolls. Obviously the king's orders to spare them had been followed. Greb could have slaughtered them when they'd been helplessly trapped in the nets. Or perhaps the commander didn't *want* their deaths to be quick. Perhaps he preferred the slow, painful, crowd-pleasing kind. Dane had seen the cold hatred in the commander's eyes and knew he was capable of such deeds. His business was killing and inflicting pain on the enemy. His village had been crushed by frost giants, hostages had been taken, and so he needed—his fellow trolls needed—retribution. It was as simple as that. It mattered none if Thrym was innocent. In Greb's mind, one frost giant was like all other frost giants. Just as in Jarl's mind one troll was like all the rest.

"Fear blinds," Dane's father had once told him, and that was why it was the cause of most of humankind's pain. That which blinds turns men irrational and foolish, often dangerously so. Men from a neighboring village had attacked Voldarstad because they'd feared hunger. It was fear of retribution that caused Godrek to try to kill Dane. Jarl hated trolls because he feared them, so why not kill them all?

Likewise, to Commander Greb, the only good frost giant was a melted one. And any human who trespassed in the troll forest deserved to have his head displayed on a pike.

And what of his mother? Dvalin said they had seen no other humans. Perhaps during the panic and confusion of the frost giant attack, Godrek's party had slipped by unseen and hidden in the woods until the giants had returned to their fortress. The anguish of not knowing her condition tore at his heart.

Dane heard the rhythmic beat of the troll drums and wondered if *his* fate had been decided long ago. Lut had said fate could be fooled, and for a while Dane had believed it. Yet if it was true that the Norns wove the web of fate, then the story of his life—and that of everyone else he knew—had been set and could not be changed. Was he to die in this pitiful troll pit, confused, cold, and starving? And what of the Valkyrie he had seen? Or thought he'd seen. Had she been real, or only a vision born of the bump on the head? Dane peered into the star-sparkled sky, the dreamlike image of the feather-cloaked beauty coming back to him. The Valkyries, he knew, as servants of the Norns, had certain foreknowledge of a person's death. So if she *had* been real, wouldn't that mean that he—

"Do you see her?"

Dane lowered his eyes to find Astrid standing next to him. "See *her*?"

"Mist, your Valkyrie."

"Uh, no, I've seen no sign of her." He knew spreading idle rumors might ruin morale.

"Because if you do—"

"I *said* I haven't seen her."

"But if you do, it doesn't mean for sure it's time for your, you know . . ."

"Death?" Dane said too loudly. This brought uneasy looks from the others, who were understandably sensitive to hearing that word right now.

"All I meant was," Astrid said, lowering her voice, "maybe a person's fate isn't written already, and if you see a stupid corpse maiden hanging around, you shouldn't instantly conclude that the game is over and you might as well give up."

"Oh, so before you accused me of being *too* brave and hogging the glory, and *now* you think I'm ready to give up? Does *anything* I do meet your approval?"

"I'm just trying to keep you alive!"

"I don't need your help for that!"

"You need it *more* than you—" Astrid bit her lip and turned away, stopping herself from saying more. She drew a breath to calm herself, turned back, and said, "If you'd like to hear it, I just might have a way to get us all out of here."

Her idea took clever advantage of the trolls' great veneration for Thor's Hammer, the weapon that had killed so many frost giants. Everyone agreed the plan was their best hope, especially Kára, who would play a key role.

Dane called to the guard at the edge of the pit, demanding to see Commander Greb. The guard laughed and said, "You'll see him soon enough. Tomorrow at your execution." On cue everyone in the pit—save for Lut, who was too dignified—erupted with insults, calling the commander the worst names they could think of.

"The commander is a dog-hearted hedge-pig!"

"Pigeon-livered scut-worm!"

"Cowardly pus-canker!"

"He dances with sheep!"

"Fat sheep at that!"

"And if you don't go tell him what a coward we think he is," Dane shouted to the guard, "you're a maggot-pie load of toad droppings!"

That did the trick. The guard hurried off, and in no time at all Commander Greb, unsteadied by drink, stood at the pit edge with a phalanx of his boisterous soldiers, who also had had a few. "Dog-hearted hedge-pig?" Greb roared. "Which of you called me *that*?" No one in the pit spoke, the only sound being that of a girl whimpering. "Come on now!" Greb snarled. "Someone want to tell me *who* is a dog-hearted hedge-pig?"

"He is someone who captures and tortures poor, defenseless girls!" Dane said. He pulled Kára into the light so Greb could see her. What a pathetic sight she affected! She stood sobbing and whimpering, tears streaming down her face.

It was such a heart-wrenching performance that even Dane started to believe her emotions were real. She looked so pitiful that the drunken soldiers were shamed and their revelry silenced.

"By the gods!" the commander shouted. "Are *all* your females so weak and pathetic?"

Now another weeper joined in. Astrid did her best to squeeze out fake tears like Kára, but all she could manage was a keening wail. Not to be outdone, Kára started to howl and screech like a stuck piglet, and Dane feared it was a bit much.

"Sir, what's the harm if we let them go?" Greb's second-in-command asked.

"*Leniency?*" Greb asked gruffly. "Would humans show any to us?"

"But sir, two girls alone in the wild? They'll die anyway, so what's the difference?"

The other soldiers grunted in agreement, clearly believing a pair of defenseless females posed nothing of a threat and that executing them was beneath their military honor. Greb wavered, not wanting to look a fool to his troops. "Very well!" the commander barked, waving a hand in dismissal. "Release them!"

Astrid and Kára were raised out of the pit and given horses, food, and a lantern to light their way out of the troll forest. Astrid demanded her axes be returned so they could defend themselves and chop wood to build a fire.

This is where Greb balked. "Or perhaps you'd use the axes against *us*."

"Yes," Astrid said, "when we make it home, I'll be sure to tell everyone how the great commander's army was threatened by two young *girls*."

Two axes were thrown at their feet. "Be gone before I change my mind!" roared Greb. After saying farewell to their friends in the pit, Astrid and Kára rode off into the moonlit woods in the direction they had come from.

"How do you fake tears like that?" Astrid asked when they were out of view of the village.

"Oh, easy. I just think of something worth crying about."

"What were you thinking to cry like *that*?"

"I pictured myself less beautiful than I am."

They rode for a time to make sure no one had been sent to follow them. Astrid halted them when she saw a fallen tree. She dismounted and saw that the log was weathered and looked to have died years ago. "This one will do," she said. Astrid set to work on the log, and Kára began chopping low-lying branches from trees and gathering them to make a sledge. Then amid her work Astrid thought she heard a sound in the brush. She signaled Kára to stop, and they listened. Nothing. Had the trolls decided to kill them anyway and sent soldiers to finish them off? Astrid waited, eyeing the thicket where the sound had come from, gripping her axe tighter, ready to kill if she had to. Nothing happened, yet still she sensed a presence. A bear? A wild boar? Or perhaps it was Mist the Valkyrie? For a moment the silence of the troll forest seemed to surround her and tighten round her throat. But she soon shook off this feeling and continued with her axe work, signaling Kára to do the same. Her friends were in trouble, and there was work to be done.

Fulnir still lay tied to the log, wide-awake and chatting away just like his old self. He hadn't had another snarling fit for a while, and his wolfen hair did not seem to have grown any thicker. It seemed strange to Dane to be sitting and having a conversation with his best friend while his friend was tied to a tree trunk, and even stranger to be thinking that he might have to kill him. But such was the nature of their situation.

"I can hear Klint," said Fulnir, cocking his ear and narrowing his eyes in discernment. "He's squawking somewhere in the village, probably eyeing their feasting pots." He caught another scent, sniffing the air. "Oh, oh, I know *that* smell. It's a musk ox, a good league away at least. No! A whole herd of them! This is amazing." And then he caught another smell, this one crinkling his nose something fierce. "Oh, what is *that*? It's awful. Part rotting corpse, part week-old rat droppings, and—*sniff, sniff*—part unwashed butt-crack. Oh, that is seriously wicked!"

Dane and Drott erupted into gleeful cackles of laughter.

"What?" said Fulnir. "What's so funny?"

"That's *you*, Fulny," said Dane. "That smell you smell is you. The 'stinking' part of Fulnir the Stinking."

Fulnir just stared back in disbelief. "No, it can't be," he said. "That's . . . *me?*" Dane and Drott broke into more laughter. "It's really that bad?"

"'Fraid so," said Dane. "But don't worry. We still love you."

The beating drums from above abruptly stopped. In the ominous silence, Dane traded looks with Jarl, Drott, and the others, wondering what was going on. Five royal troll guardsmen appeared at the pit's rim. "Runemaster!" a guard yelled down. "Lord Dvalin bids you come!" A rope ladder was unfurled into the pit from above.

Fearing for Lut's safety, Dane shouted back, "Our seer stays!"

"Our orders are to fetch him! If you resist, we will take him by force!"

Jarl waved his fist at them. "Bring it, you stinking motherless sons of—"

An arrow whistled past Jarl's ear, embedding in the pit floor.

"Hold your fire!" Lut shouted. "I will come!"

Lut picked up his leather runebag and started for the ladder, but Dane stopped him. The thought that this could be the last time he looked into his old friend's eyes was awful. Lut patted him reassuringly on the shoulder. "If the trolls wanted to eat one of us, they'd take someone plump and juicy like Ulf, not a stringy old bag of bones like me. I'll be fine, boy."

Dane prayed it was true. As the old man clung to the rope ladder, Dane watched him raised up to the rim of the pit and then, grabbed by the guards, disappear from sight.

With Lut gone, for the longest time no one spoke. Dane looked over at the dim outline of the frost giant lying still nearby. His breathing was shallow, and his great frosted exhalations had dwindled to mere puffs of mist that dissipated almost as soon as they appeared.

Much of Thrym's icy body had been hacked away and carted off by the trolls. Lut had explained that the melted ice from a frost giant was a prized drink in trolldom, for it was akin to drinking the blood of their hated enemy. The more ice they hacked and carted off, the more the frost giant's life force drained away. They would save the head for last, Lut had said, melting it slowly in a huge caldron, delighting in the giant's final wheezing gasps.

They told Lut nothing. A score of troll guardsmen, each in dyed reindeer skins and hard-leather helmets, carrying spears, clubs, and torches, escorted Lut past the village and far into the forest, at last coming upon Lord Dvalin's private lodge hall, located so deep in the forest, even the frost giants had never found it.

Lut had to duck his head crossing the threshold, but

once inside, he found himself in a surprisingly roomy main chamber, the walls lined with crude portraits of the tribal leader and his family carved into flat discs of wood, dozens of tallow candles and torches lending a cozy warmth to the place. He could hear screams coming from a nearby room. Was someone being tortured? His guards barked in guttural troll to the two trolls standing guard before a closed doorway, and moments later Lord Dvalin himself appeared. Lut was struck by the distraught look on the ruler's face and wondered what it was he wanted.

"I need a seer," said the Lord of the Trolls, "to perform a service."

"What is it Lord Dvalin would have me do?"

In a voice charged with emotion Dvalin told him that Queen Veshlah, his wife, was "with troll." She had been in painful labor for hours, he said, but the baby was refusing to be born. Now both mother and baby were in grave danger of dying. "I need a reading of the runes, seer, to learn whether the baby be male or female."

When Lut asked him why, the ruler said that if it was shown that the baby was a male, it would be cut from the mother's womb to be saved. With great delicacy Lut explained that if this were done, the mother would surely die.

"Don't you think I *know* that?" Lord Dvalin exploded, his three nostrils flaring and eyes hot with rage. The guards too reacted, and Lut suddenly found himself at spearpoint.

Regaining control of himself, the troll lord gave a nod to his men. They withdrew their spears, and Dvalin continued in a voice choked with emotion. "I am filled with unspeakable grief at the thought of losing my beloved. But I need an heir. A male heir. And if I have to choose between my wife and a male child . . . I would have to choose the child."

*Well, isn't this a fine fix,* thought Lut. His mouth went dry; he felt a sudden tightness in his chest. If the runes told him the baby was male, the mother would die. And if the runes told him the baby was female, the birth would be allowed to take its course and both mother *and* baby might die. And in his hunger-weakened state, what if he misread the runes? What then? No doubt he too would die. Lut cursed himself for having been so bold that morning, thundering that hogwash about boils and exploding eyeballs. As if he actually had the power to render such punishments.

"But have you no seer of your own?" Lut asked Dvalin.

"I'm reluctant to put the lives of my wife and baby in the hands of a stranger—a human no less—but fate has forced my hand. My royal sorceress was taken captive by the frost giants, and hence we've lost our seer." This, Lut realized, was what he had meant by his earlier lament of the trolls having lost their magic.

So the king had nowhere else to turn, and Lut knew if he refused the rune reading—or worse, if he misread the runes—whatever chance he and the others had of being spared would be dashed. Though Lut had lived a long life and did not fear death, he preferred to keep his head affixed to his neck for now. He had to find a way to improve his chances. But how?

"Well, seer?" Dvalin said with urgency. "Get on with it." Spears were again brandished, and the uncomfortable sight of them so close and so sharp helped Lut bring forth a sharp idea of his own.

"I must be in the queen's presence," Lut said, "when I throw the runes. The closer I am, the more accurate the reading will be." Lord Dvalin blinked. Lut waited. The king barked something in troll to his guards, and the spears were withdrawn. Lord Dvalin turned and opened the door, ushering Lut into his inner sanctum.

# 23

# FRIEND
# OR FOE?

Dane was in a full-blown panic. Fulnir was now worse than ever, and Dane was worried that he might actually have to do what Lut had said: put Fulnir out of his misery. Fulnir seemed now to be in a constant state of derangement, snorting and growling, his lips drawn back in a bestial snarl. And because of Dane's own lack of diligence, William had nearly been bitten.

For a good hour or more Fulnir had seemed perfectly fine, and Dane had grown lax in his vigilance. He had even fallen asleep, and dreamed that he was a tiny child climbing and playing amid the glossy strands of his father's beard. He had heard screams and awakened to find William in Fulnir's clutches, screaming for help. Dane learned later that the boy had only been trying to help Fulnir by loosening his bonds a bit, but then Fulnir had reached out with his trussed hand

and grabbed William's belt. He had drawn the boy closer and tried to bite his face. William had kicked and fought Fulnir off, managing to keep himself from getting bitten, until Drott, Vik, and Dane ran to his rescue, trying to pull him free. But even with three of them prying and pulling, Fulnir's strength was too great and, ultimately, Dane had had to beat his own friend on the head with a troll club until he finally fell unconscious and let go.

Now everyone stood a safe distance away, watching Fulnir twitch and scratch and issue his animal growls. It seemed it wouldn't be long now before his friend would cease to be human, and it pained Dane to know that something would have to be done. There was talk about which one of them would be best suited to end Fulnir's life, Jarl insisting that he alone had the strength to do it, and Rik and Vik saying that they might be willing to finish Fulnir off, but only if no one else was looking.

That's when Drott grabbed a tiny troll club and dashed to Fulnir's side. For an instant Dane thought Drott was going to do the deed himself, but he whirled to face everyone else.

"You'll have to get past me first!" Drott cried, tears in his eyes.

"Put down the club, Drott," Dane begged.

"No! Fulny's not done yet! He's got no tail and—and he still stinks like he always did! Proves he's still more human than *wulf*!"

Dane eyed Jarl, Vik, and Rik, who looked like they

might make a move on Drott. Drott saw it, too, and before they could rush him, he said, "I'll kill him myself if it comes to it, I promise. Please . . . give him more time."

Drott let the club slip from his hand and turned to gaze at Fulnir lying there comatose. "Fulny . . . I promise to make it quick," he choked out between his sobs. "You won't feel a thing. . . . It's me who'll be hurting."

But Dane knew that he was the one who would have to do it. In fact, it was a promise he had made to Fulnir. The last thing Fulnir had said to Dane when still in his right mind was "I want you to do it." Dane had dismissed it, saying that kind of talk was silly, forget about it. But Fulnir had made Dane look him in the eyes, and when he had, Fulnir said, "You know what is happening to me. If you're my friend— if you care at all—you'll do me this last favor. Kill me. Promise me you will." It had brought tears to Dane's eyes to hear him say it, but he had promised he would do as asked. Fulnir had thanked him for being such a good friend, and said, "I'll tell your father you said hello."

Now, as the night air grew colder still and he watched the figure of his friend in the gloom, Dane tried to decide. What weapon should he use? A club or a knife? It sickened him beyond words to be thinking such things, yet still the question had to be answered. Club or knife?

The queen of the trolls lay on her four-poster bed in deep distress, her face glazed in sweat. The lower half of her body was covered in a tent of linens, her breathing came in short, rhythmic bursts, and she was wailing in pain. A white-robed she-troll whom Lut took to be the midwife stood by the bed, looking scared and barking orders to a bevy of female attendants. The attendants scurried about, sponging the queen's brow and patting her hands in comfort; others looked on helplessly, not knowing what to do. Lut was deeply moved by the queen's plight. Troll or no troll, no creature should be in that much pain, no matter what the Jarls of the world might say, and he only hoped he could somehow find a way to end it.

Catching an urgent look from Dvalin, Lut knelt on the floor and drew out his leather runebag. He opened it and let the rune pieces fall into his lap. Each piece was a small, flat tablet made of bone the size of a large coin, with a single runic letter inscribed on one side. Cupping the runebones in his hands, Lut closed his eyes, going to a place deep inside himself where the tortured cries of the queen could not be heard. He began to chant the names of his forefathers, beseeching the gods for guidance, and then he threw the runes in the air, and down they came, dropping *plink, plink, plink* to the stone floor.

Saying a silent prayer of his own, Lut opened his eyes. Some of the pieces had landed rune side up, the rest blank side up. In the dim firelight Lut peered at the runes, quietly interpreting the message.

What he saw was baffling. He could not explain it. The

king demanded an answer.

"*So?* Which is it, seer? Male or female?"

Lut could only stare at the runebones in a growing panic. The gods had certainly picked a fine time to play games. *The truth lies in opposites.* What on Odin's green earth did *that* mean? All he had asked was a simple question: male or female? And the gods gave him this! He wracked his mind, desperate for a clue, some shred of illumination. But no, they had to confound him with puzzles about opposites. He suddenly wished he'd never become a seer at all. A shipbuilder. A cheese maker. Even a dung merchant. These were far more reliable trades. Why hadn't he listened to his mother and taken over his father's tannery? Sure, the odors were off-putting and the work laborious, but the hours were good and the pay reliable. No! *He* had to become a *soothsayer.* A wise man. The one everybody else looked to for answers to all their problems. What had *that* gotten him? Nothing but hassles and heartache—*and* women, he realized. Lots and lots of lonely women. So maybe it hadn't been so bad after all.

It suddenly came to him. He understood. Of course! The answer was so obvious. Why had he not seen it before? He jumped up and hurried to the queen, barking out orders to her attendants and the midwife, now knowing what he had to do. In his many years as village healer he had brought scores of babies into the world. He had even assisted birthing some of the very same kind he now faced.

"Seer!" said Lord Dvalin. "Your answer!"

Without looking up from what he was doing, Lut calmly told the troll ruler to be quiet and stay out of the way. The problem, he told him, wasn't the "baby" refusing to be born, but rather the "babies." It was twins, and they were competing to be first to enter the world.

"But—but—" Dvalin sputtered. "My wife?"

"She'll be just fine if you get out of the way!"

Lord Dvalin blanched, not used to being spoken to so rudely. But his own wife, Queen Veshlah, lifted her head from her pillow and said, "Leave him alone—he knows what he's doing." And Dvalin did as he was told.

With gentle sureness, Lut made a few adjustments in the birth canal, and sure enough, a short time later out came a squalling baby troll. . . .

"A female," said Lut, holding the bawling infant aloft and handing her to an attendant. And moments later, her equally loud and squirming baby brother appeared, wet, pink, and hairy. It was a boy *and* a girl. The *opposites* told of by the runes. The infants were wrapped in swaddling cloth and presented to the mother, and everyone oohed and aahed about how cute and adorable they were. Lut thought that the infants were about as cute and adorable as newborn mole rats, but he wisely kept this sentiment to himself.

But no one looked happier than Lord Dvalin himself. When his wife raised up her twins and laid them in his arms, and the troll lord gazed down into their pink, wrinkled faces, Lut saw Dvalin light up with a look of such love, it filled Lut with a warmth he knew to be the love he felt for every living thing, whether it be the world's tiniest insect or the world's biggest troll.

Lord Dvalin came and started to hug him, but Lut being so tall and the troll lord being so short, the troll kept hugging Lut's leg, and Lut was made a bit uncomfortable by this and finally asked Dvalin to stop.

"Thank you, seer, thank you," said the Lord of the Trolls. "How can I ever repay you?"

"Well," said Lut, "just off the top of my head, a couple things *do* come to mind."

When he put the torchlight to Fulnir's face, Dane flinched at the sight of him. Covered with dark bristles of hair, Fulnir had ceased to look like Fulnir. With his glazed-over eyes, his heavy, open-mouthed breathing, and his gray-mottled skin, Fulnir had begun to look positively feral. As Dane forced himself to look down at his friend—or the creature that *used* to be his friend—he still could not bring himself to act. He had brought out his knife but was unable to use it. All Dane could think of were the times Fulnir had saved his own life, and it felt terribly wrong to now be ending his.

It was then that he heard Drott say, "Stand aside." Turning, he saw Drott beside him, tears streaming down his face, now holding a heavy rock that had fallen into the pit, gathering the will to do the most awful thing he ever could imagine. Dane stepped aside. Drott crossed the pit floor to where their friend lay. Drott said something to Fulnir that Dane couldn't hear. Drott raised the rock to crush Fulnir's skull, Dane closed his eyes, unable to watch, and then a voice rang out. "Stop!"

With great relief Dane opened his eyes to see that it was Lut calling from the rim of the pit above, saying that he might have a cure. Moments later Lut was lowered into the pit, and from out of his cloak he produced a sheep's bladder filled with what he breathlessly explained was a *wulfdrekka,* a folk-remedy concoction of various herbs and spices used by the trollfolk to ward off the symptoms of the *wulf*-bite sickness. The troll lord, he said, had given Lut a batch of it as a thank-you for having birthed his wife's babies.

Lut came and looked at Fulnir, alarmed at how far the sickness had progressed.

"Will it work?" Dane asked.

"We have to try," Drott said, still shaken.

Lut nodded. "Yes, we will try."

Dane and the others helped hold Fulnir down while Lut forced the foul-smelling liquid down his throat. He growled and snapped, but they managed to get most of it down him, and in a matter of moments he fell into a deep, un-disturbed sleep, and for the first time Dane actually began to feel hopeful. And then he heard the voice of Dvalin calling down to them.

"I have decided to spare you!"

Fulnir, still fettered to the log, was lifted out of the pit by the troll lord's guards. With an enthusiasm bordering on giddiness, all the others climbed up a rope ladder the trolls lowered for them, Dane being the last out of the pit. And the first thing he asked Dvalin, after congratulating him on his new twin arrivals, was where they could find buckets and water.

The troll lord gave him a look and asked why. Dane said that, to try to save Thrym's life, they would need to pour large amounts of cold water on his body; the water would freeze and recrystallize his icy form.

"But there's no time for that, son," said Dvalin, explaining that Greb and his soldiers were sleeping off their night of drinking. "Soon they'll be awake and be coming to kill you all, and there'll be nothing I can do."

"But Thrym is my friend," said Dane, and he said it with such a firmness of feeling, the troll lord realized that the humans could not be persuaded to leave their frost giant.

"You realize I'm committing treason by aiding a frost giant," Dvalin complained.

"But as leader of the trolls," said Drott, "couldn't you just pardon yourself?"

Dvalin mulled this over and clapped Drott on the

shoulder, proclaiming, "*This* is truly a wise man." He then ordered his guards to show Dane and the others to the village well.

The guards and even their ruler pitched in, and a bucket brigade was formed from the well to the pit. Water was passed from troll to human and vice versa until at the pit edge, the buckets were upended and water rained down upon Thrym. The life-restoring liquid immediately froze to him, and astoundingly, his body began to gain back the ice that had been melted and hacked away.

While he worked, Dane saw Jarl in the water line, taking buckets from one troll guard and handing them to another. Jarl wore a grimace, Dane wondering if it was due to the hard work or the distasteful idea that he was touching something trolls touched. Regardless, Jarl labored without complaint, and Dane thought if ever there was a picture that proved enemies could put aside their hatreds and work together, this was it.

But it was not to last.

A loud war cry pierced the air, and everyone turned to see Commander Greb leading hundreds of troll soldiers across the meadow toward them. A squad of soldiers pushed a wagon full of flaming logs—and Dane realized they meant to dump the burning cart into the pit on top of Thrym.

Dane shouted, "Put out the fire!" and ran to intercept the cart, his only weapon the bucket of water in his hand. Drott and Ulf followed Dane's lead, and then everyone, the troll lord and his guards included, dashed with water buckets toward the onrushing cart.

Commander Greb tried to cut Dane down with his sword, but Dane used the bucket as a shield, ramming into Greb's chain-mail-covered chest, knocking him into the path of the oncoming cart. The soldiers pushing from behind saw this and swerved the cart; it tipped over, accidentally spilling its contents onto their fallen commander, who was trapped under the burning logs. Greb screamed in panic. Dane did the only thing he could do. He threw his water onto the flames. Those behind Dane charged in, too, emptying the contents of their buckets, and in moments the flames were doused enough for the soldiers to pull their singed commander out from under the logs.

Greb lay in the grass, the tunic under his chain mail still smoking. But he was alive—saved, in part, by the very humans he despised. Greb got to his feet, brushing himself off and clearing his throat, looking particularly subdued. At last, Dane thought, he has seen the error of his ways and is about to tell us that just because humans had hurt them in the past didn't mean *all* humans were out to do them harm.

"Kill the humans!" Greb screamed instead. Weapons raised, the soldiers rushed at Dane and the others—until Lord Dvalin stepped in their path, ordering them to stop. "You don't command my soldiers," Greb raged at his master. Again he ordered his soldiers to attack, but with their ruler

274

in their way, they hesitated. Dane was wondering how long this test of wills would last, when a horse galloped into their midst, forcing the soldiers to scatter.

Astrid reined her horse to a stop and shouted to all, "We have returned with the magic of the gods!" Kára's mount trotted up, pulling a small sled that carried something covered with fresh-cut pine boughs. "You have heard how the Hammer of Thor fell to earth outside our village—and how a mighty wind returned it to the heavens," Astrid said. "This sacred tool of the gods was made in ancient times by your very ancestors, is that true, Lord Dvalin?"

"It is true. It took my people two hundred years to forge the Hammer itself. The largest tree on earth was honed to serve as its handle."

"When the Hammer fell to earth," Astrid said, "a sliver of its handle chipped away. Our cart, which carried the relic, was too large to pass between your trees. So we went back and retrieved it." Astrid nodded to Kára, who removed the pine boughs to reveal a sliver of ancient wood, six feet long, that convincingly looked as if it had come from Thor's Hammer. "Thor himself touched this wood! His almighty hands grasped its surface! And he who possesses this possesses the power and favor of the gods!"

Dane saw that Dvalin and the troll soldiers were staring in awe at the fake relic. He would learn later that Astrid and Kára had spent hours singeing and rubbing dirt into the wood grain to make it appear ancient, and surprisingly Kára had not worried for a moment about breaking a nail.

"Lord Dvalin, please accept this gift from us, so it may reacquaint your people with the greatness of your past and, we hope, lead you all to a proud and powerful future," Astrid said.

Tears streamed down the faces of the trolls, and Lord Dvalin especially wept copiously as they went on their knees before the supposed relic, touching its surface with their tiny, gnarled hands. All were swept up by the emotion of the moment—all save Greb, who was fuming that a piece of wood had usurped his command.

"How do we even *know* it's real?" he asked. "It could all be a pack of lies!"

Lut stepped forward and said with the deep, mystical tones of a wise man, "Only those who believe will share in its power." Greb thought about how he could argue with that. He gave up, kicked the ground, and stalked away.

Dane smiled to himself, marveling at Lut's sagacity. Later Lut told him it didn't matter that the relic was a fake—if the trolls believed in it, if it helped them reconnect with the glories of their past and gave them strength and hope for the future, what was the harm? "Besides," Lut said, "think what neighboring trolls will pay to come and touch the relic. Faith is all-powerful, doubly so if it brings in revenue." This was the kind of wisdom you can't argue with.

# 24

# THE RUNE SWORD
# SINGS

Astrid's heart was soaring as they moved over the treetops toward the ice cliffs. Thrym was alive and well, and they were riding him again!

The water from the troll well had stirred him back to life, refreezing over the melted holes in his arms, legs, and chest, recrystallizing, and restoring him to health. How thrilled she had been, when Thrym had first come climbing out of the pit, to see the smooth solidity of his broad chest and limbs, to see him walking and talking once more.

Many of the trollfolk had cowered in fear as lambs before a wolf when they saw him again towering over them. But to put them at ease and assure them of his friendship, he had gone down on his knees, bowing before Lord Dvalin—even in this position, he still dwarfed Dvalin—and in his deep and sonorous voice Thrym solemnly promised he would go to Utgard and end the brutal war on their kind, as a gesture of peace and goodwill.

"If it's not too much trouble," Dvalin said, "could you also return the trolls taken prisoner?"

"Yes, of course," said Dane, catching a look from Thrym. "We'll do all we can to free the captives."

And then Dane heard Jarl mutter, a little too loudly, "Free dung-hearted trolls? What next? We give them piggy-back rides?"

Thrym had swung his head round and aimed an icy look at Jarl, and it had amused Astrid to see how swiftly it had chased away Jarl's unfeeling attitude.

There was still the question of what to do with Klint the raven. Their trek would take them into the windswept, frigid wastes where only men of ice could survive for long. Klint had barely survived being frozen once on this trip, so Dane decided that his friend should stay where the climate was more hospitable to feathered creatures. Astrid thought the bird would follow them anyway, such was Klint's devotion to Dane. But as they had departed the village to much fanfare—the brooding Commander Greb and his top lieutenants conspicuously absent from the cheering send-off—Astrid heard Klint's *caw! caw!* coming from high in the forest treetops. There she saw the bird perched cozily next to another shiny black raven—a female, she suspected. It seemed Klint had found a friend and was enjoying her hospitality already. He called out again, a jocular squawk that to Astrid sounded as if he were saying, "Farewell! Have fun freezing your faces off!"

Thrym leading the way, the party followed the wide path torn through the troll forest by the attacking frost giants. Since they were short on horses, Astrid, Drott, and William rode in the rope harness slung round Thrym's neck, along with the still-trussed Fulnir, who, groggy from the potion, had yet to have any more fits. The coarse wolf hairs that had sprouted on Fulnir's face were now falling out, and his fangs, which had lengthened to twice their normal size, were receding back into his gums.

"Look at you, almost human again!" Drott gushed. "We were about to start calling you Fulnir the Furry." Drott plucked at a few bristles on his friend's face, and this brought a loud growl from Fulnir. "Uh-oh—he's still got a way to go," Drott cautioned.

"That was my *own* hair you just yanked out, clotpole!" Fulnir cried.

"See?" Drott said to Astrid and William. "He *is* almost human! He sounds just like Fulny again!" This good news was relayed down, bringing cheers from everyone.

"What was it like being a wolf?" William asked.

"Did you want to sniff people's butts?" Drott asked.

"No! Well . . . yes," Fulnir admitted. "But I fought it."

"Which urge was strongest?" Drott asked. "The desire to sniff someone's rear or tear their thoat out?"

"Well, usually the throat," Fulnir replied, "but a couple

of you had particularly strong scents, and I think it best, for your own sakes, that I not answer any further."

"That," said Dane, "is most wise."

Before long, all his wolfen hair had fallen out and Fulnir seemed back to his old malodorous self. He was untied, and Astrid delighted in seeing her two friends laughing and joking again. Her spirits were lifted, but only for a moment, for the sun-white ice walls of Utgard far in the distance reminded her of the perilous task ahead. They were venturing to a place few humans had ever visited—and from which even fewer had ever returned. Worse, they were going when the giants and trolls were at war.

"How did the war with the trolls ever start in the first place?" asked Astrid.

"Trolls made Thor's Hammer, the Hammer killed giants. So the giants made war on the trolls," Thrym said.

"But that was in ancient times," Astrid said. "They're still fighting over that?"

Thrym explained that for a long while there *had* been peace between trolls and frost giants. They had engaged in lively trade, with troll artisans selling high-gloss ceramics and other wares in exchange for fish and game provided by the frost giants. There had even been an annual root vegetable festival, where troll performers dressed as turnips and beets and acted out scenes from a frost giant's epic poem. But then King Bergelmir, the giants' wise and peaceful ruler, had been killed by one of his own kind, a power-hungry frost giant named Hrut the Horrible, and it had been Hrut who had plunged them again into war.

"If I am to bring peace," Thrym said, pausing for reflection, "I must defeat Hrut in combat." From the tremor in his voice and the furrow in his brow, Astrid could see that he feared he would be facing overwhelming odds.

As they rode toward Utgard, they saw no tracks of Godrek's party in the snow. So it was true, Dane realized—Godrek had not passed through the troll valley before them. He had dropped back behind them, letting Dane lead *him* to the frost giant fortress. Dane remembered the message from the runestone:

> *Where death adorns a kingly throne*
> *Ye'll find a king as still as stone*
> *Within him rests the blade of runes*
> *To lead you to the serpent's doom*

When he had told Thrym of this rune clue, the giant had said it sounded like the Hall of Relics, a crypt deep within the fortress where the remains of their hero kings lay. There were legends of a sword buried within one of the bodies of the dead kings, and Dane surmised that if this was the other half of the rune sword he sought, it would bear the rest of the clues and lead them to the serpent's treasure. Godrek had to know this since he too had seen the message on the runestone in the cave. But if this was true, why was Whitecloak letting Dane have first chance at the blade? It made no sense. Until Dane realized that Godrek *knew* he held the ultimate bargaining advantage. He possessed Dane's mother. And that Dane would gladly give up the blade to get her back. Lut had said that Godrek needed a woman's life to unlock the treasure. Perhaps this meant that Godrek would trade the life of Dane's mother for directions to the treasure.

As all this weighed on him—the rune blade, Godrek, his mother, freeing the trolls, the impossible task of getting in and out of Utgard—they began to traverse the deep cleft in the ice cliffs, the secret entrance into the Land of the Frost Giants, when suddenly Dane began to hear things. Or *thought* he was hearing things. A faint whispering, sweet and soft like the voices of children. Soon it became stronger, an irresistible force beckoning him onward. His father had once told him of the Lorelei, beautiful maidens whose enticing songs lured sailors to their doom along rocky shores. But this could not be them, since they were far from the sea. "Do you hear—" He turned to see Jarl riding next to him.

"Voices again?" Jarl asked, smirking. He turned back and called out to everyone, "Dane the Addled-Brain is hear-ing—"

"The wind," Dane interrupted. "I *heard* the wind."

"Didn't come from me," Fulnir said from his perch atop Thrym.

"Not *that* wind. I mean—oh, forget it." They rode on, Dane trying to convince himself it *was* nothing more than the wind. He knew it was important to stay calm, if only to set a good example.

Following behind Thrym, they plunged into a dark, narrow canyon framed by sheer granite walls. It thrilled him to know he was soon to tread in a land unknown to most of humankind. And again the strange whispers came, Dane at first thinking the sounds were coming from inside the crater, bouncing off the canyon walls themselves. But then, the deeper they went through the cleft in the cliffs, the clearer and louder the sounds became. Dane felt as if they were coming from inside his very own mind. It was like beautiful music, swelling and sweet, and he became spellbound by the hypnotic sound, as if lost in a waking dream. He yearned to find the source of the music, to unite with it, and onward he rode like a starving man drawn by the enticing scent of fresh-baked bread or meat sizzling on a fire. His need to reach the source of whatever was calling him became overwhelming, and he was just about to spur his horse to gallop ahead when—

"Dane!"

Jerked from his reverie, he now saw that Lut had ridden up beside him and reached out and seized the reins of Dane's horse. "Is it the siren call you hear, son?" Lut said under his breath so as not to be overheard by the others. Dane nodded, still dazed. "It's the rune blade calling, trying to tempt you.

But you must *not* give in to it."

"But how?"

"Push it from your mind. Think of those you love."

Dane looked around at the others; no one seemed to be hearing the voices. "Why does no one else hear it?"

Lut shook his head. "You were the only one to touch it. You and Godrek. Or perhaps it calls to only those it chooses." Dane cocked his head, yearning to hear the soft, pleasing voices again. They were like sinking into a warm, soothing bath. Lut grabbed his arm.

"No! It has power to turn men mad with greed. If you are weak—if only for a moment—it will drown your soul. You'll forget everyone—your mother, your friends, all those dear to you will be cast aside in your lust for riches. Shut it out. Resist!"

With much effort Dane willed the voices away, as if slamming a door to lock them out. But like light seeping through a crack at the bottom, the whisperings did not vanish entirely.

"The closer we are to the blade, the more it will tempt you," Lut warned. "But you cannot, you *will* not give in to it."

Dane knew how easy it would be to open that door and let the seductive voices into his head again, and he feared he would not have the strength to resist their call. "Godrek said my father was a coward for not following the rune sword to the treasure. He said that's why they parted ways and why he came to hate my father."

Lut pondered this a moment. "Perhaps your father feared the sword would lead to madness . . . or maybe he had other reasons why he shut out its call."

"Is this what my dream was about? Does the serpent represent the call of the rune sword that threatens to swallow *me*?"

Lut gave a shrug. "I know only that my buttocks have grown sore in this saddle and my throat parched in thirst and I am far from the comforts of home."

"That doesn't exactly answer my question, Lut."

"Well, what do you want from a cold and tired and *starving* old man?" said Lut. He looked heavenward, asking the gods, "Is there no pleasing young folk these days? They think they know everything!"

At last the path emerged from the deep canyon, and Dane and his friends stopped and gasped in awe. They were now standing on the rim of a gargantuan crater, and filling the bowl of the crater was a vast frozen lake. And there, built upon an island in the center of the lake, was Utgard itself in all its startling, crystalline majesty. It was a gleaming, six-sided fortress, each side seeming a full league or more in length, and its massive ice-block walls rose so impossibly high that the ramparts disappeared into the heavenly mists above. Jarl began to say that he'd expected something bigger, but the words froze fast on his lips. Thrym said nothing, gazing upon his former home in dread.

"So that's the giants' fortress, is it?" Drott said, staring in wonder.

"Hope so," Ulf said, equally transfixed. "If it's just their outhouse, I'm going home."

And then Dane heard another distant sound, different from the whispers in his head, coming from the island fortress. At first he thought—again—that no one else could hear it, but Jarl asked, "What is *that*?"

"It sounds like . . . cheering," Astrid said.

"It is the *freista*," Thrym said gravely. "The battle test."

Godrek watched the troll commander strut about like a bantam rooster in front of his chieftain and lieutenants. "So it *was* a lie!" the commander crowed. "They made us out to be fools, Dvalin! And you the biggest fool of all!"

Godrek stood, backed by Svein One Brow, Thorfinn, and five of his men in the chieftain's lodge hall, having cast sufficient doubt about the supposed relic that lay on the stone floor before them. The commander kicked at the piece of wood. "A sliver from Thor's Hammer? Ha! Is it not enough that the giants destroy our village and steal our people?" he raged, pointing a finger at the chieftain, who sat looking thunderstruck. "Just when we are about to kill *one* of the enemy, *you* have him healed and released. Because they brought you this!" Again the commander kicked at the wood.

Godrek knew it was a stroke of luck that he had sent Svein One Brow ahead to spy on Dane's party. Svein had seen the two girls in the troll forest using axes to fashion the fake relic. Svein had then followed them back to the village and seen how the worshipful trolls had fallen on their knees before it. When Svein had reported back with this news, Godrek knew the truth about it would enrage the trolls— rage he would harness for his own purposes. He let the little commander strut about until he had worked himself up into a fine lather, then calmly interjected, "The frost giant you speak of—he is the one we are tracking. He has killed many men and flees to Utgard."

The stunned chieftain roused himself and said, "He says he goes to Utgard to forge a peace between us."

"Another lie!" the commander barked.

The chieftain ignored the outburst and said to Godrek, "The one known as Dane the Defiant says you have taken his mother."

"True. She is to be my wife, and he does not approve. The boy is dangerously warped and uses the frost giant as his attack dog. They both must be stopped." The Lord of the Trolls brooded on Godrek's words, unable to fathom how he had been so deceived by Dane the Defiant.

"It pains me," said Godrek, "that my own kind has wrought such a foul deception upon you. Perhaps we can take revenge."

"An alliance?" the commander said warily.

"We go to Utgard," Godrek said, "and together we will kill many frost giants."

In the troll forest near the village clearing, Ragnar sat trying to eat a bit of cheese and stale bread. His appetite had been meager of late, his stomach and mind tied in knots over what to do with Geldrun. She sat nearby, her back against a tree, refusing to eat the food that had been given her.

Through the trees he saw the troll soldiers marching around the village, chanting in unison, clearly preparing for war. Amazingly, Godrek's plan had worked.

He went to where Geldrun sat and said, "You must eat."

Her defiant eyes met his for a moment and then looked away.

"Fine! Starve for all I care!" He stalked away a few steps and stopped, his anger and frustration building. He whirled on her and hissed, "Since I was foolish enough to help you the first time, my mind has been occupied with one thing: my death poem."

"I'd like to hear it."

"You will, if I aid you again."

"Are you so afraid of Godrek?"

"With good reason, lady. If he caught us, my death would not go easy. I'd be tortured to set an example. And let me tell you, Godrek's *very* good at torture."

"If we leave now, we'll slip past him," she said quickly,

"and meet up with my son and the giant."

"So that part about him torturing me didn't stick."

"With the giant on our side, we'll be safe!"

Ragnar stood there, mind racing, guts achurn. Her horse was tied with his and the others, just a few yards away. He could take her and ride off. But then what? Every day of his life he'd fear Godrek's vengeance. He'd have to go far away. Retire from warrior work, change his name, get a little farm somewhere, and spend the rest of his days reading books and writing poetry. It didn't sound half bad, the more he thought of it.

"Ragnar! Now!" Shaken from his reverie, he hurried to her horse, untying it. He quickly led the mount to Geldrun and was about to lift her into the saddle, when Svein and Thorfinn came through the trees and saw them. For an instant Ragnar thought they had a chance to escape but realized the men were too close.

Ragnar gave a little grin to his mate Svein, hoping to deflect any suspicion. "We ready to move out?"

For a moment Ragnar thought he read a trace of unease in Svein's eyes, but it passed. "Godrek says bring the horses." Ragnar boosted Geldrun onto her roan. He, Svein, and Thorfinn mounted up and led the rest of the horses toward the troll village.

Dane knew the mission into Utgard required stealth. They would have to enter under cover of night and, quiet as mice, get in and out without attracting attention. The problem was Jarl, who usually attracted more attention than a rampaging bear in a packed mead hall. So consumed with desire to prove his courage, Jarl tended to rush thoughtlessly into dangerous situations screaming his head off. True, he was an expert bladesman, and when battling most foes Dane wanted no one else at his side. But in dealing with frost giants, Dane knew there was small margin for error. One mistake and you'd be crushed under a giant foot.

Dane announced the plan: He, Lut, Ulf, Drott, Fulnir, and Thrym would go inside. Jarl would bravely protect the rear and take command in case Dane and the others didn't make it back.

"Protect the *rear*?" Jarl said with scorn. "The only *rear* I'm concerned with are the big frosty ones I'm going to kick." He gave a whoop and bumped chests with Rik and Vik, who also had no intention of staying back. Neither did Astrid or William. If Dane was going, they were to go, too.

"*Someone* has to stay back with Kára," Dane insisted.

"What!" Kára exploded. "When will you learn I am *not* a dainty flower in need of protection?" She waved her axe, and everyone scattered for fear of injury. So Dane had to take them all, despite the fact that the more people came, the more things could go wrong, especially where Jarl was concerned.

They waited until long after sundown, when a deep violet

night shadow lay over the iced-over lake and the fortress itself was but a pearly silhouette. After Drott and Fulnir tied up their horses, concealing them among some ice-encrusted boulders, they all set out under cover of darkness, following Thrym on foot across the frozen lake toward the walls of Utgard. It occurred to Dane that if the gods were watching them, they were most probably roaring with laughter, for eleven puny humans and one as gentle-souled as Thrym did not stand a snowball's chance in summer against a fortress full of frost giants.

Remarkably, though, two things were in their favor.

Utgard was so secluded, it had not been attacked in centuries. Therefore, Thrym said, the giants had grown lackadaisical about guarding their stronghold and in all probability they would post no lookouts on the ramparts. Another stroke of good fortune, Thrym explained, was their arrival during a *freista*. All the giants would be gathered in their colossal arena within the fortress to witness and cheer the battle test, where Hrut the Horrible, the frost giants' warlord, took on all challengers in single combat.

The ice cracked and groaned as the party crept across the frozen lake. Just ahead of them a dark shape broke through the ice and rose to the height of a man. Everyone shrank away when they saw it was the head of a frost giant.

"Worry not," said Thrym. "It's quite harmless."

Indeed, Dane saw that the face of the giant was only half formed, as if a sculptor had left the details of its nose, mouth, and eyes unfinished. The head sank back under the ice, disappearing, and Thrym explained that this was the legendary Lake of Tears, where all frost giants are born. The tears of the gods fell here, he said, creating the lake, and it was from these very tears that his race was formed. To Dane's right, a huge, unhewn hand broke through the ice, floating there for a moment, then sinking back under, as if it belonged to a baby moving fitfully in its womb.

"I pray I won't have to assist *this* birth," Lut said.

"Right," said Ulf. "Imagine having to burp that thing."

With haste they continued toward the walls of Utgard, along the way glimpsing the embryonic giants beneath the ice that, Thrym explained, would not be complete for many years.

At last they made it off the shifting ice and onto the island in the center of the lake, where Utgard stood. The colossal edifice, cut from ancient glaciers, sparkled like an infinity of sky-blue diamonds. Dwarfed by the fortress, Dane craned his neck, gazing upward in amazement at the walls that went soaring into the mist. The others too stood frozen, staring upward, unable to move or speak, in awe of the massive structure and the cheering sounds coming from within it.

"Fulny, about our new nicknames . . . ," Drott said, his voice quaking with fear. "Are you still Fierce and am I still Dangerous?"

"What, you want to go back to our old names?"

"No, no, I was just checking."

Thrym, their guide and protector, trudging onward, and everyone scurried to catch up.

They crept along the wall toward the fortress gate. Moving ever closer to the rune blade, with the sound of its seductive voices surging louder in his head, Dane fought harder against it. He blocked out the rune song as best he could, the cheering sounds of the frost giants helping to drown out the call of temptation. As Lut had advised, he thought only of those he loved. His father. His friends. Astrid. And, of course, his mother, held captive in the fiendish grip of a man who cared so little for love that he would trade it for treasure. Very well, Dane thought, he too would trade—treasure for love.

*CRAAAACK!* The sound of ice breaking pierced the air, and Dane and his friends pressed back against the shadowed wall. The colossal front gates, three times higher than Thrym himself, opened with a groan, shattering the thin sheets of ice that had formed there. Two frost giants lumbered out, pulling a gigantic sled piled high with what looked to be smashed, dismembered frost giant body parts: heads, legs, arms, and torsos, some parts still moving with life. The giants picked up the pieces and threw them high in the air toward the lake. The smaller pieces smashed like glass on the ice; the heavy ones broke through, bobbed on the water for a few moments, and sank. One giant's head remained floating for a while, and Dane saw its eyes pop open and see everyone hiding in the shadows. The head opened its mouth to shout an alarm, when another giant's torso crashed down on it and both torso and head disappeared beneath the ice. When the sled was empty and their disposal work done, the giants withdrew into the fortress, pulling the doors closed behind them.

"Those are the losers of the battle test," Thrym whispered down to them, nodding to where his brethren were thrown. "Someday their parts will form into new giants."

"Imagine if we were like that, melting to form new people," marveled Drott, patting Ulf's huge stomach. "This alone would make a whole new village."

Ulf rapped his knuckles against Drott's skull. "And this would make the new village idiot."

Then came another roar from the crowd, and Dane looked to see that Thrym had found one of the doors ajar. "They'll be back," he said. "Hrut never loses." Quietly pulling open one of the doors, Thrym slipped inside. Moments later he stuck his hand out the door and, with a crooked finger, beckoned everyone inside.

As Dane passed through the arched gateway, the first thing he spied were two giants ready to attack them with enormous war axes. He and his friends stumbled backward in terror. All save for Jarl, that is. Jarl, being Jarl, drew his sword, gave a war cry, and charged the monsters. Thrym slammed his foot down in front of Jarl's path, stopping him.

"They're statues," Thrym said.

Looking again, everyone saw that the giants were indeed stone statues made of blocks of hewn granite, erected as terrifying totems at the entrance to an immense courtyard. Shamed, Jarl sheathed his sword. Rik and Vik snickered as they casually sheathed the swords they had drawn.

"You all thought they were real," Jarl fumed. "Admit it!" Dane feared Jarl might do something even *more* foolish to regain his honor. He pulled Jarl aside. "They looked real, Dane," Jarl repeated. "You saw it—"

"I did, Jarl, and that was very brave of you," Dane said solicitiously. "But think of Kára."

"Kára?"

"Someone has to protect her. Bring her safely back to Skrellborg. Whoever returns the princess will no doubt get a big runestone erected in his honor *and* collect a handsome reward from King Eldred." Dane saw the glimmer in Jarl's eyes as the idea took root. "So if you don't mind," said Dane, "I'll take that assignment."

Jarl furrowed his brow. "That's so like you, Dane," he said. "Always trying to steal the credit. Not this time. *I'm* protecting the princess." Dane pretended to argue, but Jarl adamantly insisted that he and he only be entrusted to guard Princess Kára. So Dane gave in, pleased that his ruse had worked. Now Dane hoped he'd be less inclined to go charging blindly into danger and get them all killed.

They followed Thrym past the fearsome statues, Dane

half expecting them to spring to life and crush them all. Now there were *real* giants to worry about, hundreds, if not thousands, of them. Dane heard their distant cheers swell in volume, as if the spectators had just witnessed another gruesome kill.

# 25

# TRAPPED
# IN UTGARD

Thrym tried to remember when he had last walked within the walls of Utgard. In human years perhaps hundreds, he thought, since giants marked time differently than men did, ice aging much slower than human flesh.

As Thrym led his human friends toward the arena, hugging the fringes of the courtyard, he recalled the day long, long ago when Bergelmir himself had stood on this very spot, displaying a wound he had received. The tip of the rune blade—the very one Dane and his friends now sought—was buried in his thigh, a wound he had received from a greed-maddened human who had invaded their realm in search of Draupnir.

The wise king had proclaimed to the nation of frost giants that their wars with the gods and the lesser beings must end. A new age had begun, he said, an era of peace and harmony, of brotherhood and trust. But it didn't last. In time a warmonger arose in their midst, a monster named Hrut the Horrible. Craving power and glory, Hrut challenged the king in a *freista*. In single combat, Bergelmir was destroyed. Hrut declared himself king, and then all hope for peace had died too; the giants were made to cheer only for war and death.

Now Thrym had come to contest Hrut in battle, and he knew he faced his own death. Most likely he was leading the humans to theirs, too. He did not fully understand mankind. They lived such short and painful lives, seeming to go from birth to death in a blink of a frost giant's eye. Why did they spend their precious few years warring? If he were a human like Dane, he would take Astrid and go live where war and strife would never touch her. *Was* there such a place? Probably not, he thought. They had come to the very ends of the earth, and still there was war.

They stopped outside the arena, a massive bowl structure Hrut had built to stage his gladiatorial conquests. Thrym and the others took cover behind a towering statue of the warlord himself.

"I see why he's called 'the horrible,'" Drott said, looking up at the statue's face.

As depicted on the statue, Hrut's face was hideously disfigured. Long ago, Thrym told them, Hrut's face had partially melted and then been flash-frozen in place, his rearranged features making him look savagely monstrous. But oddly, Hrut actually *liked* his gruesome visage because it frightened and intimidated his opponents. Now, eyeing the statue, Thrym felt a cold panic rise within him. If he was this afraid of his statue, how would he feel when he faced the *real* Hrut on the arena floor?

It all seemed so impossible now. Why had he followed the raven in the first place? And why had he agreed to lead them to Utgard? He was a giant made of ice, and his iron will had been easily softened by Astrid's words of challenge. Astrid! He wanted to scoop her and everyone else up into his arms and flee. But it was too late. The avalanche had started careening downhill, and nothing could stop it.

Jarl groused that he had been handed the short stick yet again. While Dane went off with Thrym, Astrid, and Lut on the glorious task of finding the other half of the legendary rune sword, Jarl was stuck with the job of leading everyone else to rescue a bunch of stinking trolls.

"I did *not* promise to free the captives!" he complained to Rik and Vik. "It was Dane! So let *him* rescue the little rat-faced cretins!" But he was comforted by the thought that at least he would have the glory—and rich reward—of bringing Kára back to Skrellborg. Dane had tried to steal that task from him too!

Jarl led his rescue party through a dark warren of tunnels beneath the arena floor, the sounds of the crowd above echoing through the passageways. Thrym had said that the captives would be found here because when Hrut was done fighting his own kind, he liked to top off the festivities by bringing trolls out to be tortured and killed.

He heard heavy footfalls approaching and motioned for everyone to take cover in an adjoining tunnel. Two frost giants lumbered by, pulling a cage full of the captured trolls. Some of the troll prisoners wailed and moaned, shaking the cage bars. Others, Jarl saw, sat quietly, looking hollow eyed and doomed. He noticed one she-troll in particular, a wrinkled old crone whose snow-white hair fell down over her cloak, nearly reaching the ground. Shaking a wooden staff in one gnarled hand and a necklace of bear's teeth in the other, she screeched and gyrated wildly, dancing and chanting strange-sounding incantations, clearly beseeching the gods for rescue. Even Jarl could not help being affected by this heartrending sight. *They may be filthy trolls, but nothing deserves to die like this,* he thought. The giants and the cage disappeared into the dim light of the tunnel ahead. Jarl signaled everyone forward, and they followed the wails of the captive trollfolk.

The tunnel abruptly ended, opening into a large chamber, and Jarl halted everyone behind him. He peered round the corner. Giants were taking the trolls from the cage and putting them into a cell. One daring young troll squirmed free and dashed toward the tunnel where Jarl and the others were hiding. A giant gave chase and caught the troll just as he ran past the crouching humans. "Bad little troll," the giant said, stroking the troll's head as if he were a pet. The crouching humans were mere footsteps away from the giant; if he turned his head, he would spy them all. Wouldn't it be—what was the word? Jarl asked himself. Laconic? Iconic? *Ironic*, that was it! Wouldn't it be ironic if he met his end because he was given away by one of the wart-faced imps he was trying to rescue?

Which is exactly what happened.

The little troll saw them hiding and screeched in fright. The giant turned his head, and Jarl and his friends all froze, stupidly thinking that staying still would make them invisible. It didn't. The giant roared, the icy blast from his breath blowing them all backward, knocking them off their feet. All except Kára, who went fleeing unseen back up the tunnel.

Now facing a real live frost giant, Jarl did the only thing he knew how to do: He drew his sword and charged. The first impulse of the others was to do the sensible thing—run. But unfortunately, when young Viking men see one of their own, no matter how foolishly, charging into battle, they tend to follow like sheep. So Rik, Vik, Drott, Fulnir, Ulf, and William attacked too. Seven humans against one mountain of ice was a mismatch, and soon they all were caged.

When the cage was lifted to be emptied, Jarl and all his friends went tumbling headfirst onto the stone floor of a dank cell. Dazed and battered from his scrap with the frost giant, Jarl took a moment to clear his head. But when he did, he was not happy. He found himself surrounded by scores of trolls, and seeing him and his friends in their midst, they all began shrieking like lunatic crows, fearing the humans were there to kill them.

"Quiet, you raving hairballs!" cried Jarl, covering his ears.

But it did no good—the cacophony of troll shrieks grew only louder.

"By the gods, be silent!" yelled Vik. "We're on your *side*!"

Suddenly the she-troll, the wrinkled one with the long white hair, raised her staff, signaling for silence. Abruptly the trolls quieted, waiting for her to speak.

"Humans on *our* side?" the she-troll said warily. "Impossible!"

"We promised Chief Dvalin to rescue you," Drott said.

"Dvalin?" the she-troll said, suddenly brightening. "Dvalin sent you?"

"It's true," William said.

"Praise the humans!" the she-troll cried. "They're here to save us!" The joyous trolls started shrieking like lunatic crows again, which Jarl found unbearable. He waved his arms wildly to make them stop, and finally they did, all staring keenly at Jarl, expecting to hear the details of the escape plan.

"Next one makes that sound again," Jarl said evenly, "I break his neck."

Dane had to concentrate or he would lose his grip on sanity. He had to think about his mother and all those he loved. If he lost sight of them in his mind, even for a moment, the bewitching call of the rune blade would engulf him. In order to find the blade, Lut had surmised, all they needed was to follow the siren call to its source. But the nearer he drew to it, the louder it became and the harder it was to resist.

Following Thrym's lead he, Lut, and Astrid had found their way into the Hall of Relics. An aisle ran down the center of the massive hall, and on each side were the funeral crypts that held the fragments of the fallen giants, be it hand, leg, arm, or head.

"Here relics of the great giants are preserved for posterity," Thrym said, "and the rest of their bodies returned to the Lake of Tears to form new citizens of Utgard."

Decorating the ceiling and walls were magnificent friezes carved into the ice, depicting the ancient history of the giants. "The largest carving," Thrym said, "portrays our creation. How the gods wept, forming the Lake of Tears, and how Ymir, the very first frost giant, rose fully formed from its waters."

As Lut and Astrid stood marveling at the sight with

Thrym, Dane felt himself being pulled away down the hall, the call of the rune blade swelling inside him. As if he were a tiny boat atop an unstoppable sea tide, he was drawn to the end of the great hall. Obeying its call, he entered a crypt with a vaulted ceiling, and there on a bier was a part of a leg, all that was left of the dead King Bergelmir. Dane moved closer, and something within the ice glistened. His eyes fell upon a gleaming shaft of steel buried in the thigh, just as Thrym had described. And drawing closer, Dane saw it was the very blade of the broken rune sword protruding from the ancient ice. Spellbound by its glitter, he felt his willpower draining away as the voices told him what to do.

Obediently he raised his sword over his head and swung it downward into the thigh with all his might. The ice shattered and fell away, and there, lying in the ice shards, was the other half of the rune blade he sought. Such a feeling swept through him! Such possessive hunger! He picked it up and felt it oddly pulsating in his hand, as if it were alive. As if it had a heart. He brushed away the slivers of ice from the metal, caressing the blade. He saw his fingers begin to bleed from the slice the rune sword made, yet he felt no pain at all, nothing but the joy of holding it. *Mine,* he thought. *All mine.*

With the power of the blade surging through him, all fear and self-doubt vanished from his mind. He had never felt so alive, so sure of himself. So invincible.

Hearing a sound, he turned to see an old man, a blond girl in a furred vest holding an axe, and a frost giant, none of whom he recognized. And he knew that if they tried to take away his blade, he would have to hurt them.

Astrid felt her throat tighten as she saw Dane looking at them with dead eyes, as if they were strangers.

"The rune blade has him spellbound," Lut whispered. He stepped forward and thundered to Dane, "You must resist, boy! I command you to resist!"

She saw Dane's hand tighten round the broken blade. The edge cut into his flesh and his blood ran down the sword, dripping onto the floor. She spoke his name, but he seemed gripped in a dream, as if he were listening to another voice altogether. And it scared her to see she had no effect on him.

Lut slammed his fist hard into Dane's face. He went sprawling; the broken blade flew from his bloody grasp across the icy floor. For a moment Astrid and Thrym just gaped, startled by the power of the old man's sudden violence. Dane sat up, rubbing his jaw, bewildered. "Did someone just hit me?"

Lut shrugged. "Had to return you to your senses."

Dane was alarmed to see blood oozing from his sliced-open hand. He asked what had happened. Astrid pulled a kerchief from her pocket and bent to wrap it tightly round Dane's wounded hand. "We lost you there for a moment," she said, gesturing to the broken blade lying at their feet.

"Can you still hear its call?" Lut asked.

Dane nodded.

"I can smack you again if you'd like," said Lut, raising his hand to strike him.

"No, no!" Dane quickly said, raising his arm to ward off the blow. "I can resist it, I know I can."

"*How* do you know?" asked Lut.

"Because when I gave in to it, it was like you said. I lost all feeling for everyone I knew. You, Astrid, my mother. I even wanted to hurt you, Lut, and I'd rather die than feel that way again."

Lut nodded, reassured that Dane was safe now from the blade's spell. Anxious to read its runic secrets, Lut knelt for a closer look at the sword that lay on the floor, the rune marks glowing like molten metal under the wet blood on the blade. Dane began to speak, but Lut shushed him, trying to decipher the markings before they faded altogether. Astrid reached out to touch it, but Lut slapped her hand away.

"Now I know," said Lut, "why none of us but you, Dane, have fallen prey to the rune song. It's the blood. When the blood touches the blade, it unleashes the curse. The blade itself comes alive, raising the runic message and corrupting anyone who comes in contact with the sword. Only you and Godrek touched the blade when it had the blood upon it, therefore only you and Godrek are touched by the curse. And if the two parts are ever joined, I fear the rune song will be impossible to resist."

It was then Dane's attention was drawn upward, to the

frieze above the bier platform. "There!" he gasped. "The serpent from my dreams!"

Carved into the ancient ice was a gigantic serpent with rows of spikes along its back and twin horns upon its hideous head. It was circled around what appeared to be a warrior's arm ring.

"It is Jörmungandr," Lut said, unable to pry his eyes from the serpent's image.

"What?" Astrid said.

"Jörmungandr," said Lut. "'Jörm' for serpent, 'gand' for magic wand. The ancients called it 'ganding,' which meant to put a spell on someone. According to this carving—and the clues on the rune sword—Jörmungandr is a kind of gatekeeper, a guardian sent by the gods."

"To guard what?" Astrid said.

Lut pointed to the arm ring circled by the serpent. "Odin's Draupnir, the very treasure Godrek seeks."

"So it's real then," Dane said gravely.

Lut nodded. "And the runes on the blade tell where it lies. On the Isle of Doom in the northernmost seas. Jörmungandr guards those waters, preying on all who dare draw near. Few are the men who've set eyes on the beast and lived to tell of it; the sea monster is said to have sunk a hundred ships in a single day and devoured all those on board, its hunger for human flesh only growing greater the more men it eats, its jaws being so large—"

"*All right,*" said Dane, "the thing's a monster, I get it. But it's not something *I'll* have to face, because we've got the rune blade now. And after I trade it to Godrek in exchange for my mother, Jörmungandr is his problem. *He'll* be facing the monster, not me. We'll be going home."

# 26

## A HORRIBLE CONFRONTATION

Kára tried to quell her panic. After escaping up the tunnel, she crept back and watched as Jarl and the others were easily overcome. She saw them gathered up and imprisoned with the trolls and then heard one of the giants tell another, "Go tell Hrut he has humans to kill."

*Humans to kill!* One of the giants lumbered up an adjoining tunnel, no doubt to convey the message of the capture of the humans. The other giant lingered behind, though, and Kára knew she would have to get past this one in order to get to the cell door. Yet even if she could, how would she open it? It was secured by a large, heavy lock far out of reach.

Feeling helpless, for a moment she wanted to cry. But no! She refused to give in to tears. *I am a princess,* she told herself.

*People rescue me, not the other way around.* She wished she were back home in Skrellborg, watching boys fight over her. Life there may have been boring and predictable, but at least it was comfortable and safe.

Eyeing her axe, she recalled the thrill she had felt when Astrid first placed it in her hand. This simple, rough-hewn tool had transformed her idea of who she could be. She need not be the highborn know-nothing of days past. No, she could be a *woman* with the courage to cut her own path through life—and woe betide anyone who would try to stop her!

She set off up the tunnel, knowing that for the first time in her life it would be up to her to come to the rescue.

Hrut the Horrible decapitated another victim, crushing the giant's head with his war axe and dismembering his frost-encrusted limbs in full view of the roaring crowd. How he relished it all. The challenge of the kill, the cold efficiency, the vigorous exercise. He took pride in his work, in knowing he had found his true purpose. And he took particular pleasure in the final conquering moment, when, with his victim on his knees, begging for mercy, he would swing his massive war axe and the whining pleas would be abruptly silenced. The head then would bounce to the ground and roll away, sometimes coming to rest with its eyes still blinking back at Hrut. And what a frolic he would have, kicking the head round the arena, further delighting the crowd as he played victor to the vanquished.

It mattered little to Hrut if his victims were truly enemies; whether a fellow frost giant wished him ill or not had no bearing on his death. The only way to retain power, Hrut knew, was to terrorize his own kind. And so whenever the mood struck, he would stage a *freista*, a sporting festival, in which any citizen of Utgard could step forward and challenge his rule in one-on-one combat. No giant was ever fool enough to challenge him, though, for they knew too well of Hrut's fearsome brutality. So Hrut then would simply point to a giant in the stands at random and summon him to the arena floor. Hrut would accuse the giant of treason or of harboring unkind thoughts against him. The giant would beg and plead and swear he was Hrut's friend. And Hrut would say, "If you are truly innocent, the gods will aid you in battle against me." The giant would be given a puny sword or dagger to fight against Hrut's three weapons of choice: his wooden club, his silver war axe, and his iron shield. And as the crowd dutifully cheered—anyone not cheering was usually the next victim—Hrut would go to work, doing what he did best.

But even a cruel, heartless warlord had his limits. And on this night, having crushed a good score or more of his brethren and tiring of large sport, Hrut decided it was time for the final spectacle: the butchery of trolls and humans. What with the war on, the killing of hated trollfolk was a rather common sight, pleasant enough but nothing special.

But humans, ah, now *that* was special.

There hadn't been humans in Utgard for quite some time, and the killing of them would be a rare pleasure for him and the crowd. Whether crushed underfoot or clubbed to death, trolls were easily smashed into a sticky green goo. Humans took longer to kill, for they were often fool enough to fight back, as if they actually believed they had any chance against Hrut the Horrible.

As the still-moving remains of his last victim were gathered up and piled on a sled for disposal, Hrut raised his arms and addressed the crowd. "My fellow *frostkjempe*!" His voice rang out, echoing across the arena. "Tonight—in addition to the traditional Troll Slaughter—you will have the rare privilege of witnessing the death of *humans* as well!" There were roars of approval and the stamping of giant feet. "And when the killing is done," he boomed, "dessert will be served!"

The cheering was thunderous. *"Blód-íss! Blód-íss! Blód-íss! Blód-íss!"*


"Exactly *when* can we expect rescue?" the she-troll asked tartly. The giant guarding the cell door had temporarily wandered away, and Jarl, Rik, and Vik were all straining to pull one of the cell bars from its footing in the rock floor. "I ask the gods to help us, they send you," the she-troll moaned. "Which proves the gods despise us."

"The gods and a few others I can think of," said Jarl through gritted teeth, straining with all his might to pull the bar free. Drott and Ulf sat on the floor nearby, playing a game of pick-up-sticks with a couple of the young trolls.

"One of us escaped," William said, trying to keep everyone's spirits up. "She'll bring Dane and Thrym. They'll save us."

But the she-troll was having none of it, which only angered Jarl more. He was about to make another rude comment when they heard a sudden thunderous chanting from the arena. . . .

*"Blód-íss! Blód-íss! Blód-íss!"*

Jarl and his friends stopped working on the cage bar, chilled by the sound of the cheer. As luck would have it, the guard giant reappeared just then, nodding his head in time with the chanting, too distracted to notice what Jarl and the others had been doing. And Drott, quite accustomed to having things explained to him, called up to the frost giant.

"What's that they're chanting?"

The giant grinned. "A special treat will be soon served. Flavored icicles."

"Flavored icicles?" said Drott, hungrily licking his lips. "Will we get some too?"

"Oh, you'll get some, all right," said the guard. And when

Drott then asked what they were made of, the giant smiled and said that the blood of all those killed in the arena was drained, mixed with ice, and pressed to form the flavored icicles and eaten with gusto. *"Blódíss,"* the giant called it. "A great delicacy in Utgard."

"'Blood ice?'" said Drott, still not clear on the notion.

"But," said Jarl more alertly, "I thought frost giants didn't *have* blood?"

"That's right," the giant said, his stupid grin growing wider.

"So whose blood do they use?" asked Drott.

The giant cleared his throat. "That of the trolls and, uh, the humans."

Drott got it. *"Us?"* he said in disbelief. *"We're* to be blood ice?" The guard giant was called away again, and as soon as his back was turned, everyone—the humans *and* the trolls— ran to the cage bars and frantically strained to loosen them, getting in each other's way and stepping on each other's feet in the mad scramble to free themselves so they would not become frozen treats.

Jarl felt the bar start to give. "It's loose! Everyone pull!" And now he wished that he'd never said a thing, for instantly he was overrun with trollfolk, their little elbows poking him in the crotch and hairy feet stepping on his, their troll odor filling his nose, a smell that could best be described as a cross between rancid goat's milk and fresh pig dung. For an awful moment he thought he would be sick, but then he felt a sudden tremor beneath his feet.

"The bar's moving!" Jarl cried. But it wasn't the bar that was moving, he realized; it was the entire floor of the cell. The whole thing was rising upward, compacting the space between the floor and the wooden planks of the ceiling.

"We'll be killed!" wailed the she-troll. She stabbed a finger at Jarl. "You bring death upon us all!"

"No, she-witch, the frost giants bring death upon you," said Jarl. "Dane and his stupid promises bring death upon *me*." The floor rose ever higher, the ceiling pressing down on them until it seemed they were to be crushed like so many grapes in a wine press. The ceiling was suddenly thrown open like a hatch, and they could see the star-brightened sky. The floor continued up until it was flush with the ground above.

Another thunderous cheer swept over him, and when Jarl raised his head, he beheld an awesome sight. He was standing on the floor of a colossal outdoor stadium, oval in shape, and carved entirely of gleaming blue ice. There were two tiers of seating benches, filled with what seemed to be a thousand frost giants, their breath frosting the night air as they cheered.

And then suddenly the cheering stopped and an eerie silence descended over the arena, the crowd of giants collectively holding their breath in expectation. Jarl saw their confiscated weapons had been piled in a heap on the ground.

"Our weapons!" he cried, rushing to retrieve them, quickly throwing swords and knives to Rik and Vik and helping William pick up his bow and quiver of arrows.

Drott asked, "Why're they giving back our— Look *out!*"

They leaped aside just before a massive war club smashed into the ground, pulping one of the trolls, its body turning to green and pink paste right before their eyes. Hrut the Horrible, his face monstrously deformed, grinned down at them. *"Blódíss is so nice."*

And down slammed Hrut's club again.


With the other half of the rune blade now in Lut's possession, Dane's spirits rose, for he knew he was closer to gaining his mother's freedom.

The plan was to meet up with Jarl and the others and—providing the rescue was successful—the freed trolls. Thrym would see them all safely away from the fortress. And then the giant would return to Utgard to do what he'd said he should have done long ago—fight the dark shadow of evil that had fallen over the realm of giants.

When they came out of the Hall of Relics, Dane saw a lone figure in the distance running toward them. It was Kára, and he realized something had gone terribly wrong.


It occurred to Jarl, in the one part of his brain still capable of reason, that they had been given weapons because Hrut *wanted* them to stand and fight—as much for his own amusement as to entertain the crowd. But Jarl knew that would be suicide. They had been easily beaten by the giant in the basement—and he hadn't had the humongous war club Hrut wielded. No, to survive, if only for a while, they must run and scatter, and stay free of the club. But how? They could not outrun Hrut forever. With one of his strides equaling ten of Jarl's own, the frost giant could stalk them relentlessly across the arena and never tire. Already Jarl had seen a half dozen or more trolls killed, their bodies turned to pulp under Hrut's club. Then they had been thrown onto a "troll press" and squeezed, their blood sluicing down into a large *blódíss* vat below it. Jarl had flinched at the sight of it. Would *his* blood be served up as a *blódíss* frozen dessert? What *else* did the gods have in store for him?

Twice Jarl had managed to outwit Hrut, once even riding atop the tip of the giant's foot, much to the crowd's delight. But now Hrut had William cornered against the far wall of the arena and was fiendishly toying with the boy as a cat would with a mouse. Jarl was sickened by the sight of the boy, stumbling in exhaustion in the shadow of the towering Hrut, and it seemed William would soon be joining the trolls in the *blódíss* vat below. Jarl watched as again he tried to run, but the giant smashed his club to the ground, blocking his way.

"So small," Hrut snickered, "yet *so* tasty." Hrut raised his club for the killing blow when Jarl leaped in front of the boy.

317

"Hey, ugly!" he cried brashly. "'Twasn't the gods' *tears* that made you! They just took a dump and called it 'Hrut'!"

The giant roared and swung his club. Jarl pushed William out of the way and hit the ground. The club smashed into the arena wall, crushing the head of a spectator giant in the first row.

Jarl sprang up and dashed away, frantic to find a place to hide. The ground beneath him shook, as behind him the monster drew nearer with each booming footfall. His heart thundering, Jarl knew escape was impossible now. This would be his final stand, his last sweet moment of life. Vivid images flashed in his mind—his body hung over the vat, his blood dripping into the ice—and he felt a sudden revulsion that his blood would be mixed with the lesser fluids of the trolls. *If I am to die,* he thought, *I want my true essence tasted in all its glory. I want the bold and heroic bite of my juices to be savored and celebrated. I want to be remembered as being the best* blódíss *ever!*

Jarl suddenly stopped and turned to face the charging beast. He was a warrior and thus would die like one. He bravely raised his sword to meet Hrut, bracing for the final blow, hoping that the next thing he saw was a Valkyrie taking him to his warrior's reward in Odin's corpse hall.

But it was not to be.

For just as Hrut raised his club for the killing blow, another huge body came rushing forth, crunching into Hrut with cataclysmic force. Hrut was sent flying backward across the arena, the distance of ten longships at least, landing with such an earth-rattling crash that Jarl thought Thor had sent down a thunderbolt.

But it was no god who had sent Hrut atumble, Jarl saw. It was none other than Thrym! The dazed frost giant lay sprawled on the ice nearby, slowly picking himself up. "Good timing, Thrym!" Jarl called up to him, relieved to still be alive. Thrym gave Jarl a shrug and a smile and turned back to face Hrut, who was rising angrily to his feet. Hrut grabbed his war club and pointed it threateningly at Thrym.

"So it is Thrym!" Hrut announced to the arena with scorn, "Thrym the exile! Thrym the coward! Thrym the murderer told never to return!"

A wave of jeers arose from the crowd, the sound so deafening Jarl had to put his hands over his ears. He watched as Thrym rose to his feet and looked up at his brethren in the stands. The crowd fell quiet, anxious to hear Thrym speak.

A cold dread came over Astrid as she first caught sight of it all—her beloved Thrym standing on the arena floor, the horrible Hrut aiming his hateful stare. When they had heard from Kára what was happening, they had all run to the arena entranceway—and arrived just in time to witness the last of Thrym's battle—and now waited for him to speak. An expectant hush fell over the crowd, Astrid feeling it all looked impossible.

"Yes, I am Thrym! The banished one!" Thrym's voice filled the stadium, and her heart thrilled at the sound of its echo. "And, yes, I caused a death. An accident I would gladly give my life to undo." Thrym paused, allowing the murmurs of the crowd to quiet. And then he turned on Hrut. "But you, Hrut—you kill for pleasure. For power. I am here to end that. Your reign is over."

There were gasps of disbelief and, to Astrid's surprise, a few scant cheers from the bravest few spectators among them. Hrut shot a deadly look at one of those who had cheered and, pointing his club, said, "I kill *you* next."

Hrut, his deformed face contorted with rage, his cold gray eyes blazing, came at the weaponless Thrym, taking great powerful strides, his war club held at his side. Thrym didn't move. Astrid screamed, terrified he would be crushed.

But with Hrut still three strides away, Thrym sprang forward with surprising swiftness—and before Hrut could raise his club, Thrym had him, arms and all, in a crushing bear hug. The crowd roared as the two giants grappled, locked as one, each trying to cut the legs out from the other, and Astrid's hopes rose at the sight of Thrym holding his own. But Hrut soon forced his foot behind Thrym's leg and delivered a tremendous head butt that sent Thrym falling backward to the floor, ice shards flying.

Hrut leaped upon him, pinning him, and, now having the advantage, the monster raised his club to crush Thrym's head. Thrym's hand shot up and caught the haft of the club before it could strike. Each tried to wrest the club from the other, and Astrid watched with growing anxiety as the two giants tumbled and rolled across the arena floor, humans and trolls scattering and diving in panic, trying not to be crushed beneath their colossal bodies. A chant arose from the crowd, *"Kill! . . . Kill! . . . Kill!"* and the sound of it frightened her even more, for she knew they were calling for Thrym's death, not Hrut's.

And then, to everyone's surprise, Thrym wrenched the club from Hrut's grasp and, rolling free, sprang to his feet, raising it over his head. Hrut, lying on the ground, raised his arms to ward off the blows he feared would soon come. The crowd suddenly stopped chanting, amazed, and there were even cheers of encouragement from a daring few. Thrym stood amid the cries of vengeance, unmoving, unable to do their bidding. *"Do it,"* Astrid urged, knowing that Hrut deserved to die, and that if it were up to her, she'd hack him into a thousand tiny pieces and dump them in the ocean so as not to have any of his evil pollute the Lake of Tears. But her heart fell as Thrym turned and flung the war club up into the stands, where it was eagerly fought over by a half dozen giants.

"Get up," Thrym said to Hrut. "For once you will fight fairly."

There were more murmurs of amazement as the crowd realized that the banished one was sacrificing himself for a principle, something they had long forgotten. On some of their faces Astrid saw looks of real hope that perhaps Thrym could win.

Hrut climbed to his feet and said with a chuckling sneer, "You should have killed me when you had the chance."

"Is that all you know, Hrut?" said Thrym. "Killing? Have you never known kindness? Or love?" This only amused Hrut all the more, and he threw back his head and laughed as he began to circle Thrym, moving in for the kill.

"Love is for the weak!" Hrut snorted. "It is war that makes us strong!"

Thrym shook his head sadly, then looked up into the faces of his fellow frost giants, pleading. "Is *that* what you all want? More killing? More death?" The closer Hrut came, the stronger Thrym's voice grew. "How long are we going to let him control us? How long are we going to live in fear?" Thrym waited. Silence. Not a single voice of protest was heard.

Hrut chuckled. "There's your answer."

"They're all too afraid to speak," said Thrym, "because they live in fear. But someday, perhaps long after I am dead, they will tire of your tyranny. And they will realize that without fear, you're nothing!"

Hrut came at Thrym wild with fury, throwing blows so hard that when they hit, shards of ice flew from Thrym's body like beads of sweat. Over and over Thrym was rocked, and backward he staggered, dazed and dizzied by the onslaught. Thrym fought back as best he could, landing a thunder shot to Hrut's face that cracked off a piece of his nose, but he was no match for the irate monster. Another crushing blow sent Thrym to his knees, and yet another knocked him flat on his back, Hrut's victory looking imminent now. Thrym lay near the entranceway where Astrid stood, and she shouted to him. At the sound of her voice, his giant head turned. Their eyes met. And for one awful moment the pain and fear she saw in his eyes turned to a plea for forgiveness, for he knew all too well that his loss meant death for her and her friends as well.

Nearby lay Hrut's war axe. He snatched it up, raising it over Thrym. Paling at the sight of his bloodthirsty sneer, Astrid closed her eyes, unwilling to watch her giant friend meet his end. But the next sound she heard wasn't that of Thrym's head cracking off. It was a new booming voice.

"Hrut! It's over!"

She opened her eyes, surprised to see that another frost giant, emboldened by Thrym's courageous stand, had climbed down into the arena and was calling to Hrut in defiance. Seeing the new challenger, Hrut merely grinned in anticipation, believing the giant easy prey. But more mutinous cries were heard, and slowly, one by one, down came more frost giants out of the stands and onto the arena floor, forming a circle around Hrut until there were ten standing in open rebellion against him. Astrid could scarce believe it; they were standing up to him! She was further amazed as slowly the chant began anew, *"Kill! . . . Kill! . . . Kill!"* and this time she knew it wasn't Thrym's death they were chanting for; it was Hrut's. And Astrid would never forget the look on Hrut's deformed face as he realized that his reign was over.

At first it thrilled Thrym to see that his words had worked! His fellow frost giants had found the strength to say no to Hrut. From where Thrym lay on the arena floor, he could see the sneer on Hrut's face turn to abject fear as the rebel giants began to attack him, taking him on two and three at a time, landing thunderous blows that cracked and cratered Hrut's face and body. Hrut tried to fight back but was too outnumbered to defend himself. And as the right side of the warlord's face shattered like glass and fell away, Hrut crumpled to the floor with a resounding boom and the chants of the crowd grew even louder, *"KILL! . . . KILL! . . . KILL!"*

As Thrym watched the whimpering warlord trying to crawl away, he could feel only pity for the beaten brute, the sight of him now so weak and defenseless seeming more sad than satisfying. More cheers rose from the crowd as the tide of fear turned and more frost giants came out of the stands, dozens upon dozens, all wanting a piece of their former dictator. Hrut went down on his knees, begging for mercy, the frenzied chants of *"Kill!"* growing louder still. And Thrym was unable to look away as the giants tore him apart.

Soon, like those of so many of his innumerable victims,

Hrut's dismembered parts were strewn about the arena floor, an arm here, a leg there. The victorious frost giants took turns holding up Hrut's smashed and decapitated head, cheering in joyous celebration! At last they were free! The brutal tyrant was dead!

Thyrm rose to his feet, elated to see Astrid waving from the entranceway, relieved to know she and her friends were safe. Bursting with pride, he moved toward her, wanting to share the moment with the one who had inspired him. But the din of raucous celebration was abruptly cut short, as from the heavens came a rain of deadly fire.

# 27

# GIANTS 34, TROLLS 3

From outside the arena the troll army launched their catapults. Clay pots full of flammable pitch were ignited and shot over the upper rim of the arena. The pots rained down upon the crowd and broke apart, splashing white ribbons of fire over the panicked giants, who furiously tried to brush the flaming pitch from their bodies; this only spread the fire onto their fingers and hands, melting them. As one giant was hit in the forehead, the fire-bomb exploded and his entire head was enveloped in flames. Within moments his horrible screams died and all that was left was a headless corpse. Another giant was hit in the legs and he tried to run, but soon his feet were eaten away and then both legs were gone and all he could do was try to drag himself away on melted stumps. The giants stampeded for the exits, only to be driven back by hailstorms of fire arrows shot by phalanxes of trolls positioned there.

From his vantage point outside the arena, Ragnar watched the troll catapults launch the flaming projectiles and heard the resultant screams of the frost giants inside. Godrek's nefarious scheme was proceeding well. He had convinced the trolls that he was their ally and that he would help them kill frost giants. Of course, it was all a subterfuge. Godrek had no plans to partner with the trolls, and cared not a whit if they were all slaughtered, for the attack was just a feint, a way of creating havoc. While the giants were locked in battle with their chief enemy, the trolls, they would be less inclined to worry about a few humans in their midst, and Godrek would have plenty of time to find the other half of the rune sword. If Geldrun's son already had it, then all the better, Godrek had told Ragnar. He would easily kill the boy and seize it without interference from the boy's frost giant protector. In one stroke he would possess the final key to finding the treasure and could at last eliminate the defiant one who had been such a thorn in his side.

The thought of the young man's death pained Ragnar, but what could he do to stop it? Take on Godrek and his liegemen single-handedly? His feelings for Dane's mother had nearly caused his demise once already. At the troll village Svein and Thorfinn had returned just before he and the woman were to make their escape. Another moment or two and they would have been seen galloping off, and there would have been a quick chase followed by his slow and painful execution. Svein had shown a sudden coldness to Ragnar after the incident, as if he suspected the Ripper's traitorous intentions, and thus had kept close watch on him and Geldrun, never leaving their side. He was with them now, camped outside the arena behind a statue of one of the giants, a monstrous-looking beast with a face right out of a nightmare.

Godrek and the others had gone off to find the rune blade's other half, the source, Ragnar suspected, of his lord's increasing mania. A mad shine had come into his lordship's eyes, and the closer they had come to Utgard, the greater grew his look of hunger. Godrek had begun to talk to himself in harsh whispers, behaving oddly, and to Ragnar it seemed as if his lordship was hearing voices no one else could hear.

Movement high atop the arena caught Ragnar's eye. A frost giant made a suicidal leap from the uppermost rim, plummeting toward a company of troll soldiers below. One of the soldiers looked up and started to cry an alarm when the giant's body crushed them all flat. Pieces of the giant's shattered body ricocheted off in all directions, killing more trolls and hitting one of the catapults just as it fired, causing the shot to go awry. The flaming bomb arced across the sky, coming straight for them, and Ragnar threw himself over Geldrun to protect her. The pot broke upon the statue, raining fiery pitch down on Svein instead, and Ragnar watched in horror as his friend ran screaming in circles, looking like a skewer of flaming meat. Ragnar leaped up and ran toward his friend, tackling him into a snowdrift. Svein rolled frantically about in the fluffs of snow as Ragnar heaped on more, but the flaming pitch was hard to put out and Ragnar's gloves caught fire. At last the pitch was extinguished and Ragnar looked into the eyes of his companion whom he had fought and drunk beside nearly all his warrior life.

"A demon has taken his lordship," Svein gasped, "so best you save yourselves and go." So it was true! Svein *had* suspected Ragnar's intentions. And now as One Brow lay dying, he was giving his friend leave to follow his heart. Slipping Svein's sword from its scabbard, Ragnar closed his comrade's hand around it. Gravely he watched as Svein took his last labored breath and his eyes fell shut with sad finality.

"May you dine at Odin's table," Ragnar uttered respectfully. "I knew none more worthy." The sounds of more explosions nearby drew him back to what was happening around him. He turned round, anxious to help Geldrun, but she was gone. And so was the knife from his belt, taken, Ragnar now realized, while he lay shielding her from the rain of flaming pitch.

Godrek loved the chaos of battle, a time when all the stifling codes of morality ceased to exist. All the virtues that weakened men—mercy, kindness, compassion—were tossed aside, replaced with a single vital need: to kill and take whatever you wanted. And what Godrek wanted was one thing: the remaining half of the rune sword. But Dane, he knew, had the giant on his side and quite possibly had already found the blade. If this was so, his task would be made even easier, for all he had to do now to find the blade was to find the boy.

His only enemy was time. The troll army could create havoc for only so long; the giants would use their superior size and numbers to soon crush them. Godrek saw a giant rush out from the arena and wipe out a score of troll archers before he was driven back by a fusillade of fire arrows. The tide was already beginning to turn, and Godrek knew that before the giants regained control, he needed to have the rest of the rune sword and already be out the gates or risk the giants' wrath.

Through the thick smoke of the burning pitch he saw one of his liegemen moving among the lines of troll soldiers. Godrek called to him. The man stopped, and Godrek saw it was Ragnar. But where was Geldrun? He saw a look of indecision flash across Ragnar's face for a moment, but it passed and he quickly hurried to join his lord and the other liegemen.

"The woman! Where is she?" Godrek demanded.

"One Brow met his end in a bombardment," the breathless Ragnar said, "and she . . . escaped."

An enraged Godrek grabbed Ragnar by the front of

his coat. *"Escaped?* Do you know what befalls those who *fail* me?"

Ragnar paled as Godrek's hand went for his sword. "Wait! My lord, I . . . caught sight of her. I think I know where she's heading."

"Then we'd best find her . . . or you'll be joining Svein."

Dane had never seen such chaos. The rain of fiery pitch, the dense smoke, the mad stampede of panicked frost giants— it had sent the arena into mass confusion and terror. Dane groped blindly, coughing as he cried out to his friends, the acrid smoke filling his lungs. Amid the din he felt the earth shake beneath him and heard thundering footfalls coming his way. From out of the billowing smoke stumbled a terrified giant, the whole top of his head melted away by flaming tar. At the last instant Dane leaped aside as the giant charged past, disappearing once more.

Again and again Dane shouted, until faintly in the distance he heard Astrid call back. Following her cries he found her and Kára crouched over the prostrate Lut, trying to help the old man up. Hearing a sudden hissing overhead, he looked up—a fireball, falling like a shooting star, was heading right at them. Dane hurried to throw Lut over his shoulder and drag him away. *Ka-bloom!* The flaming pot crashed to earth, engulfing with white-hot fire the spot where Lut had lain.

Dane knew survival depended on their finding shelter

from the charging giants and fire bombs. When the smoke cleared, he could return for the others.

They reached the outer wall of the arena and, feeling their way along it, came at last to a passageway that, though still smoky, seemed to offer some degree of shelter. His eyes burning from the smoke, Dane led them down the tunnel, feeling his way along, until the haze lifted a bit and he found himself outside the arena proper, able now to breathe easier. Pulling Kára and Astrid further into the fresh air, he could clearly see, far to the right, that the retreating trolls were scurrying to re-form their lines.

And then he heard it. *"Dane!"*

He turned. There she was—his mother—free and unfettered, emerging from a cloud of smoke. Into his arms she ran, and having her again so near, the warmth of her cheeks on his, brought him to tears. What joy to be reunited at last, to find her unharmed. Astrid too embraced her, as Geldrun excitedly spilled out an explanation of how she had escaped.

"We'll talk on the long journey home," Dane said, "but first I must gather the others." The sight of his mother's smile lit Dane with hope, and he started up the tunnel, intent on finding his friends. But a chill ran through him as a new voice rang out.

"Stay where you are!" From out of the darkness strode Godrek and his men, weapons in hand. Dane went for his sword, Astrid and Kára for their axes—but the sound of sinew stretching froze them. Three of Godrek's bowmen had arrows aimed at their chests. Godrek stepped forth and stood before Dane, his eyes twitching in impatience.

"I must thank your mother—she led us right to you." Godrek wore the same look, Dane noticed, that he had shown when he had first laid eyes on the glowing rune sword that night in the Skrellborg stables. "Where is it—my blade?"

"Hidden," Dane said. "I'll take you to it when my mother and friends are out of the gate and safely away."

"Hidden? But it's close," Godrek purred, cocking an ear to the air. "I can . . . *hear* it calling."

Commander Greb rushed up, flushed and out of breath. "Where is the manpower you promised?" he bellowed to Godrek. "My lines are breaking, my soldiers dying—and you have not lifted a sword!"

Godrek thrust his sword straight through Greb's neck and held it there for a moment, keeping the commander propped up. "I *have* lifted my sword, troll," he said with a cold grin. "Happy now?" He withdrew the blade and Greb stood for a moment, wearing a look of pained bewilderment, unable to fathom what had just happened. He collapsed like a rag doll without uttering another sound.

As if he had done nothing more than brush away a bothersome fly, Godrek now turned back to Dane.

"Time is precious, son. The blade!"

"My friends must go free," Dane demanded.

Godrek's men threw anxious looks behind them, expecting attack at any moment. They could hear troll cries of panic from out on the arena floor, as if the battle were soon to be lost.

Godrek nodded at Thorfinn, who in a lightning-quick move seized Astrid from behind, placing his knife at her throat. "Produce it *now*," Godrek said. "Or on the count of three the girl dies. Then the princess. One . . ."

Dane knew it useless to bargain with a madman. Apparently so did Lut. Before Godrek reached the count of "two," Lut produced the broken blade from under his cloak and threw it at Godrek's feet.

"It's yours now!" Geldrun said. "If there be any soul left within you, take it and free my son and his friends!"

But Godrek hadn't heard a word, the irresistible call of the blade having seized his mind and rendered him immune to anyone's pleas. Dane watched in growing alarm as Godrek, his eyes fixed upon the broken blade, reached down with his left hand and raised it above his head, whispering in unholy reverence, unaware that the blade had cut into the flesh of his hand and sent rivulets of his own blood dripping down his arm. With his right hand he took out the snake-handled half of the sword—the piece Dane had found in his father's war chest. His eyes shining madly, Godrek brought the two pieces together. The dull gray steel of the blade began to glow, once more turning a bright orange as if lit from within. The long row of runic inscriptions again became visible along the length of the blade, faintly at first, then more sharply apparent, the symbols themselves showing white-hot against the orange. There were murmurs of awe from the men. Godrek's left hand suddenly jerked away from the blade, Dane first assuming that the heat of the blade had made him let go. But then he saw what the others already had—the pieces had fused and become one! It was one unbroken blade again. The gods—or some other unseen power—had rejoined the ancient rune sword.

Godrek held it aloft, gazing up in worship at the gleaming blade, Dane fully expecting it to soon come plunging into his very chest. The mesmerized Godrek seemed to have forgotten all but the rune sword, his enraptured look telling Dane that the greed-madness had taken hold in him. Indeed, it was calling to Dane too, now louder and more alluring than ever.

Godrek ordered his men to seize Dane and his friends— he was taking them all. All but Lut, whom he told Ragnar to "take care of."

Many hours later, after the battle had subsided at last and the smoke had begun to clear, the defeated troll soldiers who had been hunted down and rounded up were brought into the arena. Fulnir had found Jarl, Drott, William, and the others still alive, and had joined them in their hiding place near the *blódíss* vat. Still missing were Dane, Kára, Astrid, and Lut, and Fulnir and the others hoped they had somehow escaped the arena unscathed.

Now Fulnir watched in fear and fascination as the frost giants debated the fate of the trolls. Understandably, the mob of giants was in a mood to massacre them all, and the first troll they brought forth to be killed was Dvalin, the troll chieftain. Looking beaten and bedraggled and resigned to his fate, he stood in stony silence as, without ado, a giant doused him with pitch and prepared to set him afire. And just as a torch was raised to ignite him, Fulnir was surprised to see Thrym burst through the crowd and protectively stand over Lord Dvalin.

"Why do you protect him?" said a giant in the crowd. "They attacked us!"

"After *we* attacked them. We destroyed their village. Can anyone here tell me what this war is about? Is there *one* thing the trolls have that you want?" he asked the giants.

The frost giants all looked at each other with blank faces, unable to think of a thing. Thrym asked the same question of the trolls, and none of them could think of one either. "This war is not about land or possessions. No, it is about one thing. Revenge. And who stoked that fire? Hrut!" Several giants nodded their heads, murmuring agreement.

"And my Commander Greb," Dvalin said. "He more than I wanted war, and now he is dead."

"Hrut too is dead. So unless someone can give me good reason why this war should continue, I am officially ending it here and now." Thrym waited, but no one, giant or troll, could think of why the war should go on.

"Does this mean we're not having *blódíss?*" one of the giants asked. Thrym proclaimed that *blódíss*, although tasty and tart, would never again be served. Giants griped and grumbled, but the peace held. Assured that they would not be turned into frozen desserts, Fulnir and his friends emerged from hiding.

Thrym saw them, and instantly his face showed alarm. "But where are Astrid and the others . . . Dane, the princess, and Lut?"

"I'm afraid," Fulnir replied gravely, "I haven't any idea."

# 28

# NORTHWARD
# TO PARTS UNKNOWN

D ane was in torment. Biting winds tore through his coat, his whole body numb from the cold, and though he had lost all feeling in his hands and toes, the bitter sting of shame and failure felt even worse. There was no denying it: He had led his mother and friends into utter disaster. And worst of it all, he feared his dearest friend, Lut the Bent, was dead.

Now as he lay on the exposed deck of the longship Godrek had seized, looking up at the gathering storm clouds, Dane clung to a single strand of hope. Their only chance for survival lay in the slim possibility that somehow Jarl and his friends had not been killed in the frost giant arena, and would bravely give chase. But if not—and if Lut had been killed by Ragnar, as he feared—he knew it spelled their doom. For now that they were Godrek's prisoners here on this longship—he, Geldrun, Astrid, and Kára—who could possibly save them?

In Utgard when Dane and the others were captured at swordpoint and spirited away, it wasn't until after they were out the fortress gates that Dane had noticed Lut wasn't with them and neither was Ragnar. An awful dread had struck Dane as he realized that the liegeman had no doubt been ordered to kill Lut, the only one who knew of Godrek's intended destination. Dane, his mother, Astrid, and Kára were tied onto the backs of horses and forced to ride hard with Godrek and his men down the western slope of the mountain. When Ragnar had joined them soon after, suspiciously alone, his face had revealed nothing, and Dane had felt a boiling rage that the old man had been killed so casually. He vowed to seek revenge on Ragnar and Godrek the first chance he had.

A day later they had reached the coastline, for it was here that the last part of their journey would begin to Ey Dauðr, the dreaded Isle of Doom, located in the northernmost seas. Desperate for a ship, Godrek and his men had commandeered one from a village of peaceful fisherfolk. Their chieftain, a toothless fat man, had tried to reason with Godrek, telling him that without the ship his people would starve. But to Dane's disgust, Godrek had wordlessly plunged the rune sword into the poor man's belly and, ripping it sideways, spilled out the man's vitals. The villagers—along with Astrid, Geldrun, and Kára—had gaped in shock as the chieftain collapsed, writhing in death spasms. Even Godrek's men had appeared taken aback by his brutality, since it was clear the boat could have been taken without violence. But Godrek strode, unruffled, aboard the ship without looking back—and it was then Dane had realized that the rune sword had completely poisoned his heart, and whatever humanity had once existed within the man was gone. Dane and the other captives had been herded onto the ship and tied securely, Astrid and Kára tied to oarlocks in the stern, Dane and his mother at the bow, and there they had stayed, pondering their fate.

Now, as the boat made its way north through ice-choked seas and wet flakes of snow began to fall, Dane felt a great wave of despair. How could he have been so naïve to think he could ever best a warrior like Godrek? King Eldred had warned him, but Dane, in all his foolhardy recklessness, had thought he could prevail. What a Rune Warrior he had turned out to be! If his rash and foolish exploits were ever carved into stone, it would surely be only as a dire warning to future Norsefolk, a lesson to all: how Dane the Defiant's actions brought ruin and death to his brethren, or something to that effect.

Dane watched Godrek, a soulless husk of a man, stride the deck like a glowering monster, mumbling and muttering foul curses under his breath. Dane saw that the men shared uneasy looks behind Godrek's back, as if they too were alarmed by their liege lord's transformation. And when

Godrek gave an order, the men swiftly hopped to as if fearing the thrust of his blade if they dawdled for even half a moment.

Dane looked at his mother, who sat with her back to the mast some distance away, arms tied behind her, looking to starboard, a fiery determination still in her eyes. "I will not go like a lamb to slaughter," she had whispered to him as they had been herded aboard the ship hours ago. This was so like his mother, Dane thought. Even when times were at their worst, she was never one to sink into despair and wait for the axe to fall. She expected him to fight back, but how? They were bound hand and foot, without weapons, and at the mercy of a pitiless madman and his hired killers. Even if they managed an escape, how could they swim through freezing waters?

And then Dane thought of what lay *under* the water— the thing that had for so long invaded his dreams and robbed him of peace. The serpent Jörmungandr. He knew now that his dreams were a premonition and that his journey was destined to end where the gigantic beast dwelled, hungry and waiting. "Life feeds on life," his father had always told him, all living things food for something else. Something larger, tougher, hungrier. The trick was to last as long as you could without getting eaten yourself. Well, soon it would all be over. He was being drawn ever closer to the thing he feared most, perhaps into the very belly of the beast itself. His best efforts had failed, so perhaps he deserved to die in this fashion. Men were not meant to live forever. How different things would be if he had only followed Lut's sage advice and never opened the trunk at all.

Astrid had never felt so cold and angry and twisted up inside. To feel so powerless, unable to fight back—it was as if the Norns had been toying with her all along. Each time Dane had faced danger and survived—against the ghost-wolves, in the troll village, and in Utgard—Astrid thought the peril could not possibly get any worse.

But it had. Much worse.

Oh, the cruel-hearted Skuld! Was this how the Wyrd Sisters got their jollies? Holding out hope and then cruelly yanking it away? And what of Lut? She feared his life had been snuffed out on Godrek's orders. Beside her she heard Kára loudly sniffling. "I doubt that tears will soften them," Astrid said, as she saw Thorfinn eyeing the two girls wolfishly.

"I'm *not* crying," Kára shot back. "The cold makes my nose run." Turning to Thorfinn she said, "You there! Untie me so I can dab my nose." But all Thorfinn did was give her a chilling leer and turn away, which only riled the princess further. "Rude!" she cried after the brute. "When I get my hands on an axe, you'll be dealt with! Your impudence will *not* be tolerated—"

It was at that moment that Astrid leaned over and, with her own sleeve, wiped Kára's runny nose, as much to shut her up as to clean her face.

"I doubt that insults will help us either, Kára."

"Well, I don't intend to sit here and be treated like rabble until I'm ransomed."

"Ransomed? Is that why you think Godrek took you?"

"I'm certain of it. As a royal I'm worth more than the combined treasuries of several small kingdoms." And then, not wanting Astrid's feelings to be hurt too badly, she said, "Oh, and I'm sure that you will fetch a pretty sum as well. A dozen cows and pigs, perhaps."

Holding her tongue, Astrid realized that perhaps Kára was right. As a princess she could command a queenly sum. But what of a commoner like Astrid? What fate did Godrek have in store for her if not to ransom? She wasn't naïve; she knew there were terrible things that could befall young women in the company of such savage men. Lying forward, she caught sight of the sling of axes that had been taken from her. If only she could get to them some way, she thought, at least she would go down fighting.


Although his beard was frosted with ice and he shivered in the cold, Lut was very much alive. Adrift on the frigid sea in a leaky boat, Lut clung to the hope that his life had been spared for a reason. He was tempted to throw the runes but frightened of what the gods might foretell. Was their mission doomed, or were the gods on their side? And what of that pain in his lower back? Would that ever go away?

343

Back in Utgard, after Godrek had taken Dane and the others, when the scarred one had come at him, Lut had been sure his end was near. So it had surprised him when, instead of dispensing a swift knife to his throat, Ragnar had taken him into the shadows and waited until he was sure Godrek was gone.

"Godrek ordered you to kill me," Lut had said.

"It is not in my creed to kill defenseless old men," Ragnar had answered.

"A creed I admire," Lut had said. Ragnar had told Lut he had to tie him and gag him to make sure he would remain silent and not alert Godrek that Ragnar had disobeyed. He had then asked Lut if he knew of Godrek's destination.

"I do," Lut had said. "The Isle of Doom."

"Well, perhaps our paths will meet again." From the bodies of dead trolls lying nearby Ragnar had found enough leather belts to secure Lut's hands and feet and left the old man in an alcove of the arena and disappeared.

Many hours later, when Lut at last had been found by Fulnir and Drott, Lut had been untied and happily reunited with his villagers. When Thrym learned of Godrek's destination, eager to smash the brigands who had kidnapped his beloved Astrid, the giant had given chase immediately. Carrying Lut and all the others in a sling on his back, he had quickly found Godrek's trail down the mountain and followed it to the same coastal village Whitecloak had terrorized. But alas, they had arrived many hours too late, the fisherfolk explained, telling of their chieftain's murder and the theft of their only seaworthy ship.

Fulnir had spied another craft, a weather-beaten, woe-begone flea-scow of a ship, lying beached on the pebble-strewn shore. Half the length of the usual longship, it boasted a single tattered sail and there were gaps in its gunwale planking. Aboard the ship was a small, coal-fired brazier used to heat pots of pitch that had been used to repair the boat's caulking, a job, they were later to find, that had not yet been completed. "If you lend us this boat, we will pursue the one who killed your leader," Fulnir had told them. Jarl, Rik, and Vik had doubted the craft was sea-worthy, but when they considered the load of silver that awaited them for the return of the princess and Godrek's head to King Eldred, they had agreed it worth the risk. Asked about their destination, Lut had told them they were going to Ey Dauði. The villagers had gasped and clutched the Thor's Hammer amulets around their necks, for the Isle of Doom was a place of dread from which no one returned.

Thrym being unable to accompany them any farther, they said their good-byes to the giant and climbed into the ship. Thrym gave it a push and stood watching and waving as they oared away. And just as their ship was disappearing into the sea mist, Lut had looked back to see the giant's face etched in apprehension, as if the frosted fellow knew only too well that this could be the last he would see of his friends.

Now they were hours at sea, rowing through an ever-thickening obstacle course of icebergs that threatened to smash their boat and send it to the bottom. Though there was wind, to be under sail would be too dangerous, given the icebergs, so they were forced to oar instead.

"Lut!" Jarl cried, manning the tiller, trying to steer the craft away from growlers, the word seafarers used to describe the house-size chunks of floating ice. "What say the gods? Are they with us?" The others kept to their work but cocked their ears to hear Lut's response. William bailed water, trying to keep up with the constant seepage through the ship's rotted caulking, while Rik, Vik, Fulnir, Drott, and Ulf strained at the oars.

"The runes say we must press on," Lut lied. "The signs are favorable."

"You already threw them?" said Jarl with suspicion. "I didn't see you do that."

"Uh," said Lut, searching for an answer, "I did it while you weren't looking."

"Starboard ice!" cried William. Jarl jammed the tiller, the bow lurched to port, the starboard rowers quickly pulled in their oars so they wouldn't be broken, and the ship narrowly passed a chunk of ice that would've crushed it.

Lut saw the frightened, ashen faces looking to him for reassurance. "Fear not!" he boomed. "The gods will protect us!" At that moment a wave crested the gunwale, splashing Lut in the face, dousing him with freezing seawater.

"That's some protection, Lut," chuckled Ulf, and this brought laughter from the group. Were the gods scolding him for evoking their names without consent? Perhaps, but he wanted to believe the gods *were* on their side.

A sudden *screek* snapped Dane from his stupor. The longship had just scraped an iceberg along its portside gunwale and now Godrek's men were scurrying about, using oars to push the berg away from the ship. His mother signaled him, and as he caught her eye, she began mouthing words to him, covertly glancing at Godrek and his men to be sure they were not watching. Dane tried to make out what she was saying, but reading lips was not one of his talents. He shook his head to tell her he didn't understand. Exasperated, she mouthed the words again. He thought he understood one of them. *Friend . . . friend,* she seemed to be saying. Friend? What did it mean?

She began nodding toward the aft part of the ship. What did *that* mean? That a "friend" was on board? But the wordless conversation abruptly ended when Godrek strode forward between them to the bow, where he stood gazing out at the seas ahead, the mad shine in his eyes now like a fever. Godrek wore the rune sword at his waist, sheathed in its scabbard, his hand caressing the bronze serpent's head on its protruding hilt. Dane stared in fear at the rune sword so dangerously close, feeling again its fearsome power, feeling the pull of its call.

"Where we go, a monster dwells," uttered Godrek, peering into the snow-laden mist. "Do you fear it?"

"Sane men do," Dane said.

Godrek turned his head and pointed his lethal gaze at Dane. "Sane men? Or men who fear the gods? With Odin's ring I'll *be* a god." Godrek drew forth the rune sword, raising it before his eyes and running a finger lovingly along the length of the blade, gazing at his own reflection in the steel. "This," he said hotly, "*this* is what binds us, boy!" He brought the rune sword down with sudden swiftness and laid it flat it against Dane's brow, pressing it there. Dane felt instantly electrified, a surge of energy pulsing through him, overtaken by the scream of the rune song, his mind drowning in the sound and fury of it, every fiber of his body alive and vibrating. Dane realized with horror that it was the very madness of Godrek himself flowing into him! The terror! Helpless to stop it, tied as he was, he tried to resist, to block it out. But like a furious river it flowed, a torrent of mad desire, the urge to kill and possess and dominate and destroy. But, oh, the power he felt! The same sweet invincibility! "You feel it now, don't you?" he heard Godrek purr madly. "The power? The glory of it? We are bound together now, boy, joined in united purpose, you and I melded as one, free and fearless and one!"

Godrek abruptly drew the blade away, sheathing it in his scabbard. Dane slumped against the gunwale, shaken and feeling suddenly empty.

"*That's* what your father lacked the courage to grasp," Godrek said, dripping disdain. "And what *you* no doubt lack as well, though it pains me to say it." Godrek swept away, leaving Dane lying on the icy deck, more bereft than ever.

# 29

# A BEASTLY
# SACRIFICE

Godrek's ship sailed ever northward, the air
growing colder, their sea path increasingly
blocked by icebergs large and small. A sudden
flare of light caught Dane's eye, and looking to the port side,
he saw that oil lamps were being lit and hung at intervals
along the gunwales of the ship. Soon he learned the reason
for this, for he overheard a man saying that Jörmungandr
was repelled by firelight. So we have entered the realm of
the beast, Dane realized with dread. The Isle of Doom was
near.

The scarred one known as Ragnar approached, hanging a
lamp on the bow. For an instant he flicked a look at Dane,
his face illuminated by the amber lamplight. "The old one
lives," he whispered, and then moved on. Lut was *alive*?
Could it be true? Dane's heart leaped with hope. If so—and

if Jarl and his friends had not been killed in the Utgard arena—Dane knew there was a chance now, however slim, of rescue.

He looked over at his mother. Again she mouthed the word "friend" and nodded toward Ragnar. And now he realized their chances for survival had suddenly improved. They had an ally on board.

"Land ho!"

Men scrambled about, peering ahead into the thick curtains of mist. It first appeared as a ghostly suggestion, an otherworldly apparition. But soon its outline solidified, a craggy gray spike of an island rising up out of the black flatness of the sea, its one thorny peak shining silver in the moonlight. And as the boat came abeam, the dark shape of Godrek himself stood out in silhouette over the view of the island, and it seemed a mystical foreshadowing of fate itself, as man and island merged into one striking image.

Within moments the ship was anchored and a small shore boat put into the water. Dane, his mother, Astrid, and Kára, their hands bound tightly in front of them, were lifted up and loaded in with Godrek and five of his liegemen. Ragnar, Dane was disappointed to see, was ordered to stay aboard the main ship and keep watch, so it seemed the one man they were counting on for help would not even be with them.

Godrek urged his oarsmen on, lashing them with curses as he sat caressing his rune sword in worship, and a short time later they reached the isle. Disembarking onto land, such as it was, Dane saw they were standing on a small, flat chunk of windswept ice broken only by the craggy spire of rock that rose at its center. Now so close to the treasure of his dreams, Godrek strode ahead with mad purpose. Dane and the women were herded onward by the five liegemen. When they arrived at the spire, they discovered a large crack in its side, and Godrek entered without trepidation, the captives pushed in after him.

Torchlight danced upon the cavern walls as everyone crept forward into darkness. At last the cave walls grew higher and wider, and Dane saw the true nature of the place. It was a soaring, many-chambered cavern, the sides of which were covered with a thick, sea-washed frost. Huge stalactites hung from the ceiling a good distance above their heads, and embedded in these were crystals such as he had never laid eyes on, flecked green and orange in the flickering torchlight. As they were moved onward, the splashing of water was heard, and peering ahead across the dimly lit floor of ice, Dane saw that the sea itself had entered through a side chasm and filled the far side of the chamber.

At the rim of the misty pool, Godrek lifted his torch higher, and the light from it illuminated the entire cavern. "There!" he cried. "Over there!" Dane could see the faint outline of a passageway cut into the wall on the far side of the dark pool.

It was the entrance to the vault, Dane realized, his heart quickening. Could Odin's Draupnir actually exist within? Godrek hurried forward, intending to cross to the other side via a narrow walkway along the right wall of the cavern. But he suddenly froze and hurried backward, shouting to his men to stand back.

Something was in the water.

Kára gasped. Then Dane saw it—the tail of an enormous sea beast rising straight out of the water, black and glistening in the amber firelight—and he knew they were in the lair of Jörmungandr, the hideous monster of his nightmares.

Everyone shrank away, Godrek and his men drawing weapons. The serpent's tail came forward, slithering along the surface of the lake and right up onto the ice floor itself, dripping water and bits of seaweed as it snaked left and right in search of a warm body to snatch. Dane saw the monster's scaly spikes protruding along its undulating spine, spikes so sharp, he was sure they could puncture a man straight through.

In terror everyone scrambled backward and stood with weapons raised and torch fires brandished in self-defense.

"My lord, it will not let us pass," Thorfinn said. Godrek was undeterred.

"It must feed," he said, more fascinated than afraid. "The very thing I prepared for." A sick grin crossed his face, and he nodded toward Astrid and Kára. "Which of you wishes to be first?"

For a moment Dane and the women were struck dumb.

"Godrek, you can't be serious!" Dane gasped.

"I'll let *you* choose, " Godrek said to Dane. "Which one?"

"By the gods!" cried Geldrun. "What depravity has poisoned you?"

"Wait! You—you brought me here to be—to be *food?*" Kára sputtered. "I am not food! I am of royal blood! I deserve to be ransomed! Not eaten!"

Godrek appeared to consider her argument. "You are entirely correct, princess. Perhaps the beast prefers blondes, anyway." He gestured to Thorfinn, who grabbed Astrid, his forearm around her neck.

"No!" Dane cried, coming at Godrek. He too was grabbed from behind, as were Geldrun and Kára. Astrid struggled like a wildcat, screaming curses, but Thorfinn's grip was too strong, for he was a warrior who had killed opponents with his bare hands and enjoyed it. He pulled her toward the pool.

Hearing a sharp cry of pain, Dane saw that Kára had sunk her teeth into the hand of the liegeman restraining her. And in the instant the howling man loosened his grip, Kára swung round and gave him a ferocious kick in the groin, which made him bellow in agony. She squirmed free and, before Godrek could stop her, ran toward Thorfinn, shrieking like a she-demon. As Thorfinn looked up in distraction, Astrid viciously whipped her head back into his nose, shattering it. Blind with pain, blood spraying from his nose, he stumbled backward. Righting himself, he drew his knife from his belt and screamed, "You daughter of Hel, I'll kill you—"

His words were cut short when Kára charged and head butted him in the chest, knocking him into the pool. Thorfinn gave a hideous cry, and Dane saw he had landed upon one of the creature's tail spikes, impaling him back to front. Pinned there on the beast's tail, helpless, a look of horrified disbelief on his face, Thorfinn disappeared under the water as the creature sank to the depths, no doubt to enjoy a hearty repast.

Dane expected Godrek to explode in fury and exact retribution for his man's death. But as the bubbles of Thorfinn's last breaths broke the surface, all Godrek said was "Well, *that* was a surprise." Intent only on Draupnir and seeing the path to it now clear, he commanded everyone onward. They advanced across the narrow walkway until Dane found himself standing on the threshold of the inner sanctum itself.

*We're lost,* Lut thought. *I hate being lost.* A heavy mist had swallowed them hours before, obscuring any sight of land. Worse, it obscured the massive ice floes that loomed in their path like giant battering rams, threatening to sink them with a single collision. The seawater, he saw, was seeping in between the rotten keel planks even faster than before, now near to his ankles. And from where he sat in the bow, helping William bail with buckets, he kept watch for icebergs ahead.

Lut was not a praying man. He thought such pleas rarely moved the gods to intervene in human affairs, either in help or in hindrance. But being in so dire a plight, he cast aside his doubts and said a silent prayer. *Merciful Odin, I beseech thee . . . spare the lives of these courageous men and boys. . . .*

His prayer was cut short. "Look—fire!" Fulnir cried, stabbing a finger at something just over the port bow. Lut peered into the mist, and, by the gods, there it was. An orange glow! At the rudder, Jarl steered the ship to port and they slowly drew closer. It was a ship, a large one, ringed with the light of a dozen or so torches. Lut spied a figure on deck, one side of his face made momentarily visible by the torchlight. It was Ragnar, one of the liegemen. They had found Godrek!

Jarl ordered the rowing be stopped, for if they came any closer, they risked being seen through the mist. A dim outline of land appeared, and they now saw that the torchlit ship lay anchored near a small, forbidding-looking rise of rock and ice.

"Oh, look," said Drott dryly, "it's . . . the Isle of Gloom."

"It's the Isle of *Doom*, idiot," said Jarl, always quick to criticize.

"I got the 'isle' part right, didn't I?" said Drott with an air of pride.

But Jarl ignored him, already asking Lut why Godrek's ship was ringed with torches. Lut paused, anxious over the answer he was about to give.

"Legend has it that fire is the only thing it fears," said Lut.

Drott asked the only question on everyone's mind. *"It?"*

Lut could hold off no longer. "The deadly sea serpent seen on the rune sword itself," he said. "Jörmungandr." The very utterance of its name brought sudden looks of fear to their faces.

"It's . . . *real?*" Ulf asked, his voice aquiver.

"Apparently so," Lut said grimly. "As guardian of the treasure, it forever haunts and hunts in these waters, intent on keeping men away. Ever vigilant, ever ravenous. So seeing as how it is we who are trespassing in its realm," Lut said, dropping his voice to a cautionary whisper, "I think it wise we stay as quiet as possible and hope its hunger finds bigger prey."

"And exactly how big might this Jörmunblundergunder be?" asked Vik. "Roughly. I mean, is it bigger than, say, this ship?"

Lut gave a grim nod.

"Bigger than *two* of our boats?"

Again Lut nodded.

Vik gulped and looked at his brother, Rik. "So," said Rik, "if I'm catching what you're saying, you're saying—"

"He's saying it's *big!*" hissed Jarl, at last exploding, but never raising his voice above a harsh whisper. "Huge! Big enough to eat us all and still be hungry for more! But if I hear anyone say they want to turn round and go home, they'll have to answer to me. 'Cause I want that reward for Godrek's head."

"You sure that's what you're after, Jarl?" teased Drott.

"Why *else* would I be here?" Jarl shot back. "Not because I enjoy *your* company."

"We all know whose company you love," Fulnir said. "Impossible as it seems, there's someone you're more sweet on than yourself."

Jarl just stared at them for a moment, waiting for everyone to stop their snickering. "What are you getting at?"

"Come on! You're smitten with the princess—admit it," said Drott.

"Smitten? With that stuck-up harpy? If anyone is smitten with anyone, *she's* smitten with *me*," Jarl said, throwing back his lustrous hair. "And for good reason." Jarl stood and made his way back to the rudder. The others sat there a moment, not knowing what to say. Then Ulf spoke.

"Not that I don't find the whole 'who is smitten with whom' thing fascinating . . . but on another subject—Lut, you think the *next* time we sail into ice-choked seas in a leaky boat, you could maybe tell us about the humungous man-eating monster *beforehand*?"

"Yes," said Lut, "I'll make it a top priority."

# 30

# INTO THE JAWS
# OF FATE

Godrek urging them onward, they passed through an ice-rimmed hole in the wall. Soon the path plunged downward along a perilous series of crumbling steps, and Dane realized their descent was taking them into the very innards of the isle, below the waterline. Finally the steps ended in a chamber that was perhaps thirty paces across and a good ten paces high.

"The door! Find it!" Godrek demanded.

His men spread out as commanded, holding their torches aloft as they searched along the walls. "Over here!" a man cried, and there in the torchlight Dane saw a massive iron door set in the rock. Scarred and encrusted with rust, the door looked ancient, perhaps many centuries old.

Godrek excitedly brushed away the accumulated bits of dust and rust to reveal the door's keyhole, the size and shape of a scabbard opening. He unsheathed the rune sword, and Dane now realized that the blade itself was the "key" to opening the door! But instead of inserting it into the lock, Godrek turned to face the captives, his eyes shining with diabolical calculation.

"The blade needs blood," he murmured. "Hold the others!" The liegemen sprang to seize Dane, Astrid, and Kára. Godrek now came at Geldrun with a slow, stalking gait, holding the rune sword before him.

Struggling to free himself, Dane shouted, "If it's blood you need, take mine!"

"Only your mother's will do," Godrek uttered, backing a terrified Geldrun into a corner.

Dane's mind shot back to Lut's warning: Succumbing to the rune sword meant sacrificing those you loved. Did the sword need *proof* of such a sacrifice to unlock the door to the treasure? Dane saw Godrek raise the rune sword to strike down his mother—and realized the madman had forgotten one thing.

"But you don't love her!" Dane cried.

Godrek froze, the sword poised. "She is the only woman alive I loved."

"Long ago, perhaps," Dane said. "But that love is gone. Killing her will be no sacrifice, if that's what the sword demands of you. There's *no one* in this world you love, Godrek. Which means you've come all this way for nothing."

Godrek lowered the sword. He turned to Dane. Instead

of a look of defeat on his face, he wore a malevolent smile. "Cut him loose," he ordered. The liegeman cut Dane's bonds, freeing him. "There is someone *else* who loves her," Godrek said. And before Dane could even absorb these words, Godrek threw him the rune sword. With the hilt end of it coming straight at him, Dane had no time to think— he instinctively caught the sword in his hand, gripping its hilt. Too late. Instantly jolted, he felt his whole body give way, once again overtaken by the torrent, the surging rune song now stronger and more irresistible than ever. Waves of sound and light swept through him and gave rise to a kind of chilling, all-commanding voice. *Kill,* it told him. *Resist! Resist,* he told himself. But the old part of him grew smaller and smaller as the new part grew ever more omnipotent.

He saw figures standing before him in the flickering light. Three women, two young ones and an older one, their faces unfamiliar. They meant nothing to him. But the man, the one with the gleaming white cloak, he was the one Dane was drawn to. Bathed in light, his cloak like a glowing aura behind him, this man seemed a part of him somehow, a figure of fatherly protection. The people in the room were talking to him yelling, it seemed—but he could not hear a word of what they were saying. Suddenly the only voice he could hear was that of the white-cloaked one standing before him—Godrek, yes, that was his name—and then other voices entered his mind. Gruff and howling voices, some speaking strange and ancient languages, and instantly

Dane knew who they were: the voices of all the others who had ever held the rune sword! Such was the magic of the blade! He moved toward the older woman, his only impulse being a desire to kill her, to end her life as quickly as possible, the chanting voices inside urging him on, their bloodlust filling his ears. Another step forward, the woman seeming faintly familiar—then a new voice spoke to him, one he instantly recognized. It was a more recent holder of the rune blade—his own father! *Dare not, son!* the voice of Voldar commanded. *Kill and lose the very thing you seek! It is love that gives one strength, not riches! The cloaked one is your enemy—trust him not.* . . . In a momentary flash the face of the woman was revealed to him—his mother. And with new eyes, resisting the call, blocking out the voices, he turned toward the cloaked one, knowing what he had to do, the thing his father had given him the strength to do—

As Dane grabbed the rune sword, Astrid saw the shock go through his body, the force of it knocking him backward. She saw his eyes go dead, drained of all kindness and feeling. It was the same look he had worn when first under the spell of the broken rune blade, but now even scarier.

"Dane! Drop the sword! Resist it!" Astrid cried.

He looked at her as if she were a stranger who meant nothing.

"You're with me now, Dane," Godrek crowed. "You're the man your father was afraid to become."

"Don't listen to him, Dane!" Astrid begged.

"We'll ride together, Dane. Conquer worlds! Be kings! You want that, don't you, son?"

An alien voice came from him; it said, "Yes."

"We'll have it all . . . if you will do one thing," Godrek purred. "The blade demands a sacrifice." He pointed at Geldrun and said, "Kill her."

Dane turned to face his mother. For an instant Astrid saw a flicker of something in his eyes, his emotions straining to act. But his face deadened again, becoming a cold mask—and at that moment Astrid knew the rune sword had seized all control of his mind and that he was going to kill his own mother.

And then it all happened so fast. Compelled by something deep inside, with a sudden surge of superhuman strength, she broke free of her guard and ran at Dane, grabbing the hilt of the sword, wrestling with him for control of the blade. Their eyes met. She saw a flash of raw terror—and the bloodthirst of a monster. Having surprised him, she had gained a firm hold on the hilt of the sword, both of their hands now gripping the handle, whipping it back and forth through the air, each trying to wrest control of it from the other. Godrek's guards advanced, but in the struggle she whipped the sword in circles, holding them at bay. She felt his hot breath upon her; worse, she felt the power of the rune song surging through her, filling her with new urges. With an animal growl, Dane tried to wrench the sword away, and in the ensuing struggle she heard a scream.

Next she knew, she was alarmed to see Dane sprawled on the floor, blood flowing from what looked to be a mortal wound in his side. She was further horrified to find the rune sword clutched in her hand, the blade wet with Dane's fresh blood, the runes upon it glowing white hot. What had happened? What had she done? Her head spun. She heard Dane's mother scream. She heard another voice say, *It is time. . . .* Everyone in the room seemed to have frozen in place as if time itself were standing still. A light flashed. A moment later, Astrid found herself standing beside the pool beneath the sacred tree Yggdrasil, startled to find herself once again in the moss-hung grotto of the Norns.

"How ironic," cackled Skuld. Astrid turned to see the three Wyrd Sisters sitting comfortably on the bank. "She asks to spare the boy's life, then kills him with her own hand."

"Do you take joy in your cruelty?" Astrid asked, her voice ringing with anger.

"Life is cruel," said Verdandi with a shrug. She gestured to the water. There in the reflection Astrid saw Dane lying motionless where he had fallen, blood pooling around him, the light in his eyes dimming. "Now to the business at hand. When last you were here, need I remind you, we made a little deal: At the time of his death, you could spare him by pledging your life to Odin. Well, the time has come, my dear. He lies at death's door. What is your decision?"

364

"You tricked me!" Astrid cried in tears. "You knew he wasn't going to kill his mother, but you made me believe it was up to me to stop him!"

"Still," said Skuld, "he is going to die."

Astrid gazed down at the image of Dane in the pool, anguished by the choice she had to make. If she spared him, she was giving up her human existence. She would become a Valkyrie, forever apart from Dane, her father, and all her friends in the village. She would never be a wife or have children. And worst of all, she would never again experience the joy of being loved.

"Answer now!" demanded Skuld. Astrid saw the Book of Life before Skuld. The Norn tapped a finger upon an opened page. "Answer before the ink is dry, or the boy will be gone forever!"

Astrid gazed again at Dane's lifeless body and knew she could never live with herself if she did not save him. "May I return to him?" she murmured sadly. "Just for a while?"

The Sisters shared a look, made gleeful by Astrid's submission. "You may return," Skuld said. "When it is time, we will summon you." Skuld flicked a hand at the page, and *pliff!* It burst into flames and was gone.

Astrid blinked and found herself back in the ice dungeon, standing over Dane, the pool of blood now strangely fading away. Geldrun, Kára, and their liegemen guards stared in befuddlement for a moment, as if all awaking from a dream. The rune sword lay at her feet, still wet with blood. Stirred

365

by the sight of it, Godrek snatched up the sword, hurried to the door, and thrust the blade into the keyhole. It fit. He turned it. There was the sound of rusted gears moaning within its ancient mechanism. The door groaned open, and fetid air trapped for centuries rushed out. A golden glow radiated from within, a light so blindingly bright that Godrek and the others had to shield their eyes. And the look on his face as he entered the vault of Draupnir was one of invincible rapture.

"Astrid . . ."

She looked down to see it was Dane, awake now, the wound in his side no longer there at all. She knelt beside him as he opened his eyes in confusion. "Did I . . . die?"

Astrid tearfully hugged him and whispered, "No, Dane, you didn't. . . . You're very much alive." And the joy of it brought tears.

# 31

## HALFWAY
## TO COURAGEOUS

Feeling the icy wind in his face, William listened to the fevered discussion as to how exactly they might go about rescuing Dane, Geldrun, Astrid, and Kára without attracting Jörmungandr. Through the mist, they could see five men aboard the ship, which meant Godrek had taken the prisoners and the rest of his men ashore. A small launch was beached there on an ice bar. And though the odds were definitely in their favor—their seven against Godrek's five—Jarl said a frontal assault was suicide. Because the sides of the larger ship were much higher than their craft, climbing aboard her would be near impossible. And if they were spotted, they'd be under deadly arrow fire from above.

William piped up. "What if we had two boats? One to

attack and one to go ashore for the rescue." Jarl told the boy to shut up, because they plainly didn't *have* two boats. "But we do," said William. "Look." He pointed to a small ice floe that had floated between their boat and Godrek's. "From there I can shoot arrows at them while you slip through the mist to the far side of the isle and get ashore."

It was an audacious plan and, although perilous, probably their best chance. The growler floated maybe fifty paces from Godrek's ship, well within William's range. Although Lut was hesitant to subject the boy to such danger, he saw that the growler was so small, anyone else set upon the berg risked capsizing it.

Fortunately there was the brazier and pot of pitch aboard ship, and so Lut started a fire with his fire-steel. Quietly the boat was rowed alongside the iceberg, and William, his bow slung over his shoulder with a quiver of arrows, was deposited upon it along with the brazier and pitch pot. The ice floe, a mere four paces across, dipped in the water as he stepped upon it, and William had to quickly center himself on it so as not to flip it over. "Good luck, my lad," Lut whispered. "May your aim be true."

Watching the boat disappear into the briny mist, William felt his stomach tighten and he fought the urge to cry, "Come back!" But then he remembered what Dane oft told him: Courage, he had said, wasn't the lack of fear; it was acting *despite* one's fear. Well, if that was true, he was halfway to courageous. He was floating alone on a tiny cake of ice in the dark seas of a merciless man-eating monster; he had the fear part covered. Now the hard part—forcing himself to act.

But he had to wait. He could not shoot before he gave his friends enough time to row the boat to the other side of the isle, so when Godrek and his men ran to save their ship, his cohorts would have opportunity to find Dane and the others.

The pitch now bubbling atop the brazier fire, he dipped an arrow-point into the pot, tarring its tip with a thick dollop of the flammable stuff, raising it up again and watching it quickly dry in the chill wind. Soon he would dip the iron tip into the brazier fire and set it aflame, but only right before he was ready to shoot.

He heard the sound of rippling water. An enormous fin broke the surface of the water twenty paces to his left. Another fin rose. Then six more, all in one continuous line and moving straight for him. And in a flash William realized these were not fins but hornlike spikes. Jörmungandr! One by one the angular spikes dove beneath his fragile little ice floe and disappeared. He felt a jarring bump—the creature had dealt the underside a glancing blow—that made his berg begin to drift *away* from Godrek's ship! His horror at having seen the monster was eclipsed only by the sudden realization that he had to shoot his arrows *before* drifting out of range. But it was too soon! His friends hadn't reached the other side of the isle yet. *It was now or never,* he thought. *Act, William, act!* He thrust his arrowhead into the brazier fire, allowing the tip to take flame. Pulling the arrow back in his bow, the bowstring drawn taut, he took aim and let fly his fire arrow at the largest target—the sail of Godrek's ship.

Godrek gazed at the glittering mountain of gold, staggered by the enormity of the treasure piled before him. Hundreds—nay, thousands—of solid gold arm rings lay heaped atop each other inside the immense cavern. Oh, glory! Bending down, he saw that each gleaming ring was identical to the others—replicas of the serpent Jörmungandr swallowing its tail—and large enough to fit round a grown man's upper arm. Marveling at the wonder of it all, another thought occurred, and he lifted his gaze. There atop the summit of this impossible hoard was Draupnir itself, the magical mother ring that had spawned them all. For centuries it had been in this place, and every ninth day Draupnir had dripped eight identical rings, miniature duplicates of the massive mother ring.

Drawn upward, Godrek scrambled up the mountain of gold. He cared not that each step he took landed him upon enough rings to make him wealthy for a lifetime. Mad with greed, he lusted after the godly source of it all.

He reached the peak. Above him hung Draupnir itself,

suspended from the cavern ceiling by two thick iron rods fastened to opposite sides of the ring. Now so near to it, Godrek gasped, seeing the size of the ring—large enough perhaps to fit round a horse's belly! And then before his eyes, the magic of Draupnir revealed itself. From out of the serpent's mouth dripped a stream of pure liquid gold, the golden stream squirming like a snake, as if alive, and just as quickly curling back onto itself, forming a circle and dropping down onto the mountain of rings below. Moments later the ring hardened into the very image of Jörmungandr, identical to the multitude of golden rings it now lay upon.

But he barely noticed the mountain of gold beneath him. Raising the rune sword, he began hacking at the iron bands to free Draupnir. The ancient iron chipped away, but not fast enough for Godrek. Shooting a look down at his men, he saw they had roused themselves and were eagerly scooping up rings, slipping them over their arms until each arm was covered with the glittering gold.

"Up here!" Godrek barked. "We must free Odin's ring!"

The men looked perplexed. "But my lord, we have all this," one man said, gesturing to the mountain. "That is only one ring."

"It's the one I want most of all!"

As he ran in with urgent news for Lord Godrek, Ragnar stopped cold at the sight of it. A mountain of golden rings gleaming in the torchlight. At the very top of the heap he spied Godrek and the men madly cutting away at something—and as Godrek shrieked in joy, down it came, an ever-larger ring rolling right for him, a huge serpentine circle of gold as big and round as a wagon wheel careening toward him. Ragnar spun aside, and the giant ring smashed into the cavern wall and fell to the ground with a resounding otherworldly clang.

For a moment Ragnar could scarce believe his eyes. Draupnir!

Godrek came scrambling down the vast hoard of rings to where Draupnir had come to rest, quickly inspecting the sacred ring to find that, remarkably, its gleaming surface was unscathed.

"The ship, my lord—" Ragnar said, eager to deliver his news. "It's on fire!"

Godrek swung his head round to face Ragnar now. "Fire! How?"

"We're under attack, m'lord! Flaming arrows. We're trying to douse it, but—"

Alarmed, his men immediately started out, but Godrek ordered them to stop. "The ring! We must get the ring to the ship."

Ragnar exchanged urgent looks with the others. "My lord," he said, "we can come back for it. If we lose our ship, we'll die here. All this gold will be worthless in Valhalla!" For an anxious moment, Godrek stood there looking at

Draupnir, then at the panicked faces of his men. Somehow the need to save the ship penetrated his irrational fog of greed, and he hurried off with them.

Each time William shot a flaming arrow, he knew he was giving away his position. He would hear shouts of "There!" from the men aboard Godrek's ship, and in an instant the hiss of their arrows flying back would fill the air. After each volley he hugged the ice, making himself as small a target as possible. The hail of arrows fell short and went over his head, and some stung the berg itself, nearly hitting him. These he dipped into the pitch, lit, and fired back. How many arrows had he sent? Fifteen? Twenty? He wasn't sure. After a time he was aware his growler had drifted even farther from Godrek's ship; too far for his arrows to reach it or for the return arrows to reach him. Through swirls of mist he saw the dim glow of the ship on fire and heard the echoing shouts of the men, and then even those sights and sounds vanished into the night.

*Now I'm alone,* he thought. *But I've done my job. I've shown courage.* And even if his act of bravery would prove to be his last, at least he had tried to rescue his friends. He sat on his tiny bread crust of an iceberg, drifting into the misty oblivion, going farther and farther away from all who knew and loved him. He was surprised at how peaceful he felt.

And then the dim outline of a new shape appeared,

looming before him. Drifting closer, he saw the object was enormous, with soaring white spires towering as high as the walls of a castle. And it was not until the last instant before impact that he realized it was as if his little berg were reuniting with its mother.

# 32

# THE ETERNAL HUNGER
# OF JÖRMUNGANDR

Ragnar the Ripper knew this was his best chance to escape his liege lord forever. He would sail away with those who had come to rescue the captives. And he would take with him treasure that would make him wealthy beyond his wildest dreams—rich enough to buy a small country in some faraway corner of the world, where he could while away his remaining days reading books and writing epic poetry.

But he had to act fast.

After delivering the news of their ship being on fire, he had hurried out of the cave with Godrek and the other liegemen, making for the launch boat. Just before they piled into the boat, Ragnar lagged behind and hid behind a boulder. The men were in such a hurry to return to the burning ship, Ragnar's absence wasn't noticed. As the men rowed away, he took off running back toward the cave entrance.

When Dane heard that Godrek's ship was under attack, his hopes had brightened—it had to be Jarl and his friends to the rescue! But the man left behind to guard them—a hatchet-faced cutthroat named Smek the Gaunt—forced them all facedown on the cold stone floor, retying their hands behind their backs and binding their ankles together so they could not run off.

"It's over," taunted Smek, his face close to Dane's. His breath smelled like rancid milk, and Dane saw most of his teeth were rotted stumps. "You'll be in the belly of the serpent before your friends ever find you. Now stay here while I take a gander at what's beyond that door."

Smek disappeared though the great iron door. Immediately, Dane and the others worked feverishly to loosen their bonds. "Gah!" Dane spat. "I'd rather be eaten by Jörmungandr than smell his breath again."

He heard a sound. Ragnar was standing before them. He held a knife in his hand, and Dane wasn't sure if he was here to save them or slice their throats.

"Ragnar—at last!" Geldrun gasped. "Free us!"

"On one condition," he said.

A long moment passed and Kára blurted, "You want us to *guess*? We don't have all day!"

"Odin's ring is just beyond that door. I'm taking it with us."

"Fine!" agreed Kára. "A tiny ring. Now cut our bonds— me first."

Ragnar quickly cut through the ropes, and they were free. He told Geldrun, Astrid, and Kára to wait there and signaled Dane to follow him. They crept to the iron door. Ragnar turned to Dane and whispered, "*Don't* make a sound." Dane nodded and followed Ragnar through the door.

The instant Dane beheld the mountain of gold, he gave a loud gasp. Smek, halfway up the mountain's slope, turned and saw them. Ragnar shot Dane a pained look.

"Sorry," Dane said.

"Ragnar, what are you doing there?" asked Smek.

"I'm taking Odin's ring and locking you inside," replied Ragnar.

Smek let out a bellow and took off down the mountain toward them, falling, cartwheeling as if he were on a snow-clad slope.

Ragnar pointed to Draupnir, which lay close by the door. "Hurry!" he said to Dane. "Help me with this!"

It was incredibly heavy. Dane and Ragnar righted it and rolled it out the door. Dane looked back and saw Smek was almost upon them. Ragnar put both hands on the ancient iron door and pushed with all his might. It closed with a deep *kuh-lunnngg!* just before Smek slammed into the other side. Locked in with a mountain of gold, Smek let fly curses that were but faint, faraway murmurings.

Dane turned. The women stared in disbelief at the enormous piece of godly jewelry standing on its side before them. "Glad we're not bringing the matching earrings," Kára said.

The women emerged from the crack in the spire, followed by Dane and Ragnar, rolling the cumbersome ring between them. They could see that the fire on the ship had almost been extinguished, but the sail was gone. Godrek too could be spied through the mist, standing on the bow, shouting orders. Although Dane felt a strong urge for revenge, he knew this was not the time for it.

"Pssst! Over here!" Dane turned to see Drott, Fulnir, and Jarl peeking out from the cover of a boulder, and behind them were Rik and Vik. Kára rushed into Jarl's embrace, and Dane, Astrid, and Geldrun were equally overjoyed to see their friends.

"Glad to see me, huh?" Jarl said to the princess in his arms.

Kára instantly turned aloof again. "I'd be glad to see a one-eyed ogre," she said, turning away, "if he were here to save me."

Jarl shot a wary look at Ragnar.

"He's the one who freed us," Dane explained. "He's no longer Whitecloak's. He's with us now." Everyone's eyes went to the giant gold ring, and Ragnar quickly disabused them of any thoughts it was community property. "This is mine, and I kill anyone who thinks it isn't."

"I think that's fair," Drott said.

Suddenly a sharp cry was heard from Godrek's ship. They'd been spotted.

"Quick! To the boat!" Fulnir said. They hurried off, Dane and Ragnar lagging behind, rolling the ring. Glancing back, Dane saw Godrek and his men were already into the launch craft, furiously rowing to shore.

"The ring is slowing us down!" Dane shouted.

"Keep rolling!" Ragnar barked.

Lut had never beheld a happier sight. There they were—Geldrun, Astrid, and Kára—all alive and emerging from the mist, running toward the boat with Jarl and the others. His heart leaped. But he realized Dane was not among them. Moments later he made out two dim figures who seemed to be struggling with an object of some kind. They were arguing and swearing at each other and Lut saw that one of them was Dane! The other . . . was that Ragnar? He saw the object they were rolling—a massive gold ring. By the gods! Could it be?

And then Lut saw that closing fast behind them were Godrek and his men.

The craft bobbed in the water next to a crumbling ice shelf. Astrid and the others hurried across the shelf without stopping and jumped into the moving ship. Kára balked, so Jarl picked her up and unceremoniously threw her at the boat just as it dipped—and she would've flown over it into the water if Ulf had not caught her.

Everyone looked back and saw that Godrek and his men were making up ground quickly behind Dane and Ragnar, who frantically rolled the ring as fast as they could.

"Leave the ring!" cried Geldrun.

"Not a chance!" Ragnar yelled back.

Just as they reached the ice shelf, the boat rose and the ring rolled right on board and fell over, narrowly missing Lut. Dane and Ragnar pushed the boat off and jumped in just as arrows hissed past. By the time the pursuers arrived at the ice shelf, the boat was a good distance from shore. More arrows came, but everyone in the craft ducked below the gunwale and no one was struck. Soon the arrows stopped, and peeking over the gunwale, Lut saw Godrek and his men now running in the other direction toward their ship. He heard Jarl give a shout to the group, and soon the rowers sat and began to pull at the oars and Jarl, at the tiller, steered the boat north.

"Why north?" Dane asked. "Go south! Godrek's ship has lost its sail—they'll have to row. We're smaller and faster, so we can outrun them."

"I wondered how soon you'd start giving orders," Jarl sneered. "This is *my* command."

"You're going the wrong way!"

"We cannot leave as yet," Lut said, stepping between them. "Not without William."

Now Dane noticed that, indeed, the boy was missing. He grabbed the front of Lut's cloak, his voice rising in panic. "Where is he? What happened?" Lut told him how the boy was the one who'd set Godrek's ship on fire as a diversion so they could get ashore.

"Why did you let him do that? He's just a boy—"

"He's proven more than a boy, son," Lut replied gently. "He's resourceful and brave, as the name you gave him attests."

Their craft headed for the northern tip of the island, Jarl's strategy being that Godrek, thinking their ship would flee southward, would naturally go south as well, and so by the time they circled the isle to reach William, Godrek would be gone. Lut agreed that this was a sound plan, and Jarl seemed pleased by this endorsement, rising to an even greater height as he stood at the rear and piloted the craft. Dane told Lut of their brush with Jörmungandr, and about the fabulous mountain of gold spawned by the ring now being jealously guarded by Ragnar.

"The monster may come for it," Lut whispered. "Perhaps we should cast it into the sea." They looked at Ragnar, who stood over the ring, his hand gripping the haft of his sword, ready to strike at anyone who threatened his ownership.

"There'll be blood if we try," Dane said.

"Well, perhaps the monster won't find us," Lut said with an air of false optimism.

"And if he does? I've brought you all to where it dwells."

"It wasn't only you we came to rescue, Dane. Besides, the gods are protecting us."

Dane brightened at this. "Is that what the runes say?"

"Would I lie?"


Though his situation was still dire, William was glad at least to be off the tiny growler. It had drifted into a much larger iceberg and, as if going from a rowboat to a longship, William had easily stepped upon it, bringing his weapons, brazier, and pitch pot with him.

He guessed this larger berg was a hundred paces across. The place he was now standing on was flat, like a beach lapped by small waves. There were two pinnacles of ice that rose as tall as a frost giant on opposite sides. Maybe seventy paces behind him the flat part had eroded away, sloping down like a funnel into a watery channel. It was a stroke of luck that his tiny drifting floe had been stopped by this larger berg, for if it hadn't, he knew he would be farther away from land now, without hope for rescue.

But *when* would it come?

He warmed his freezing hands on the brazier coals, knowing that when they died, all he would have for warmth would be his tattered coat. Then *crraaacckk!!* A startling sound from deep within the ice. Again the ice groaned and snapped as if the berg itself were alive, its bones and joints creaking and cracking as the churning sea thrashed it about.

And then he heard a new sound from out in the mist.

*Sploop, sploosh.* Followed by an ominous silence. Was it Jörmungandr? Instinctively he backed away from the edge, seized with a sudden chill of panic, staring helplessly into the clouds of mist.

From somewhere beyond the mist he now heard the rhythmic splash of oars hitting water. "William!" It was the voice of Dane. "William! Where are you?"

What should he do? Should he keep quiet so they would row away? No! They would only come back. He must warn them. "Go away!" he shouted into the mist. "The monster is here! Go away!" He listened, but the pace of the oars only quickened and grew louder. "No! Go back! Go back!"

The ship appeared from out of the mist, moving swiftly toward him, the figure of Dane standing tall in the prow. William realized his warnings were useless, for Dane and the others would never abandon him, even if huge, scary beasts *were* lurking about. As the craft came closer William saw Dane wore the stern look of a father ready to punish his son. "William the Brave, eh? We'll have to change that name." Dane broke into a big grin. "How 'bout William the *Insanely* Brave?"

William had always yearned for Dane's approval, and he wanted to say something in return. But the words caught in his throat, for he saw, rising high out of the water, as high as the top of the ship's mast itself, a sinuous serpent's tail bearing long, daggerlike spikes. And a cry of "Look out!" was all William could manage.

The tail came crashing down behind the stern, and the huge wave it made lifted the entire ship up out of the water and onto the ice. For a moment Dane and his friends just sat there, glad the ship was still intact and they were in it. And then the tail rose again, even higher than before, and as it came down, everyone dove from the ship onto the ice. *Krrr-splamm!* The tail crushed the craft, turning it to splinters. For a chaotic moment everyone scrambled away from the writhing tail. William looked back and to his horror saw that Rik had been skewered like a piece of meat by one of the beast's tail spikes. The tail plunged under the water, taking Rik with it.

Rik's twin, Vik, bellowed in agony as if mortally wounded himself. He tried to leap into the sea to save his brother, but Dane and Jarl held him back. Vik beat at them, trying to free himself—when William saw the tail again break the surface, excited to see Rik hanging on to the creature's tail, stabbing into its scales with his knife!

"He's alive!" William cried, pointing.

Indeed, Rik rode the tail as if it were a bucking horse, stabbing and cutting its flesh. But when the beast finally shook him free, Rik's body went catapulting skyward, arcing high overhead until, hitting one of the upraised ice pinnacles, his body slid down its smooth, curved side and soon came to rest at the very feet of his brother, Vik. For a moment no one spoke, believing Rik dead. And then they heard laughter. And when Vik rolled his brother onto his back, he saw it was Rik who was laughing, his cloak bearing a large rip in the side where the monster's spike had stabbed, missing his body completely. Pulled to his feet, Rik was soaked and shivering. Nevertheless, he shook his head to clear it, grinned, and said, "That was fun. Can I go again?"

Astrid, Dane, and William dashed to the destroyed ship, looking for weapons. Astrid found a knife and Dane a long-handled fishing gaff. A hand grasped his shoulder and swung him around to face Ragnar's glaring eyes.

"The ring is mine!" he growled.

"I don't want it!" Dane yelled back. "The monster does! Give it to him and maybe he'll go!"

But Ragnar wasn't listening. He was sifting through the broken timbers to find Draupnir when a jarring quake knocked everyone off their feet.

The sea monster was attacking the iceberg itself—hacking away with its massive spiked tail, as if the berg were a ship it could splinter and send to the bottom. Thunderous whacks cracked the ice, sending large chunks of the berg flying off and splashing into the sea. Dane knew if this went on any longer, their ice shelter would be smashed to bits and all lives lost.

"William! Any arrows left?"

"Just three."

The brazier, Dane saw, was lying on its side, some of its still-glowing coals spilled out on the ice. He coated the three

arrows in pitch and lit them, and—in rapid succession—
William grabbed each one and shot at the tail. The first
one missed, but the next two sank into its scaly hide. There
was the sizzle of fire on flesh, and the tail jerked in pain and
quickly plunged underwater.

"Killer aim, Will."

"If only I had more arrows." The boiling sea calmed, as if
the monster had dived far below to lick its wounds. But was
it gone for good? "I thought of what you said," said William.
"About having courage . . . about acting *through* the fear. I
guess it worked."

"*Guess* it worked? Without you I'd still be a prisoner." He
gave William a brotherly fist to the shoulder. "And I saw
you trying to warn us, thinking more of our safety than your
own. The act of a true Rune Warrior."

"Me?" said William, his face alighting in awe. "A *Rune*
Warrior?"

"At only ten years old. What'll you do when you hit
eleven?"

The berg shuddered violently again. The monster was
now attacking from the other side. It had snaked its way into
the channel eroded by seawater—which meant there was
no place on the berg that was safe. The creature's glistening spiked tail uncoiled upward, rising high overhead, then
came slamming down like a felled redwood—*KA-BAM!*—
landing with a thunderous crash right on the spot where
they had just been standing, the crushing weight of its tail

so intense that the ice cracked beneath it.

Now they were split into two groups, one on either side of the tail, and they quickly backed away in opposite directions, Jarl and Dane on the right side, everyone else on the left. But the tip of the tail curled round to the left, trapping everyone on that side, and threatening, Dane saw, to enclose them and pull them back into the sea.

"William!" cried Dane. "Make a torch!"

William grabbed an oar and thrust the handle end into the pitch pot, then into the brazier fire, lighting it. He bravely ran at the slithering tail, touched the flame to the hide, and jumped away. Instantly the creature jerked away its tail.

But this stratagem backfired, for then the snaking tail went sliding the other way, curling back around to the right and trapping Jarl and Dane on an even smaller section of ice. As the tail snaked close, Jarl hacked at it with his sword, Dane stabbed with the sharp, hooked gaff, but the thing dodged their weapons as if it had a mind of its own.

And then Dane saw, astonishingly, near the tip of the tail a black orb that could only be one thing: an eye!

"It sees us!" Dane cried.

"A tail can't see!"

Dane thrust the gaff at it; the tail ducked and swerved, lunging with its spikes at Dane's head. He parried the attack, slashing with his weapon.

"The end! Go for the end of the tail!" shouted Dane.

As Dane fought furiously, trying to keep the thing's attention on him, Jarl crept to the side, his blade held high, waiting to strike. With the long, deadly tail spikes thrusting toward him, it was as if Dane were fighting six swordsmen at once. *Swoosh! Swoosh!*

"Any time now, Jarl!"

The tail whipped sideways, knocking Dane off his feet. Again he saw it rise, ready to slam its spikes into his body—but Jarl gave a war cry, and in a flash of his blade he had severed the end of the thing's tail. Dane rolled as the tail slammed down blindly, missing him. The tail jerked and writhed, wildly whipping around like a frenzied blind man trying to ward off attackers. Then it retreated, slithering back across the ice, disappearing beneath the black water.

The severed end of the tail, bearing the single black-orbed eye, lay twitching on the ice. "I shall hang it over my hearth to honor my victory," Jarl proclaimed. He cocked a look at Dane, in case his rival was thinking of stealing his trophy.

"No argument here," Dane conceded.

Hefting the twitching tail, Jarl brought it back to where everyone stood. He held his trophy high, boasted loudly, "I have slain the monster!"

Jarl's boastings were usually overblown, and this time was no different. With a roar Jörmungandr shot headfirst from the channel, landing with cataclysmic force upon the ice. Everyone was thrown off their feet, and the berg began to tip upward under the monster's enormous weight.

In a mad scramble, they all reached out and clutched one another's hands, legs, and clothing so as not to slide toward the monster. Jarl had Kára. Ulf grabbed Dane and Astrid. Geldrun grabbed Lut, who held William's hand. Drott and Fulnir anchored themselves by sinking their knives into the ice and called out for others to hold on to them. Ragnar had also anchored himself with his knife and was clutching his precious ring to prevent its sliding away.

The ice sheet angled higher and higher, but the human web seemed to be holding. The beast below them hissed and snorted, blowing gusts of hot air from its nostrils. Below him Dane saw the black maw of its mouth and the sharp, pointed horns atop its reptilian head, its eyes twin orbs of green smoke and fire that burned with an all-seeing malevolence.

Dane heard a cry. Astrid had lost her grip and was sliding right past him. He flung out his leg, and at the last instant, she grabbed his foot, hanging on precariously.

"Don't let go!" Dane shouted.

"I won't!"

To shake its prey free, below them the monster reared its head up and smashed it onto the ice. The berg shook, and Astrid lost her grip and tumbled downward.

Astrid clawed frantically at the ice to stop her slide. *If I die, must I still be a Valkyrie? If not, where will I go? Is Valhalla strictly a males-only afterlife? That seems rather unfair. . . .*

Then she realized she still had a knife. She grabbed it from her waist and stabbed at the ice, but down she kept sliding. Again and again, she plunged it in, until finally it held and she jerked to a stop.

Clutching the knife handle with both hands, she hazarded a look below—she hung a mere two body lengths above the beast's black, cavernous jaws.

"*This* time don't let go!" she heard Dane cry.

"That was my intention!" she cried in answer.

Below Dane the monster smashed its black jaw onto the ice, shaking the berg like a bear shakes a tree to dislodge low-hanging fruit. Dane saw that the reverberations were swinging Astrid to and fro from her precarious handhold. Another jolt might shake her free. "Form a chain!" Dane yelled to those nearest him. "We can reach her!"

Above him he saw one of the ship's long-shafted oars had gotten lodged in the knot of arms and legs. "The oar!" he yelled. "Fulnir, give me the oar!" Quickly the oar was handed down to him. Dane took one last look at his mother, who clung to Lut beside him, and he let go of Ulf's grasp and slid away, the oar in hand.

He knew if he collided with Astrid, they'd both tumble into the monster's mouth. So he dug the oar into the ice like a rudder as he slid, steering himself just a bit to the left of her. Astrid grabbed at him as he shot past—missing—and Dane went sliding feetfirst toward the monster. He rammed into its lower jaw, its breath steaming over him. He rolled and kicked, trying to elude its massive fangs, the sudden nearness of its jaws flooding him with panic. In moments, he'd be eaten. He swatted the creature's snout with his oar shaft—once! twice!—and the thing growled and opened its jaws even wider, hungry to finish Dane off. But as its jaws came down, they suddenly locked—for Dane had wedged the oar shaft inside its mouth, propping it up between the roof of its mouth and the bottom.

The sea monster violently slammed the ice, intent on dislodging the oar. But Astrid was jolted loose instead and, plunging past Dane, she went tumbling into the beast's open mouth and onto its slick black tongue. Her knife still in hand, she began stabbing it upward into the roof of the beast's mouth, the creature bleating in pain. Dane could see its blood spurting onto Astrid, her arms awash in crimson. Thrusting himself halfway into the beast's mouth, he seized her hand to stop her from disappearing down its throat.

"Get out!" she cried, insisting he save himself. But nothing would make him let go—he'd go into the belly of the beast itself if he had to. Jerking a look up to those still hanging precariously above him, he spied the dim gleam of Draupnir—yes! This was his chance! "Ragnar!" Dane cried. "Let it go!" Their eyes met, Dane sensing some new feeling there. Ragnar released his grip on Odin's Draupnir, and Dane saw the ring skate down the sheet of ice just past him, its golden glint disappearing with a splash into the sea.

Having seen the golden ring go past, the monster made a move to retreat after it into the sea but then stopped, unable, Dane realized, to go underwater with its mouth wide open. Still hung halfway in its jaws, reaching in for Astrid, Dane saw her knifing the flesh of the beast's throat, Jörmungandr swallowing its own blood. Coughs then came from the beast, great choking spasms. Its whole body shook. Dane saw terror in Astrid's eyes as they both realized at the same moment what was about to happen.

And then, with sudden force, a great wave of putrescence shot up Jörmungandr's throat, the stream of vomit propelling Dane and Astrid out of the mouth and tumbling down on the now-righted iceberg in a steaming-hot pool of sea brine and sour puke.

Dane sat up, dripping. Moaning beside him, Astrid wiped away the foul, soupy regurgitation from her eyes. "Well, *that* was interesting," she said.

He hugged her as if she were the most beautiful girl in the world, for to him, even covered head to toe with sea-monster vomit, she was.

But where were the others? He turned, shocked to see Godrek's ship beside the berg; his men had Dane's beleaguered friends surrounded, spears and swords held at their necks. Accompanied by one of his men, Godrek strode forth, brandishing the rune sword, his eyes mad with avarice. The liegeman grabbed Astrid, and Godrek put the sword tip to Dane's neck.

"Odin's ring? Where is it, boy? My *ring!*"

"Gone, my lord," Ragnar said, behind them. Godrek slowly turned to face his man. "I let it slip into the sea for the serpent to retrieve. He would've killed us all had I not let go."

Godrek began to shake and quiver with rage, a volcano about to blow. "No . . . no . . . *NO!* It *can't* be gone!" he wailed. In a frenzy he began to beat at his temples with his fists. "It can't be! It can't be!"

His liegemen gave each other uneasy looks.

"My lord . . . ," a liegeman said, "all the other gold . . . surely that's enough."

"No!" Godrek raged. "It will *never* be enough!"

"Just the lesson my father learned," Dane said. "There would never be enough gold in the world to make up for losing those he loved. He was no coward, Whitecloak; he was stronger and richer than you'll ever be."

Godrek stood motionless, everyone watching, his eyes jerking back and forth in their sockets, listening to the mad jumble of voices in his head. He began mumbling a stream of unintelligible words, as if carrying on a conversation with the very demon that had cursed the rune sword. Dane had had a burning desire for revenge against this man, but now he felt only pity. Godrek had been a leader, a warrior; he had bravely fought beside Dane's father and experienced more than most men could ever dream of. But now he had succumbed to the curse of the rune sword—the incurable disease of greed. Like a man whose sole companion is his ale cup, eventually he winds up alone, empty cup in hand, friendless, loveless, gibbering to himself like an idiot.

"We need spill no more blood," Ragnar said to the liegemen. The men exchanged looks, nodded, and sheathed their weapons. Godrek too sheathed the rune sword. And then, with a mad howl, he ran at Dane, seizing him by the throat, his fingers squeezing with inhuman strength, Dane choking, unable to breathe. Dane saw flecks of foam at the corners of Godrek's mouth, and was just as frightened by the sheer madness in the man's gaze as he was to be so near death. Others came at Godrek, trying to stop him, but suddenly they froze, backing away in terror, and Dane thought it only too fitting an end, to die at the hands of the very man he once looked to for wisdom. His world going dark as he began losing his vision, a sudden sound filled his head. A hissing snort. And then, just before his sight completely deserted him, he looked over Godrek's shoulder and spied a chilling sight—Jörmungandr rising slick and gleaming from the sea.

The beast's head rose from the water, dripping and majestic, the oar shaft gone from inside its jaws, the weight of its neck and belly cracking the ice as it rested against the rim of the berg, its glassy green eyes as big and round as war shields, gazing down at no one but Godrek. And then, as if to tease and taunt him, the sea creature's tail rose behind it and, snaking its way up onto the flat surface of the ice, displayed its prize. The ring! Draupnir itself! Its golden glow shimmered as if lit from within, bathing the monster's black hide in amber light. Hung from its tail, hooked to one of its spikes, the ring beckoned. Dane had the eerie realization that Jörmungandr was no senseless beast. Like a dog with a bone, the sea serpent had retrieved the ring from the sea and was now parading it in front of them, as if showing them all that he had won, Dane detecting a trace of a grin round the creature's mouth.

"It's mine!" cried Godrek. Mad to possess it again, Godrek thrust his sword upward and charged the creature, leaping off the ice and onto the back of its head, slashing at it with the rune sword and bellowing curses. Jörmungandr gave a mighty shake of its head, flinging Godrek high in the air. Godrek screamed, his white cloak flapping like the wings of a dying bird, and fell headfirst into the monster's mouth; the serpent cocked back its head and swallowed him like a clam, letting him slide right down its slimy throat. Again the creature slipped beneath the waves, and Dane sank to his knees in exhaustion. Finally it was over.

Well, almost.

Moments later, the creature ascended again, rising over the ice, its giant head descending toward Dane. Fixed in its gaze, he saw its jaws open, felt its hideous breath blow over him. This would be his final moment of life, he thought. Strange, the peace he felt. The serpent spat something out onto the ice, and then, opening its jaws wider, it blew out a fierce roar, the force so great, it knocked Dane backward onto the ice. He lay there, looking up at the thing, understanding then that he would not, in the end, be eaten at all. That he had won. And after a final snort of defiance, the serpent sank beneath the waves, taking Draupnir and its meal of Whitecloak with it.

Dane slumped to the ice. Hearing his cohorts cheering Godrek's demise, it was then he saw it, the object lying beside him on the ice. Somehow it seemed a fitting end; there were some things too monstrous even for Jörmungandr to consume. And so, with sad finality, Dane gazed upon the head of the now most definitely dead Godrek Whitecloak, serpent slime dripping down his cheeks, his pale lips frozen in a grisly grimace, those same mad eyes forever open as if staring out in wistful and painful contemplation of the rich life that had so nearly been his.

# 33

# THE LONG TREK
# HOMEWARD

A mysterious thing happened when they tried to return to the Isle of Doom.

It seemed to have simply vanished.

The surviving liegemen and those from Voldarstad agreed that if they were to reach home, they must make peace and band together. Firstly, there was the issue of all that gold for the taking. Lut tried to tell them that without the rune sword, entrance to the vault would be an impossibility. But the liegemen, and even Jarl and Vik, said that with such treasure within reach, they had to try. Then a thick curtain of fog had settled in. They rowed and rowed for two days and two nights trying to find the isle again, with no luck. Twice they heard loud splashes and hissing snorts somewhere out in the fog, and once their ship was rocked as Jörmungandr passed under it. Lut concluded that the monster was either mocking them or warning them that its patience was wearing thin and they should make haste to vacate its realm. There was much argument, heated at times, but in a vote of fourteen to five, it was agreed they must strike for home.

Now, as dawn broke, Dane stood on the prow of the ship as it headed south, relieved to realize that his long nightmare was over. "Drink this," said Lut, sidling up and handing him a jar of hot barley cider. "It'll put some hair on your chest, and other places, too." Dane took the cider, smiling, enjoying the sensation of sunshine on his face and the feeling of being alive.

"Did you sleep well?" Lut asked.

Dane nodded. "I dreamed of poor Smek, locked in that vault of gold for eternity."

"That would have been a fitting end for Godrek. He would've died happy, surrounded by the one thing he loved."

"What I don't understand," Dane said, "is if my father knew the rune sword could turn men mad, why did he leave it in the chest and not destroy it?"

"My guess is he left the sword there when he was young, perhaps too young to know that the love he found later with your mother and you would make the temptations of Odin's Draupnir fade from his mind."

Dane sipped his steaming drink as the ship's prow cut through the water, brought awake by the bracing breeze on his face. Behind them the morning rowing shift was hard at work. It was great to see the two groups toiling in unison with nary a complaint—just days before, they had been enemies, and all because of the madness of one man. This gave Dane a sobering thought.

"I could've been just like Godrek, Lut. I could've succumbed too."

"You could never be like him." When Dane asked why, Lut said, "Because he did not have what you have, Dane. People you love, and who love you." As if on invisible cue, their attention was then drawn away by more raucous bickering from Jarl and Kára.

"There are many competitors for my hand, Jarl. I suppose you can get in line."

"What a spoiled, silly girl! Just because I saved your skin, what makes you think I'd want your hand too?"

"Confess it—you love me."

"You say it first: You love me."

"No, *you* first."

"No, *you* first."

"Say it!"

"*You* say it!"

"Enough!" said Ragnar the Ripper, erupting in anger. "Either profess your love or shut your holes! Keep it up and I'll cut *both* your throats!" That did the trick; they shut up. Everyone on board *knew* they had fallen in love, but both Jarl and Kára were too proud and pigheaded to admit it. So they each went to opposite sides of the ship and refused to speak to each other, which was a big relief for the crew. Until it began all over again less than an hour later.

What kind of future might they have? Dane wondered. Kára had grown up a lot since their journey had begun, yet too often still believed the world revolved around her. Of course, so did Jarl. All things considered, they were perfectly matched, although Dane foresaw hand-to-hand combat for the mirror and hair combs.

And what of Dane's future with Astrid? She was standing at the ship's railing, looking vexed, peering at the skies as if waiting for a lightning bolt from Thor, although the weather was clear and cloudless. He wanted to ask why she wore such a worried look, but Lut told him to let her be. She needed to be alone with her thoughts. Dane could not escape the nagging sense that something was wrong, but for now he would follow Lut's advice and not press her in the matter.

The trip back to Skrellborg was a peaceful one. In Utgard Dane was delighted to hear that Thrym had been elected leader of the frost giants and had forged a peace treaty between troll and giant. Thrym proudly showed off his spacious new home with plush, wall-to-wall frost and introduced them to his new girlfriend, Glacia, who served them a delicious meal of berry-flavored sleet.

At the troll village they learned there were plans to erect

a monument to honor Jarl the Fair for his brave action in saving troll lives in Utgard. Such was Jarl's desperate need for accolades that even though he despised trollkind—or "the maggoty fur balls," as he called them—he eagerly agreed to make a personal appearance in their village come spring. Klint, the raven, who had had a brief fling with a female raven in the troll forest, decided to rejoin Dane's troop. There were a lot of ruffled feathers and squawking when Klint flew the roost, but it seemed that he, like Jarl, was not fond of life in the proximity of trolls.

They arrived in Skrellborg to much cheering and acclaim. King Eldred welcomed them on the steps of his great lodge hall. For the safe return of the princess he generously awarded one thousand pieces of silver to the people of Voldarstad; for Godrek's head he gave one thousand more. As chief elder of Voldarstad, Lut graciously accepted the gifts, promising that part of the funds would be spent building a private outhouse for each village family, complete with his and hers seats.

As before, a great banquet was held to honor the heroes. Dane was asked to regale the packed mead hall with the tale of their thrilling quest. Instead, he turned the floor over to his friends. Fulnir hissed and made scary faces, playing the part of the fearsome Jörmungandr so well that some small children ran from the room screaming. Drott drew hearty laughter portraying Fulnir snarling, biting, and scratching during his *varúlfur* transformation. William too gave a hair-raising performance depicting his narrow escape from the jaws of the giant glowing insect. And Rik and Vik wrestled and head butted, giving a lively performance of Thrym's victory over Hrut. Topping off the entertainment, Ragnar gave a reading of his epic poem that told the story of the Isle of Doom, Draupnir, the mountain of gold, and Godrek's demise. When he finished, the room exploded in applause and Ragnar's eyes filled with tears, so touched was he by the people's appreciation of his creative skill.

The king was so impressed by Ragnar's story, he offered him the title of liege lord plus all of Godrek's properties. Ragnar thought for a long moment, then said he was greatly honored by the king's offer but did not want to be a warrior any longer. All he desired was a small piece of land where he could retire, raise prize pigs, and indulge in scholarly pursuits. Eldred granted his wish.

The prize of the evening, Dane thought, was seeing Drott and Fulnir surrounded by adoring girls. In telling their stories, they had not tried to hide who they were. They proudly announced their names to all, Drott the Dim and Fulnir the Stinking, and carried themselves with confidence and good humor. The result was that the people naturally liked and respected them, as Dane knew they would.

In the wane of the evening, Dane was summoned to see the king. He was led into the royal chambers and the door closed behind him. Eldred wore a grave look and bade Dane sit in one of two high-backed cedar chairs that stood before a warming fire. Dane sat, but the king remained standing, his back to Dane, staring in silence at the fire. Dane said nothing, having learned that a king should not be prompted by a lesser's queries but rather only speak when he bloody well chose to.

"There is something of a delicate matter I need to discuss." The king turned to face Dane, his brows low and knotted. "About the future of my kingdom. Your friend, the one they call the Fair One?"

"Jarl?"

"Yes. My niece tells me he . . . well . . . for some inexplicable reason she has lost her heart to him. Does this Jarl return her feelings?"

"I believe he does, my lord," said Dane.

"But he's bigheaded, is he not? A braggart? Much given to shows of vanity and smugness?"

"At times he's guilty of self-worship, yes. But he is a fine man; he'd make a fine husband in time, too, if that's what you're asking. For though he may have his faults—as do we all—he does not lie, my lord, and his bravery knows no bounds. He would die to protect anyone he loved; I trust him with my life."

"Yes, yes, yes," said the king, somewhat annoyed by Dane's defense of Jarl. "So the man is of recommendable character, fine, fine. But you? What about you, son?"

"My lord?"

"Please, enough with the humility. *You* inspired confidence in your cohorts. You led them. When the chips were down, you gave them strength."

"Strength? No, that's what they gave *me*. Without them—"

"Come now! I hate modesty! It all too often beclouds the true mettle of a man." The king sat and abruptly bent forward so that his eyes were but inches from Dane's and his stare bored into him. "I heard the stories, Dane. Frost giants. Trolls. Ghostwolves. Man-eating insects. And Jörmungandr itself! You led them through it all. That's why I want you to go back."

Dane was gob-smacked. Was he hearing correctly? He had just returned from a nightmare and Eldred wanted him to go *back*?

"Take as many men and ships as you want. I'll give you half of all the gold you return with. Half! And when you return, I will appoint you prince and heir to my throne."

Dane didn't know what to say. This was lunacy.

"Do you feel no loyalty to *me*? Have you no sense of duty to enrich the one responsible for giving you the rune sword in the first place?"

"My lord, even if I *did* want to return, there's no guarantee we'd even find the isle again. We tried for two days. And without the rune sword to unlock the treasure—"

404

"We can dig our way in!" the king snapped. "I'm offering you my kingdom and you give me excuses? You, Dane the Defiant, son of Voldar the Vile, have the temerity to stand there and reject the riches I bestow on you?! *GIVE ME ONE REASON WHY YOU DO THIS!*"

Dane looked the king straight in the eye, showing not a flinch in the face of his outburst. "Because," said Dane calmly, "I *am* the son of Voldar the Vile, and the village he built is where I belong. With the families I love and have sworn to protect."

The king's stare continued to bore into him. Dane began to panic. Had his boldness been an irrational miscalculation? Dane was relieved to see the king sink back in his chair with a sigh. The king's anger seemed to melt away as tears welled in his eyes. Eldred sat up and grasped Dane by both shoulders, saying, "I'm so happy to hear you say that, son. My friend Voldar rejected wealth and power as well. He found the secret to happiness . . . and so shall you, my boy. So shall you."

Days later, when at last they reached home, they were given an even more tumultuous welcome, received with hugs and kisses by the villagers of Voldarstad and given a grand celebration. Everyone gathered on Thor's Hill behind the village, the place where Thor's Hammer had fallen to earth. Dane and his friends who together had braved the long road of adversity stood in front of the assemblage as Gorm the Grumpy came forth.

"I have an important announcement!" Gorm announced.

Dane saw that Gorm's expression was slightly less grouchy than normal, perhaps because he had just learned of the new outhouse he was to receive.

"It is my pleasure to announce that the elders of the village have decided that on this spot where we stand, a runestone is to be erected to honor the courageous men and women who stand before you! Their names and deeds shall be carved into a great slab of granite so that for all time those who pass here will know of their exploits! Fellow villagers, be proud! For I give you . . . the Rune Warriors of Voldarstad!"

The villagers cheered. Dane saw tears streaming down his mother's face, and this brought thoughts of his father. If only Voldar had lived to see his own prophecy come true . . . his son *had* become a Rune Warrior, just as he had once predicted. Dane had been tempted by the rune sword's call of greed, but like his father, he had come to realize that love was infinitely more valuable than soulless glitter.

Later at the village feasting, Dane sat before the great outdoor fire, his belly stuffed with fine food and drink, watching the festivities with bemusement. Amid a crowd of local girls, each one more adoring than the next, Fulnir and Ulf were drumming a table with their hands and singing a heroic war chant, clearly enjoying the attention. Kára and Jarl were a very cozy-looking couple, Jarl so entranced with her, he gave scant notice to Rik and Vik, who were drunkenly arm-wrestling each other at the far end of the table, drawing an even larger crowd.

Dane realized he felt completely at peace, save for the one thing he cared for most: Astrid. During the whole trip back, she had said very little, busying herself with taking care of the others, showing special attention, it seemed, to everyone but Dane. Now, with his back to the fire, watching the festivities, he scanned the crowd, searching for the one face that would truly make him smile: hers.

There! He saw her standing alone on the far side of the crowd, statuesque and stoic, her beauty still a powerful piece of poetry. He smiled and waved, but she was too busy watching Drott performing handstands on the dance floor to notice. For a moment he too watched the silly performance, and when he looked back, she was gone. He soon caught sight of her; she had turned her back on the revelers and was threading her way past the perimeter of torchlights, disappearing into the darkness. Why was she walking away? Where was she going? Something about the way she had looked, the finality on her face, had seemed disturbing.

Dane found her in the woods where he had given her the Thor's Hammer locket she still wore. Alerted by his footsteps in the crusted snow, she turned to face him as he approached, and he saw the shine in her eyes, a sign that she'd been crying. Coming closer, he thought he glimpsed another figure nearby, but now as he drew near, he saw that she was alone. Her eyes were puffy and red and she wore a look of such distress, it made Dane worry even more.

"What's going on?" he asked. "Who were you talking to?"

It took a long time for her to answer.

"I didn't know how to tell you. The thought of it was . . . too awful."

"Tell me? Tell me *what*?"

"I wanted to—so many times—but I had no idea how. I was going to leave without even telling you, but now . . ."

"Oh, for Odin's sake, *tell* him!"

Dane looked around. Where was that voice coming from? Then he and Astrid were standing in a sudden pool of light, the reflected glow, he saw, from a figure who hung suspended above them. It was Mist, he realized. The Valkyrie.

"Why are *you* here?" He looked from Mist to Astrid and back to Mist again. Seeing that Astrid was still too tearful to speak, Mist saw that she would have to.

"I fault myself for some of this," said Mist apologetically. "You were fated to die—"

"You saved my life," said Dane. "Twice."

"Yes, but the Sisters found out and ordered me to take

408

your life for real. And then she took my feather cloak and forced me to take her to the Sisters, and *they* said—"

"Sisters?" said Dane, confused.

"The Wyrd Sisters. The Norns, the Goddesses of Time, the Keepers of the Book? And they said no, absolutely not, they would not intercede, rules were rules, but your friend here, Ester—"

"Astrid," said Astrid.

"Astrid—she pitched quite a fit, you should've seen it, and well, they finally agreed to the deal and that's why I'm here and it's time to go."

"Deal? What deal? I still have *no* idea what you're talking about."

"She gave her life for yours."

For a moment Dane was too stunned to speak. He looked into Astrid's teary eyes. "No . . . no, it's impossible. You can't die!"

"She's *not* going to die," Mist said. "She'll merely live on a higher plane, serving Odin as a corpse maiden, a Valkyrie. She'll have all the perks and powers that come with the position, including flying, invisibility, a nice horse—"

Dane took an angry step toward Mist. "No! You will take me instead! I was supposed to die, so take *me*, not *her*!"

"I'm afraid it's decided," Mist said. "It is her fate to have saved you from yours."

He gazed at Astrid as if for the first time realizing how

truly beautiful she was, and it broke his heart all over again. She ran to him, into his arms, and he kissed her. Tears streamed down his face as he held her and felt his whole future with her slipping away.

"You're mine, Astrid," he whispered, holding her tightly, "always and forever."

But then she was gone from his arms. Gazing upward, he saw her astride a beautiful golden-maned stallion, his hide as smooth as satin, his head tossed back in pride, Mist floating beside her on another mighty steed. And seeing his Astrid, bathed in a glowing light that gave her more beauty than ever, a deep pain arose in him as if his very vitals were being torn from his body, as if she were a piece of him ripping away.

"I love you!" he called to her.

*"And I you . . . ,"* he heard her whisper in response. But strangely, it seemed she had spoken without even moving her lips. It was as if she were speaking to him from inside his mind, as if her voice had come to him from another realm. The stallions let out otherworldly whinnies, and up they went. As he watched her fly up and away into the night sky, growing smaller and smaller atop the stallion, her glowing image seen through his tears made it seem as though she had begun to sparkle just like one of the frosty stars in the sky. And when he wiped the tears from his eyes to look again, the light of her in the sky was gone

altogether, and Dane felt a great, gaping hole in his world, a wound in his heart that would never heal as long as he drew breath.

He slumped to the ground, too weak to make a sound, his head a whirl of emotions. He wanted to weep. He wanted to scream. He wanted to run and tell his mother what had happened and cry like an infant in her arms. He had an overwhelming impulse to jump into the sea and drown himself. And he probably would have had he not heard approaching footsteps.

It was Lut the Bent walking toward him, his figure silvered by the moon. Upon his face Dane saw an ineffable sadness, and in his voice he heard the echo of his own torment. "At times like these," Lut said, "a man wishes he were dead, so that he will not have to feel the pain of loss and lamentation."

"Did you know?" Dane asked. Lut nodded. "She gave up her life for *me*—*because* of me. How can I live knowing that it is at her expense? Were it not for me and my so-called heroics, she would be right here beside me and we would have a life together."

"But who's to say *you* would have lived? The Norns had foretold that you would die on your rune sword journey. But through sheer force of will, she has given you another chance at life. Don't throw it away."

"But how can I live without her?"

411

"Courage comes to those who need it most," said Lut, laying a hand on Dane's shoulder. "But only if you choose to live. To embrace the new possibilities that lie before you. To devote yourself to those who love you. Those who need you. Your mother. Your friends. The elderly and infirm. Me, for instance."

"Devote myself to those I love?" Dane said bitterly. "Like Astrid? Look what my love for her has caused!"

Lut kept silent for a moment. "Hope," he said, "is the food we feed the ailing heart." Knowing the boy was in too great a pain to engage in further conversation, Lut laid a hand on Dane's shoulder and left him there alone to wrestle with his anger and grief. Dane watched the old one walk slowly back to the village, recalling the many gems of wisdom he had imparted. The answers would come by living the questions? What kind of life philosophy was that?

The music and merriment of the village celebration drifted back to him on the cold night air, and to Dane these sounds were like further stabs to his heart.

Staring again into the stars, he found himself talking aloud to Astrid. He could not accept a life without her, he said, and he vowed he would spend the rest of his days trying to find a way to be with her again. If not in life, then perhaps in death. For if he were to end his life valiantly, defending his people in battle, would it not be possible to reunite with her up in Valhalla, the realm in which she now dwelled? And live with her there, in the heavens among the gods themselves? *Yes!* And the thought of a reunion with his dear one, a reunion even in death, filled his heart with new hope. For he knew with sudden certainty that he would someday see her and hold her again. Alive or dead, he would make it so.

# ABOUT THE AUTHORS

**JAMES JENNEWEIN** lives in a bloodthirsty, barbaric land filled with evil tyrants, slimy monsters, and comely maidens. It is called Los Angeles.

**TOM S. PARKER**, who has Viking ancestors on his Swedish mother's side, enjoys pillaging now and then with his pet Chihuahua, Tony. He lives in a moated fortress in Topanga, California.

Visit the authors at www.runewarriors.net.

31901051059352